A PASSAGE TO INDIA

A Clash of Cultures in British India

E.M. FORSTER

GENERAL PRESS

Published by
GENERAL PRESS
4805/24, Fourth Floor, Krishna House
Ansari Road, Daryaganj, New Delhi - 110002
Ph : 011-23282971, 45795759
E-mail : generalpressindia@gmail.com

www.generalpress.in

First Edition : 2020

ISBN : 9789354990205

Published by Azeem Ahmad Khan for General Press

BESTSELLING FICTION

- 1984 by George Orwell
  Literature & Fiction, ISBN: 9789380914947
- A Passage to India by E.M. Forster
  Literature & Fiction, ISBN: 9789354990205
- A Room of One's Own by Virginia Woolf
  Literature & Fiction, ISBN: 9789354990281
- A Wrinkle in Time by Madeleine L'Engle
  Literature & Fiction, ISBN: 9789354991066
- Animal Farm by George Orwell
  Literature & Fiction, ISBN: 9789380914701
- Anthem by Ayn Rand
  Literature & Fiction, ISBN: 9789389157079
- As a Man Thinketh by James Allen
  Literature & Fiction, ISBN: 9788180320262
- As I Lay Dying by William Faulkner
  Literature & Fiction, ISBN: 9789390492381
- Demian by Hermann Hesse
  Literature & Fiction, ISBN: 9789387669567
- Lost Horizon by James Hilton
  Literature & Fiction, ISBN: 9789389716313
- Mansarover 1 (Hindi) by Premchand
  Literature & Fiction, ISBN: 9789380914978
- One, None and a Hundred Thousand by Luigi Pirandello
  Literature & Fiction, ISBN: 9789389716337

Search the book by its ISBN

BESTSELLING FICTION

- Siddhartha by Hermann Hesse
  Literature & Fiction, ISBN: 9789380914145
- Tales from Shakespeare by Charles Lamb & Mary Lamb
  Literature & Fiction, ISBN: 9789380914367
- The Mysterious Affair at Styles by Agatha Christie
  Literature & Fiction, ISBN: 9789390492510
- The Plague by Albert Camus
  Literature & Fiction, ISBN: 9788194764892
- The Prophet by Kahlil Gibran
  Literature & Fiction, ISBN: 9789380914022
- The Railway Children by E Nesbit
  Literature & Fiction, ISBN: 9789354990960
- The Sound and the Fury by William Faulkner
  Literature & Fiction, ISBN: 9789390492572
- The Stranger by Albert Camus
  Literature & Fiction, ISBN: 9789390492589
- The Sun Also Rises by Ernest Hemingway
  Literature & Fiction, ISBN: 9789354990984
- Their Eyes Were Watching God by Zora Neale Hurston
  Literature & Fiction, ISBN: 9788194764885
- To the Lighthouse by Virginia Woolf
  Literature & Fiction, ISBN: 9789390492190
- World's Best Short Stories: Volume 1 by Various Authors
  Literature & Fiction, ISBN: 9789390492275

Search the book by its ISBN

Contents

PART 1

MOSQUE

Chapter 1

Except for the Marabar Caves—and they are twenty miles off—the city of Chandrapore presents nothing extraordinary. Edged rather than washed by the river Ganges, it trails for a couple of miles along the bank, scarcely distinguishable from the rubbish it deposits so freely. There are no bathing-steps on the river front, as the Ganges happens not to be holy here; indeed there is no river front, and bazaars shut out the wide and shifting panorama of the stream. The streets are mean, the temples ineffective, and though a few fine houses exist they are hidden away in gardens or down alleys whose filth deters all but the invited guest. Chandrapore was never large or beautiful, but two hundred years ago it lay on the road between Upper India, then imperial, and the sea, and the fine houses date from that period. The zest for decoration stopped in the eighteenth century, nor was it ever democratic. There is no painting and scarcely any carving in the bazaars. The very wood seems made of mud, the inhabitants of mud moving. So abased, so monotonous is everything that meets the eye, that when the Ganges comes down it might be expected to wash the excrescence back into the soil. Houses do fall, people are drowned and left rotting, but the general outline of the town persists, swelling here, shrinking there, like some low but indestructible form of life.

Inland, the prospect alters. There is an oval Maidan, and a long sallow hospital. Houses belonging to Eurasians stand on the high ground by the railway station. Beyond the railway—which runs parallel to the river—the land sinks, then rises again rather steeply. On the second rise is laid out the little civil station, and viewed hence Chandrapore appears to be a totally different place. It is a city of gardens. It is no city, but a forest sparsely scattered with huts. It is a tropical pleasaunce washed by a noble river. The toddy palms and neem trees and mangoes and pepul that were hidden behind the bazaars now become visible and in their turn hide the bazaars. They rise from the gardens where ancient tanks nourish them, they burst out of stifling purlieus and unconsidered temples. Seeking, light and air, and endowed with more strength than man or his works, they soar above the lower deposit to greet one another with branches and beckoning leaves, and to build a city for the birds. Especially after the rains do they screen what passes below, but at all times, even when scorched or leafless, they glorify the city to the English people who inhabit the rise, so that new-comers cannot believe it to be as meagre as it is described, and have to be driven down to acquire disillusionment. As for the civil station itself, it provokes no emotion. It charms not, neither does it repel. It is sensibly planned, with a red-brick club on its brow, and farther back a grocer's and a cemetery, and the bungalows are disposed along roads that intersect at right angles. It has nothing hideous in it, and only the view is beautiful; it shares nothing with the city except the overarching sky.

The sky too has its changes, but they are less marked than those of the vegetation and the river. Clouds map it up at times, but it is normally a dome of blending tints, and the main tint blue. By day the blue will pale down into white where it touches the white of the land, after sunset it has a new circumference—orange, melting upwards into tenderest purple. But the core of blue persists, and so it is by night. Then the stars hang like lamps from the immense vault. The distance between the vault and them is as nothing to the distance behind them, and that farther distance, though beyond colour, last freed itself from blue.

The sky settles everything—not only climates and seasons but when the earth shall be beautiful. By herself she can do little—only feeble outbursts of flowers. But when the sky chooses, glory can rain into the Chandrapore bazaars or a benediction pass from horizon to horizon. The sky can do this because it is so strong and so enormous. Strength comes from the sun, infused in it daily, size from the prostrate earth. No mountains infringe on the curve. League after league the earth lies flat, heaves a little, is flat again. Only in the south, where a group of fists and fingers are thrust up through the soil, is the endless expanse interrupted. These fists and fingers are the Marabar Hills, containing the extraordinary caves.

CHAPTER 2

Abandoning his bicycle, which fell before a servant could catch it, the young man sprang up on to the verandah. He was all animation. "Hamidullah, Hamidullah! am I late?" he cried.

"Do not apologize," said his host. "You are always late."

"Kindly answer my question. Am I late? Has Mahmoud Ali eaten all the food? If so I go elsewhere. Mr. Mahmoud Ali, how are you?"

"Thank you, Dr. Aziz, I am dying."

"Dying before your dinner? Oh, poor Mahmoud Ali!"

"Hamidullah here is actually dead. He passed away just as you rode up on your bike."

"Yes, that is so," said the other. "Imagine us both as addressing you from another and a happier world."

"Does there happen to be such a thing as a hookah in that happier world of yours?"

"Aziz, don't chatter. We are having a very sad talk."

The hookah had been packed too tight, as was usual in his friend's house, and bubbled sulkily. He coaxed it. Yielding at last, the tobacco jetted up into his lungs and nostrils, driving out the smoke of burning cow dung that had filled them as he rode through the bazaar. It was delicious. He lay in a trance, sensuous but healthy, through which the talk of the two others did not seem particularly sad—they were discussing as to whether or no it is possible to be friends with an Englishman. Mahmoud Ali argued that it was not, Hamidullah disagreed, but with so many reservations that there was no friction between them. Delicious indeed to lie on the broad verandah with the moon rising in front and the servants preparing dinner behind, and no trouble happening.

"Well, look at my own experience this morning."

"I only contend that it is possible in England," replied Hamidullah, who had been to that country long ago, before the big rush, and had received a cordial welcome at Cambridge.

"It is impossible here. Aziz! The red-nosed boy has again insulted me in Court. I do not blame him. He was told that he ought to insult me. Until lately he was quite a nice boy, but the others have got hold of him."

"Yes, they have no chance here, that is my point. They come out intending to be gentlemen, and are told it will not do. Look at Lesley, look at Blakiston, now it is your red-nosed boy, and Fielding will go next. Why, I remember when Turton came out first. It was in another part of the Province. You fellows will not believe me, but I have driven with Turton in his carriage—Turton! Oh yes, we were once quite intimate. He has shown me his stamp collection."

"He would expect you to steal it now. Turton! But red-nosed boy will be far worse than Turton!"

"I do not think so. They all become exactly the same, not worse, not better. I give any Englishman two years, be he Turton or Burton. It is only the difference of a letter. And I give any Englishwoman six months. All are exactly alike. Do you not agree with me?"

"I do not," replied Mahmoud Ali, entering into the bitter fun, and feeling both pain and amusement at each word that was uttered. "For my own part I find such profound differences among our rulers. Red-nose mumbles, Turton talks distinctly, Mrs. Turton takes bribes, Mrs. Red-nose does not and cannot, because so far there is no Mrs. Red-nose."

"Bribes?"

"Did you not know that when they were lent to Central India over a Canal Scheme, some Rajah or other gave her a sewing machine in solid gold so that the water should run through his state."

"And does it?"

"No, that is where Mrs. Turton is so skilful. When we poor blacks take bribes, we perform what we are bribed to perform, and the law discovers us in consequence. The English take and do nothing. I admire them."

"We all admire them. Aziz, please pass me the hookah."

"Oh, not yet—hookah is so jolly now."

"You are a very selfish boy." He raised his voice suddenly, and shouted for dinner. Servants shouted back that it was ready. They meant that they wished it was ready, and were so understood, for nobody moved. Then Hamidullah continued, but with changed manner and evident emotion.

"But take my case—the case of young Hugh Bannister. Here is the son of my dear, my dead friends, the Reverend and Mrs. Bannister, whose goodness to me in England I shall never forget or describe. They were father and mother to me, I talked to them as I do now. In the vacations their Rectory became my home. They entrusted all their children to me—I often carried little Hugh about—I took him up to the Funeral of Queen Victoria, and held him in my arms above the crowd."

"Queen Victoria was different," murmured Mahmoud Ali.

"I learn now that this boy is in business as a leather merchant at Cawnpore. Imagine how I long to see him and to pay his fare that this house may be his home. But it is useless. The other Anglo-Indians will have got hold of him long ago. He will probably think that

I want something, and I cannot face that from the son of my old friends. Oh, what in this country has gone wrong with everything, Vakil Sahib? I ask you."

Aziz joined in. "Why talk about the English? Brrrr...! Why be either friends with the fellows or not friends? Let us shut them out and be jolly. Queen Victoria and Mrs. Bannister were the only exceptions, and they're dead."

"No, no, I do not admit that, I have met others."

"So have I," said Mahmoud Ali, unexpectedly veering. "All ladies are far from alike." Their mood was changed, and they recalled little kindnesses and courtesies. "She said 'Thank you so much' in the most natural way." "She offered me a lozenge when the dust irritated my throat." Hamidullah could remember more important examples of angelic ministration, but the other, who only knew Anglo-India, had to ransack his memory for scraps, and it was not surprising that he should return to "But of course all this is exceptional. The exception does not prove the rule. The average woman is like Mrs. Turton, and, Aziz, you know what she is." Aziz did not know, but said he did. He too generalized from his disappointments—it is difficult for members of a subject race to do otherwise. Granted the exceptions, he agreed that all Englishwomen are haughty and venal. The gleam passed from the conversation, whose wintry surface unrolled and expanded interminably.

A servant announced dinner. They ignored him. The elder men had reached their eternal politics, Aziz drifted into the garden. The trees smelt sweet—green-blossomed champak—and scraps of Persian poetry came into his head. Dinner, dinner, dinner... but when he returned to the house for it, Mahmoud Ali had drifted away in his turn, to speak to his sais. "Come and see my wife a little then," said Hamidullah, and they spent twenty minutes behind the purdah. Hamidullah Begum was a distant aunt of Aziz, and the only female relative he had in Chandrapore, and she had much to say to him on this occasion about a family circumcision that had been celebrated with imperfect pomp. It was difficult to get away, because until they had had their dinner she would not begin hers, and consequently prolonged her remarks in case they should suppose she was impatient. Having censured the circumcision, she bethought her of kindred topics, and asked Aziz when he was going to be married.

Respectful but irritated, he answered, "Once is enough."

"Yes, he has done his duty," said Hamidullah. "Do not tease him so. He carries on his family, two boys and their sister."

"Aunt, they live most comfortably with my wife's mother, where she was living when she died. I can see them whenever I like. They are such very, very small children."

"And he sends them the whole of his salary and lives like a low-grade clerk, and tells no one the reason. What more do you require him to do?"

But this was not Hamidullah Begum's point, and having courteously changed the conversation for a few moments she returned and made it. She said, "What is to become of all our daughters if men refuse to marry? They will marry beneath them, or——" And she began the oft-told tale of a lady of Imperial descent who could find no husband in the narrow circle where her pride permitted her to mate, and had lived on unwed, her age now thirty, and would die unwed, for no one would have her now. While the tale was in progress, it convinced the two men, the tragedy seemed a slur on the whole community; better polygamy almost, than that a woman should die without the joys God has intended her to receive. Wedlock, motherhood, power in the house—for what else is she born, and how can the man who has denied them to her stand up to face her creator and his own at the last day? Aziz took his leave saying "Perhaps... but later..."—his invariable reply to such an appeal.

"You mustn't put off what you think right," said Hamidullah. "That is why India is in such a plight, because we put off things." But seeing that his young relative looked worried, he added a few soothing words, and thus wiped out any impression that his wife might have made.

During their absence, Mahmoud Ali had gone off in his carriage leaving a message that he should be back in five minutes, but they were on no account to wait. They sat down to meat with a distant cousin of the house, Mohammed Latif, who lived on Hamidullah's bounty and who occupied the position neither of a servant nor of an equal. He did not speak unless spoken to, and since no one spoke kept unoffended silence. Now and then he belched, in compliment to the richness of the food. A gentle, happy and dishonest old man; all his life he had never done a stroke of work. So long as some one of his relatives had a house he was sure of a home, and it was unlikely that so large a family would all go bankrupt. His wife led a similar existence some hundreds of miles away—he did not visit her, owing to the expense of the railway ticket. Presently Aziz chaffed him, also the servants, and then began quoting poetry, Persian, Urdu, a little Arabic. His memory was good, and for so young a man he had read largely; the themes he preferred were the decay of Islam and the brevity of love. They listened delighted, for they took the public view of poetry, not the private which obtains in England. It never bored them to hear words, words; they breathed them with the cool night air, never stopping to analyse; the name of the poet, Hafiz, Hali, Iqbal, was sufficient guarantee. India—a hundred Indias—whispered outside beneath the indifferent moon, but for the time India seemed one and their own, and they regained their departed greatness by hearing its departure lamented, they felt young again because reminded that youth must fly. A servant in scarlet interrupted him; he was the chuprassi of the Civil Surgeon, and he handed Aziz a note.

"Old Callendar wants to see me at his bungalow," he said, not rising. "He might have the politeness to say why."

"Some case, I daresay."

"I daresay not, I daresay nothing. He has found out our dinner hour, that's all, and chooses to interrupt us every time, in order to show his power."

"On the one hand he always does this, on the other it may be a serious case, and you cannot know," said Hamidullah, considerately paving the way towards obedience. "Had you not better clean your teeth after pan?"

"If my teeth are to be cleaned, I don't go at all. I am an Indian, it is an Indian habit to take pan. The Civil Surgeon must put up with it. Mohammed Latif, my bike, please."

The poor relation got up. Slightly immersed in the realms of matter, he laid his hand on the bicycle's saddle, while a servant did the actual wheeling. Between them they took it over a tintack. Aziz held his hands under the ewer, dried them, fitted on his green felt hat, and then with unexpected energy whizzed out of Hamidullah's compound.

"Aziz, Aziz, imprudent boy..." But he was far down the bazaar, riding furiously. He had neither light nor bell nor had he a brake, but what use are such adjuncts in a land where the cyclist's only hope is to coast from face to face, and just before he collides with each it vanishes? And the city was fairly empty at this hour. When his tyre went flat, he leapt off and shouted for a tonga.

He did not at first find one, and he had also to dispose of his bicycle at a friend's house. He dallied furthermore to clean his teeth. But at last he was rattling towards the civil lines, with a vivid sense of speed. As he entered their arid tidiness, depression suddenly seized him. The roads, named after victorious generals and intersecting at right angles, were symbolic of the net Great Britain had thrown over India. He felt caught in their meshes. When he turned into Major Callendar's compound he could with difficulty restrain himself from getting down from the tonga and approaching the bungalow on foot, and this not because his soul was servile but because his feelings—the sensitive edges of him—

feared a gross snub. There had been a "case" last year—an Indian gentleman had driven up to an official's house and been turned back by the servants and been told to approach more suitably—only one case among thousands of visits to hundreds of officials, but its fame spread wide. The young man shrank from a repetition of it. He compromised, and stopped the driver just outside the flood of light that fell across the verandah.

The Civil Surgeon was out.

"But the sahib has left me some message?"

The servant returned an indifferent "No." Aziz was in despair. It was a servant whom he had forgotten to tip, and he could do nothing now because there were people in the hall. He was convinced that there was a message, and that the man was withholding it out of revenge. While they argued, the people came out. Both were ladies. Aziz lifted his hat. The first, who was in evening dress, glanced at the Indian and turned instinctively away.

"Mrs. Lesley, it *is* a tonga," she cried.

"Ours?" enquired the second, also seeing Aziz, and doing likewise.

"Take the gifts the gods provide, anyhow," she screeched, and both jumped in. "O Tonga wallah, club, club. Why doesn't the fool go?"

"Go, I will pay you to-morrow," said Aziz to the driver, and as they went off he called courteously, "You are most welcome, ladies." They did not reply, being full of their own affairs.

So it had come, the usual thing—just as Mahmoud Ali said. The inevitable snub—his bow ignored, his carriage taken. It might have been worse, for it comforted him somehow that Mesdames Callendar and Lesley should both be fat and weigh the tonga down behind. Beautiful women would have pained him. He turned to the servant, gave him a couple of rupees, and asked again whether there was a message. The man, now very civil, returned the same answer. Major Callendar had driven away half an hour before.

"Saying nothing?"

He had as a matter of fact said, "Damn Aziz"—words that the servant understood, but was too polite to repeat. One can tip too much as well as too little, indeed the coin that buys the exact truth has not yet been minted.

"Then I will write him a letter."

He was offered the use of the house, but was too dignified to enter it. Paper and ink were brought on to the verandah. He began: "Dear Sir,—At your express command I have hastened as a subordinate should——" and then stopped. "Tell him I have called, that is sufficient," he said, tearing the protest up. "Here is my card. Call me a tonga."

"Huzoor, all are at the club."

"Then telephone for one down to the railway station." And since the man hastened to do this he said, "Enough, enough, I prefer to walk." He commandeered a match and lit a cigarette. These attentions, though purchased, soothed him. They would last as long as he had rupees, which is something. But to shake the dust of Anglo-India off his feet! To escape from the net and be back among manners and gestures that he knew! He began a walk, an unwonted exercise.

He was an athletic little man, daintily put together, but really very strong. Nevertheless walking fatigued him, as it fatigues everyone in India except the new-comer. There is something hostile in that soil. It either yields, and the foot sinks into a depression, or else it is unexpectedly rigid and sharp, pressing stones or crystals against the tread. A series of these little surprises exhausts; and he was wearing pumps, a poor preparation for any country. At the edge of the civil station he turned into a mosque to rest.

He had always liked this mosque. It was gracious, and the arrangement pleased him. The courtyard—entered through a ruined gate—contained an ablution tank of fresh clear water, which was always in motion, being indeed part of a conduit that supplied the city. The courtyard was paved with broken slabs. The covered part of the mosque was deeper than is usual; its effect was that of an English parish church whose side has been taken out. Where he sat, he looked into three arcades whose darkness was illuminated by a small hanging lamp and by the moon. The front—in full moonlight—had the appearance of marble, and the ninety-nine names of God on the frieze stood out black, as the frieze stood out white against the sky. The contest between this dualism and the contention of shadows within pleased Aziz, and he tried to symbolize the whole into some truth of religion or love. A mosque by winning his approval let loose his imagination. The temple of another creed, Hindu, Christian, or Greek, would have bored him and failed to awaken his sense of beauty. Here was Islam, his own country, more than a Faith, more than a battle-cry, more, much more... Islam, an attitude towards life both exquisite and durable, where his body and his thoughts found their home.

His seat was the low wall that bounded the courtyard on the left. The ground fell away beneath him towards the city, visible as a blur of trees, and in the stillness he heard many small sounds. On the right, over in the club, the English community contributed an amateur orchestra. Elsewhere some Hindus were drumming—he knew they were Hindus, because the rhythm was uncongenial to him,—and others were bewailing a corpse—he knew whose, having certified it in the afternoon. There were owls, the Punjab mail... and flowers smelt deliciously in the station-master's garden. But the mosque—that alone signified, and he returned to it from the complex appeal of the night, and decked it with meanings the builder had never intended. Some day he too would build a mosque, smaller than this but in perfect taste, so that all who passed by should experience the happiness he felt now. And near it, under a low dome, should be his tomb, with a Persian inscription:

Alas, without me for thousands of years
The Rose will blossom and the Spring will bloom,
But those who have secretly understood my heart—
They will approach and visit the grave where I lie.

He had seen the quatrain on the tomb of a Deccan king, and regarded it as profound philosophy—he always held pathos to be profound. The secret understanding of the heart! He repeated the phrase with tears in his eyes, and as he did so one of the pillars of the mosque seemed to quiver. It swayed in the gloom and detached itself. Belief in ghosts ran in his blood, but he sat firm. Another pillar moved, a third, and then an Englishwoman stepped out into the moonlight. Suddenly he was furiously angry and shouted: "Madam! Madam! Madam!"

"Oh! Oh!" the woman gasped.

"Madam, this is a mosque, you have no right here at all; you should have taken off your shoes; this is a holy place for Moslems."

"I have taken them off."

"You have?"

"I left them at the entrance."

"Then I ask your pardon."

Still startled, the woman moved out, keeping the ablution-tank between them. He called after her, "I am truly sorry for speaking."

"Yes, I was right, was I not? If I remove my shoes, I am allowed?"

"Of course, but so few ladies take the trouble, especially if thinking no one is there to see."

"That makes no difference. God is here."

"Madam!"

"Please let me go."

"Oh, can I do you some service now or at any time?"

"No, thank you, really none—good night."

"May I know your name?"

She was now in the shadow of the gateway, so that he could not see her face, but she saw his, and she said with a change of voice, "Mrs. Moore."

"Mrs.——" Advancing, he found that she was old.

A fabric bigger than the mosque fell to pieces, and he did not know whether he was glad or sorry. She was older than Hamidullah Begum, with a red face and white hair. Her voice had deceived him.

"Mrs. Moore, I am afraid I startled you. I shall tell my community—our friends—about you. That God is here—very good, very fine indeed. I think you are newly arrived in India."

"Yes—how did you know?"

"By the way you address me. No, but can I call you a carriage?"

"I have only come from the club. They are doing a play that I have seen in London, and it was so hot."

"What was the name of the play?"

"Cousin Kate."

"I think you ought not to walk at night alone, Mrs. Moore. There are bad characters about and leopards may come across from the Marabar Hills. Snakes also."

She exclaimed; she had forgotten the snakes.

"For example, a six-spot beetle," he continued, "You pick it up, it bites, you die."

"But you walk about yourself."

"Oh, I am used to it."

"Used to snakes?"

They both laughed. "I'm a doctor," he said. "Snakes don't dare bite me." They sat down side by side in the entrance, and slipped on their evening shoes. "Please may I ask you a question now? Why do you come to India at this time of year, just as the cold weather is ending?"

"I intended to start earlier, but there was an unavoidable delay."

"It will soon be so unhealthy for you! And why ever do you come to Chandrapore?"

"To visit my son. He is the City Magistrate here."

"Oh no, excuse me, that is quite impossible. Our City Magistrate's name is Mr. Heaslop. I know him intimately."

"He's my son all the same," she said, smiling.

"But, Mrs. Moore, how can he be?"

"I was married twice."

"Yes, now I see, and your first husband died."

"He did, and so did my second husband."

"Then we are in the same box," he said cryptically. "Then is the City Magistrate the entire of your family now?"

"No, there are the younger ones—Ralph and Stella in England."

"And the gentleman here, is he Ralph and Stella's half-brother?"

"Quite right."

"Mrs. Moore, this is all extremely strange, because like yourself I have also two sons and a daughter. Is not this the same box with a vengeance?"

"What are their names? Not also Ronny, Ralph, and Stella, surely?"

The suggestion delighted him. "No, indeed. How funny it sounds! Their names are quite different and will surprise you. Listen, please. I am about to tell you my children's names. The first is called Ahmed, the second is called Karim, the third—she is the eldest—Jamila. Three children are enough. Do not you agree with me?"

"I do."

They were both silent for a little, thinking of their respective families. She sighed and rose to go.

"Would you care to see over the Minto Hospital one morning?" he enquired. "I have nothing else to offer at Chandrapore."

"Thank you, I have seen it already, or I should have liked to come with you very much."

"I suppose the Civil Surgeon took you."

"Yes, and Mrs. Callendar."

His voice altered. "Ah! A very charming lady."

"Possibly, when one knows her better."

"What? What? You didn't like her?"

"She was certainly intending to be kind, but I did not find her exactly charming."

He burst out with: "She has just taken my tonga without my permission—do you call that being charming?—and Major Callendar interrupts me night after night from where I am dining with my friends and I go at once, breaking up a most pleasant entertainment, and he is not there and not even a message. Is this charming, pray? But what does it matter? I can do nothing and he knows it. I am just a subordinate, my time is of no value, the verandah is good enough for an Indian, yes, yes, let him stand, and Mrs. Callendar takes my carriage and cuts me dead..."

She listened.

He was excited partly by his wrongs, but much more by the knowledge that someone sympathized with them. It was this that led him to repeat, exaggerate, contradict. She had proved her sympathy by criticizing her fellow-countrywoman to him, but even earlier he had known. The flame that not even beauty can nourish was springing up, and though his words were querulous his heart began to glow secretly. Presently it burst into speech.

"You understand me, you know what others feel. Oh, if others resembled you!"

Rather surprised, she replied: "I don't think I understand people very well. I only know whether I like or dislike them."

"Then you are an Oriental."

She accepted his escort back to the club, and said at the gate that she wished she was a member, so that she could have asked him in.

"Indians are not allowed into the Chandrapore Club even as guests," he said simply. He did not expatiate on his wrongs now, being happy. As he strolled downhill beneath the lovely moon, and again saw the lovely mosque, he seemed to own the land as much as anyone owned it. What did it matter if a few flabby Hindus had preceded him there, and a few chilly English succeeded?

CHAPTER 3

The third act of *Cousin Kate* was well advanced by the time Mrs. Moore re-entered the club. Windows were barred, lest the servants should see their mem-sahibs acting, and the heat was consequently immense. One electric fan revolved like a wounded bird, another was out of order. Disinclined to return to the audience, she went into the billiard room, where she was greeted by "I want to see the *real* India," and her appropriate life came back with a rush. This was Adela Quested, the queer, cautious girl whom Ronny had commissioned her to bring from England, and Ronny was her son, also cautious, whom Miss Quested would probably though not certainly marry, and she herself was an elderly lady.

"I want to see it too, and I only wish we could. Apparently the Turtons will arrange something for next Tuesday."

"It'll end in an elephant ride, it always does. Look at this evening. *Cousin Kate!* Imagine, *Cousin Kate!* But where have you been off to? Did you succeed in catching the moon in the Ganges?"

The two ladies had happened, the night before, to see the moon's reflection in a distant channel of the stream. The water had drawn it out, so that it had seemed larger than the real moon, and brighter, which had pleased them.

"I went to the mosque, but I did not catch the moon."

"The angle would have altered—she rises later."

"Later and later," yawned Mrs. Moore, who was tired after her walk. "Let me think—we don't see the other side of the moon out here, no."

"Come, India's not as bad as all that," said a pleasant voice. "Other side of the earth, if you like, but we stick to the same old moon." Neither of them knew the speaker nor did they ever see him again. He passed with his friendly word through red-brick pillars into the darkness.

"We aren't even seeing the other side of the world; that's our complaint," said Adela. Mrs. Moore agreed; she too was disappointed at the dullness of their new life. They had made such a romantic voyage across the Mediterranean and through the sands of Egypt to the harbour of Bombay, to find only a gridiron of bungalows at the end of it. But she did not take the disappointment as seriously as Miss Quested, for the reason that she was forty years older, and had learnt that Life never gives us what we want at the moment that we consider appropriate. Adventures do occur, but not punctually. She said again that she hoped that something interesting would be arranged for next Tuesday.

"Have a drink," said another pleasant voice. "Mrs. Moore—Miss Quested—have a drink, have two drinks." They knew who it was this time—the Collector, Mr. Turton, with whom they had dined. Like themselves, he had found the atmosphere of *Cousin Kate* too hot. Ronny, he told them, was stage-managing in place of Major Callendar, whom some native subordinate or other had let down, and doing it very well; then he turned to Ronny's other merits, and in quiet, decisive tones said much that was flattering. It wasn't that the young man was particularly good at the games or the lingo, or that he had much notion of the Law, but—apparently a large but—Ronny was dignified.

Mrs. Moore was surprised to learn this, dignity not being a quality with which any mother credits her son. Miss Quested learnt it with anxiety, for she had not decided whether she liked dignified men. She tried indeed to discuss this point with Mr. Turton, but he silenced her with a good-humoured motion of his hand, and continued what he had come to say. "The long and the short of it is Heaslop's a sahib; he's the type we want, he's one of us," and another civilian who was leaning over the billiard table said, "Hear, hear!" The matter was thus placed beyond doubt, and the Collector passed on, for other duties called him.

Meanwhile the performance ended, and the amateur orchestra played the National Anthem. Conversation and billiards stopped, faces stiffened. It was the Anthem of the Army of Occupation. It reminded every member of the club that he or she was British and in exile. It produced a little sentiment and a useful accession of will-power. The meagre tune, the curt series of demands on Jehovah, fused into a prayer unknown in England, and though they perceived neither Royalty nor Deity they did perceive something, they were strengthened to resist another day. Then they poured out, offering one another drinks.

"Adela, have a drink; mother, a drink."

They refused—they were weary of drinks—and Miss Quested, who always said exactly what was in her mind, announced anew that she was desirous of seeing the real India.

Ronny was in high spirits. The request struck him as comic, and he called out to another passer-by: "Fielding! how's one to see the real India?"

"Try seeing Indians," the man answered, and vanished.

"Who was that?"

"Our schoolmaster—Government College."

"As if one could avoid seeing them," sighed Mrs. Lesley.

"I've avoided," said Miss Quested. "Excepting my own servant, I've scarcely spoken to an Indian since landing."

"Oh, lucky you."

"But I want to see them."

She became the centre of an amused group of ladies. One said, "Wanting to see Indians! How new that sounds!" Another, "Natives! why, fancy!" A third, more serious, said, "Let me explain. Natives don't respect one any the more after meeting one, you see."

"That occurs after so many meetings."

But the lady, entirely stupid and friendly, continued: "What I mean is, I was a nurse before my marriage, and came across them a great deal, so I know. I really do know the truth about Indians. A most unsuitable position for any Englishwoman—I was a nurse in a Native State. One's only hope was to hold sternly aloof."

"Even from one's patients?"

"Why, the kindest thing one can do to a native is to let him die," said Mrs. Callendar.

"How if he went to heaven?" asked Mrs. Moore, with a gentle but crooked smile.

"He can go where he likes as long as he doesn't come near me. They give me the creeps."

"As a matter of fact I have thought what you were saying about heaven, and that is why I am against Missionaries," said the lady who had been a nurse. "I am all for Chaplains, but all against Missionaries. Let me explain."

But before she could do so, the Collector intervened.

"Do you really want to meet the Aryan Brother, Miss Quested? That can be easily fixed up. I didn't realize he'd amuse you." He thought a moment. "You can practically see any type you like. Take your choice. I know the Government people and the landowners, Heaslop here can get hold of the barrister crew, while if you want to specialize on education, we can come down on Fielding."

"I'm tired of seeing picturesque figures pass before me as a frieze," the girl explained. "It was wonderful when we landed, but that superficial glamour soon goes."

Her impressions were of no interest to the Collector; he was only concerned to give her a good time. Would she like a Bridge Party?

He explained to her what that was—not the game, but a party to bridge the gulf between East and West; the expression was his own invention, and amused all who heard it.

"I only want those Indians whom you come across socially—as your friends."

"Well, we don't come across them socially," he said, laughing. "They're full of all the virtues, but we don't, and it's now eleven-thirty, and too late to go into the reasons."

"Miss Quested, what a name!" remarked Mrs. Turton to her husband as they drove away. She had not taken to the new young lady, thinking her ungracious and cranky. She trusted that she hadn't been brought out to marry nice little Heaslop, though it looked like it, Her husband agreed with her in his heart, but he never spoke against an Englishwoman if he could avoid doing so, and he only said that Miss Quested naturally made mistakes. He added: "India does wonders for the judgment, especially during the hot weather; it has even done wonders for Fielding." Mrs. Turton closed her eyes at this name and remarked that Mr. Fielding wasn't pukka, and had better marry Miss Quested, for she wasn't pukka. Then they reached their bungalow, low and enormous, the oldest and most uncomfortable bungalow in the civil station, with a sunk soup plate of a lawn, and they had one drink more, this time of barley water, and went to bed. Their withdrawal from the club had broken up the evening, which, like all gatherings, had an official tinge. A community that bows the knee to a Viceroy and believes that the divinity that hedges a king can be transplanted, must feel some reverence for any viceregal substitute. At Chandrapore the Turtons were little gods; soon they would retire to some suburban villa, and die exiled from glory.

"It's decent of the Burra Sahib," chattered Ronny, much gratified at the civility that had been shown to his guests. "Do you know he's never given a Bridge Party before? Coming on top of the dinner too! I wish I could have arranged something myself, but when you know the natives better you'll realize it's easier for the Burra Sahib than for me. They know him—they know he can't be fooled—I'm still fresh comparatively. No one can even begin to think of knowing this country until he has been in it twenty years.—Hullo, the mater! Here's your cloak.—Well: for an example of the mistakes one makes. Soon after I came out I asked one of the Pleaders to have a smoke with me—only a cigarette, mind. I found afterwards that he had sent touts all over the bazaar to announce the fact—told all the litigants, 'Oh, you'd better come to my Vakil Mahmoud Ali—he's in with the City Magistrate.' Ever since then I've dropped on him in Court as hard as I could. It's taught me a lesson, and I hope him."

"Isn't the lesson that you should invite all the Pleaders to have a smoke with you?"

"Perhaps, but time's limited and the flesh weak. I prefer my smoke at the club amongst my own sort, I'm afraid."

"Why not ask the Pleaders to the club?" Miss Quested persisted.

"Not allowed." He was pleasant and patient, and evidently understood why she did not understand. He implied that he had once been as she, though not for long. Going to the verandah, he called firmly to the moon. His sais answered, and without lowering his head, he ordered his trap to be brought round.

Mrs. Moore, whom the club had stupefied, woke up outside. She watched the moon, whose radiance stained with primrose the purple of the surrounding sky. In England the moon had seemed dead and alien; here she was caught in the shawl of night together with earth and all the other stars. A sudden sense of unity, of kinship with the heavenly bodies, passed into the old woman and out, like water through a tank, leaving a strange freshness behind. She did not dislike *Cousin Kate* or the National Anthem, but their note had died into a new one, just as cocktails and cigars had died into invisible flowers. When the mosque, long and domeless, gleamed at the turn of the road, she exclaimed, "Oh, yes—that's where I got to—that's where I've been."

"Been there when?" asked her son.

"Between the acts."

"But, mother, you can't do that sort of thing."

"Can't mother?" she replied.

"No, really not in this country. It's not done. There's the danger from snakes for one thing. They are apt to lie out in the evening."

"Ah yes, so the young man there said."

"This sounds very romantic," said Miss Quested, who was exceedingly fond of Mrs. Moore, and was glad she should have had this little escapade. "You meet a young man in a mosque, and then never let me know!"

"I was going to tell you, Adela, but something changed the conversation and I forgot. My memory grows deplorable."

"Was he nice?"

She paused, then said emphatically: "Very nice."

"Who was he?" Ronny enquired.

"A doctor. I don't know his name."

"A doctor? I know of no young doctor in Chandrapore. How odd! What was he like?"

"Rather small, with a little moustache and quick eyes. He called out to me when I was in the dark part of the mosque—about my shoes. That was how we began talking. He was afraid I had them on, but I remembered luckily. He told me about his children, and then we walked back to the club. He knows you well."

"I wish you had pointed him out to me. I can't make out who he is."

"He didn't come into the club. He said he wasn't allowed to."

Thereupon the truth struck him, and he cried "Oh, good gracious! Not a Mohammedan? Why ever didn't you tell me you'd been talking to a native? I was going all wrong."

"A Mohammedan! How perfectly magnificent!" exclaimed Miss Quested. "Ronny, isn't that like your mother? While we talk about seeing the real India, she goes and sees it, and then forgets she's seen it."

But Ronny was ruffled. From his mother's description he had thought the doctor might be young Muggins from over the Ganges, and had brought out all the comradely emotions. What a mix-up! Why hadn't she indicated by the tone of her voice that she was talking about an Indian? Scratchy and dictatorial, he began to question her. "He called to you in the mosque, did he? How? Impudently? What was he doing there himself at that time of night?—No, it's not their prayer time."—This in answer to a suggestion of Miss Quested's, who showed the keenest interest. "So he called to you over your shoes. Then it was impudence. It's an old trick. I wish you had had them on."

"I think it was impudence, but I don't know about a trick," said Mrs. Moore. "His nerves were all on edge—I could tell from his voice. As soon as I answered he altered."

"You oughtn't to have answered."

"Now look here," said the logical girl, "wouldn't you expect a Mohammedan to answer if you asked him to take off his hat in church?"

"It's different, it's different; you don't understand."

"I know I don't, and I want to. What is the difference, please?"

He wished she wouldn't interfere. His mother did not signify—she was just a globe-trotter, a temporary escort, who could retire to England with what impressions she chose. But Adela, who meditated spending her life in the country, was a more serious matter; it would be tiresome if she started crooked over the native question. Pulling up the mare, he said, "There's your Ganges."

Their attention was diverted. Below them a radiance had suddenly appeared. It belonged neither to water nor moonlight, but stood like a luminous sheaf upon the fields of darkness. He told them that it was where the new sand-bank was forming, and that the dark ravelled bit at the top was the sand, and that the dead bodies floated down that way from Benares, or would if the crocodiles let them. "It's not much of a dead body that gets down to Chandrapore."

"Crocodiles down in it too, how terrible!" his mother murmured. The young people glanced at each other and smiled; it amused them when the old lady got these gentle creeps, and harmony was restored between them consequently. She continued: "What a terrible river! what a wonderful river!" and sighed. The radiance was already altering, whether through shifting of the moon or of the sand; soon the bright sheaf would be gone, and a circlet, itself to alter, be burnished upon the streaming void. The women discussed whether they would wait for the change or not, while the silence broke into patches of unquietness and the mare shivered. On her account they did not wait, but drove on to the City Magistrate's bungalow, where Miss Quested went to bed, and Mrs. Moore had a short interview with her son.

He wanted to enquire about the Mohammedan doctor in the mosque. It was his duty to report suspicious characters and conceivably it was some disreputable hakim who had prowled up from the bazaar. When she told him that it was someone connected with the Minto Hospital, he was relieved, and said that the fellow's name must be Aziz, and that he was quite all right, nothing against him at all.

"Aziz! what a charming name!"

"So you and he had a talk. Did you gather he was well disposed?"

Ignorant of the force of this question, she replied, "Yes, quite, after the first moment."

"I meant, generally. Did he seem to tolerate us—the brutal conqueror, the sundried bureaucrat, that sort of thing?"

"Oh, yes, I think so, except the Callendars—he doesn't care for the Callendars at all."

"Oh. So he told you that, did he? The Major will be interested. I wonder what was the aim of the remark."

"Ronny, Ronny! you're never going to pass it on to Major Callendar?"

"Yes, rather. I must, in fact!"

"But, my dear boy——"

"If the Major heard I was disliked by any native subordinate of mine, I should expect him to pass it on to me."

"But, my dear boy—a private conversation!"

"Nothing's private in India. Aziz knew that when he spoke out, so don't you worry. He had some motive in what he said. My personal belief is that the remark wasn't true."

"How not true?"

"He abused the Major in order to impress you."

"I don't know what you mean, dear."

"It's the educated native's latest dodge. They used to cringe, but the younger generation believe in a show of manly independence. They think it will pay better with the itinerant M.P. But whether the native swaggers or cringes, there's always something behind every remark he makes, always something, and if nothing else he's trying to increase his izzat—in plain Anglo-Saxon, to score. Of course there are exceptions."

"You never used to judge people like this at home."

"India isn't home," he retorted, rather rudely, but in order to silence her he had been using phrases and arguments that he had picked up from older officials, and he did not feel quite sure of himself. When he said "of course there are exceptions" he was quoting Mr. Turton, while "increasing the izzat" was Major Callendar's own. The phrases worked and were in current use at the club, but she was rather clever at detecting the first from the second hand, and might press him for definite examples.

She only said, "I can't deny that what you say sounds very sensible, but you really must not hand on to Major Callendar anything I have told you about Doctor Aziz."

He felt disloyal to his caste, but he promised, adding, "In return please don't talk about Aziz to Adela."

"Not talk about him? Why?"

"There you go again, mother—I really can't explain everything. I don't want Adela to be worried, that's the fact; she'll begin wondering whether we treat the natives properly, and all that sort of nonsense."

"But she came out to be worried—that's exactly why she's here. She discussed it all on the boat. We had a long talk when we went on shore at Aden. She knows you in play, as she put it, but not in work, and she felt she must come and look round, before she decided—and before you decided. She is very, very fair-minded."

"I know," he said dejectedly.

The note of anxiety in his voice made her feel that he was still a little boy, who must have what he liked, so she promised to do as he wished, and they kissed good night. He had not forbidden her to think about Aziz, however, and she did this when she retired to her room. In the light of her son's comment she reconsidered the scene at the mosque, to see whose impression was correct. Yes, it could be worked into quite an unpleasant scene. The doctor had begun by bullying her, had said Mrs. Callendar was nice, and then—finding the ground safe—had changed; he had alternately whined over his grievances and patronized her, had run a dozen ways in a single sentence, had been unreliable, inquisitive, vain. Yes, it was all true, but how false as a summary of the man; the essential life of him had been slain.

Going to hang up her cloak, she found that the tip of the peg was occupied by a small wasp. She had known this wasp or his relatives by day; they were not as English wasps, but had long yellow legs which hung down behind when they flew. Perhaps he mistook the peg for a branch—no Indian animal has any sense of an interior. Bats, rats, birds, insects will as soon nest inside a house as out; it is to them a normal growth of the eternal jungle, which alternately produces houses trees, houses trees. There he clung, asleep, while jackals in the plain bayed their desires and mingled with the percussion of drums.

"Pretty dear," said Mrs. Moore to the wasp. He did not wake, but her voice floated out, to swell the night's uneasiness.

CHAPTER 4

The Collector kept his word. Next day he issued invitation cards to numerous Indian gentlemen in the neighbourhood, stating that he would be at home in the garden of the club between the hours of five and seven on the following Tuesday, also that Mrs. Turton would be glad to receive any ladies of their families who were out of purdah. His action caused much excitement and was discussed in several worlds.

"It is owing to orders from the L.G.," was Mahmoud Ali's explanation. "Turton would never do this unless compelled. Those high officials are different—they sympathize, the Viceroy sympathizes, they would have us treated properly. But they come too seldom and live too far away. Meanwhile——"

"It is easy to sympathize at a distance," said an old gentleman with a beard. "I value more the kind word that is spoken close to my ear. Mr. Turton has spoken it, from whatever cause. He speaks, we hear. I do not see why we need discuss it further." Quotations followed from the Koran.

"We have not all your sweet nature, Nawab Bahadur, nor your learning."

"The Lieutenant-Governor may be my very good friend, but I give him no trouble.—How do you do, Nawab Bahadur?—Quite well, thank you, Sir Gilbert; how are you?—And all is over. But I can be a thorn in Mr. Turton's flesh, and if he asks me I accept the invitation. I shall come in from Dilkusha specially, though I have to postpone other business."

"You will make yourself chip," suddenly said a little black man.

There was a stir of disapproval. Who was this ill-bred upstart, that he should criticize the leading Mohammedan landowner of the district? Mahmoud Ali, though sharing his opinion, felt bound to oppose it. "Mr. Ram Chand!" he said, swaying forward stiffly with his hands on his hips.

"Mr. Mahmoud Ali!"

"Mr. Ram Chand, the Nawab Bahadur can decide what is cheap without our valuation, I think."

"I do not expect I shall make myself cheap," said the Nawab Bahadur to Mr. Ram Chand, speaking very pleasantly, for he was aware that the man had been impolite and he desired to shield him from the consequences. It had passed through his mind to reply, "I expect I shall make myself cheap," but he rejected this as the less courteous alternative. "I do not see why we should make ourselves cheap. I do not see why we should. The invitation is worded very graciously." Feeling that he could not further decrease the social gulf between himself and his auditors, he sent his elegant grandson, who was in attendance on him, to fetch his car. When it came, he repeated all that he had said before, though at greater length, ending up with "Till Tuesday, then, gentlemen all, when I hope we may meet in the flower gardens of the club."

This opinion carried great weight. The Nawab Bahadur was a big proprietor and a philanthropist, a man of benevolence and decision. His character among all the communities in the province stood high. He was a straightforward enemy and a staunch friend, and his hospitality was proverbial. "Give, do not lend; after death who will thank you?" was his favourite remark. He held it a disgrace to die rich. When such a man was prepared to motor twenty-five miles to shake the Collector's hand, the entertainment took another aspect.

For he was not like some eminent men, who give out that they will come, and then fail at the last moment, leaving the small fry floundering. If he said he would come, he would come, he would never deceive his supporters. The gentlemen whom he had lectured now urged one another to attend the party, although convinced at heart that his advice was unsound.

He had spoken in the little room near the Courts where the pleaders waited for clients; clients, waiting for pleaders, sat in the dust outside. These had not received a card from Mr. Turton. And there were circles even beyond these—people who wore nothing but a loincloth, people who wore not even that, and spent their lives in knocking two sticks together before a scarlet doll—humanity grading and drifting beyond the educated vision, until no earthly invitation can embrace it.

All invitations must proceed from heaven perhaps; perhaps it is futile for men to initiate their own unity, they do but widen the gulfs between them by the attempt. So at all events thought old Mr. Graysford and young Mr. Sorley, the devoted missionaries who lived out beyond the slaughterhouses, always travelled third on the railways, and never came up to the club. In our Father's house are many mansions, they taught, and there alone will the incompatible multitudes of mankind be welcomed and soothed. Not one shall be turned away by the servants on that verandah, be he black or white, not one shall be kept standing who approaches with a loving heart. And why should the divine hospitality cease here? Consider, with all reverence, the monkeys. May there not be a mansion for the monkeys also? Old Mr. Graysford said No, but young Mr. Sorley, who was advanced, said Yes; he saw no reason why monkeys should not have their collateral share of bliss, and he had sympathetic discussions about them with his Hindu friends. And the jackals? Jackals were indeed less to Mr. Sorley's mind, but he admitted that the mercy of God, being infinite, may well embrace all mammals. And the wasps? He became uneasy during the descent to wasps, and was apt to change the conversation.

And oranges, cactuses, crystals and mud? and the bacteria inside Mr. Sorley? No, no, this is going too far. We must exclude someone from our gathering, or we shall be left with nothing.

CHAPTER 5

The Bridge Party was not a success—at least it was not what Mrs. Moore and Miss Quested were accustomed to consider a successful party. They arrived early, since it was given in their honour, but most of the Indian guests had arrived even earlier, and stood massed at the farther side of the tennis lawns, doing nothing.

"It is only just five," said Mrs. Turton. "My husband will be up from his office in a moment and start the thing. I have no idea what we have to do. It's the first time we've ever given a party like this at the club. Mr. Heaslop, when I'm dead and gone will you give parties like this? It's enough to make the old type of Burra Sahib turn in his grave."

Ronny laughed deferentially. "You wanted something not picturesque and we've provided it," he remarked to Miss Quested. "What do you think of the Aryan Brother in a topi and spats?"

Neither she nor his mother answered. They were gazing rather sadly over the tennis lawn. No, it was not picturesque; the East, abandoning its secular magnificence, was descending into a valley whose farther side no man can see.

"The great point to remember is that no one who's here matters; those who matter don't come. Isn't that so, Mrs. Turton?"

"Absolutely true," said the great lady, leaning back. She was "saving herself up," as she called it—not for anything that would happen that afternoon or even that week, but for some vague future occasion when a high official might come along and tax her social strength. Most of her public appearances were marked by this air of reserve.

Assured of her approbation, Ronny continued: "The educated Indians will be no good to us if there's a row, it's simply not worth while conciliating them, that's why they don't matter. Most of the people you see are seditious at heart, and the rest 'ld run squealing. The cultivator—he's another story. The Pathan—he's a man if you like. But these people—don't imagine they're India." He pointed to the dusky line beyond the court, and here and there it flashed a pince-nez or shuffled a shoe, as if aware that he was despising it. European costume had lighted like a leprosy. Few had yielded entirely, but none were untouched. There was a silence when he had finished speaking, on both sides of the court; at least, more ladies joined the English group, but their words seemed to die as soon as uttered. Some kites hovered overhead, impartial, over the kites passed the mass of a vulture, and with an impartiality exceeding all, the sky, not deeply coloured but translucent, poured light from its whole circumference. It seemed unlikely that the series stopped here. Beyond the sky must not there be something that overarches all the skies, more impartial even than they? Beyond which again...

They spoke of *Cousin Kate.*

They had tried to reproduce their own attitude to life upon the stage, and to dress up as the middle-class English people they actually were. Next year they would do *Quality Street* or *The Yeomen of the Guard.* Save for this annual incursion, they left literature alone. The men had no time for it, the women did nothing that they could not share with the men. Their ignorance of the Arts was notable, and they lost no opportunity of proclaiming it to one another; it was the Public School attitude, flourishing more vigorously than it can yet hope to do in England. If Indians were shop, the Arts were bad form, and Ronny had repressed his mother when she enquired after his viola; a viola was almost a demerit, and certainly not the sort of instrument one mentioned in public. She noticed now how tolerant and conventional his judgments had become; when they had seen *Cousin Kate* in London together in the past, he had scorned it; now he pretended that it was a good play, in order to hurt nobody's feelings. An "unkind notice" had appeared in the local paper, "the sort of thing no white man could have written," as Mrs. Lesley said. The play was praised, to be sure, and so were the stage management and the performance as a whole, but the notice contained the following sentence: "Miss Derek, though she charmingly looked her part, lacked the necessary experience, and occasionally forgot her words." This tiny breath of genuine criticism had given deep offence, not indeed to Miss Derek, who was as hard as nails, but to her friends. Miss Derek did not belong to Chandrapore. She was stopping for a fortnight with the McBrydes, the police people, and she had been so good as to fill up a gap in the cast at the last moment. A nice impression of local hospitality she would carry away with her.

"To work, Mary, to work," cried the Collector, touching his wife on the shoulder with a switch.

Mrs. Turton got up awkwardly. "What do you want me to do? Oh, those purdah women! I never thought any would come. Oh dear!"

A little group of Indian ladies had been gathering in a third quarter of the grounds, near a rustic summer-house in which the more timid of them had already taken refuge. The rest stood with their backs to the company and their faces pressed into a bank of shrubs. At a little distance stood their male relatives, watching the venture. The sight was significant: an island bared by the turning tide, and bound to grow.

"I consider they ought to come over to me."

"Come along, Mary, get it over."

"I refuse to shake hands with any of the men, unless it has to be the Nawab Bahadur."

"Whom have we so far?" He glanced along the line. "H'm! h'm! much as one expected. We know why he's here, I think—over that contract, and he wants to get the right side of me for Mohurram, and he's the astrologer who wants to dodge the municipal building regulations, and he's that Parsi, and he's—Hullo! there he goes—smash into our hollyhocks. Pulled the left rein when he meant the right. All as usual."

"They ought never to have been allowed to drive in; it's so bad for them," said Mrs. Turton, who had at last begun her progress to the summer-house, accompanied by Mrs. Moore, Miss Quested, and a terrier. "Why they come at all I don't know. They hate it as much as we do. Talk to Mrs. McBryde. Her husband made her give purdah parties until she struck."

"This isn't a purdah party," corrected Miss Quested.

"Oh, really," was the haughty rejoinder.

"Do kindly tell us who these ladies are," asked Mrs. Moore.

"You're superior to them, anyway. Don't forget that. You're superior to everyone in India except one or two of the Ranis, and they're on an equality."

Advancing, she shook hands with the group and said a few words of welcome in Urdu. She had learnt the lingo, but only to speak to her servants, so she knew none of the politer forms and of the verbs only the imperative mood. As soon as her speech was over, she enquired of her companions, "Is that what you wanted?"

"Please tell these ladies that I wish we could speak their language, but we have only just come to their country."

"Perhaps we speak yours a little," one of the ladies said.

"Why, fancy, she understands!" said Mrs. Turton.

"Eastbourne, Piccadilly, High Park Corner," said another of the ladies.

"Oh yes, they're English-speaking."

"But now we can talk: how delightful!" cried Adela, her face lighting up.

"She knows Paris also," called one of the onlookers.

"They pass Paris on the way, no doubt," said Mrs. Turton, as if she was describing the movements of migratory birds. Her manner had grown more distant since she had discovered that some of the group was Westernized, and might apply her own standards to her.

"The shorter lady, she is my wife, she is Mrs. Bhattacharya," the onlooker explained. "The taller lady, she is my sister, she is Mrs. Das."

The shorter and the taller ladies both adjusted their saris, and smiled. There was a curious uncertainty about their gestures, as if they sought for a new formula which neither East nor West could provide. When Mrs. Bhattacharya's husband spoke, she turned away from him, but she did not mind seeing the other men. Indeed all the ladies were uncertain, cowering, recovering, giggling, making tiny gestures of atonement or despair at all that was said, and alternately fondling the terrier or shrinking from him. Miss Quested now had her desired opportunity; friendly Indians were before her, and she tried to make them talk, but she failed, she strove in vain against the echoing walls of their civility. Whatever she said produced a murmur of deprecation, varying into a murmur of concern when she dropped her pocket-handkerchief. She tried doing nothing, to see what that produced, and they too did nothing. Mrs. Moore was equally unsuccessful. Mrs. Turton waited for them with a detached expression; she had known what nonsense it all was from the first.

When they took their leave, Mrs. Moore had an impulse, and said to Mrs. Bhattacharya, whose face she liked, "I wonder whether you would allow us to call on you some day."

"When?" she replied, inclining charmingly.

"Whenever is convenient."

"All days are convenient."

"Thursday..."

"Most certainly."

"We shall enjoy it greatly, it would be a real pleasure. What about the time?"

"All hours."

"Tell us which you would prefer. We're quite strangers to your country; we don't know when you have visitors," said Miss Quested.

Mrs. Bhattacharya seemed not to know either. Her gesture implied that she had known, since Thursdays began, that English ladies would come to see her on one of them, and so always stayed in. Everything pleased her, nothing surprised. She added, "We leave for Calcutta to-day."

"Oh, do you?" said Adela, not at first seeing the implication. Then she cried, "Oh, but if you do we shall find you gone."

Mrs. Bhattacharya did not dispute it. But her husband called from the distance, "Yes, yes, you come to us Thursday."

"But you'll be in Calcutta."

"No, no, we shall not." He said something swiftly to his wife in Bengali. "We expect you Thursday."

"Thursday..." the woman echoed.

"You can't have done such a dreadful thing as to put off going for our sake?" exclaimed Mrs. Moore.

"No, of course not, we are not such people." He was laughing.

"I believe that you have. Oh, please—it distresses me beyond words."

Everyone was laughing now, but with no suggestion that they had blundered. A shapeless discussion occurred, during which Mrs. Turton retired, smiling to herself. The upshot was that they were to come Thursday, but early in the morning, so as to wreck the Bhattacharya plans as little as possible, and Mr. Bhattacharya would send his carriage to fetch them, with servants to point out the way. Did he know where they lived? Yes, of course he knew, he knew everything; and he laughed again. They left among a flutter of compliments and smiles, and three ladies, who had hitherto taken no part in the reception, suddenly shot out of the summer-house like exquisitely coloured swallows, and salaamed them.

Meanwhile the Collector had been going his rounds. He made pleasant remarks and a few jokes, which were applauded lustily, but he knew something to the discredit of nearly every one of his guests, and was consequently perfunctory. When they had not cheated, it was bhang, women, or worse, and even the desirables wanted to get something out of him. He believed that a "Bridge Party" did good rather than harm, or he would not have given one, but he was under no illusions, and at the proper moment he retired to the English side of the lawn. The impressions he left behind him were various. Many of the guests, especially the humbler and less anglicized, were genuinely grateful. To be addressed by so high an official was a permanent asset. They did not mind how long they stood, or how little happened, and when seven o'clock struck, they had to be turned out. Others were grateful with more intelligence. The Nawab Bahadur, indifferent for himself and for the distinction with which he was greeted, was moved by the mere kindness that must have prompted the invitation. He knew the difficulties. Hamidullah also thought that the Collector had played up well. But others, such as Mahmoud Ali, were cynical; they were firmly convinced that Turton had been made to give the party by his official superiors and was all the time consumed with impotent rage, and they infected some who were inclined to a healthier view. Yet even Mahmoud Ali was glad he had come. Shrines are fascinating, especially when rarely opened, and it amused him to note the ritual of the English club, and to caricature it afterwards to his friends.

After Mr. Turton, the official who did his duty best was Mr. Fielding, the Principal of the little Government College. He knew little of the district and less against the inhabitants, so he was in a less cynical state of mind. Athletic and cheerful, he romped about, making numerous mistakes which the parents of his pupils tried to cover up, for he was popular among them. When the moment for refreshments came, he did not move back to the English side, but burnt his mouth with gram. He talked to anyone and he ate anything. Amid much that was alien, he learnt that the two new ladies from England had been a great success, and that their politeness in wishing to be Mrs. Bhattacharya's guests had pleased not only her but all Indians who heard of it. It pleased Mr. Fielding also. He scarcely knew the two new ladies, still he decided to tell them what pleasure they had given by their friendliness.

He found the younger of them alone. She was looking through a nick in the cactus hedge at the distant Marabar Hills, which had crept near, as was their custom at sunset; if the sunset had lasted long enough, they would have reached the town, but it was swift, being tropical. He gave her his information, and she was so much pleased and thanked him so heartily that he asked her and the other lady to tea.

"I'ld like to come very much indeed, and so would Mrs. Moore, I know."

"I'm rather a hermit, you know."

"Much the best thing to be in this place."

"Owing to my work and so on, I don't get up much to the club."

"I know, I know, and we never get down from it. I envy you being with Indians."

"Do you care to meet one or two?"

"Very, very much indeed; it's what I long for. This party to-day makes me so angry and miserable. I think my countrymen out here must be mad. Fancy inviting guests and not treating them properly! You and Mr. Turton and perhaps Mr. McBryde are the only people who showed any common politeness. The rest make me perfectly ashamed, and it's got worse and worse."

It had. The Englishmen had intended to play up better, but had been prevented from doing so by their women folk, whom they had to attend, provide with tea, advise about dogs, etc. When tennis began, the barrier grew impenetrable. It had been hoped to have some sets between East and West, but this was forgotten, and the courts were monopolized by the usual club couples. Fielding resented it too, but did not say so to the girl, for he found something theoretical in her outburst. Did she care about Indian music? he enquired; there was an old professor down at the College, who sang.

"Oh, just what we wanted to hear. And do you know Doctor Aziz?"

"I know all about him. I don't know him. Would you like him asked too?"

"Mrs. Moore says he is so nice."

"Very well, Miss Quested. Will Thursday suit you?"

"Indeed it will, and that morning we go to this Indian lady's. All the nice things are coming Thursday."

"I won't ask the City Magistrate to bring you. I know he'll be busy at that time."

"Yes, Ronny is always hard-worked," she replied, contemplating the hills. How lovely they suddenly were! But she couldn't touch them. In front, like a shutter, fell a vision of her married life. She and Ronny would look into the club like this every evening, then drive home to dress; they would see the Lesleys and the Callendars and the Turtons and the Burtons, and invite them and be invited by them, while the true India slid by unnoticed. Colour would remain—the pageant of birds in the early morning, brown bodies, white turbans, idols whose flesh was scarlet or blue—and movement would remain as long as there were crowds in the bazaar and bathers in the tanks. Perched up on the seat of a dogcart, she would see them. But the force that lies behind colour and movement would escape her even more effectually than it did now. She would see India always as a frieze, never as a spirit, and she assumed that it was a spirit of which Mrs. Moore had had a glimpse.

And sure enough they did drive away from the club in a few minutes, and they did dress, and to dinner came Miss Derek and the McBrydes, and the menu was: Julienne soup full of bullety bottled peas, pseudo-cottage bread, fish full of branching bones, pretending to be plaice, more bottled peas with the cutlets, trifle, sardines on toast: the menu of Anglo-India. A dish might be added or subtracted as one rose or fell in the official scale, the peas might rattle less or more, the sardines and the vermouth be imported by a different firm, but the tradition remained; the food of exiles, cooked by servants who did not understand it. Adela thought of the young men and women who had come out before her, P. & O. full after P. & O. full, and had been set down to the same food and the same ideas, and been snubbed in the same good-humoured way until they kept to the accredited themes and began to snub others. "I should never get like that," she thought, for she was young herself; all the same she knew that she had come up against something that was both insidious and tough, and against which she needed allies. She must gather around her at Chandrapore a few people who felt as she did, and she was glad to have met Mr. Fielding and the Indian lady with the unpronounceable name. Here at all events was a nucleus; she should know much better where she stood in the course of the next two days.

Miss Derek—she companioned a Maharani in a remote Native State. She was genial and gay and made them all laugh about her leave, which she had taken because she felt she deserved it, not because the Maharani said she might go. Now she wanted to take the Maharajah's motor-car as well; it had gone to a Chiefs' Conference at Delhi, and she had a great scheme for burgling it at the junction as it came back in the train. She was also very funny about the Bridge Party—indeed she regarded the entire peninsula as a comic opera. "If one couldn't see the laughable side of these people one 'ld be done for," said Miss Derek. Mrs. McBryde—it was she who had been the nurse—ceased not to exclaim, "Oh, Nancy, how topping! Oh, Nancy, how killing! I wish I could look at things like that." Mr. McBryde did not speak much; he seemed nice.

When the guests had gone, and Adela gone to bed, there was another interview between mother and son. He wanted her advice and support—while resenting interference. "Does Adela talk to you much?" he began. "I'm so driven with work, I don't see her as much as I hoped, but I hope she finds things comfortable."

"Adela and I talk mostly about India. Dear, since you mention it, you're quite right—you ought to be more alone with her than you are."

"Yes, perhaps, but then people'ld gossip."

"Well, they must gossip sometime! Let them gossip."

"People are so odd out here, and it's not like home—one's always facing the footlights, as the Burra Sahib said. Take a silly little example: when Adela went out to the boundary of the club compound, and Fielding followed her. I saw Mrs. Callendar notice it. They notice everything, until they're perfectly sure you're their sort."

"I don't think Adela 'll ever be quite their sort—she's much too individual."

"I know, that's so remarkable about her," he said thoughtfully. Mrs. Moore thought him rather absurd. Accustomed to the privacy of London, she could not realize that India, seemingly so mysterious, contains none, and that consequently the conventions have greater force. "I suppose nothing's on her mind," he continued.

"Ask her, ask her yourself, my dear boy."

"Probably she's heard tales of the heat, but of course I should pack her off to the Hills every April—I'm not one to keep a wife grilling in the Plains."

"Oh, it wouldn't be the weather."

"There's nothing in India but the weather, my dear mother; it's the Alpha and Omega of the whole affair."

"Yes, as Mr. McBryde was saying, but it's much more the Anglo-Indians themselves who are likely to get on Adela's nerves. She doesn't think they behave pleasantly to Indians, you see."

"What did I tell you?" he exclaimed, losing his gentle manner. "I knew it last week. Oh, how like a woman to worry over a side-issue!"

She forgot about Adela in her surprise. "A side-issue, a side-issue?" she repeated. "How can it be that?"

"We're not out here for the purpose of behaving pleasantly!"

"What do you mean?"

"What I say. We're out here to do justice and keep the peace. Them's my sentiments. India isn't a drawing-room."

"Your sentiments are those of a god," she said quietly, but it was his manner rather than his sentiments that annoyed her.

Trying to recover his temper, he said, "India likes gods."

"And Englishmen like posing as gods."

"There's no point in all this. Here we are, and we're going to stop, and the country's got to put up with us, gods or no gods. Oh, look here," he broke out, rather pathetically, "what do you and Adela want me to do? Go against my class, against all the people I respect and admire out here? Lose such power as I have for doing good in this country because my behaviour isn't pleasant? You neither of you understand what work is, or you 'ld never talk such eyewash. I hate talking like this, but one must occasionally. It's morbidly sensitive to go on as Adela and you do. I noticed you both at the club to-day—after the Burra Sahib had been at all that trouble to amuse you. I am out here to work, mind, to hold this wretched country by force. I'm not a missionary or a Labour Member or a vague sentimental sympathetic literary man. I'm just a servant of the Government; it's the profession you wanted me to choose myself, and that's that. We're not pleasant in India, and we don't intend to be pleasant. We've something more important to do."

He spoke sincerely. Every day he worked hard in the court trying to decide which of two untrue accounts was the less untrue, trying to dispense justice fearlessly, to protect the weak against the less weak, the incoherent against the plausible, surrounded by lies and flattery. That morning he had convicted a railway clerk of overcharging pilgrims for their tickets, and a Pathan of attempted rape. He expected no gratitude, no recognition for this, and both clerk and Pathan might appeal, bribe their witnesses more effectually in the interval, and get their sentences reversed. It was his duty. But he did expect sympathy from his own people, and except from new-comers he obtained it. He did think he ought not to be worried about "Bridge Parties" when the day's work was over and he wanted to play tennis with his equals or rest his legs upon a long chair.

He spoke sincerely, but she could have wished with less gusto. How Ronny revelled in the drawbacks of his situation! How he did rub it in that he was not in India to behave pleasantly, and derived positive satisfaction there from! He reminded her of his public-schooldays. The traces of young-man humanitarianism had sloughed off, and he talked like an intelligent and embittered boy. His words without his voice might have impressed her, but when she heard the self-satisfied lilt of them, when she saw the mouth moving so complacently and competently beneath the little red nose, she felt, quite illogically, that this was not the last word on India. One touch of regret—not the canny substitute but the true regret from the heart—would have made him a different man, and the British Empire a different institution.

"I'm going to argue, and indeed dictate," she said, clinking her rings. "The English are out here to be pleasant."

"How do you make that out, mother?" he asked, speaking gently again, for he was ashamed of his irritability.

"Because India is part of the earth. And God has put us on the earth in order to be pleasant to each other. God... is... love." She hesitated, seeing how much he disliked the argument, but something made her go on. "God has put us on earth to love our neighbours and to show it, and He is omnipresent, even in India, to see how we are succeeding."

He looked gloomy, and a little anxious. He knew this religious strain in her, and that it was a symptom of bad health; there had been much of it when his stepfather died. He thought, "She is certainly ageing, and I ought not to be vexed with anything she says."

"The desire to behave pleasantly satisfies God... The sincere if impotent desire wins His blessing. I think everyone fails, but there are so many kinds of failure. Good will and more good will and more good will. Though I speak with the tongues of..."

He waited until she had done, and then said gently, "I quite see that. I suppose I ought to get off to my files now, and you'll be going to bed."

"I suppose so, I suppose so." They did not part for a few minutes, but the conversation had become unreal since Christianity had entered it. Ronny approved of religion as long as it endorsed the National Anthem, but he objected when it attempted to influence his life. Then he would say in respectful yet decided tones, "I don't think it does to talk about these things, every fellow has to work out his own religion," and any fellow who heard him muttered, "Hear!"

Mrs. Moore felt that she had made a mistake in mentioning God, but she found him increasingly difficult to avoid as she grew older, and he had been constantly in her thoughts since she entered India, though oddly enough he satisfied her less. She must needs pronounce his name frequently, as the greatest she knew, yet she had never found it less efficacious. Outside the arch there seemed always an arch, beyond the remotest echo a silence. And she regretted afterwards that she had not kept to the real serious subject that had caused her to visit India—namely the relationship between Ronny and Adela. Would they, or would they not, succeed in becoming engaged to be married?

Chapter 6

Aziz had not gone to the Bridge Party. Immediately after his meeting with Mrs. Moore he was diverted to other matters. Several surgical cases came in, and kept him busy. He ceased to be either outcaste or poet, and became the medical student, very gay, and full of details of operations which he poured into the shrinking ears of his friends. His profession fascinated him at times, but he required it to be exciting, and it was his hand, not his mind, that was scientific. The knife he loved and used skilfully, and he also liked pumping in the latest serums. But the boredom of regime and hygiene repelled him, and after inoculating a man for enteric, he would go away and drink unfiltered water himself. "What can you expect from the fellow?" said dour Major Callendar. "No grits, no guts." But in his heart he knew that if Aziz and not he had operated last year on Mrs. Graysford's appendix, the old lady would probably have lived. And this did not dispose him any better towards his subordinate.

There was a row the morning after the mosque—they were always having rows. The Major, who had been up half the night, wanted damn well to know why Aziz had not come promptly when summoned.

"Sir, excuse me, I did. I mounted my bike, and it bust in front of the Cow Hospital. So I had to find a tonga."

"Bust in front of the Cow Hospital, did it? And how did you come to be there?"

"I beg your pardon?"

"Oh Lord, oh Lord! When I live here"—he kicked the gravel—"and you live there—not ten minutes from me—and the Cow Hospital is right ever so far away the other side of you—*there*—then how did you come to be passing the Cow Hospital on the way to me? Now do some work for a change."

He strode away in a temper, without waiting for the excuse, which as far as it went was a sound one: the Cow Hospital was in a straight line between Hamidullah's house and his own, so Aziz had naturally passed it. He never realized that the educated Indians visited one another constantly, and were weaving, however painfully, a new social fabric. Caste "or something of the sort" would prevent them. He only knew that no one ever told him the truth, although he had been in the country for twenty years.

Aziz watched him go with amusement. When his spirits were up he felt that the English are a comic institution, and he enjoyed being misunderstood by them. But it was an amusement of the emotions and nerves, which an accident or the passage of time might destroy; it was apart from the fundamental gaiety that he reached when he was with those whom he trusted. A disobliging simile involving Mrs. Callendar occurred to his fancy. "I must tell that to Mahmoud Ali, it'll make him laugh," he thought. Then he got to work. He was competent and indispensable, and he knew it. The simile passed from his mind while he exercised his professional skill.

During these pleasant and busy days, he heard vaguely that the Collector was giving a party, and that the Nawab Bahadur said every one ought to go to it. His fellow-assistant, Doctor Panna Lal, was in ecstasies at the prospect, and was urgent that they should attend it together in his new tum-tum. The arrangement suited them both. Aziz was spared the indignity of a bicycle or the expense of hiring, while Dr. Panna Lal, who was timid and elderly, secured someone who could manage his horse. He could manage it himself, but only just, and he was afraid of the motors and of the unknown turn into the club grounds. "Disaster may come," he said politely, "but we shall at all events get there safe, even if we do not get back." And with more logic: "It will, I think, create a good impression should two doctors arrive at the same time."

But when the time came, Aziz was seized with a revulsion, and determined not to go. For one thing his spell of work, lately concluded, left him independent and healthy. For another, the day chanced to fall on the anniversary of his wife's death. She had died soon after he had fallen in love with her; he had not loved her at first. Touched by Western feeling, he disliked union with a woman whom he had never seen; moreover, when he did see her, she disappointed him, and he begat his first child in mere animality. The change began after its birth. He was won by her love for him, by a loyalty that implied something more than submission, and by her efforts to educate herself against that lifting of the purdah that would come in the next generation if not in theirs. She was intelligent, yet had old-fashioned grace. Gradually he lost the feeling that his relatives had chosen wrongly for him. Sensuous enjoyment—well, even if he had had it, it would have dulled in a year, and he had gained something instead, which seemed to increase the longer they lived together. She became the mother of a son... and in giving him a second son she died. Then he realized what he had lost, and that no woman could ever take her place; a friend would come nearer to her than another woman. She had gone, there was no one like her, and what is that uniqueness but love? He amused himself, he forgot her at times: but at other times he felt that she had sent all the beauty and joy of the world into Paradise, and he meditated suicide. Would he meet her beyond the tomb? Is there such a meeting-place? Though orthodox, he did not know. God's unity was indubitable and indubitably announced, but on all other points he wavered like the average Christian; his belief in the life to come would pale to a hope, vanish, reappear, all in a single sentence or a dozen heart-beats, so that the corpuscles of his blood rather than he seemed to decide which opinion he should hold, and for how long. It was so with all his opinions. Nothing stayed, nothing passed that did not return; the circulation was ceaseless and kept him young, and he mourned his wife the more sincerely because he mourned her seldom.

It would have been simpler to tell Dr. Lal that he had changed his mind about the party, but until the last minute he did not know that he had changed it; indeed, he didn't change it, it changed itself. Unconquerable aversion welled. Mrs. Callendar, Mrs. Lesley—no, he couldn't stand them in his sorrow: they would guess it—for he dowered the British matron with strange insight—and would delight in torturing him, they would mock him to their husbands. When he should have been ready, he stood at the Post Office, writing a telegram to his children, and found on his return that Dr. Lal had called for him, and gone on. Well, let him go on, as befitted the coarseness of his nature. For his own part, he would commune with the dead.

And unlocking a drawer, he took out his wife's photograph. He gazed at it, and tears spouted from his eyes. He thought, "How unhappy I am!" But because he really was unhappy, another emotion soon mingled with his self-pity: he desired to remember his wife and could not. Why could he remember people whom he did not love? They were always so vivid to him, whereas the more he looked at this photograph, the less he saw. She had eluded him thus, ever since they had carried her to her tomb. He had known that she would pass from his hands and eyes, but had thought she could live in his mind, not realizing that the very fact that we have loved the dead increases their unreality, and that the more passionately we invoke them the further they recede. A piece of brown cardboard and three children—that was all that was left of his wife. It was unbearable, and he thought again, "How unhappy I am!" and became happier. He had breathed for an instant the mortal air that surrounds Orientals and all men, and he drew back from it with a gasp, for he was young. "Never, never shall I get over this," he told himself. "Most certainly my career is a failure, and my sons will be badly brought up." Since it was certain, he strove to avert it, and looked at some notes he had made on a case at the hospital. Perhaps someday a rich person might require this particular operation, and he gain a large sum. The notes interesting him on their own account, he locked the photograph up again. Its moment was over, and he did not think about his wife any more.

After tea his spirits improved, and he went round to see Hamidullah. Hamidullah had gone to the party, but his pony had not, so Aziz borrowed it, also his friend's riding breeches and polo mallet. He repaired to the Maidan. It was deserted except at its rim, where some bazaar youths were training. Training for what? They would have found it hard to say, but the word had got into the air. Round they ran, weedy and knock-kneed—the local physique was wretched—with an expression on their faces not so much of determination as of a determination to be determined. "Maharajah, salaam," he called for a joke. The youths stopped and laughed. He advised them not to exert themselves. They promised they would not, and ran on.

Riding into the middle, he began to knock the ball about. He could not play, but his pony could, and he set himself to learn, free from all human tension. He forgot the whole damned business of living as he scurried over the brown platter of the Maidan, with the evening wind on his forehead, and the encircling trees soothing his eyes. The ball shot away towards a stray subaltern who was also practising; he hit it back to Aziz and called, "Send it along again."

"All right."

The new-comer had some notion of what to do, but his horse had none, and forces were equal. Concentrated on the ball, they somehow became fond of one another, and smiled when they drew rein to rest. Aziz liked soldiers—they either accepted you or swore at you, which was preferable to the civilian's hauteur—and the subaltern liked anyone who could ride.

"Often play?" he asked.

"Never."

"Let's have another chukker."

As he hit, his horse bucked and off he went, cried, "Oh God!" and jumped on again. "Don't you ever fall off?"

"Plenty."

"Not you."

They reined up again, the fire of good fellowship in their eyes. But it cooled with their bodies, for athletics can only raise a temporary glow. Nationality was returning, but before it could exert its poison they parted, saluting each other. "If only they were all like that," each thought.

Now it was sunset. A few of his co-religionists had come to the Maidan, and were praying with their faces towards Mecca. A Brahminy Bull walked towards them, and Aziz, though disinclined to pray himself, did not see why they should be bothered with the clumsy and idolatrous animal. He gave it a tap with his polo mallet. As he did so, a voice from the road hailed him: it was Dr. Panna Lal, returning in high distress from the Collector's party.

"Dr. Aziz, Dr. Aziz, where you been? I waited ten full minutes' time at your house, then I went."

"I am so awfully sorry—I was compelled to go to the Post Office."

One of his own circle would have accepted this as meaning that he had changed his mind, an event too common to merit censure. But Dr. Lal, being of low extraction, was not sure whether an insult had not been intended, and he was further annoyed because Aziz had buffeted the Brahminy Bull. "Post Office? Do you not send your servants?" he said.

"I have so few—my scale is very small."

"Your servant spoke to me. I saw your servant."

"But, Dr. Lal, consider. How could I send my servant when you were coming: you come, we go, my house is left alone, my servant comes back perhaps, and all my portable property has been carried away by bad characters in the meantime. Would you have that? The cook is deaf—I can never count on my cook—and the boy is only a little boy. Never, never do I and Hassan leave the house at the same time together. It is my fixed rule." He said all this and much more out of civility, to save Dr. Lal's face. It was not offered as truth and should not have been criticized as such. But the other demolished it—an easy and ignoble task. "Even if this so, what prevents leaving a chit saying where you go?" and so on. Aziz detested ill breeding, and made his pony caper. "Farther away, or mine will start out of sympathy," he wailed, revealing the true source of his irritation. "It has been so rough and wild this afternoon. It spoiled some most valuable blossoms in the club garden, and had to be dragged back by four men. English ladies and gentlemen looking on, and the Collector Sahib himself taking a note. But, Dr. Aziz, I'll not take up your valuable time. This will not interest you, who have so many engagements and telegrams. I am just a poor old doctor who thought right to pay my respects when I was asked and where I was asked. Your absence, I may remark, drew commentaries."

"They can damn well comment."

"It is fine to be young. Damn well! Oh, very fine. Damn whom?"

"I go or not as I please."

"Yet you promise me, and then fabricate this tale of a telegram. Go forward, Dapple."

They went, and Aziz had a wild desire to make an enemy for life. He could do it so easily by galloping near them. He did it. Dapple bolted. He thundered back on to the Maidan. The glory of his play with the subaltern remained for a little, he galloped and swooped till he poured with sweat, and until he returned the pony to Hamidullah's stable he felt the equal of any man. Once on his feet, he had creeping fears. Was he in bad odour with the powers that be? Had he offended the Collector by absenting himself? Dr. Panna Lal was a person of no importance, yet was it wise to have quarrelled even with him? The complexion of his mind turned from human to political. He thought no longer, "Can I get on with people?" but "Are they stronger than I?" breathing the prevalent miasma.

At his home a chit was awaiting him, bearing the Government stamp. It lay on his table like a high explosive, which at a touch might blow his flimsy bungalow to bits. He was going to be cashiered because he had not turned up at the party. When he opened the note, it proved to be quite different; an invitation from Mr. Fielding, the Principal of Government College, asking him to come to tea the day after to-morrow. His spirits revived with violence. They would have revived in any case, for he possessed a soul that could suffer but not stifle, and led a steady life beneath his mutability. But this invitation gave him particular joy, because Fielding had asked him to tea a month ago, and he had forgotten about it—never answered, never gone, just forgotten.

And here came a second invitation, without a rebuke or even an allusion to his slip. Here was true courtesy—the civil deed that shows the good heart—and snatching up his pen he wrote an affectionate reply, and hurried back for news to Hamidullah's. For he had never met the Principal, and believed that the one serious gap in his life was going to be filled. He longed to know everything about the splendid fellow—his salary, preferences, antecedents, how best one might please him. But Hamidullah was still out, and Mahmoud Ali, who was in, would only make silly rude jokes about the party.

CHAPTER 7

This Mr. Fielding had been caught by India late. He was over forty when he entered that oddest portal, the Victoria Terminus at Bombay, and—having bribed a European ticket inspector—took his luggage into the compartment of his first tropical train. The journey remained in his mind as significant. Of his two carriage companions one was a youth, fresh to the East like himself, the other a seasoned Anglo-Indian of his own age. A gulf divided him from either; he had seen too many cities and men to be the first or to become the second. New impressions crowded on him, but they were not the orthodox new impressions; the past conditioned them, and so it was with his mistakes. To regard an Indian as if he were an Italian is not, for instance, a common error, nor perhaps a fatal one, and Fielding often attempted analogies between this peninsula and that other, smaller and more exquisitely shaped, that stretches into the classic waters of the Mediterranean.

His career, though scholastic, was varied, and had included going to the bad and repenting thereafter. By now he was a hard-bitten, good-tempered, intelligent fellow on the verge of middle age, with a belief in education. He did not mind whom he taught; public schoolboys, mental defectives and policemen, had all come his way, and he had no objection to adding Indians. Through the influence of friends, he was nominated Principal of the little college at Chandrapore, liked it, and assumed he was a success. He did succeed with his pupils, but the gulf between himself and his countrymen, which he had noticed in the train, widened distressingly. He could not at first see what was wrong. He was not unpatriotic, he always got on with Englishmen in England, all his best friends were English, so why was it not the same out here? Outwardly of the large shaggy type, with sprawling limbs and blue eyes, he appeared to inspire confidence until he spoke. Then something in his manner puzzled people and failed to allay the distrust which his profession naturally inspired. There needs must be this evil of brains in India, but woe to him through whom they are increased! The feeling grew that Mr. Fielding was a disruptive force, and rightly, for ideas are fatal to caste, and he used ideas by that most potent method—interchange. Neither a missionary nor a student, he was happiest in the give-and-take of a private conversation. The world, he believed, is a globe of men who are trying to reach one another and can best do so by the help of good will plus culture and intelligence—a creed ill suited to Chandrapore, but he had come out too late to lose it. He had no racial feeling—not because he was superior to his brother civilians, but because he had matured in a different atmosphere, where the herd-instinct does not flourish. The remark that did him most harm at the club was a silly aside to the effect that the so-called white races are really pinko-grey. He only said this to be cheery, he did not realize that "white" has no more to do with a colour than "God save the King" with a god, and that it is the height of impropriety to consider what it does connote. The pinko-grey male whom he addressed was subtly scandalized; his sense of insecurity was awoken, and he communicated it to the rest of the herd.

Still, the men tolerated him for the sake of his good heart and strong body; it was their wives who decided that he was not a sahib really. They disliked him. He took no notice of them, and this, which would have passed without comment in feminist England, did him harm in a community where the male is expected to be lively and helpful. Mr. Fielding never advised one about dogs or horses, or dined, or paid his midday calls, or decorated trees for one's children at Christmas, and though he came to the club, it was only to get his tennis or billiards, and to go. This was true. He had discovered that it is possible to keep in with Indians and Englishmen, but that he who would also keep in with Englishwomen must drop the Indians. The two wouldn't combine. Useless to blame either party, useless to blame them for blaming one another. It just was so, and one had to choose. Most Englishmen preferred their own kinswomen, who, coming out in increasing numbers, made life on the home pattern yearly more possible. He had found it convenient and pleasant to associate with Indians and he must pay the price. As a rule no Englishwoman entered the College except for official functions, and if he invited Mrs. Moore and Miss Quested to tea, it was because they were new-comers who would view everything with an equal if superficial eye, and would not turn on a special voice when speaking to his other guests.

The College itself had been slapped down by the Public Works Department, but its grounds included an ancient garden and a garden-house, and here he lived for much of the year. He was dressing after a bath when Dr. Aziz was announced. Lifting up his voice, he shouted from the bedroom, "Please make yourself at home." The remark was unpremeditated, like most of his actions; it was what he felt inclined to say.

To Aziz it had a very definite meaning. "May I really, Mr. Fielding? It's very good of you," he called back; "I like unconventional behaviour so extremely." His spirits flared up, he glanced round the living-room. Some luxury in it, but no order—nothing to intimidate poor Indians. It was also a very beautiful room, opening into the garden through three high arches of wood. "The fact is I have long wanted to meet you," he continued. "I have heard so much about your warm heart from the Nawab Bahadur. But where is one to meet in a wretched hole like Chandrapore?" He came close up to the door. "When I was greener here, I'll tell you what. I used to wish you to fall ill so that we could meet that way." They laughed, and encouraged by his success he began to improvise. "I said to myself, How does Mr. Fielding look this morning? Perhaps pale. And the Civil Surgeon is pale too, he will not be able to attend upon him when the shivering commences. I should have been sent for instead. Then we would have had jolly talks, for you are a celebrated student of Persian poetry."

"You know me by sight, then."

"Of course, of course. You know me?"

"I know you very well by name."

"I have been here such a short time, and always in the bazaar. No wonder you have never seen me, and I wonder you know my name. I say, Mr. Fielding?"

"Yes?"

"Guess what I look like before you come out. That will be a kind of game."

"You're five feet nine inches high," said Fielding, surmising this much through the ground glass of the bedroom door.

"Jolly good. What next? Have I not a venerable white beard?"

"Blast!"

"Anything wrong?"

"I've stamped on my last collar stud."

"Take mine, take mine."

"Have you a spare one?"

"Yes, yes, one minute."

"Not if you're wearing it yourself."

"No, no, one in my pocket." Stepping aside, so that his outline might vanish, he wrenched off his collar, and pulled out of his shirt the back stud, a gold stud, which was part of a set that his brother-in-law had brought him from Europe. "Here it is," he cried.

"Come in with it if you don't mind the unconventionality."

"One minute again." Replacing his collar, he prayed that it would not spring up at the back during tea. Fielding's bearer, who was helping him to dress, opened the door for him.

"Many thanks." They shook hands smiling. He began to look round, as he would have with any old friend. Fielding was not surprised at the rapidity of their intimacy. With so emotional a people it was apt to come at once or never, and he and Aziz, having heard only good of each other, could afford to dispense with preliminaries.

"But I always thought that Englishmen kept their rooms so tidy. It seems that this is not so. I need not be so ashamed." He sat down gaily on the bed; then, forgetting himself entirely, drew up his legs and folded them under him. "Everything ranged coldly on shelves was what *I* thought.—I say, Mr. Fielding, is the stud going to go in?"

"I hae ma doots."

"What's that last sentence, please? Will you teach me some new words and so improve my English?"

Fielding doubted whether "everything ranged coldly on shelves" could be improved. He was often struck with the liveliness with which the younger generation handled a foreign tongue. They altered the idiom, but they could say whatever they wanted to say quickly; there were none of the babuisms ascribed to them up at the club. But then the club moved slowly; it still declared that few Mohammedans and no Hindus would eat at an Englishman's table, and that all Indian ladies were in impenetrable purdah. Individually it knew better; as a club it declined to change.

"Let me put in your stud. I see... the shirt back's hole is rather small and to rip it wider a pity."

"Why in hell does one wear collars at all?" grumbled Fielding as he bent his neck.

"We wear them to pass the Police."

"What's that?"

"If I'm biking in English dress—starch collar, hat with ditch—they take no notice. When I wear a fez, they cry, 'Your lamp's out!' Lord Curzon did not consider this when he urged natives of India to retain their picturesque costumes.—Hooray! Stud's gone in.—Sometimes I shut my eyes and dream I have splendid clothes again and am riding into battle behind Alamgir. Mr. Fielding, must not India have been beautiful then, with the Mogul Empire at its height and Alamgir reigning at Delhi upon the Peacock Throne?"

"Two ladies are coming to tea to meet you—I think you know them."

"Meet me? I know no ladies."

"Not Mrs. Moore and Miss Quested?"

"Oh yes—I remember." The romance at the mosque had sunk out of his consciousness as soon as it was over. "An excessively aged lady; but will you please repeat the name of her companion?"

"Miss Quested."

"Just as you wish." He was disappointed that other guests were coming, for he preferred to be alone with his new friend.

"You can talk to Miss Quested about the Peacock Throne if you like—she's artistic, they say."

"Is she a Post Impressionist?"

"Post Impressionism, indeed! Come along to tea. This world is getting too much for me altogether."

Aziz was offended. The remark suggested that he, an obscure Indian, had no right to have heard of Post Impressionism—a privilege reserved for the Ruling Race, that. He said stiffly, "I do not consider Mrs. Moore my friend, I only met her accidentally in my mosque," and was adding "a single meeting is too short to make a friend," but before he could finish the sentence the stiffness vanished from it, because he felt Fielding's fundamental good will. His own went out to it, and grappled beneath the shifting tides of emotion which can alone bear the voyager to an anchorage but may also carry him across it on to the rocks. He was safe really—as safe as the shore-dweller who can only understand stability and supposes that every ship must be wrecked, and he had sensations the shore-dweller cannot know. Indeed, he was sensitive rather than responsive. In every remark he found a meaning, but not always the true meaning, and his life though vivid was largely a dream. Fielding, for instance, had not meant that Indians are obscure, but that Post Impressionism is; a gulf divided his remark from Mrs. Turton's "Why, they speak English," but to Aziz the two sounded alike. Fielding saw that something had gone wrong, and equally that it had come right, but he didn't fidget, being an optimist where personal relations were concerned, and their talk rattled on as before.

"Besides the ladies I am expecting one of my assistants—Narayan Godbole."

"Oho, the Deccani Brahman!"

"He wants the past back too, but not precisely Alamgir."

"I should think not. Do you know what Deccani Brahmans say? That England conquered India from them—from them, mind, and not from the Moguls. Is not that like their cheek? They have even bribed it to appear in text-books, for they are so subtle and immensely rich. Professor Godbole must be quite unlike all other Deccani Brahmans from all I can hear say. A most sincere chap."

"Why don't you fellows run a club in Chandrapore, Aziz?"

"Perhaps—some day... just now I see Mrs. Moore and—what's her name—coming."

How fortunate that it was an "unconventional" party, where formalities are ruled out! On this basis Aziz found the English ladies easy to talk to, he treated them like men. Beauty would have troubled him, for it entails rules of its own, but Mrs. Moore was so old and Miss Quested so plain that he was spared this anxiety. Adela's angular body and the freckles on her face were terrible defects in his eyes, and he wondered how God could have been so unkind to any female form. His attitude towards her remained entirely straightforward in consequence.

"I want to ask you something, Dr. Aziz," she began. "I heard from Mrs. Moore how helpful you were to her in the mosque, and how interesting. She learnt more about India in those few minutes' talk with you than in the three weeks since we landed."

"Oh, please do not mention a little thing like that. Is there anything else I may tell you about my country?"

"I want you to explain a disappointment we had this morning; it must be some point of Indian etiquette."

"There honestly is none," he replied. "We are by nature a most informal people."

"I am afraid we must have made some blunder and given offence," said Mrs. Moore.

"That is even more impossible. But may I know the facts?"

"An Indian lady and gentleman were to send their carriage for us this morning at ninc. It has never come. We waited and waited and waited; we can't think what happened."

"Some misunderstanding," said Fielding, seeing at once that it was the type of incident that had better not be cleared up.

"Oh no, it wasn't that," Miss Quested persisted. "They even gave up going to Calcutta to entertain us. We must have made some stupid blunder, we both feel sure."

"I wouldn't worry about that."

"Exactly what Mr. Heaslop tells me," she retorted, reddening a little. "If one doesn't worry, how's one to understand?"

The host was inclined to change the subject, but Aziz took it up warmly, and on learning fragments of the delinquents' name pronounced that they were Hindus.

"Slack Hindus—they have no idea of society; I know them very well because of a doctor at the hospital. Such a slack, unpunctual fellow! It is as well you did not go to their house, for it would give you a wrong idea of India. Nothing sanitary. I think for my own part they grew ashamed of their house and that is why they did not send."

"That's a notion," said the other man.

"I do so hate mysteries," Adela announced.

"We English do."

"I dislike them not because I'm English, but from my own personal point of view," she corrected.

"I like mysteries but I rather dislike muddles," said Mrs. Moore.

"A mystery is a muddle."

"Oh, do you think so, Mr. Fielding?"

"A mystery is only a high-sounding term for a muddle. No advantage in stirring it up, in either case. Aziz and I know well that India's a muddle."

"India's—— Oh, what an alarming idea!"

"There'll be no muddle when you come to see me," said Aziz, rather out of his depth. "Mrs. Moore and everyone—I invite you all—oh, please."

The old lady accepted: she still thought the young doctor excessively nice; moreover, a new feeling, half languor, half excitement, bade her turn down any fresh path. Miss Quested accepted out of adventure. She also liked Aziz, and believed that when she knew him better he would unlock his country for her. His invitation gratified her, and she asked him for his address.

Aziz thought of his bungalow with horror. It was a detestable shanty near a low bazaar. There was practically only one room in it, and that infested with small black flies. "Oh, but we will talk of something else now," he exclaimed. "I wish I lived here. See this beautiful room! Let us admire it together for a little. See those curves at the bottom of the arches. What delicacy! It is the architecture of Question and Answer. Mrs. Moore, you are in India; I am not joking." The room inspired him. It was an audience hall built in the eighteenth century for some high official, and though of wood had reminded Fielding of the Loggia de' Lanzi at Florence. Little rooms, now Europeanized, clung to it on either side, but the central hall was unpapered and unglassed, and the air of the garden poured in freely. One sat in public—on exhibition, as it were—in full view of the gardeners who were screaming at the birds and of the man who rented the tank for the cultivation of water chestnut. Fielding let the mango trees too—there was no knowing who might not come in—and his servants sat on his steps night and day to discourage thieves. Beautiful certainly, and the Englishman had not spoilt it, whereas Aziz in an occidental moment would have hung Maude Goodmans on the walls. Yet there was no doubt to whom the room really belonged...

"I am doing justice here. A poor widow who has been robbed comes along and I give her fifty rupees, to another a hundred, and so on and so on. I should like that."

Mrs. Moore smiled, thinking of the modern method as exemplified in her son. "Rupees don't last forever, I'm afraid," she said.

"Mine would. God would give me more when he saw I gave. Always be giving, like the Nawab Bahadur. My father was the same, that is why he died poor." And pointing about the room he peopled it with clerks and officials, all benevolent because they lived long ago. "So we would sit giving for ever—on a carpet instead of chairs, that is the chief change between now and then, but I think we would never punish anyone."

The ladies agreed.

"Poor criminal, give him another chance. It only makes a man worse to go to prison and be corrupted." His face grew very tender—the tenderness of one incapable of administration, and unable to grasp that if the poor criminal is let off he will again rob the poor widow. He was tender to everyone except a few family enemies whom he did not consider human: on these he desired revenge. He was even tender to the English; he knew at the bottom of his heart that they could not help being so cold and odd and circulating like an ice stream through his land. "We punish no one, no one," he repeated, "and in the evening we will give a great banquet with a nautch and lovely girls shall shine on every side of the tank with fireworks in their hands, and all shall be feasting and happiness until the next day, when there shall be justice as before—fifty rupees, a hundred, a thousand—till peace comes. Ah, why didn't we live in that time?—But are you admiring Mr. Fielding's house? Do look how the pillars are painted blue, and the verandah's pavilions—what do you call them?—that are above us inside are blue also. Look at the carving on the pavilions. Think of the hours it took. Their little roofs are curved to imitate bamboo. So pretty—and the bamboos waving by the tank outside. Mrs. Moore! Mrs. Moore!"

"Well?" she said, laughing.

"You remember the water by our mosque? It comes down and fills this tank—a skilful arrangement of the Emperors. They stopped here going down into Bengal. They loved water. Wherever they went they created fountains, gardens, hammams. I was telling Mr. Fielding I would give anything to serve them."

He was wrong about the water, which no Emperor, however skilful, can cause to gravitate uphill; a depression of some depth together with the whole of Chandrapore lay between the mosque and Fielding's house. Ronny would have pulled him up, Turton would have wanted to pull him up, but restrained himself. Fielding did not even want to pull him up; he had dulled his craving for verbal truth and cared chiefly for truth of mood. As for Miss Quested, she accepted everything Aziz said as true verbally. In her ignorance, she regarded him as "India," and never surmised that his outlook was limited and his method inaccurate, and that no one is India.

He was now much excited, chattering away hard, and even saying damn when he got mixed up in his sentences. He told them of his profession, and of the operations he had witnessed and performed, and he went into details that scared Mrs. Moore, though Miss Quested mistook them for proofs of his broad-mindedness; she had heard such talk at home in advanced academic circles, deliberately free. She supposed him to be emancipated as well as reliable, and placed him on a pinnacle which he could not retain. He was high enough for the moment, to be sure, but not on any pinnacle. Wings bore him up, and flagging would deposit him.

The arrival of Professor Godbole quieted him somewhat, but it remained his afternoon. The Brahman, polite and enigmatic, did not impede his eloquence, and even applauded it. He took his tea at a little distance from the outcasts, from a low table placed slightly behind him, to which he stretched back, and as it were encountered food by accident; all feigned indifference to Professor Godbole's tea. He was elderly and wizen with a grey moustache and grey-blue eyes, and his complexion was as fair as a European's. He wore a turban that looked like pale purple macaroni, coat, waistcoat, dhoti, socks with clocks. The clocks matched the turban, and his whole appearance suggested harmony—as if he had reconciled the products of East and West, mental as well as physical, and could never be discomposed. The ladies were interested in him, and hoped that he would supplement Dr. Aziz by saying something about religion. But he only ate—ate and ate, smiling, never letting his eyes catch sight of his hand.

Leaving the Mogul Emperors, Aziz turned to topics that could distress no one. He described the ripening of the mangoes, and how in his boyhood he used to run out in the Rains to a big mango grove belonging to an uncle and gorge there. "Then back with water streaming over you and perhaps rather a pain inside. But I did not mind. All my friends were paining with me. We have a proverb in Urdu: 'What does unhappiness matter when we are all unhappy together?' which comes in conveniently after mangoes. Miss Quested, do wait for mangoes. Why not settle altogether in India?"

"I'm afraid I can't do that," said Adela. She made the remark without thinking what it meant. To her, as to the three men, it seemed in key with the rest of the conversation, and not for several minutes—indeed, not for half an hour—did she realize that it was an important remark, and ought to have been made in the first place to Ronny.

"Visitors like you are too rare."

"They are indeed," said Professor Godbole. "Such affability is seldom seen. But what can we offer to detain them?"

"Mangoes, mangoes."

They laughed. "Even mangoes can be got in England now," put in Fielding. "They ship them in ice-cold rooms. You can make India in England apparently, just as you can make England in India."

"Frightfully expensive in both cases," said the girl.

"I suppose so."

"And nasty."

But the host wouldn't allow the conversation to take this heavy turn. He turned to the old lady, who looked flustered and put out—he could not imagine why—and asked about her own plans. She replied that she should like to see over the College. Everyone immediately rose, with the exception of Professor Godbole, who was finishing a banana.

"Don't you come too, Adela; you dislike institutions."

"Yes, that is so," said Miss Quested, and sat down again.

Aziz hesitated. His audience was splitting up. The more familiar half was going, but the more attentive remained. Reflecting that it was an "unconventional" afternoon, he stopped.

Talk went on as before. Could one offer the visitors unripe mangoes in a fool? "I speak now as a doctor: no." Then the old man said, "But I will send you up a few healthy sweets. I will give myself that pleasure."

"Miss Quested, Professor Godbole's sweets are delicious," said Aziz sadly, for he wanted to send sweets too and had no wife to cook them. "They will give you a real Indian treat. Ah, in my poor position I can give you nothing."

"I don't know why you say that, when you have so kindly asked us to your house."

He thought again of his bungalow with horror. Good heavens, the stupid girl had taken him at his word! What was he to do? "Yes, all that is settled," he cried.

"I invite you all to see me in the Marabar Caves."

"I shall be delighted."

"Oh, that is a most magnificent entertainment compared to my poor sweets. But has not Miss Quested visited our caves already?"

"No. I've not even heard of them."

"Not heard of them?" both cried. "The Marabar Caves in the Marabar Hills?"

"We hear nothing interesting up at the club. Only tennis and ridiculous gossip."

The old man was silent, perhaps feeling that it was unseemly of her to criticize her race, perhaps fearing that if he agreed she would report him for disloyalty. But the young man uttered a rapid "I know."

"Then tell me everything you will, or I shall never understand India. Are they the hills I sometimes see in the evening? What are these caves?"

Aziz undertook to explain, but it presently appeared that he had never visited the caves himself—had always been "meaning" to go, but work or private business had prevented him, and they were so far. Professor Godbole chaffed him pleasantly. "My dear young sir, the pot and the kettle! Have you ever heard of that useful proverb?"

"Are they large caves?" she asked.

"No, not large."

"Do describe them, Professor Godbole."

"It will be a great honour." He drew up his chair and an expression of tension came over his face. Taking the cigarette box, she offered to him and to Aziz, and lit up herself. After an impressive pause he said: "There is an entrance in the rock which you enter, and through the entrance is the cave."

"Something like the caves at Elephanta?"

"Oh no, not at all; at Elephanta there are sculptures of Siva and Parvati. There are no sculptures at Marabar."

"They are immensely holy, no doubt," said Aziz, to help on the narrative.

"Oh no, oh no."

"Still, they are ornamented in some way."

"Oh no."

"Well, why are they so famous? We all talk of the famous Marabar Caves. Perhaps that is our empty brag."

"No, I should not quite say that."

"Describe them to this lady, then."

"It will be a great pleasure." He forewent the pleasure, and Aziz realized that he was keeping back something about the caves. He realized because he often suffered from similar inhibitions himself. Sometimes, to the exasperation of Major Callendar, he would pass over the one relevant fact in a position, to dwell on the hundred irrelevant. The Major accused him of disingenuousness, and was roughly right, but only roughly. It was rather that a power he couldn't control capriciously silenced his mind. Godbole had been silenced now; no doubt not willingly, he was concealing something. Handled subtly, he might regain control and announce that the Marabar Caves were—full of stalactites, perhaps; Aziz led up to this, but they weren't.

The dialogue remained light and friendly, and Adela had no conception of its underdrift. She did not know that the comparatively simple mind of the Mohammedan was encountering Ancient Night. Aziz played a thrilling game. He was handling a human toy that refused to work—he knew that much. If it worked, neither he nor Professor Godbole would be the least advantaged, but the attempt enthralled him and was akin to abstract thought. On he chattered, defeated at every move by an opponent who would not even admit that a move had been made, and further than ever from discovering what, if anything, was extraordinary about the Marabar Caves.

Into this Ronny dropped.

With an annoyance he took no trouble to conceal, he called from the garden: "What's happened to Fielding? Where's my mother?"

"Good evening!" she replied coolly.

"I want you and mother at once. There's to be polo."

"I thought there was to be no polo."

"Everything's altered. Some soldier men have come in. Come along and I'll tell you about it."

"Your mother will return shortly, sir," said Professor Godbole, who had risen with deference. "There is but little to see at our poor college."

Ronny took no notice, but continued to address his remarks to Adela; he had hurried away from his work to take her to see the polo, because he thought it would give her pleasure. He did not mean to be rude to the two men, but the only link he could be conscious of with an Indian was the official, and neither happened to be his subordinate. As private individuals he forgot them.

Unfortunately Aziz was in no mood to be forgotten. He would not give up the secure and intimate note of the last hour. He had not risen with Godbole, and now, offensively friendly, called from his seat, "Come along up and join us, Mr. Heaslop; sit down till your mother turns up."

Ronny replied by ordering one of Fielding's servants to fetch his master at once.

"He may not understand that. Allow me——" Aziz repeated the order idiomatically.

Ronny was tempted to retort; he knew the type; he knew all the types, and this was the spoilt Westernized. But he was a servant of the Government, it was his job to avoid "incidents," so he said nothing, and ignored the provocation that Aziz continued to offer. Aziz was provocative. Everything he said had an impertinent flavour or jarred. His wings were failing, but he refused to fall without a struggle. He did not mean to be impertinent to Mr. Heaslop, who had never done him harm, but here was an Anglo-Indian who must become a man before comfort could be regained. He did not mean to be greasily confidential to Miss Quested, only to enlist her support; nor to be loud and jolly towards Professor Godbole. A strange quartette—he fluttering to the ground, she puzzled by the sudden ugliness, Ronny fuming, the Brahman observing all three, but with downcast eyes and hands folded, as if nothing was noticeable. A scene from a play, thought Fielding, who now saw them from the distance across the garden grouped among the blue pillars of his beautiful hall.

"Don't trouble to come, mother," Ronny called; "we're just starting." Then he hurried to Fielding, drew him aside and said with pseudo-heartiness, "I say, old man, do excuse me, but I think perhaps you oughtn't to have left Miss Quested alone."

"I'm sorry, what's up?" replied Fielding, also trying to be genial.

"Well... I'm the sun-dried bureaucrat, no doubt; still, I don't like to see an English girl left smoking with two Indians."

"She stopped, as she smokes, by her own wish, old man."

"Yes, that's all right in England."

"I really can't see the harm."

"If you can't see, you can't see... Can't you see that fellow's a bounder?"

Aziz flamboyant, was patronizing Mrs. Moore.

"He isn't a bounder," protested Fielding. "His nerves are on edge, that's all."

"What should have upset his precious nerves?"

"I don't know. He was all right when I left."

"Well, it's nothing I've said," said Ronny reassuringly. "I never even spoke to him."

"Oh well, come along now, and take your ladies away; the catastrophe over."

"Fielding... don't think I'm taking it badly, or anything of that sort... I suppose you won't come on to the polo with us? We should all be delighted."

"I'm afraid I can't, thanks all the same. I'm awfully sorry you feel I've been remiss. I didn't mean to be."

So the leave-taking began. Everyone was cross or wretched. It was as if irritation exuded from the very soil. Could one have been so petty on a Scotch moor or an Italian alp? Fielding wondered afterwards. There seemed no reserve of tranquillity to draw upon in India.

Either none, or else tranquillity swallowed up everything, as it appeared to do for Professor Godbole. Here was Aziz all shoddy and odious, Mrs. Moore and Miss Quested both silly, and he himself and Heaslop both decorous on the surface, but detestable really, and detesting each other.

"Good-bye, Mr. Fielding, and thank you so much... What lovely College buildings!"

"Good-bye, Mrs. Moore."

"Good-bye, Mr. Fielding. Such an interesting afternoon..."

"Good-bye, Miss Quested."

"Good-bye, Dr. Aziz."

"Good-bye, Mrs. Moore."

"Good-bye, Dr. Aziz."

"Good-bye, Miss Quested." He pumped her hand up and down to show that he felt at ease. "You'll jolly jolly well not forget those caves, won't you? I'll fix the whole show up in a jiffy."

"Thank you...

Inspired by the devil to a final effort, he added, "What a shame you leave India so soon! Oh, do reconsider your decision, do stay."

"Good-bye, Professor Godbole," she continued, suddenly agitated. "It's a shame we never heard you sing."

"I may sing now," he replied, and did.

His thin voice rose, and gave out one sound after another. At times there seemed rhythm, at times there was the illusion of a Western melody. But the ear, baffled repeatedly, soon lost any clue, and wandered in a maze of noises, none harsh or unpleasant, none intelligible. It was the song of an unknown bird. Only the servants understood it. They began to whisper to one another. The man who was gathering water chestnut came naked out of the tank, his lips parted with delight, disclosing his scarlet tongue. The sounds continued and ceased after a few moments as casually as they had begun—apparently half through a bar, and upon the subdominant.

"Thanks so much: what was that?" asked Fielding.

"I will explain in detail. It was a religious song. I placed myself in the position of a milk maiden. I say to Shri Krishna, 'Come! come to me only.' The god refuses to come. I grow humble and say: 'Do not come to me only. Multiply yourself into a hundred Krishnas, and let one go to each of my hundred companions, but one, O Lord of the Universe, come to me.' He refuses to come. This is repeated several times. The song is composed in a raga appropriate to the present hour, which is the evening."

"But He comes in some other song, I hope?" said Mrs. Moore gently.

"Oh no, he refuses to come," repeated Godbole, perhaps not understanding her question. "I say to Him, Come, come, come, come, come, come. He neglects to come."

Ronny's steps had died away, and there was a moment of absolute silence. No ripple disturbed the water, no leaf stirred.

CHAPTER 8

Although Miss Quested had known Ronny well in England, she felt well advised to visit him before deciding to be his wife. India had developed sides of his character that she had never admired. His self-complacency, his censoriousness, his lack of subtlety, all grew vivid beneath a tropic sky; he seemed more indifferent than of old to what was passing in the minds of his fellows, more certain that he was right about them or that if he was wrong it didn't matter. When proved wrong, he was particularly exasperating; he always managed to suggest that she needn't have bothered to prove it. The point she made was never the relevant point, her arguments conclusive but barren, she was reminded that he had expert knowledge and she none, and that experience would not help her because she could not interpret it. A Public School, London University, a year at a crammer's, a particular sequence of posts in a particular province, a fall from a horse and a touch of fever were presented to her as the only training by which Indians and all who reside in their country can be understood; the only training she could comprehend, that is to say, for of course above Ronny there stretched the higher realms of knowledge, inhabited by Callendars and Turtons, who had been not one year in the country but twenty and whose instincts were superhuman. For himself he made no extravagant claims; she wished he would. It was the qualified bray of the callow official, the "I am not perfect, but——" that got on her nerves.

How gross he had been at Mr. Fielding's—spoiling the talk and walking off in the middle of the haunting song! As he drove them away in the tum-tum, her irritation became unbearable, and she did not realize that much of it was directed against herself. She longed for an opportunity to fly out at him, and since he felt cross too, and they were both in India, an opportunity soon occurred. They had scarcely left the College grounds before she heard him say to his mother, who was with him on the front seat, "What was that about caves?" and she promptly opened fire.

"Mrs. Moore, your delightful doctor has decided on a picnic, instead of a party in his house; we are to meet him out there—you, myself, Mr. Fielding, Professor Godbole—exactly the same party."

"Out where?" asked Ronny.

"The Marabar Caves."

"Well, I'm blessed," he murmured after a pause. "Did he descend to any details?"

"He did not. If you had spoken to him, we could have arranged them."

He shook his head laughing.

"Have I said anything funny?"

"I was only thinking how the worthy doctor's collar climbed up his neck."

"I thought you were discussing the caves."

"So I am. Aziz was exquisitely dressed, from tie-pin to spats, but he had forgotten his back collar-stud, and there you have the Indian all over: inattention to detail; the fundamental slackness that reveals the race. Similarly, to 'meet' in the caves as if they were the clock at Charing Cross, when they're miles from a station and each other."

"Have you been to them?"

"No, but I know all about them, naturally."

"Oh naturally!"

"Are you too pledged to this expedition, mother?"

"Mother is pledged to nothing," said Mrs. Moore, rather unexpectedly. "Certainly not to this polo. Will you drive up to the bungalow first, and drop me there, please? I prefer to rest."

"Drop me too," said Adela. "I don't want to watch polo either, I'm sure."

"Simpler to drop the polo," said Ronny. Tired and disappointed, he quite lost self-control, and added in a loud lecturing voice, "I won't have you messing about with Indians anymore! If you want to go to the Marabar Caves, you'll go under British auspices."

"I've never heard of these caves, I don't know what or where they are," said Mrs. Moore, "but I really can't have"—she tapped the cushion beside her—"so much quarrelling and tiresomeness!"

The young people were ashamed. They dropped her at the bungalow and drove on together to the polo, feeling it was the least they could do. Their crackling bad humour left them, but the heaviness of their spirit remained; thunderstorms seldom clear the air. Miss Quested was thinking over her own behaviour, and didn't like it at all. Instead of weighing Ronny and herself, and coming to a reasoned conclusion about marriage, she had incidentally, in the course of a talk about mangoes, remarked to mixed company that she didn't mean to stop in India. Which meant that she wouldn't marry Ronny: but what a way to announce it, what a way for a civilized girl to behave! She owed him an explanation, but unfortunately there was nothing to explain. The "thorough talk" so dear to her principles and temperament had been postponed until too late. There seemed no point in being disagreeable to him and formulating her complaints against his character at this hour of the day, which was the evening... The polo took place on the Maidan near the entrance of Chandrapore city. The sun was already declining and each of the trees held a premonition of night. They walked away from the governing group to a distant seat, and there, feeling that it was his due and her own, she forced out of herself the undigested remark: "We must have a thorough talk, Ronny, I'm afraid."

"My temper's rotten, I must apologize," was his reply. "I didn't mean to order you and mother about, but of course the way those Bengalis let you down this morning annoyed me, and I don't want that sort of thing to keep happening."

"It's nothing to do with them that I..."

"No, but Aziz would make some similar muddle over the caves. He meant nothing by the invitation, I could tell by his voice; it's just their way of being pleasant."

"It's something very different, nothing to do with caves, that I wanted to talk over with you." She gazed at the colourless grass. "I've finally decided we are not going to be married, my dear boy."

The news hurt Ronny very much. He had heard Aziz announce that she would not return to the country, but had paid no attention to the remark, for he never dreamt that an Indian could be a channel of communication between two English people. He controlled himself and said gently, "You never said we should marry, my dear girl; you never bound either yourself or me—don't let this upset you."

She felt ashamed. How decent he was! He might force his opinions down her throat, but did not press her to an "engagement," because he believed, like herself, in the sanctity of personal relationships: it was this that had drawn them together at their first meeting, which had occurred among the grand scenery of the English Lakes. Her ordeal was over, but she felt it should have been more painful and longer. Adela will not marry Ronny. It seemed slipping away like a dream. She said, "But let us discuss things; it's all so frightfully important, we mustn't make false steps. I want next to hear your point of view about me—it might help us both."

His manner was unhappy and reserved. "I don't much believe in this discussing—besides, I'm so dead with all this extra work Mohurram's bringing, if you'll excuse me."

"I only want everything to be absolutely clear between us, and to answer any questions you care to put to me on my conduct."

"But I haven't got any questions. You've acted within your rights, you were quite right to come out and have a look at me doing my work, it was an excellent plan, and anyhow it's no use talking further—we should only get up steam." He felt angry and bruised; he was too proud to tempt her back, but he did not consider that she had behaved badly, because where his compatriots were concerned he had a generous mind.

"I suppose that there is nothing else; it's unpardonable of me to have given you and your mother all this bother," said Miss Quested heavily, and frowned up at the tree beneath which they were sitting. A little green bird was observing her, so brilliant and neat that it might have hopped straight out of a shop. On catching her eye it closed its own, gave a small skip and prepared to go to bed. Some Indian wild bird. "Yes, nothing else," she repeated, feeling that a profound and passionate speech ought to have been delivered by one or both of them. "We've been awfully British over it, but I suppose that's all right."

"As we are British, I suppose it is."

"Anyhow we've not quarrelled, Ronny."

"Oh, that would have been too absurd. Why should we quarrel?"

"I think we shall keep friends."

"I know we shall."

"Quite so."

As soon as they had exchanged this admission, a wave of relief passed through them both, and then transformed itself into a wave of tenderness, and passed back. They were softened by their own honesty, and began to feel lonely and unwise. Experiences, not character, divided them; they were not dissimilar, as humans go; indeed, when compared with the people who stood nearest to them in point of space they became practically identical. The Bhil who was holding an officer's polo pony, the Eurasian who drove the Nawab Bahadur's car, the Nawab Bahadur himself, the Nawab Bahadur's debauched grandson—none would have examined a difficulty so frankly and coolly. The mere fact of examination caused it to diminish. Of course they were friends, and forever. "Do you know what the name of that green bird up above us is?" she asked, putting her shoulder rather nearer to his.

"Bee-eater."

"Oh no, Ronny, it has red bars on its wings."

"Parrot," he hazarded.

"Good gracious no."

The bird in question dived into the dome of the tree. It was of no importance, yet they would have liked to identify it, it would somehow have solaced their hearts.

But nothing in India is identifiable, the mere asking of a question causes it to disappear or to merge in something else.

"McBryde has an illustrated bird book," he said dejectedly. "I'm no good at all at birds, in fact I'm useless at any information outside my own job. It's a great pity."

"So am I. I'm useless at everything."

"What do I hear?" shouted the Nawab Bahadur at the top of his voice, causing both of them to start. "What most improbable statement have I heard? An English lady useless? No, no, no, no, no." He laughed genially, sure, within limits, of his welcome.

"Hallo, Nawab Bahadur! Been watching the polo again?" said Ronny tepidly.

"I have, sahib, I have."

"How do you do?" said Adela, likewise pulling herself together. She held out her hand. The old gentleman judged from so wanton a gesture that she was new to his country, but he paid little heed.

Women who exposed their face became by that one act so mysterious to him that he took them at the valuation of their men folk rather than at his own. Perhaps they were not immoral, and anyhow they were not his affair. On seeing the City Magistrate alone with a maiden at twilight, he had borne down on them with hospitable intent. He had a new little car, and wished to place it at their disposal; the City Magistrate would decide whether the offer was acceptable.

Ronny was by this time rather ashamed of his curtness to Aziz and Godbole, and here was an opportunity of showing that he could treat Indians with consideration when they deserved it. So he said to Adela, with the same sad friendliness that he had employed when discussing the bird, "Would half an hour's spin entertain you at all?"

"Oughtn't we to get back to the bungalow."

"Why?" He gazed at her.

"I think perhaps I ought to see your mother and discuss future plans."

"That's as you like, but there's no hurry, is there?"

"Let me take you to the bungalow, and first the little spin," cried the old man, and hastened to the car.

"He may show you some aspect of the country I can't, and he's a real loyalist. I thought you might care for a bit of a change."

Determined to give him no more trouble, she agreed, but her desire to see India had suddenly decreased. There had been a factitious element in it.

How should they seat themselves in the car? The elegant grandson had to be left behind. The Nawab Bahadur got up in front, for he had no intention of neighbouring an English girl. "Despite my advanced years, I am learning to drive," he said. "Man can learn everything if he will but try." And foreseeing a further difficulty, he added, "I do not do the actual steering. I sit and ask my chauffeur questions, and thus learn the reason for everything that is done before I do it myself. By this method serious and I may say ludicrous accidents, such as befell one of my compatriots during that delightful reception at the English Club, are avoided. Our good Panna Lal! I hope, sahib, that great damage was not done to your flowers. Let us have our little spin down the Gangavati road. Half one league onwards!" He fell asleep.

Ronny instructed the chauffeur to take the Marabar road rather than the Gangavati, since the latter was under repair, and settled himself down beside the lady he had lost. The car made a burring noise and rushed along a chaussée that ran upon an embankment above melancholy fields. Trees of a poor quality bordered the road, indeed the whole scene was inferior, and suggested that the country-side was too vast to admit of excellence. In vain did each item in it call out, "Come, come."

There was not enough god to go round. The two young people conversed feebly and felt unimportant. When the darkness began, it seemed to well out of the meagre vegetation, entirely covering the fields each side of them before it brimmed over the road. Ronny's face grew dim—an event that always increased her esteem for his character. Her hand touched his, owing to a jolt, and one of the thrills so frequent in the animal kingdom passed between them, and announced that all their difficulties were only a lovers' quarrel. Each was too proud to increase the pressure, but neither withdrew it, and a spurious unity descended on them, as local and temporary as the gleam that inhabits a firefly. It would vanish in a moment, perhaps to reappear, but the darkness is alone durable. And the night that encircled them, absolute as it seemed, was itself only a spurious unity, being modified by the gleams of day that leaked up round the edges of the earth, and by the stars.

They gripped... bump, jump, a swerve, two wheels lifted in the air, breaks on, bump with tree at edge of embankment, standstill. An accident. A slight one. Nobody hurt. The Nawab Bahadur awoke. He cried out in Arabic, and violently tugged his beard.

"What's the damage?" enquired Ronny, after the moment's pause that he permitted himself before taking charge of a situation. The Eurasian, inclined to be flustered, rallied to the sound of his voice, and, every inch an Englishman, replied, "You give me five minutes' time, I'll take you any dam anywhere."

"Frightened, Adela?" He released her hand.

"Not a bit."

"I consider not to be frightened the height of folly," cried the Nawab Bahadur quite rudely.

"Well, it's all over now, tears are useless," said Ronny, dismounting. "We had some luck butting that tree."

"All over... oh yes, the danger is past, let us smoke cigarettes, let us do anything we please. Oh yes... enjoy ourselves—oh my merciful God..." His words died into Arabic again.

"Wasn't the bridge. We skidded."

"We didn't skid," said Adela, who had seen the cause of the accident, and thought everyone must have seen it too. "We ran into an animal."

A loud cry broke from the old man: his terror was disproportionate and ridiculous.

"An animal?"

"A large animal rushed up out of the dark on the right and hit us."

"By Jove, she's right," Ronny exclaimed. "The paint's gone."

"By Jove, sir, your lady is right," echoed the Eurasian. Just by the hinges of the door was a dent, and the door opened with difficulty.

"Of course I'm right. I saw its hairy back quite plainly."

"I say, Adela, what was it?"

"I don't know the animals any better than the birds here—too big for a goat."

"Exactly, too big for a goat..." said the old man.

Ronny said, "Let's go into this; let's look for its tracks."

"Exactly; you wish to borrow this electric torch."

The English people walked a few steps back into the darkness, united and happy. Thanks to their youth and upbringing, they were not upset by the accident. They traced back the writhing of the tyres to the source of their disturbance. It was just after the exit from a bridge; the animal had probably come up out of the nullah. Steady and smooth ran the marks of the car, ribbons neatly nicked with lozenges, then all went mad. Certainly some external force had impinged, but the road had been used by too many objects for any one track to be legible, and the torch created such high lights and black shadows that they could not interpret what it revealed. Moreover, Adela in her excitement knelt and swept her skirts about, until it was she if anyone who appeared to have attacked the car. The incident was a great relief to them both. They forgot their abortive personal relationship, and felt adventurous as they muddled about in the dust.

"I believe it was a buffalo," she called to their host, who had not accompanied them.

"Exactly."

"Unless it was a hyena."

Ronny approved this last conjecture. Hyenas prowl in nullahs and headlights dazzle them.

"Excellent, a hyena," said the Indian with an angry irony and a gesture at the night. "Mr. Harris!"

"Half a mo-ment. Give me ten minutes' time."

"Sahib says hyena."

"Don't worry Mr. Harris. He saved us from a nasty smash. Harris, well done!"

"A smash, sahib, that would not have taken place had he obeyed and taken us Gangavati side, instead of Marabar."

"My fault that. I told him to come this way because the road's better. Mr. Lesley has made it pukka right up to the hills."

"Ah, now I begin to understand." Seeming to pull himself together, he apologized slowly and elaborately for the accident. Ronny murmured, "Not at all," but apologies were his due, and should have started sooner: because English people are so calm at a crisis, it is not to be assumed that they are unimportant. The Nawab Bahadur had not come out very well.

At that moment a large car approached from the opposite direction. Ronny advanced a few steps down the road, and with authority in his voice and gesture stopped it. It bore the inscription "Mudkul State" across its bonnet. All friskiness and friendliness, Miss Derek sat inside.

"Mr. Heaslop, Miss Quested, what are you holding up an innocent female for?"

"We've had a breakdown."

"But how putrid!"

"We ran into a hyena!"

"How absolutely rotten!"

"Can you give us a lift?"

"Yes, indeed."

"Take me too," said the Nawab Bahadur.

"Heh, what about me?" cried Mr. Harris.

"Now what's all this? I'm not an omnibus," said Miss Derek with decision. "I've a harmonium and two dogs in here with me as it is. I'll take three of you if one'll sit in front and nurse a pug. No more."

"I will sit in front," said the Nawab Bahadur.

"Then hop in: I've no notion who you are."

"Heh no, what about my dinner? I can't be left alone all the night." Trying to look and feel like a European, the chauffeur interposed aggressively. He still wore a topi, despite the darkness, and his face, to which the Ruling Race had contributed little beyond bad teeth, peered out of it pathetically, and seemed to say, "What's it all about? Don't worry me so, you blacks and whites. Here I am, stuck in dam India same as you, and you got to fit me in better than this."

"Nussu will bring you out some suitable dinner upon a bicycle," said the Nawab Bahadur, who had regained his usual dignity. "I shall despatch him with all possible speed. Meanwhile, repair my car."

They sped off, and Mr. Harris, after a reproachful glance, squatted down upon his hams. When English and Indians were both present, he grew self-conscious, because he did not know to whom he belonged. For a little he was vexed by opposite currents in his blood, then they blended, and he belonged to no one but himself.

But Miss Derek was in tearing spirits. She had succeeded in stealing the Mudkul car. Her Maharajah would be awfully sick, but she didn't mind, he could sack her if he liked. "I don't believe in these people letting you down," she said. "If I didn't snatch like the devil, I should be nowhere. He doesn't want the car, silly fool! Surely it's to the credit of his State I should be seen about in it at Chandrapore during my leave. He ought to look at it that way. Anyhow he's got to look at it that way. My Maharani's different—my Maharani's a dear. That's her fox terrier, poor little devil. I fished them out both with the driver. Imagine taking dogs to a Chiefs' Conference! As sensible as taking Chiefs, perhaps." She shrieked with laughter. "The harmonium—the harmonium's my little mistake, I own. They rather had me over the harmonium. I meant it to stop on the train. Oh lor'!"

Ronny laughed with restraint. He did not approve of English people taking service under the Native States, where they obtain a certain amount of influence, but at the expense of the general prestige. The humorous triumphs of a free lance are of no assistance to an administrator, and he told the young lady that she would outdo Indians at their own game if she went on much longer.

"They always sack me before that happens, and then I get another job. The whole of India seethes with Maharanis and Ranis and Begums who clamour for such as me."

"Really. I had no idea."

"How could you have any idea, Mr. Heaslop? What should he know about Maharanis, Miss Quested? Nothing. At least I should hope not."

"I understand those big people are not particularly interesting," said Adela, quietly, disliking the young woman's tone. Her hand touched Ronny's again in the darkness, and to the animal thrill there was now added a coincidence of opinion.

"Ah, there you're wrong. They're priceless."

"I would scarcely call her wrong," broke out the Nawab Bahadur, from his isolation on the front seat, whither they had relegated him. "A Native State, a Hindu State, the wife of a ruler of a Hindu State, may beyond doubt be a most excellent lady, and let it not be for a moment supposed that I suggest anything against the character of Her Highness the Maharani of Mudkul. But I fear she will be uneducated, I fear she will be superstitious. Indeed, how could she be otherwise? What opportunity of education has such a lady had? Oh, superstition is terrible, terrible! oh, it is the great defect in our Indian character!"—and as if to point his criticism, the lights of the civil station appeared on a rise to the right. He grew more and more voluble. "Oh, it is the duty of each and every citizen to shake superstition off, and though I have little experience of Hindu States, and none of this particular one, namely Mudkul (the Ruler, I fancy, has a salute of but eleven guns)—yet I cannot imagine that they have been as successful as British India, where we see reason and orderliness spreading in every direction, like a most health-giving flood!"

Miss Derek said "Golly!"

Undeterred by the expletive, the old man swept on. His tongue had been loosed and his mind had several points to make. He wanted to endorse Miss Quested's remark that big people are not interesting, because he was bigger himself than many an independent chief; at the same time, he must neither remind nor inform her that he was big, lest she felt she had committed a discourtesy. This was the groundwork of his oration; worked in with it was his gratitude to Miss Derek for the lift, his willingness to hold a repulsive dog in his arms, and his general regret for the trouble he had caused the human race during the evening. Also he wanted to be dropped near the city to get hold of his cleaner, and to see what mischief his grandson was up to. As he wove all these anxieties into a single rope, he suspected that his audience felt no interest, and that the City Magistrate fondled either maiden behind the cover of the harmonium, but good breeding compelled him to continue; it was nothing to him if they were bored, because he did not know what boredom is, and it was nothing to him if they were licentious, because God has created all races to be different. The accident was over, and his life, equably useful, distinguished, happy, ran on as before and expressed itself in streams of well-chosen words.

When this old geyser left them, Ronny made no comment, but talked lightly about polo; Turton had taught him that it is sounder not to discuss a man at once, and he reserved what he had to say on the Nawab's character until later in the evening. His hand, which he had removed to say good-bye, touched Adela's again; she caressed it definitely, he responded, and their firm and mutual pressure surely meant something. They looked at each other when they reached the bungalow, for Mrs. Moore was inside it. It was for Miss Quested to speak, and she said nervously, "Ronny, I should like to take back what I said on the Maidan." He assented, and they became engaged to be married in consequence.

Neither had foreseen such a consequence. She had meant to revert to her former condition of important and cultivated uncertainty, but it had passed out of her reach at its appropriate hour. Unlike the green bird or the hairy animal, she was labelled now. She felt humiliated again, for she deprecated labels, and she felt too that there should have been another scene between her lover and herself at this point, something dramatic and lengthy. He was pleased instead of distressed, he was surprised, but he had really nothing to say. What indeed is there to say? To be or not to be married, that was the question, and they had decided it in the affirmative.

"Come along and let's tell the mater all this"—opening the perforated zinc door that protected the bungalow from the swarms of winged creatures. The noise woke the mater up. She had been dreaming of the absent children who were so seldom mentioned, Ralph and Stella, and did not at first grasp what was required of her. She too had become used to thoughtful procrastination, and felt alarmed when it came to an end.

When the announcement was over, he made a gracious and honest remark. "Look here, both of you, see India if you like and as you like—I know I made myself rather ridiculous at Fielding's, but... it's different now. I wasn't quite sure of myself."

"My duties here are evidently finished, I don't want to see India now; now for my passage back," was Mrs. Moore's thought. She reminded herself of all that a happy marriage means, and of her own happy marriages, one of which had produced Ronny. Adela's parents had also been happily married, and excellent it was to see the incident repeated by the younger generation. On and on! the number of such unions would certainly increase as education spread and ideals grew loftier, and characters firmer. But she was tired by her visit to Government College, her feet ached, Mr. Fielding had walked too fast and far, the young people had annoyed her in the tum-tum, and given her to suppose they were breaking with each other, and though it was all right now she could not speak as enthusiastically of wedlock or of anything as she should have done. Ronny was suited, now she must go home and help the others, if they wished. She was past marrying herself, even unhappily; her function was to help others, her reward to be informed that she was sympathetic. Elderly ladies must not expect more than this.

They dined alone. There was much pleasant and affectionate talk about the future. Later on they spoke of passing events, and Ronny reviewed and recounted the day from his own point of view. It was a different day from the women's, because while they had enjoyed themselves or thought, he had worked. Mohurram was approaching, and as usual the Chandrapore Mohammedans were building paper towers of a size too large to pass under the branches of a certain pepul tree. One knew what happened next; the tower stuck, a Mohammedan climbed up the pepul and cut the branch off, the Hindus protested, there was a religious riot, and Heaven knew what, with perhaps the troops sent for. There had been deputations and conciliation committees under the auspices of Turton, and all the normal work of Chandrapore had been hung up. Should the procession take another route, or should the towers be shorter? The Mohammedans offered the former, the Hindus insisted on the latter. The Collector had favoured the Hindus, until he suspected that they had artificially bent the tree nearer the ground. They said it sagged naturally. Measurements, plans, an official visit to the spot. But Ronny had not disliked his day, for it proved that the British were necessary to India; there would certainly have been bloodshed without them. His voice grew complacent again; he was here not to be pleasant but to keep the peace, and now that Adela had promised to be his wife, she was sure to understand.

"What does our old gentleman of the car think?" she asked, and her negligent tone was exactly what he desired.

"Our old gentleman is helpful and sound, as he always is over public affairs. You've seen in him our show Indian."

"Have I really?"

"I'm afraid so. Incredible, aren't they, even the best of them? They're all—they all forget their back collar studs sooner or later.

You've had to do with three sets of Indians to-day, the Bhattacharyas, Aziz, and this chap, and it really isn't a coincidence that they've all let you down."

"I like Aziz, Aziz is my real friend," Mrs. Moore interposed.

"When the animal runs into us the Nawab loses his head, deserts his unfortunate chauffeur, intrudes upon Miss Derek... no great crimes, no great crimes, but no white man would have done it."

"What animal?"

"Oh, we had a small accident on the Marabar road. Adela thinks it was a hyena."

"An accident?" she cried.

"Nothing; no one hurt. Our excellent host awoke much rattled from his dreams, appeared to think it was our fault, and chanted exactly, exactly."

Mrs. Moore shivered, "A ghost!" But the idea of a ghost scarcely passed her lips. The young people did not take it up, being occupied with their own outlooks, and deprived of support it perished, or was reabsorbed into the part of the mind that seldom speaks.

"Yes, nothing criminal," Ronny summed up, "but there's the native, and there's one of the reasons why we don't admit him to our clubs, and how a decent girl like Miss Derek can take service under natives puzzles me... But I must get on with my work. Krishna!" Krishna was the peon who should have brought the files from his office. He had not turned up, and a terrific row ensued. Ronny stormed, shouted, howled, and only the experienced observer could tell that he was not angry, did not much want the files, and only made a row because it was the custom. Servants, quite understanding, ran slowly in circles, carrying hurricane lamps. Krishna the earth, Krishna the stars replied, until the Englishman was appeased by their echoes, fined the absent peon eight annas, and sat down to his arrears in the next room.

"Will you play Patience with your future mother-in-law, dear Adela, or does it seem too tame?"

"I should like to—I don't feel a bit excited—I'm just glad it's settled up at last, but I'm not conscious of vast changes. We are all three the same people still."

"That's much the best feeling to have." She dealt out the first row of "demon."

"I suppose so," said the girl thoughtfully.

"I feared at Mr. Fielding's that it might be settled the other way... black knave on a red queen..." They chatted gently about the game.

Presently Adela said: "You heard me tell Aziz and Godbole I wasn't stopping in their country. I didn't mean it, so why did I say it? I feel I haven't been—frank enough, attentive enough, or something. It's as if I got everything out of proportion. You have been so very good to me, and I meant to be good when I sailed, but somehow I haven't been... Mrs. Moore, if one isn't absolutely honest, what is the use of existing?"

She continued to lay out her cards. The words were obscure, but she understood the uneasiness that produced them. She had experienced it twice herself, during her own engagements—this vague contrition and doubt. All had come right enough afterwards and doubtless would this time—marriage makes most things right enough. "I wouldn't worry," she said. "It's partly the odd surroundings; you and I keep on attending to trifles instead of what's important; we are what the people here call 'new.'"

"You mean that my bothers are mixed up with India?"

"India's——" She stopped.

"What made you call it a ghost?"

"Call what a ghost?"

"The animal thing that hit us. Didn't you say 'Oh, a ghost,' in passing."

"I couldn't have been thinking of what I was saying."

"It was probably a hyena, as a matter of fact."

"Ah, very likely."

And they went on with their Patience. Down in Chandrapore the Nawab Bahadur waited for his car. He sat behind his town house (a small unfurnished building which he rarely entered) in the midst of the little court that always improvises itself round Indians of position. As if turbans were the natural product of darkness a fresh one would occasionally froth to the front, incline itself towards him, and retire. He was preoccupied, his diction was appropriate to a religious subject. Nine years previously, when first he had had a car, he had driven it over a drunken man and killed him, and the man had been waiting for him ever since. The Nawab Bahadur was innocent before God and the Law, he had paid double the compensation necessary; but it was no use, the man continued to wait in an unspeakable form, close to the scene of his death. None of the English people knew of this, nor did the chauffeur; it was a racial secret communicable more by blood than speech. He spoke now in horror of the particular circumstances; he had led others into danger, he had risked the lives of two innocent and honoured guests. He repeated, "If I had been killed, what matter? it must happen sometime; but they who trusted me——"

The company shuddered and invoked the mercy of God. Only Aziz held aloof, because a personal experience restrained him: was it not by despising ghosts that he had come to know Mrs. Moore? "You know, Nureddin," he whispered to the grandson—an effeminate youth whom he seldom met, always liked, and invariably forgot—"you know, my dear fellow, we Moslems simply must get rid of these superstitions, or India will never advance. How long must I hear of the savage pig upon the Marabar Road?" Nureddin looked down. Aziz continued: "Your grandfather belongs to another generation, and I respect and love the old gentleman, as you know. I say nothing against him, only that it is wrong for us, because we are young. I want you to promise me—Nureddin, are you listening?—not to believe in Evil Spirits, and if I die (for my health grows very weak) to bring up my three children to disbelieve in them too." Nureddin smiled, and a suitable answer rose to his pretty lips, but before he could make it the car arrived, and his grandfather took him away.

The game of Patience up in the civil lines went on longer than this. Mrs. Moore continued to murmur "Red ten on a black knave," Miss Quested to assist her, and to intersperse among the intricacies of the play details about the hyena, the engagement, the Maharani of Mudkul, the Bhattacharyas, and the day generally, whose rough desiccated surface acquired as it receded a definite outline, as India itself might, could it be viewed from the moon. Presently the players went to bed, but not before other people had woken up elsewhere, people whose emotions they could not share, and whose existence they ignored. Never tranquil, never perfectly dark, the night wore itself away, distinguished from other nights by two or three blasts of wind, which seemed to fall perpendicularly out of the sky and to bounce back into it, hard and compact, leaving no freshness behind them: the hot weather was approaching.

CHAPTER 9

Aziz fell ill as he foretold—slightly ill. Three days later he lay abed in his bungalow, pretending to be very ill. It was a touch of fever, which he would have neglected if there was anything important at the hospital. Now and then he groaned and thought he should die, but did not think so for long, and a very little diverted him. It was Sunday, always an equivocal day in the East, and an excuse for slacking. He could hear church bells as he drowsed, both from the civil station and from the missionaries out beyond the slaughter house—different bells and rung with different intent, for one set was calling firmly to Anglo-India, and the other feebly to mankind. He did not object to the first set; the other he ignored, knowing their inefficiency. Old Mr. Graysford and young Mr. Sorley made converts during a famine, because they distributed food; but when times improved they were naturally left alone again, and though surprised and aggrieved each time this happened, they never learnt wisdom. "No Englishman understands us except Mr. Fielding," he thought; "but how shall I see him again? If he entered this room the disgrace of it would kill me." He called to Hassan to clear up, but Hassan, who was testing his wages by ringing them on the step of the verandah, found it possible not to hear him; heard and didn't hear, just as Aziz had called and hadn't called. "That's India all over... how like us... there we are..." He dozed again, and his thoughts wandered over the varied surface of life.

Gradually they steadied upon a certain spot—the Bottomless Pit according to missionaries, but he had never regarded it as more than a dimple. Yes, he did want to spend an evening with some girls, singing and all that, the vague jollity that would culminate in voluptuousness. Yes, that was what he did want. How could it be managed? If Major Callendar had been an Indian, he would have remembered what young men are, and granted two or three days' leave to Calcutta without asking questions. But the Major assumed either that his subordinates were made of ice, or that they repaired to the Chandrapore bazaars—disgusting ideas both. It was only Mr. Fielding who——

"Hassan!"

The servant came running.

"Look at those flies, brother;" and he pointed to the horrible mass that hung from the ceiling. The nucleus was a wire which had been inserted as a homage to electricity. Electricity had paid no attention, and a colony of eye-flies had come instead and blackened the coils with their bodies.

"Huzoor, those are flies."

"Good, good, they are, excellent, but why have I called you?"

"To drive them elsewhere," said Hassan, after painful thought.

"Driven elsewhere, they always return."

"Huzoor."

"You must make some arrangement against flies; that is why you are my servant," said Aziz gently.

Hassan would call the little boy to borrow the step-ladder from Mahmoud Ali's house; he would order the cook to light the Primus stove and heat water; he would personally ascend the steps with a bucket in his arms, and dip the end of the coil into it.

"Good, very good. Now what have you to do?"

"Kill flies."

"Good. Do it."

Hassan withdrew, the plan almost lodged in his head, and began to look for the little boy. Not finding him, his steps grew slower, and he stole back to his post on the verandah, but did not go on testing his rupees, in case his master heard them clink. On twittered the Sunday bells; the East had returned to the East via the suburbs of England, and had become ridiculous during the detour.

Aziz continued to think about beautiful women.

His mind here was hard and direct, though not brutal. He had learnt all he needed concerning his own constitution many years ago, thanks to the social order into which he had been born, and when he came to study medicine he was repelled by the pedantry and fuss with which Europe tabulates the facts of sex. Science seemed to discuss everything from the wrong end. It didn't interpret his experiences when he found them in a German manual, because by being there they ceased to be his experiences. What he had been told by his father or mother or had picked up from servants—it was information of that sort that he found useful, and handed on as occasion offered to others.

But he must not bring any disgrace on his children by some silly escapade. Imagine if it got about that he was not respectable! His professional position too must be considered, whatever Major Callendar thought. Aziz upheld the proprieties, though he did not invest them with any moral halo, and it was here that he chiefly differed from an Englishman. His conventions were social. There is no harm in deceiving society as long as she does not find you out, because it is only when she finds you out that you have harmed her; she is not like a friend or God, who are injured by the mere existence of unfaithfulness. Quite clear about this, he meditated what type of lie he should tell to get away to Calcutta, and had thought of a man there who could be trusted to send him a wire and a letter that he could show to Major Callendar, when the noise of wheels was heard in his compound. Someone had called to enquire. The thought of sympathy increased his fever, and with a sincere groan he wrapped himself in his quilt.

"Aziz, my dear fellow, we are greatly concerned," said Hamidullah's voice. One, two, three, four bumps, as people sat down upon his bed.

"When a doctor falls ill it is a serious matter," said the voice of Mr. Syed Mohammed, the assistant engineer.

"When an engineer falls ill, it is equally important," said the voice of Mr. Haq, a police inspector.

"Oh yes, we are all jolly important, our salaries prove it."

"Dr. Aziz took tea with our Principal last Thursday afternoon," piped Rafi, the engineer's nephew. "Professor Godbole, who also attended, has sickened too, which seems rather a curious thing, sir, does it not?"

Flames of suspicion leapt up in the breast of each man.

"Humbug!" exclaimed Hamidullah, in authoritative tones, quenching them.

"Humbug, most certainly," echoed the others, ashamed of themselves. The wicked schoolboy, having failed to start a scandal, lost confidence and stood up with his back to the wall.

"Is Professor Godbole ill?" enquired Aziz, penetrated by the news. "I am sincerely sorry." Intelligent and compassionate, his face peeped out of the bright crimson folds of the quilt. "How do you do, Mr. Syed Mohammed, Mr. Haq? How very kind of you to enquire after my health! How do you do, Hamidullah? But you bring me bad news. What is wrong with him, the excellent fellow?"

"Why don't you answer, Rafi? You're the great authority," said his uncle.

"Yes, Rafi's the great man," said Hamidullah, rubbing it in. "Rafi is the Sherlock Holmes of Chandrapore. Speak up, Rafi."

Less than the dust, the schoolboy murmured the word "Diarrhœa," but took courage as soon as it had been uttered, for it improved his position. Flames of suspicion shot up again in the breasts of his elders, though in a different direction. Could what was called diarrhœa really be an early case of cholera?

"If this is so, this is a very serious thing: this is scarcely the end of March. Why have I not been informed?" cried Aziz.

"Dr. Panna Lal attends him, sir."

"Oh yes, both Hindus; there we have it; they hang together like flies and keep everything dark. Rafi, come here. Sit down. Tell me all the details. Is there vomiting also?"

"Oh yes indeed, sir, and the serious pains."

"That settles it. In twenty-four hours he will be dead."

Everybody looked and felt shocked, but Professor Godbole had diminished his appeal by linking himself with a co-religionist. He moved them less than when he had appeared as a suffering individual. Before long they began to condemn him as a source of infection. "All illness proceeds from Hindus," Mr. Haq said. Mr. Syed Mohammed had visited religious fairs, at Allahabad and at Ujjain, and described them with biting scorn. At Allahabad there was flowing water, which carried impurities away, but at Ujjain the little river Sipra was banked up, and thousands of bathers deposited their germs in the pool. He spoke with disgust of the hot sun, the cow-dung and marigold flowers, and the encampment of saddhus, some of whom strode stark naked through the streets. Asked what was the name of the chief idol at Ujjain, he replied that he did not know, he had disdained to enquire, he really could not waste his time over such trivialities. His outburst took some time, and in his excitement he fell into Punjabi (he came from that side) and was unintelligible.

Aziz liked to hear his religion praised. It soothed the surface of his mind, and allowed beautiful images to form beneath. When the engineer's noisy tirade was finished, he said, "That is exactly my own view." He held up his hand, palm outward, his eyes began to glow, his heart to fill with tenderness. Issuing still farther from his quilt, he recited a poem by Ghalib. It had no connection with anything that had gone before, but it came from his heart and spoke to theirs. They were overwhelmed by its pathos; pathos, they agreed, is the highest quality in art; a poem should touch the hearer with a sense of his own weakness, and should institute some comparison between mankind and flowers. The squalid bedroom grew quiet; the silly intrigues, the gossip, the shallow discontent were stilled, while words accepted as immortal filled the indifferent air. Not as a call to battle, but as a calm assurance came the feeling that India was one; Moslem; always had been; an assurance that lasted until they looked out of the door. Whatever Ghalib had felt, he had anyhow lived in India, and this consolidated it for them: he had gone with his own tulips and roses, but tulips and roses do not go. And the sister kingdoms of the north—Arabia, Persia, Ferghana, Turkestan—stretched out their hands as he sang, sadly, because all beauty is sad, and greeted ridiculous Chandrapore, where every street and house was divided against itself, and told her that she was a continent and a unity.

Of the company, only Hamidullah had any comprehension of poetry. The minds of the others were inferior and rough. Yet they listened with pleasure, because literature had not been divorced from their civilization. The police inspector, for instance, did not feel that Aziz had degraded himself by reciting, nor break into the cheery guffaw with which an Englishman averts the infection of beauty. He just sat with his mind empty, and when his thoughts, which were mainly ignoble, flowed back into it they had a pleasant freshness. The poem had done no "good" to anyone, but it was a passing reminder, a breath from the divine lips of beauty, a nightingale between two worlds of dust. Less explicit than the call to Krishna, it voiced our loneliness nevertheless, our isolation, our need for the Friend who never comes yet is not entirely disproved. Aziz it left thinking about women again, but in a different way: less definite, more intense. Sometimes poetry had this effect on him, sometimes it only increased his local desires, and he never knew beforehand which effect would ensue: he could discover no rule for this or for anything else in life.

Hamidullah had called in on his way to a worrying committee of notables, nationalist in tendency, where Hindus, Moslems, two Sikhs, two Parsis, a Jain, and a Native Christian tried to like one another more than came natural to them. As long as someone abused the English, all went well, but nothing constructive had been achieved, and if the English were to leave India, the committee would vanish also. He was glad that Aziz, whom he loved and whose family was connected with his own, took no interest in politics, which ruin the character and career, yet nothing can be achieved without them. He thought of Cambridge—sadly, as of another poem that had ended. How happy he had been there, twenty years ago! Politics had not mattered in Mr. and Mrs. Bannister's rectory. There, games, work, and pleasant society had interwoven, and appeared to be sufficient substructure for a national life. Here all was wire-pulling and fear. Messrs. Syed Mohammed and Haq—he couldn't even trust them, although they had come in his carriage, and the schoolboy was a scorpion. Bending down, he said, "Aziz, Aziz, my dear boy, we must be going, we are already late. Get well quickly, for I do not know what our little circle would do without you."

"I shall not forget those affectionate words," replied Aziz.

"Add mine to them," said the engineer.

"Thank you, Mr. Syed Mohammed, I will."

"And mine," "And, sir, accept mine," cried the others, stirred each according to his capacity towards goodwill. Little ineffectual unquenchable flames! The company continued to sit on the bed and to chew sugarcane, which Hassan had run for into the bazaar, and Aziz drank a cup of spiced milk. Presently there was the sound of another carriage. Dr. Panna Lal had arrived, driven by horrid Mr. Ram Chand. The atmosphere of a sick-room was at once re-established, and the invalid retired under his quilt.

"Gentlemen, you will excuse, I have come to enquire by Major Callendar's orders," said the Hindu, nervous of the den of fanatics into which his curiosity had called him.

"Here he lies," said Hamidullah, indicating the prostrate form.

"Dr. Aziz, Dr, Aziz, I come to enquire."

Aziz presented an expressionless face to the thermometer.

"Your hand also, please." He took it, gazed at the flies on the ceiling, and finally announced "Some temperature."

"I think not much," said Ram Chand, desirous of fomenting trouble.

"Some; he should remain in bed," repeated Dr. Panna Lal, and shook the thermometer down, so that its altitude remained for ever unknown. He loathed his young colleague since the disasters with Dapple, and he would have liked to do him a bad turn and report to Major Callendar that he was shamming. But he might want a day in bed himself soon,—besides, though Major Callendar always believed the worst of natives, he never believed them when they carried tales about one another. Sympathy seemed the safer course. "How is stomach?" he enquired, "how head?" And catching sight of the empty cup, he recommended a milk diet.

"This is a great relief to us, it is very good of you to call, Doctor Sahib," Said Hamidullah, buttering him up a bit.

"It is only my duty."

"We know how busy you are."

"Yes, that is true."

"And how much illness there is in the city."

The doctor suspected a trap in this remark; if he admitted that there was or was not illness, either statement might be used against him. "There is always illness," he replied, "and I am always busy—it is a doctor's nature."

"He has not a minute, he is due double sharp at Government College now," said Ram Chand.

"You attend Professor Godbole there perhaps?"

The doctor looked professional and was silent.

"We hope his diarrhœa is ceasing."

"He progresses, but not from diarrhœa."

"We are in some anxiety over him—he and Dr. Aziz are great friends. If you could tell us the name of his complaint we should be grateful to you."

After a cautious pause he said, "Hæmorrhoids."

"And so much, my dear Rafi, for your cholera," hooted Aziz, unable to restrain himself.

"Cholera, cholera, what next, what now?" cried the doctor, greatly fussed. "Who spreads such untrue reports about my patients?"

Hamidullah pointed to the culprit.

"I hear cholera, I hear bubonic plague, I hear every species of lie. Where will it end, I ask myself sometimes. This city is full of misstatements, and the originators of them ought to be discovered and punished authoritatively."

"Rafi, do you hear that? Now why do you stuff us up with all this humbug?"

The schoolboy murmured that another boy had told him, also that the bad English grammar the Government obliged them to use often gave the wrong meaning for words, and so led scholars into mistakes.

"That is no reason you should bring a charge against a doctor," said Ram Chand.

"Exactly, exactly," agreed Hamidullah, anxious to avoid an unpleasantness. Quarrels spread so quickly and so far, and Messrs. Syed Mohammed and Haq looked cross, and ready to fly out. "You must apologize properly, Rafi, I can see your uncle wishes it," he said. "You have not yet said that you are sorry for the trouble you have caused this gentleman by your carelessness."

"It is only a boy," said Dr. Panna Lal, appeased.

"Even boys must learn," said Ram Chand.

"Your own son failing to pass the lowest standard, I think," said Syed Mohammed suddenly.

"Oh, indeed? Oh yes, perhaps. He has not the advantage of a relative in the Prosperity Printing Press."

"Nor you the advantage of conducting their cases in the Courts any longer."

Their voices rose. They attacked one another with obscure allusions and had a silly quarrel. Hamidullah and the doctor tried to make peace between them. In the midst of the din someone said, "I say! Is he ill or isn't he ill?" Mr. Fielding had entered unobserved. All rose to their feet, and Hassan, to do an Englishman honour, struck with a sugar-cane at the coil of flies.

Aziz said, "Sit down," coldly. What a room! What a meeting! Squalor and ugly talk, the floor strewn with fragments of cane and nuts, and spotted with ink, the pictures crooked upon the dirty walls, no punkah! He hadn't meant to live like this or among these third-rate people. And in his confusion he thought only of the insignificant Rafi, whom he had laughed at, and allowed to be teased. The boy must be sent away happy, or hospitality would have failed, along the whole line.

"It is good of Mr. Fielding to condescend to visit our friend," said the police inspector. "We are touched by this great kindness."

"Don't talk to him like that, he doesn't want it, and he doesn't want three chairs; he's not three Englishmen," he flashed. "Rafi, come here. Sit down again. I'm delighted you could come with Mr. Hamidullah, my dear boy; it will help me to recover, seeing you."

"Forgive my mistakes," said Rafi, to consolidate himself.

"Well, are you ill, Aziz, or aren't you?" Fielding repeated.

"No doubt Major Callendar has told you that I am shamming."

"Well, are you?" The company laughed, friendly and pleased. "An Englishman at his best," they thought; "so genial."

"Enquire from Dr. Panna Lal."

"You're sure I don't tire you by stopping?"

"Why, no! There are six people present in my small room already. Please remain seated, if you will excuse the informality." He turned away and continued to address Rafi, who was terrified at the arrival of his Principal, remembered that he had tried to spread slander about him, and yearned to get away.

"He is ill and he is not ill," said Hamidullah, offering a cigarette. "And I suppose that most of us are in that same case."

Fielding agreed; he and the pleasant sensitive barrister got on well. They were fairly intimate and beginning to trust each other.

"The whole world looks to be dying, still it doesn't die, so we must assume the existence of a beneficent Providence."

"Oh, that is true, how true!" said the policeman, thinking religion had been praised.

"Does Mr. Fielding think it's true?."

"Think which true? The world isn't dying. I'm certain of that!"

"No, no—the existence of Providence."

"Well, I don't believe in Providence."

"But how then can you believe in God?" asked Syed Mohammed.

"I don't believe in God."

A tiny movement as of "I told you so!" passed round the company, and Aziz looked up for an instant, scandalized. "Is it correct that most are atheists in England now?" Hamidullah enquired.

"The educated thoughtful people? I should say so, though they don't like the name. The truth is that the West doesn't bother much over belief and disbelief in these days. Fifty years ago, or even when you and I were young, much more fuss was made."

"And does not morality also decline?"

"It depends what you call—yes, yes, I suppose morality does decline."

"Excuse the question, but if this is the case, how is England justified in holding India?"

There they were! Politics again. "It's a question I can't get my mind on to," he replied. "I'm out here personally because I needed a job. I cannot tell you why England is here or whether she ought to be here. It's beyond me."

"Well-qualified Indians also need jobs in the educational."

"I guess they do; I got in first," said Fielding, smiling.

"Then excuse me again—is it fair an Englishman should occupy one when Indians are available? Of course I mean nothing personally. Personally we are delighted you should be here, and we benefit greatly by this frank talk."

There is only one answer to a conversation of this type: "England holds India for her good." Yet Fielding was disinclined to give it. The zeal for honesty had eaten him up. He said, "I'm delighted to be here too—that's my answer, there's my only excuse. I can't tell you anything about fairness. It mayn't have been fair I should have been born. I take up some other fellow's air, don't I, whenever I breathe? Still, I'm glad it's happened, and I'm glad I'm out here. However big a badmash one is—if one's happy in consequence, that is some justification."

The Indians were bewildered. The line of thought was not alien to them, but the words were too definite and bleak. Unless a sentence paid a few compliments to Justice and Morality in passing, its grammar wounded their ears and paralysed their minds. What they said and what they felt were (except in the case of affection) seldom the same. They had numerous mental conventions and when these were flouted they found it very difficult to function. Hamidullah bore up best. "And those Englishmen who are not delighted to be in India—have they no excuse?" he asked.

"None. Chuck 'em out."

"It may be difficult to separate them from the rest," he laughed.

"Worse than difficult, wrong," said Mr. Ram Chand. "No Indian gentleman approves chucking out as a proper thing. Here we differ from those other nations. We are so spiritual."

"Oh that is true, how true!" said the police inspector.

"Is it true, Mr. Haq? I don't consider us spiritual. We can't co-ordinate, we can't co-ordinate, it only comes to that. We can't keep engagements, we can't catch trains. What more than this is the so-called spirituality of India? You and I ought to be at the Committee of Notables, we're not; our friend Dr. Lal ought to be with his patients, he isn't. So we go on, and so we shall continue to go, I think, until the end of time."

"It is not the end of time, it is scarcely ten-thirty, ha, ha!" cried Dr. Panna Lal, who was again in confident mood. "Gentlemen, if I may be allowed to say a few words, what an interesting talk, also thankfulness and gratitude to Mr. Fielding in the first place teaches our sons and gives them all the great benefits of his experience and judgment——"

"Dr. Lal!"

"Dr. Aziz?"

"You sit on my leg."

"I beg pardon, but some might say your leg kicks."

"Come along, we tire the invalid in either case," said Fielding, and they filed out—four Mohammedans, two Hindus and the Englishman. They stood on the verandah while their conveyances were summoned out of various patches of shade.

"Aziz has a high opinion of you, he only did not speak because of his illness."

"I quite understand," said Fielding, who was rather disappointed with his call. The Club comment, "making himself cheap as usual," passed through his mind. He couldn't even get his horse brought up. He had liked Aziz so much at their first meeting, and had hoped for developments.

CHAPTER 10

The heat had leapt forward in the last hour, the street was deserted as if a catastrophe had cleaned off humanity during the inconclusive talk. Opposite Aziz' bungalow stood a large unfinished house belonging to two brothers, astrologers, and a squirrel hung head-downwards on it, pressing its belly against burning scaffolding and twitching a mangy tail. It seemed the only occupant of the house, and the squeals it gave were in tune with the infinite, no doubt, but not attractive except to other squirrels. More noises came from a dusty tree, where brown birds creaked and floundered about looking for insects; another bird, the invisible coppersmith, had started his "ponk ponk." It matters so little to the majority of living beings what the minority, that calls itself human, desires or decides. Most of the inhabitants of India do not mind how India is governed. Nor are the lower animals of England concerned about England, but in the tropics the indifference is more prominent, the inarticulate world is closer at hand and readier to resume control as soon as men are tired. When the seven gentlemen who had held such various opinions inside the bungalow came out of it, they were aware of a common burden, a vague threat which they called "the bad weather coming." They felt that they could not do their work, or would not be paid enough for doing it. The space between them and their carriages, instead of being empty, was clogged with a medium that pressed against their flesh, the carriage cushions scalded their trousers, their eyes pricked, domes of hot water accumulated under their head-gear and poured down their cheeks. Salaaming feebly, they dispersed for the interior of other bungalows, to recover their self-esteem and the qualities that distinguished them from each other.

All over the city and over much of India the same retreat on the part of humanity was beginning, into cellars, up hills, under trees. April, herald of horrors, is at hand. The sun was returning to his kingdom with power but without beauty—that was the sinister feature. If only there had been beauty! His cruelty would have been tolerable then. Through excess of light, he failed to triumph, he also; in his yellowy-white overflow not only matter, but brightness itself lay drowned. He was not the unattainable friend, either of men or birds or other suns, he was not the eternal promise, the never-withdrawn suggestion that haunts our consciousness; he was merely a creature, like the rest, and so debarred from glory.

CHAPTER 11

Although the Indians had driven off, and Fielding could see his horse standing in a small shed in the corner of the compound, no one troubled to bring it to him. He started to get it himself, but was stopped by a call from the house. Aziz was sitting up in bed, looking dishevelled and sad. "Here's your home," he said sardonically. "Here's the celebrated hospitality of the East. Look at the flies. Look at the chunam coming off the walls. Isn't it jolly? Now I suppose you want to be off, having seen an Oriental interior."

"Anyhow, you want to rest."

"I can rest the whole day, thanks to worthy Dr. Lal. Major Callendar's spy, I suppose you know, but this time it didn't work. I am allowed to have a slight temperature."

"Callendar doesn't trust anyone, English or Indian: that's his character, and I wish you weren't under him; but you are, and that's that."

"Before you go, for you are evidently in a great hurry, will you please unlock that drawer? Do you see a piece of brown paper at the top?"

"Yes."

"Open it."

"Who is this?"

"She was my wife. You are the first Englishman she has ever come before. Now put her photograph away."

He was astonished, as a traveller who suddenly sees, between the stones of the desert, flowers. The flowers have been there all the time, but suddenly he sees them. He tried to look at the photograph, but in itself it was just a woman in a sari, facing the world. He muttered, "Really, I don't know why you pay me this great compliment, Aziz, but I do appreciate it."

"Oh, it's nothing, she was not a highly educated woman or even beautiful, but put it away. You would have seen her, so why should you not see her photograph?"

"You would have allowed me to see her?"

"Why not? I believe in the purdah, but I should have told her you were my brother, and she would have seen you. Hamidullah saw her, and several others."

"Did she think they were your brothers?"

"Of course not, but the word exists and is convenient. All men are my brothers, and as soon as one behaves as such he may see my wife."

"And when the whole world behaves as such, there will be no more purdah?"

"It is because you can say and feel such a remark as that, that I show you the photograph," said Aziz gravely.

"It is beyond the power of most men. It is because you behave well while I behave badly that I show it you. I never expected you to come back just now when I called you. I thought, 'He has certainly done with me; I have insulted him.' Mr. Fielding, no one can ever realize how much kindness we Indians need, we do not even realize it ourselves. But we know when it has been given. We do not forget, though we may seem to. Kindness, more kindness, and even after that more kindness. I assure you it is the only hope." His voice seemed to arise from a dream. Altering it, yet still deep below his normal surface, he said, "We can't build up India except on what we feel. What is the use of all these reforms, and Conciliation Committees for Mohurram, and shall we cut the tazia short or shall we carry it another route, and Councils of Notables and official parties where the English sneer at our skins?"

"It's beginning at the wrong end, isn't it? I know, but institutions and the governments don't." He looked again at the photograph. The lady faced the world at her husband's wish and her own, but how bewildering she found it, the echoing contradictory world!

"Put her away, she is of no importance, she is dead," said Aziz gently. "I showed her to you because I have nothing else to show. You may look round the whole of my bungalow now, and empty everything. I have no other secrets, my three children live away with their grandmamma, and that is all."

Fielding sat down by the bed, flattered at the trust reposed in him, yet rather sad. He felt old. He wished that he too could be carried away on waves of emotion. The next time they met, Aziz might be cautious and standoffish. He realized this, and it made him sad that he should realize it. Kindness, kindness, and more kindness—yes, that he might supply, but was that really all that the queer nation needed? Did it not also demand an occasional intoxication of the blood? What had he done to deserve this outburst of confidence, and what hostage could he give in exchange? He looked back at his own life. What a poor crop of secrets it had produced! There were things in it that he had shown to no one, but they were so uninteresting, it wasn't worth while lifting a purdah on their account. He'd been in love, engaged to be married, lady broke it off, memories of her and thoughts about her had kept him from other women for a time; then indulgence, followed by repentance and equilibrium. Meagre really except the equilibrium, and Aziz didn't want to have that confided to him—he would have called it "everything ranged coldly on shelves."

"I shall not really be intimate with this fellow," Fielding thought, and then "nor with anyone." That was the corollary.

And he had to confess that he really didn't mind, that he was content to help people, and like them as long as they didn't object, and if they objected pass on serenely. Experience can do much, and all that he had learnt in England and Europe was an assistance to him, and helped him towards clarity, but clarity prevented him from experiencing something else.

"How did you like the two ladies you met last Thursday?" he asked.

Aziz shook his head distastefully. The question reminded him of his rash remark about the Marabar Caves.

"How do you like Englishwomen generally?"

"Hamidullah liked them in England. Here we never look at them. Oh no, much too careful. Let's talk of something else."

"Hamidullah's right: they are much nicer in England. There's something that doesn't suit them out here."

Aziz after another silence said, "Why are you not married?"

Fielding was pleased that he had asked. "Because I have more or less come through without it," he replied.

"I was thinking of telling you a little about myself some day if I can make it interesting enough. The lady I liked wouldn't marry me—that is the main point, but that's fifteen years ago and now means nothing."

"But you haven't children."

"None."

"Excuse the following question: have you any illegitimate children?"

"No. I'd willingly tell you if I had."

"Then your name will entirely die out."

"It must."

"Well." He shook his head. "This indifference is what the Oriental will never understand."

"I don't care for children."

"Caring has nothing to do with it," he said impatiently.

"I don't feel their absence, I don't want them weeping around my death-bed and being polite about me afterwards, which I believe is the general notion. I'd far rather leave a thought behind me than a child. Other people can have children. No obligation, with England getting so chock-a-block and overrunning India for jobs."

"Why don't you marry Miss Quested?"

"Good God! why, the girl's a prig."

"Prig, prig? Kindly explain. Isn't that a bad word?"

"Oh, I don't know her, but she struck me as one of the more pathetic products of Western education. She depresses me."

"But prig, Mr. Fielding? How's that?"

"She goes on and on as if she's at a lecture—trying ever so hard to understand India and life, and occasionally taking a note."

"I thought her so nice and sincere."

"So she probably is," said Fielding, ashamed of his roughness: any suggestion that he should marry always does produce over-statements on the part of the bachelor, and a mental breeze. "But I can't marry her if I wanted to, for she has just become engaged to the City Magistrate."

"Has she indeed? I am so glad!" he exclaimed with relief, for this exempted him from the Marabar expedition: he would scarcely be expected to entertain regular Anglo-Indians.

"It's the old mother's doing. She was afraid her dear boy would choose for himself, so she brought out the girl on purpose, and flung them together until it happened."

"Mrs. Moore did not mention that to me among her plans."

"I may have got it wrong—I'm out of club gossip. But anyhow they're engaged to be married."

"Yes, you're out of it, my poor chap," he smiled. "No Miss Quested for Mr. Fielding. However, she was not beautiful. She has practically no breasts, if you come to think of it."

He smiled too, but found a touch of bad taste in the reference to a lady's breasts.

"For the City Magistrate they shall be sufficient perhaps, and he for her. For you I shall arrange a lady with breasts like mangoes..."

"No, you won't."

"I will not really, and besides your position makes it dangerous for you." His mind had slipped from matrimony to Calcutta. His face grew grave. Fancy if he had persuaded the Principal to accompany him there, and then got him into trouble! And abruptly he took up a new attitude towards his friend, the attitude of the protector who knows the dangers of India and is admonitory. "You can't be too careful in every way, Mr. Fielding; whatever you say or do in this damned country there is always some envious fellow on the look-out. You may be surprised to know that there were at least three spies sitting here when you came to enquire. I was really a good deal upset that you talked in that fashion about God. They will certainly report it."

"To whom?"

"That's all very well, but you spoke against morality also, and you said you had come to take other people's jobs. All that was very unwise. This is an awful place for scandal. Why, actually one of your own pupils was listening."

"Thanks for telling me that; yes, I must try and be more careful. If I'm interested, I'm apt to forget myself. Still, it doesn't do real harm."

"But speaking out may get you into trouble."

"It's often done so in the past."

"There, listen to that! But the end of it might be that you lost your job."

"If I do, I do. I shall survive it. I travel light."

"Travel light! You are a most extraordinary race," said Aziz, turning away as if he were going to sleep, and immediately turning back again. "Is it your climate, or what?"

"Plenty of Indians travel light too—saddhus and such. It's one of the things I admire about your country. Any man can travel light until he has a wife or children. That's part of my case against marriage. I'm a holy man minus the holiness. Hand that on to your three spies, and tell them to put it in their pipes."

Aziz was charmed and interested, and turned the new idea over in his mind. So this was why Mr. Fielding and a few others were so fearless! They had nothing to lose. But he himself was rooted in society and Islam. He belonged to a tradition which bound him, and he had brought children into the world, the society of the future. Though he lived so vaguely in this flimsy bungalow, nevertheless he was placed, placed.

"I can't be sacked from my job, because my job's Education. I believe in teaching people to be individuals, and to understand other individuals. It's the only thing I do believe in. At Government College, I mix it up with trigonometry, and so on. When I'm a saddhu, I shall mix it up with something else."

He concluded his manifesto, and both were silent. The eye-flies became worse than ever and danced close up to their pupils, or crawled into their ears. Fielding hit about wildly. The exercise made him hot, and he got up to go.

"You might tell your servant to bring my horse. He doesn't seem to appreciate my Urdu."

"I know. I gave him orders not to. Such are the tricks we play on unfortunate Englishmen. Poor Mr. Fielding! But I will release you now. Oh dear! With the exception of yourself and Hamidullah, I have no one to talk to in this place. You like Hamidullah, don't you?"

"Very much."

"Do you promise to come at once to us when you are in trouble?"

"I never can be in trouble."

"There goes a queer chap, I trust he won't come to grief," thought Aziz, left alone. His period of admiration was over, and he reacted towards patronage. It was difficult for him to remain in awe of anyone who played with all his cards on the table. Fielding, he discovered on closer acquaintance, was truly warm-hearted and unconventional, but not what can be called wise. That frankness of speech in the presence of Ram Chand, Rafi and Co. was dangerous and inelegant. It served no useful end.

But they were friends, brothers. That part was settled, their compact had been subscribed by the photograph, they trusted one another, affection had triumphed for once in a way. He dropped off to sleep amid the happier memories of the last two hours—poetry of Ghalib, female grace, good old Hamidullah, good Fielding, his honoured wife and dear boys. He passed into a region where these joys had no enemies but bloomed harmoniously in an eternal garden, or ran down water shoots of ribbed marble, or rose into domes where under were inscribed, black against white, the ninety-nine attributes of God.

Part 2

Caves

CHAPTER 12

The Ganges, though flowing from the foot of Vishnu and through Siva's hair, is not an ancient stream. Geology, looking further than religion, knows of a time when neither the river nor the Himalayas that nourished it existed, and an ocean flowed over the holy places of Hindustan. The mountains rose, their debris silted up the ocean, the gods took their seats on them and contrived the river, and the India we call immemorial came into being. But India is really far older. In the days of the prehistoric ocean the southern part of the peninsula already existed, and the high places of Dravidia have been land since land began, and have seen on the one side the sinking of a continent that joined them to Africa, and on the other the upheaval of the Himalayas from a sea. They are older than anything in the world. No water has ever covered them, and the sun who has watched them for countless æons may still discern in their outlines forms that were his before our globe was torn from his bosom. If flesh of the sun's flesh is to be touched anywhere, it is here, among the incredible antiquity of these hills.

Yet even they are altering. As Himalayan India rose, this India, the primal, has been depressed, and is slowly re-entering the curve of the earth. It may be that in æons to come an ocean will flow here too, and cover the sun-born rocks with slime. Meanwhile the plain of the Ganges encroaches on them with something of the sea's action.

They are sinking beneath the newer lands. Their main mass is untouched, but at the edge their outposts have been cut off and stand knee-deep, throat-deep, in the advancing soil. There is something unspeakable in these outposts. They are like nothing else in the world, and a glimpse of them makes the breath catch. They rise abruptly, insanely, without the proportion that is kept by the wildest hills elsewhere, they bear no relation to anything dreamt or seen. To call them "uncanny" suggests ghosts, and they are older than all spirit. Hinduism has scratched and plastered a few rocks, but the shrines are unfrequented, as if pilgrims, who generally seek the extraordinary, had here found too much of it. Some saddhus did once settle in a cave, but they were smoked out, and even Buddha, who must have passed this way down to the Bo Tree of Gya, shunned a renunciation more complete than his own, and has left no legend of struggle or victory in the Marabar.

The caves are readily described. A tunnel eight feet long, five feet high, three feet wide, leads to a circular chamber about twenty feet in diameter. This arrangement occurs again and again throughout the group of hills, and this is all, this is a Marabar Cave. Having seen one such cave, having seen two, having seen three, four, fourteen, twenty-four, the visitor returns to Chandrapore uncertain whether he has had an interesting experience or a dull one or any experience at all. He finds it difficult to discuss the caves, or to keep them apart in his mind, for the pattern never varies, and no carving, not even a bees'-nest or a bat distinguishes one from another. Nothing, nothing attaches to them, and their reputation—for they have one—does not depend upon human speech. It is as if the surrounding plain or the passing birds have taken upon themselves to exclaim "extraordinary," and the word has taken root in the air, and been inhaled by mankind.

They are dark caves. Even when they open towards the sun, very little light penetrates down the entrance tunnel into the circular chamber. There is little to see, and no eye to see it, until the visitor arrives for his five minutes, and strikes a match.

Immediately another flame rises in the depths of the rock and moves towards the surface like an imprisoned spirit: the walls of the circular chamber have been most marvellously polished. The two flames approach and strive to unite, but cannot, because one of them breathes air, the other stone. A mirror inlaid with lovely colours divides the lovers, delicate stars of pink and grey interpose, exquisite nebulæ, shadings fainter than the tail of a comet or the midday moon, all the evanescent life of the granite, only here visible. Fists and fingers thrust above the advancing soil—here at last is their skin, finer than any covering acquired by the animals, smoother than windless water, more voluptuous than love. The radiance increases, the flames touch one another, kiss, expire. The cave is dark again, like all the caves.

Only the wall of the circular chamber has been polished thus. The sides of the tunnel are left rough, they impinge as an afterthought upon the internal perfection. An entrance was necessary, so mankind made one. But elsewhere, deeper in the granite, are there certain chambers that have no entrances? Chambers never unsealed since the arrival of the gods. Local report declares that these exceed in number those that can be visited, as the dead exceed the living—four hundred of them, four thousand or million. Nothing is inside them, they were sealed up before the creation of pestilence or treasure; if mankind grew curious and excavated, nothing, nothing would be added to the sum of good or evil. One of them is rumoured within the boulder that swings on the summit of the highest of the hills; a bubble-shaped cave that has neither ceiling nor floor, and mirrors its own darkness in every direction infinitely. If the boulder falls and smashes, the cave will smash too—empty as an Easter egg. The boulder because of its hollowness sways in the wind, and even moves when a crow perches upon it: hence its name and the name of its stupendous pedestal: the Kawa Dol.

CHAPTER 13

These hills look romantic in certain lights and at suitable distances, and seen of an evening from the upper verandah of the club they caused Miss Quested to say conversationally to Miss Derek that she should like to have gone, that Dr. Aziz at Mr. Fielding's had said he would arrange something, and that Indians seem rather forgetful. She was overheard by the servant who offered them vermouths. This servant understood English. And he was not exactly a spy, but he kept his ears open, and Mahmoud Ali did not exactly bribe him, but did encourage him to come and squat with his own servants, and would happen to stroll their way when he was there. As the story travelled, it accreted emotion and Aziz learnt with horror that the ladies were deeply offended with him, and had expected an invitation daily. He thought his facile remark had been forgotten. Endowed with two memories, a temporary and a permanent, he had hitherto relegated the caves to the former. Now he transferred them once for all, and pushed the matter through. They were to be a stupendous replica of the tea party. He began by securing Fielding and old Godbole, and then commissioned Fielding to approach Mrs. Moore and Miss Quested when they were alone—by this device Ronny, their official protector, could be circumvented. Fielding didn't like the job much; he was busy, caves bored him, he foresaw friction and expense, but he would not refuse the first favour his friend had asked from him, and did as required. The ladies accepted. It was a little inconvenient in the present press of their engagements, still, they hoped to manage it after consulting Mr. Heaslop. Consulted, Ronny raised no objection, provided Fielding undertook full responsibility for their comfort. He was not enthusiastic about the picnic, but, then, no more were the ladies—no one was enthusiastic, yet it took place.

Aziz was terribly worried. It was not a long expedition—a train left Chandrapore just before dawn, another would bring them back for tiffin—but he was only a little official still, and feared to acquit himself dishonourably. He had to ask Major Callendar for half a day's leave, and be refused because of his recent malingering; despair; renewed approach of Major Callendar through Fielding, and contemptuous snarling permission. He had to borrow cutlery from Mahmoud Ali without inviting him. Then there was the question of alcohol; Mr. Fielding, and perhaps the ladies, were drinkers, so must he provide whisky-sodas and ports? There was the problem of transport from the wayside station of Marabar to the caves. There was the problem of Professor Godbole and his food, and of Professor Godbole and other people's food—two problems, not one problem. The Professor was not a very strict Hindu—he would take tea, fruit, soda-water and sweets, whoever cooked them, and vegetables and rice if cooked by a Brahman; but not meat, not cakes lest they contained eggs, and he would not allow anyone else to eat beef: a slice of beef upon a distant plate would wreck his happiness. Other people might eat mutton, they might eat ham. But over ham Aziz' own religion raised its voice: he did not fancy other people eating ham. Trouble after trouble encountered him, because he had challenged the spirit of the Indian earth, which tries to keep men in compartments.

At last the moment arrived.

His friends thought him most unwise to mix himself up with English ladies, and warned him to take every precaution against unpunctuality. Consequently he spent the previous night at the station.

The servants were huddled on the platform, enjoined not to stray. He himself walked up and down with old Mohammed Latif, who was to act as major-domo. He felt insecure and also unreal. A car drove up, and he hoped Fielding would get out of it, to lend him solidity. But it contained Mrs. Moore, Miss Quested, and their Goanese servant. He rushed to meet them, suddenly happy. "But you've come, after all. Oh how very very kind of you!" he cried. "This is the happiest moment in all my life."

The ladies were civil. It was not the happiest moment in their lives, still, they looked forward to enjoying themselves as soon as the bother of the early start was over. They had not seen him since the expedition was arranged, and they thanked him adequately.

"You don't require tickets—please stop your servant. There are no tickets on the Marabar branch line; it is its peculiarity. You come to the carriage and rest till Mr. Fielding joins us. Did you know you are to travel purdah? Will you like that?"

They replied that they should like it. The train had come in, and a crowd of dependents were swarming over the seats of the carriage like monkeys. Aziz had borrowed servants from his friends, as well as bringing his own three, and quarrels over precedence were resulting. The ladies' servant stood apart, with a sneering expression on his face. They had hired him while they were still globe-trotters, at Bombay. In a hotel or among smart people he was excellent, but as soon as they consorted with anyone whom he thought second-rate he left them to their disgrace.

The night was still dark, but had acquired the temporary look that indicates its end. Perched on the roof of a shed, the station-master's hens began to dream of kites instead of owls. Lamps were put out, in order to save the trouble of putting them out later; the smell of tobacco and the sound of spitting arose from third-class passengers in dark corners; heads were unshrouded, teeth cleaned on the twigs of a tree. So convinced was a junior official that another sun would rise, that he rang a bell with enthusiasm. This upset the servants. They shrieked that the train was starting, and ran to both ends of it to intercede. Much had still to enter the purdah carriage—a box bound with brass, a melon wearing a fez, a towel containing guavas, a step-ladder and a gun. The guests played up all right. They had no race-consciousness—Mrs. Moore was too old, Miss Quested too new—and they behaved to Aziz as to any young man who had been kind to them in the country. This moved him deeply. He had expected them to arrive with Mr. Fielding, instead of which they trusted themselves to be with him a few moments alone.

"Send back your servant," he suggested. "He is unnecessary. Then we shall all be Moslems together."

"And he is such a horrible servant. Antony, you can go; we don't want you," said the girl impatiently.

"Master told me to come."

"Mistress tells you to go."

"Master says, keep near the ladies all the morning."

"Well, your ladies won't have you." She turned to the host. "Do get rid of him, Dr. Aziz!"

"Mohammed Latif!" he called.

The poor relative exchanged fezzes with the melon, and peeped out of the window of the railway carriage, whose confusion he was superintending.

"Here is my cousin, Mr. Mohammed Latif. Oh no, don't shake hands. He is an Indian of the old-fashioned sort, he prefers to salaam. There, I told you so. Mohammed Latif, how beautifully you salaam. See, he hasn't understood; he knows no English."

"You spick lie," said the old man gently.

"I spick a lie! Oh, jolly good. Isn't he a funny old man? We will have great jokes with him later. He does all sorts of little things. He is not nearly as stupid as you think, and awfully poor. It's lucky ours is a large family." He flung an arm round the grubby neck. "But you get inside, make yourselves at home; yes, you lie down."

The celebrated Oriental confusion appeared at last to be at an end. "Excuse me, now I must meet our other two guests!"

He was getting nervous again, for it was ten minutes to the time. Still, Fielding was an Englishman, and they never do miss trains, and Godbole was a Hindu and did not count, and, soothed by this logic, he grew calmer as the hour of departure approached. Mohammed Latif had bribed Antony not to come. They walked up and down the platform, talking usefully. They agreed that they had overdone the servants, and must leave two or three behind at Marabar station. And Aziz explained that he might be playing one or two practical jokes at the caves—not out of unkindness, but to make the guests laugh. The old man assented with slight sideway motions of the head: he was always willing to be ridiculed, and he bade Aziz not spare him. Elated by his importance, he began an indecent anecdote.

"Tell me another time, brother, when I have more leisure, for now, as I have already explained, we have to give pleasure to non-Moslems. Three will be Europeans, one a Hindu, which must not be forgotten. Every attention must be paid to Professor Godbole, lest he feel that he is inferior to my other guests."

"I will discuss philosophy with him."

"That will be kind of you; but the servants are even more important. We must not convey an impression of disorganization. It can be done, and I expect you to do it..."

A shriek from the purdah carriage. The train had started.

"Merciful God!" cried Mohammed Latif. He flung himself at the train, and leapt on to the footboard of a carriage. Aziz did likewise. It was an easy feat, for a branch-line train is slow to assume special airs. "We're monkeys, don't worry," he called, hanging on to a bar and laughing. Then he howled, "Mr. Fielding! Mr. Fielding!"

There were Fielding and old Godbole, held up at the level-crossing. Appalling catastrophe! The gates had been closed earlier than usual. They leapt from their tonga; they gesticulated, but what was the good. So near and yet so far! As the train joggled past over the points, there was time for agonized words.

"Bad, bad, you have destroyed me."

"Godbole's pujah did it," cried the Englishman.

The Brahman lowered his eyes, ashamed of religion. For it was so: he had miscalculated the length of a prayer.

"Jump on, I must have you," screamed Aziz, beside himself.

"Right, give a hand."

"He's not to, he'll kill himself," Mrs. Moore protested. He jumped, he failed, missed his friend's hand, and fell back on to the line. The train rumbled past. He scrambled on to his feet, and bawled after them, "I'm all right, you're all right, don't worry," and then they passed beyond range of his voice.

"Mrs. Moore, Miss Quested, our expedition is a ruin." He swung himself along the footboard, almost in tears.

"Get in, get in; you'll kill yourself as well as Mr. Fielding. I see no ruin."

"How is that? Oh, explain to me!" he said piteously, like a child.

"We shall be all Moslems together now, as you promised."

She was perfect as always, his dear Mrs. Moore. All the love for her he had felt at the mosque welled up again, the fresher for forgetfulness. There was nothing he would not do for her. He would die to make her happy.

"Get in, Dr. Aziz, you make us giddy," the other lady called. "If they're so foolish as to miss the train, that's their loss, not ours."

"I am to blame. I am the host."

"Nonsense, go to your carriage. We're going to have a delightful time without them."

Not perfect like Mrs. Moore, but very sincere and kind. Wonderful ladies, both of them, and for one precious morning his guests. He felt important and competent. Fielding was a loss personally, being a friend, increasingly dear, yet if Fielding had come, he himself would have remained in leading-strings. "Indians are incapable of responsibility," said the officials, and Hamidullah sometimes said so too. He would show those pessimists that they were wrong. Smiling proudly, he glanced outward at the country, which was still invisible except as a dark movement in the darkness; then upwards at the sky, where the stars of the sprawling Scorpion had begun to pale. Then he dived through a window into a second-class carriage.

"Mohammed Latif, by the way, what is in these caves, brother? Why are we all going to see them?"

Such a question was beyond the poor relative's scope. He could only reply that God and the local villagers knew, and that the latter would gladly act as guides.

CHAPTER 14

Most of life is so dull that there is nothing to be said about it, and the books and talk that would describe it as interesting are obliged to exaggerate, in the hope of justifying their own existence. Inside its cocoon of work or social obligation, the human spirit slumbers for the most part, registering the distinction between pleasure and pain, but not nearly as alert as we pretend. There are periods in the most thrilling day during which nothing happens, and though we continue to exclaim, "I do enjoy myself," or, "I am horrified," we are insincere. "As far as I feel anything, it is enjoyment, horror"—it's no more than that really, and a perfectly adjusted organism would be silent.

It so happened that Mrs. Moore and Miss Quested had felt nothing acutely for a fortnight. Ever since Professor Godbole had sung his queer little song, they had lived more or less inside cocoons, and the difference between them was that the elder lady accepted her own apathy, while the younger resented hers. It was Adela's faith that the whole stream of events is important and interesting, and if she grew bored she blamed herself severely and compelled her lips to utter enthusiasms. This was the only insincerity in a character otherwise sincere, and it was indeed the intellectual protest of her youth. She was particularly vexed now because she was both in India and engaged to be married, which double event should have made every instant sublime.

India was certainly dim this morning, though seen under the auspices of Indians. Her wish had been granted, but too late. She could not get excited over Aziz and his arrangements. She was not the least unhappy or depressed, and the various odd objects that surrounded her—the comic "purdah" carriage, the piles of rugs and bolsters, the rolling melons, the scent of sweet oils, the ladder, the brass-bound box, the sudden irruption of Mahmoud Ali's butler from the lavatory with tea and poached eggs upon a tray—they were all new and amusing, and led her to comment appropriately, but they wouldn't bite into her mind. So she tried to find comfort by reflecting that her main interest would henceforward be Ronny.

"What a nice cheerful servant! What a relief after Antony!"

"They startle one rather. A strange place to make tea in," said Mrs. Moore, who had hoped for a nap.

"I want to sack Antony. His behaviour on the platform has decided me."

Mrs. Moore thought that Antony's better self would come to the front at Simla. Miss Quested was to be married at Simla; some cousins, with a house looking straight on to Thibet, had invited her.

"Anyhow, we must get a second servant, because at Simla you will be at the hotel, and I don't think Ronny's Baldeo..." She loved plans.

"Very well, you get another servant, and I'll keep Antony with me. I am used to his unappetizing ways. He will see me through the Hot Weather."

"I don't believe in the Hot Weather. People like Major Callendar who always talk about it—it's in the hope of making one feel inexperienced and small, like their everlasting, 'I've been twenty years in this country.'"

"I believe in the Hot Weather, but never did I suppose it would bottle me up as it will." For owing to the sage leisureliness of Ronny and Adela, they could not be married till May, and consequently Mrs. Moore could not return to England immediately after the wedding, which was what she had hoped to do. By May a barrier of fire would have fallen across India and the adjoining sea, and she would have to remain perched up in the Himalayas waiting for the world to get cooler.

"I won't be bottled up," announced the girl. "I've no patience with these women here who leave their husbands grilling in the plains. Mrs. McBryde hasn't stopped down once since she married; she leaves her quite intelligent husband alone half the year, and then's surprised she's out of touch with him."

"She has children, you see."

"Oh yes, that's true," said Miss Quested, disconcerted.

"It is the children who are the first consideration. Until they are grown up, and married off. When that happens one has again the right to live for oneself—in the plains or the hills, as suits."

"Oh yes, you're perfectly right. I never thought it out."

"If one has not become too stupid and old." She handed her empty cup to the servant.

"My idea now is that my cousins shall find me a servant in Simla, at all events to see me through the wedding, after which Ronny means to reorganize his staff entirely. He does it very well for a bachelor; still, when he is married no doubt various changes will have to be made—his old servants won't want to take their orders from me, and I don't blame them."

Mrs. Moore pushed up the shutters and looked out. She had brought Ronny and Adela together by their mutual wish, but really she could not advise them further. She felt increasingly (vision or nightmare?) that, though people are important, the relations between them are not, and that in particular too much fuss has been made over marriage; centuries of carnal embracement, yet man is no nearer to understanding man. And to-day she felt this with such force that it seemed itself a relationship, itself a person who was trying to take hold of her hand.

"Anything to be seen of the hills?"

"Only various shades of the dark."

"We can't be far from the place where my hyena was." She peered into the timeless twilight. The train crossed a nullah. "Pomper, pomper, pomper," was the sound that the wheels made as they trundled over the bridge, moving very slowly. A hundred yards on came a second nullah, then a third, suggesting the neighbourhood of higher ground. "Perhaps this is mine; anyhow, the road runs parallel with the railway." Her accident was a pleasant memory; she felt in her dry, honest way that it had given her a good shake up, and taught her Ronny's true worth. Then she went back to her plans; plans had been a passion with her from girlhood. Now and then she paid tribute to the present, said how friendly and intelligent Aziz was, ate a guava, couldn't eat a fried sweet, practised her Urdu on the servant; but her thoughts ever veered to the manageable future, and to the Anglo-Indian life she had decided to endure. And as she appraised it with its adjuncts of Turtons and Burtons, the train accompanied her sentences, "pomper, pomper," the train half asleep, going nowhere in particular and with no passenger of importance in any of its carriages, the branch-line train, lost on a low embankment between dull fields. Its message—for it had one—avoided her well-equipped mind. Far away behind her, with a shriek that meant business, rushed the Mail, connecting up important towns such as Calcutta and Lahore, where interesting events occur and personalities are developed. She understood that. Unfortunately, India has few important towns. India is the country, fields, fields, then hills, jungle, hills, and more fields. The branch line stops, the road is only practicable for cars to a point, the bullock-carts lumber down the side tracks, paths fray out into the cultivation, and disappear near a splash of red paint. How can the mind take hold of such a country? Generations of invaders have tried, but they remain in exile. The important towns they build are only retreats, their quarrels the malaise of men who cannot find their way home. India knows of their trouble. She knows of the whole world's trouble, to its uttermost depth. She calls "Come" through her hundred mouths, through objects ridiculous and august. But come to what? She has never defined. She is not a promise, only an appeal.

"I will fetch you from Simla when it's cool enough. I will unbottle you in fact," continued the reliable girl. "We then see some of the Mogul stuff—how appalling if we let you miss the Taj!—and then I will see you off at Bombay. Your last glimpse of this country really shall be interesting." But Mrs. Moore had fallen asleep, exhausted by the early start. She was in rather low health, and ought not to have attempted the expedition, but had pulled herself together in case the pleasure of the others should suffer. Her dreams were of the same texture, but there it was her other children who were wanting something, Stella and Ralph, and she was explaining to them that she could not be in two families at once. When she awoke, Adela had ceased to plan, and leant out of a window, saying, "They're rather wonderful."

Astonishing even from the rise of the civil station, here the Marabar were gods to whom earth is a ghost. Kawa Dol was nearest. It shot up in a single slab, on whose summit one rock was poised—if a mass so great can be called one rock. Behind it, recumbent, were the hills that contained the other caves, isolated each from his neighbour by broad channels of the plain. The assemblage, ten in all, shifted a little as the train crept past them, as if observing its arrival.

"I'ld not have missed this for anything," said the girl, exaggerating her enthusiasm. "Look, the sun's rising—this'll be absolutely magnificent—come quickly—look. I wouldn't have missed this for anything. We should never have seen it if we'd stuck to the Turtons and their eternal elephants."

As she spoke, the sky to the left turned angry orange. Colour throbbed and mounted behind a pattern of trees, grew in intensity, was yet brighter, incredibly brighter, strained from without against the globe of the air. They awaited the miracle. But at the supreme moment, when night should have died and day lived, nothing occurred. It was as if virtue had failed in the celestial fount. The hues in the east decayed, the hills seemed dimmer though in fact better lit, and a profound disappointment entered with the morning breeze. Why, when the chamber was prepared, did the bridegroom not enter with trumpets and shawms, as humanity expects? The sun rose without splendour. He was presently observed trailing yellowish behind the trees, or against insipid sky, and touching the bodies already at work in the fields.

"Ah, that must be the false dawn—isn't it caused by dust in the upper layers of the atmosphere that couldn't fall down during the night? I think Mr. McBryde said so. Well, I must admit that England has it as regards sunrises. Do you remember Grasmere?"

"Ah, dearest Grasmere!" Its little lakes and mountains were beloved by them all. Romantic yet manageable, it sprang from a kindlier planet. Here an untidy plain stretched to the knees of the Marabar.

"Good morning, good morning, put on your topis," shouted Aziz from farther down the train. "Put on your topis at once, the early sun is highly dangerous for heads. I speak as a doctor."

"Good morning, good morning, put on your own."

"Not for my thick head," he laughed, banging it and holding up pads of his hair.

"Nice creature he is," murmured Adela.

"Listen—Mohammed Latif says 'Good morning' next." Various pointless jests.

"Dr. Aziz, what's happened to your hills? The train has forgotten to stop."

"Perhaps it is a circular train and goes back to Chandrapore without a break. Who knows!"

Having wandered off into the plain for a mile, the train slowed up against an elephant. There was a platform too, but it shrivelled into insignificance. An elephant, waving her painted forehead at the morn! "Oh, what a surprise!" called the ladies politely. Aziz said nothing, but he nearly burst with pride and relief. The elephant was the one grand feature of the picnic, and God alone knew what he had gone through to obtain her. Semi-official, she was best approached through the Nawab Bahadur, who was best approached through Nureddin, but he never answered letters, but his mother had great influence with him and was a friend of Hamidullah Begum's, who had been excessively kind and had promised to call on her provided the broken shutter of the purdah carriage came back soon enough from Calcutta. That an elephant should depend from so long and so slender a string filled Aziz with content, and with humorous appreciation of the East, where the friends of friends are a reality, where everything gets done sometime, and sooner or later everyone gets his share of happiness. And Mohammed Latif was likewise content, because two of the guests had missed the train, and consequently he could ride on the howdah instead of following in a cart, and the servants were content because an elephant increased their self-esteem, and they tumbled out the luggage into the dust with shouts and bangs, issuing orders to one another, and convulsed with goodwill.

"It takes an hour to get there, an hour to get back, and two hours for the caves, which we will call three," said Aziz, smiling charmingly. There was suddenly something regal about him. "The train back is at eleven-thirty, and you will be sitting down to your tiffin in Chandrapore with Mr. Heaslop at exactly your usual hour, namely, one-fifteen. I know everything about you. Four hours—quite a small expedition—and an hour extra for misfortunes, which occur somewhat frequently among my people. My idea is to plan everything without consulting you; but you, Mrs. Moore, or Miss Quested, you are at any moment to make alterations if you wish, even if it means giving up the caves. Do you agree? Then mount this wild animal."

The elephant had knelt, grey and isolated, like another hill. They climbed up the ladder, and he mounted shikar fashion, treading first on the sharp edge of the heel and then into the looped-up tail. When Mohammed Latif followed him, the servant who held the end of the tail let go of it according to previous instructions, so that the poor relative slipped and had to cling to the netting over the buttocks. It was a little piece of Court buffoonery, and distressed only the ladies, whom it was intended to divert. Both of them disliked practical jokes. Then the beast rose in two shattering movements, and poised them ten feet above the plain. Immediately below was the scurf of life that an elephant always collects round its feet—villagers, naked babies. The servants flung crockery into tongas. Hassan annexed the stallion intended for Aziz, and defied Mahmoud Ali's man from its altitude. The Brahman who had been hired to cook for Professor Godbole was planted under an acacia tree, to await their return. The train, also hoping to return, wobbled away through the fields, turning its head this way and that like a centipede. And the only other movement to be seen was a movement as of antennae, really the counterpoises of the wells which rose and fell on their pivots of mud all over the plain and dispersed a feeble flow of water. The scene was agreeable rather than not in the mild morning air, but there was little colour in it, and no vitality.

As the elephant moved towards the hills (the pale sun had by this time saluted them to the base, and pencilled shadows down their creases) a new quality occurred, a spiritual silence which invaded more senses than the ear. Life went on as usual, but had no consequences, that is to say, sounds did not echo or thoughts develop. Everything seemed cut off at its root, and therefore infected with illusion. For instance, there were some mounds by the edge of the track, low, serrated, and touched with whitewash.

What were these mounds—graves, breasts of the goddess Parvati? The villagers beneath gave both replies. Again, there was a confusion about a snake which was never cleared up. Miss Quested saw a thin, dark object reared on end at the farther side of a watercourse, and said, "A snake!" The villagers agreed, and Aziz explained: yes, a black cobra, very venomous, who had reared himself up to watch the passing of the elephant, But when she looked through Ronny's field-glasses, she found it wasn't a snake, but the withered and twisted stump of a toddy-palm. So she said, "It isn't a snake." The villagers contradicted her. She had put the word into their minds, and they refused to abandon it. Aziz admitted that it looked like a tree through the glasses, but insisted that it was a black cobra really, and improvised some rubbish about protective mimicry. Nothing was explained, and yet there was no romance. Films of heat, radiated from the Kawa Dol precipices, increased the confusion. They came at irregular intervals and moved capriciously. A patch of field would jump as if it was being fried, and then lie quiet. As they drew closer the radiation stopped.

The elephant walked straight at the Kawa Dol as if she would knock for admission with her forehead, then swerved, and followed a path round its base. The stones plunged straight into the earth, like cliffs into the sea, and while Miss Quested was remarking on this, and saying that it was striking, the plain quietly disappeared, peeled off, so to speak, and nothing was to be seen on either side but the granite, very dead and quiet. The sky dominated as usual, but seemed unhealthily near, adhering like a ceiling to the summits of the precipices. It was as if the contents of the corridor had never been changed. Occupied by his own munificence, Aziz noticed nothing. His guests noticed a little. They did not feel that it was an attractive place or quite worth visiting, and wished it could have turned into some Mohammedan object, such as a mosque, which their host would have appreciated and explained. His ignorance became evident, and was really rather a drawback. In spite of his gay, confident talk, he had no notion how to treat this particular aspect of India; he was lost in it without Professor Godbole, like themselves.

The corridor narrowed, then widened into a sort of tray. Here, more or less, was their goal. A ruined tank held a little water which would do for the animals, and close above the mud was punched a black hole—the first of the caves. Three hills encircled the tray. Two of them pumped out heat busily, but the third was in shadow, and here they camped.

"A horrid, stuffy place really," murmured Mrs. Moore to herself.

"How quick your servants are!" Miss Quested exclaimed. For a cloth had already been laid, with a vase of artificial flowers in its centre, and Mahmoud Ali's butler offered them poached eggs and tea for the second time.

"I thought we would eat this before our caves, and breakfast after."

"Isn't this breakfast?"

"This breakfast? Did you think I should treat you so strangely?" He had been warned that English people never stop eating, and that he had better nourish them every two hours until a solid meal was ready.

"How very well it is all arranged."

"That you shall tell me when I return to Chandrapore. Whatever disgraces I bring upon myself, you remain my guests." He spoke gravely now. They were dependent on him for a few hours, and he felt grateful to them for placing themselves in such a position. All was well so far; the elephant held a fresh cut bough to her lips, the tonga shafts stuck up into the air, the kitchen-boy peeled potatoes, Hassan shouted, and Mohammed Latif stood as he ought, with a peeled switch in his hand. The expedition was a success, and it was Indian; an obscure young man had been allowed to show courtesy to visitors from another country, which is what all Indians long to do—even cynics like Mahmoud Ali—but they never have the chance. Hospitality had been achieved, they were "his" guests; his honour was involved in their happiness, and any discomfort they endured would tear his own soul.

Like most Orientals, Aziz overrated hospitality, mistaking it for intimacy, and not seeing that it is tainted with the sense of possession. It was only when Mrs. Moore or Fielding was near him that he saw further, and knew that it is more blessed to receive than to give. These two had strange and beautiful effects on him—they were his friends, his forever, and he theirs for ever; he loved them so much that giving and receiving became one. He loved them even better than the Hamidullahs, because he had surmounted obstacles to meet them, and this stimulates a generous mind. Their images remained somewhere in his soul up to his dying day, permanent additions. He looked at her now as she sat on a deck-chair, sipping his tea, and had for a moment a joy that held the seeds of its own decay, for it would lead him to think, "Oh, what more can I do for her?" and so back to the dull round of hospitality. The black bullets of his eyes filled with soft expressive light, and he said, "Do you ever remember our mosque, Mrs. Moore?"

"I do. I do," she said, suddenly vital and young.

"And how rough and rude I was, and how good you were."

"And how happy we both were."

"Friendships last longest that begin like that, I think. Shall I ever entertain your other children?"

"Do you know about the others? She will never talk about them to me," said Miss Quested, unintentionally breaking a spell.

"Ralph and Stella, yes, I know everything about them. But we must not forget to visit our caves. One of the dreams of my life is accomplished in having you both here as my guests. You cannot imagine how you have honoured me. I feel like the Emperor Babur."

"Why like him?" she enquired, rising.

"Because my ancestors came down with him from Afghanistan. They joined him at Herat. He also had often no more elephants than one, none sometimes, but he never ceased showing hospitality. When he fought or hunted or ran away, he would always stop for a time among hills, just like us; he would never let go of hospitality and pleasure, and if there was only a little food, he would have it arranged nicely, and if only one musical instrument, he would compel it to play a beautiful tune. I take him as my ideal. He is the poor gentleman, and he became a great king."

"I thought another Emperor is your favourite—I forget the name—you mentioned him at Mr. Fielding's: what my book calls Aurangzebe."

"Alamgir? Oh yes, he was of course the more pious. But Babur—never in his whole life did he betray a friend, so I can only think of him this morning. And you know how he died? He laid down his life for his son. A death far more difficult than battle. They were caught in the heat. They should have gone back to Kabul for the bad weather, but could not for reasons of state, and at Agra Humayun fell sick. Babur walked round the bed three times, and said, 'I have borne it away,' and he did bear it away; the fever left his son and came to him instead, and he died. That is why I prefer Babur to Alamgir. I ought not to do so, but I do. However, I mustn't delay you. I see you are ready to start."

"Not at all," she said, sitting down by Mrs. Moore again. "We enjoy talk like this very much." For at last he was talking about what he knew and felt, talking as he had in Fielding's garden-house; he was again the Oriental guide whom they appreciated.

"I always enjoy conversing about the Moguls. It is the chief pleasure I know. You see, those first six emperors were all most wonderful men, and as soon as one of them is mentioned, no matter which, I forget everything else in the world except the other five. You could not find six such kings in all the countries of the earth, not, I mean, coming one after the other—father, son."

"Tell us something about Akbar."

"Ah, you have heard the name of Akbar. Good. Hamidullah—whom you shall meet—will tell you that Akbar is the greatest of all. I say, 'Yes, Akbar is very wonderful, but half a Hindu; he was not a true Moslem,' which makes Hamidullah cry, 'No more was Babur, he drank wine.' But Babur always repented afterwards, which makes the entire difference, and Akbar never repented of the new religion he invented instead of the Holy Koran."

"But wasn't Akbar's new religion very fine? It was to embrace the whole of India."

"Miss Quested, fine but foolish. You keep your religion, I mine. That is the best. Nothing embraces the whole of India, nothing, nothing, and that was Akbar's mistake."

"Oh, do you feel that, Dr. Aziz?" she said thoughtfully. "I hope you're not right. There will have to be something universal in this country—I don't say religion, for I'm not religious, but something, or how else are barriers to be broken down?"

She was only recommending the universal brotherhood he sometimes dreamed of, but as soon as it was put into prose it became untrue.

"Take my own case," she continued—it was indeed her own case that had animated her. "I don't know whether you happen to have heard, but I'm going to marry Mr. Heaslop."

"On which my heartiest congratulations."

"Mrs. Moore, may I put our difficulty to Dr. Aziz—I mean our Anglo-Indian one?"

"It is your difficulty, not mine, my dear."

"Ah, that's true. Well, by marrying Mr. Heaslop, I shall become what is known as an Anglo-Indian."

He held up his hand in protest. "Impossible. Take back such a terrible remark."

"But I shall; it's inevitable. I can't avoid the label. What I do hope to avoid is the mentality. Women like——" She stopped, not quite liking to mention names; she would boldly have said "Mrs. Turton and Mrs. Callendar" a fortnight ago. "Some women are so—well, ungenerous and snobby about Indians, and I should feel too ashamed for words if I turned like them, but—and here's my difficulty—there's nothing special about me, nothing specially good or strong, which will help me to resist my environment and avoid becoming like them. I've most lamentable defects. That's why I want Akbar's 'universal religion' or the equivalent to keep me decent and sensible. Do you see what I mean?"

Her remarks pleased him, but his mind shut up tight because she had alluded to her marriage. He was not going to be mixed up in that side of things. "You are certain to be happy with any relative of Mrs. Moore's," he said with a formal bow.

"Oh, my happiness—that's quite another problem. I want to consult you about this Anglo-Indian difficulty. Can you give me any advice?"

"You are absolutely unlike the others, I assure you. You will never be rude to my people."

"I am told we all get rude after a year."

"Then you are told a lie," he flashed, for she had spoken the truth and it touched him on the raw; it was itself an insult in these particular circumstances. He recovered himself at once and laughed, but her error broke up their conversation—their civilization it had almost been—which scattered like the petals of a desert flower, and left them in the middle of the hills. "Come along," he said, holding out a hand to each. They got up a little reluctantly, and addressed themselves to sightseeing.

The first cave was tolerably convenient. They skirted the puddle of water, and then climbed up over some unattractive stones, the sun crashing on their backs. Bending their heads, they disappeared one by one into the interior of the hills. The small black hole gaped where their varied forms and colours had momentarily functioned. They were sucked in like water down a drain. Bland and bald rose the precipices; bland and glutinous the sky that connected the precipices; solid and white, a Brahminy kite flapped between the rocks with a clumsiness that seemed intentional. Before man, with his itch for the seemly, had been born, the planet must have looked thus. The kite flapped away... Before birds, perhaps... And then the hole belched and humanity returned.

A Marabar cave had been horrid as far as Mrs. Moore was concerned, for she had nearly fainted in it, and had some difficulty in preventing herself from saying so as soon as she got into the air again. It was natural enough: she had always suffered from faintness, and the cave had become too full, because all their retinue followed them. Crammed with villagers and servants, the circular chamber began to smell. She lost Aziz and Adela in the dark, didn't know who touched her, couldn't breathe, and some vile naked thing struck her face and settled on her mouth like a pad. She tried to regain the entrance tunnel, but an influx of villagers swept her back. She hit her head. For an instant she went mad, hitting and gasping like a fanatic. For not only did the crush and stench alarm her; there was also a terrifying echo.

Professor Godbole had never mentioned an echo; it never impressed him, perhaps. There are some exquisite echoes in India; there is the whisper round the dome at Bijapur; there are the long, solid sentences that voyage through the air at Mandu, and return unbroken to their creator. The echo in a Marabar cave is not like these, it is entirely devoid of distinction. Whatever is said, the same monotonous noise replies, and quivers up and down the walls until it is absorbed into the roof. "Boum" is the sound as far as the human alphabet can express it, or "bou-oum," or "ou-boum,"—utterly dull. Hope, politeness, the blowing of a nose, the squeak of a boot, all produce "boum." Even the striking of a match starts a little worm coiling, which is too small to complete a circle but is eternally watchful. And if several people talk at once, an overlapping howling noise begins, echoes generate echoes, and the cave is stuffed with a snake composed of small snakes, which writhe independently.

After Mrs. Moore all the others poured out. She had given the signal for the reflux. Aziz and Adela both emerged smiling and she did not want him to think his treat was a failure, so smiled too. As each person emerged she looked for a villain, but none was there, and she realized that she had been among the mildest individuals, whose only desire was to honour her, and that the naked pad was a poor little baby, astride its mother's hip. Nothing evil had been in the cave, but she had not enjoyed herself; no, she had not enjoyed herself, and she decided not to visit a second one.

"Did you see the reflection of his match—rather pretty?" asked Adela.

"I forget..."

"But he says this isn't a good cave, the best are on the Kawa Dol."

"I don't think I shall go on to there. I dislike climbing."

"Very well, let's sit down again in the shade until breakfast's ready."

"Ah, but that'll disappoint him so; he has taken such trouble. You should go on; you don't mind."

"Perhaps I ought to," said the girl, indifferent to what she did, but desirous of being amiable.

The servants, etc., were scrambling back to the camp, pursued by grave censures from Mohammed Latif. Aziz came to help the guests over the rocks. He was at the summit of his powers, vigorous and humble, too sure of himself to resent criticism, and he was sincerely pleased when he heard they were altering his plans. "Certainly, Miss Quested, so you and I will go together, and leave Mrs. Moore here, and we will not be long, yet we will not hurry, because we know that will be her wish."

"Quite right. I'm sorry not to come too, but I'm a poor walker."

"Dear Mrs. Moore, what does anything matter so long as you are my guests? I am very glad you are *not* coming, which sounds strange, but you are treating me with true frankness, as a friend."

"Yes, I am your friend," she said, laying her hand on his sleeve, and thinking, despite her fatigue, how very charming, how very good, he was, and how deeply she desired his happiness. "So may I make another suggestion? Don't let so many people come with you this time. I think you may find it more convenient."

"Exactly, exactly," he cried, and, rushing to the other extreme, forbade all except one guide to accompany Miss Quested and him to the Kawa Dol. "Is that all right?" he enquired.

"Quite right, now enjoy yourselves, and when you come back tell me all about it." And she sank into the deck-chair.

If they reached the big pocket of caves, they would be away nearly an hour. She took out her writing-pad, and began, "Dear Stella, Dear Ralph," then stopped, and looked at the queer valley and their feeble invasion of it. Even the elephant had become a nobody. Her eye rose from it to the entrance tunnel. No, she did not wish to repeat that experience. The more she thought over it, the more disagreeable and frightening it became. She minded it much more now than at the time. The crush and the smells she could forget, but the echo began in some indescribable way to undermine her hold on life. Coming at a moment when she chanced to be fatigued, it had managed to murmur, "Pathos, piety, courage—they exist, but are identical, and so is filth. Everything exists, nothing has value." If one had spoken vileness in that place, or quoted lofty poetry, the comment would have been the same—"ou-boum." If one had spoken with the tongues of angels and pleaded for all the unhappiness and misunderstanding in the world, past, present, and to come, for all the misery men must undergo whatever their opinion and position, and however much they dodge or bluff—it would amount to the same, the serpent would descend and return to the ceiling. Devils are of the North, and poems can be written about them, but no one could romanticize the Marabar because it robbed infinity and eternity of their vastness, the only quality that accommodates them to mankind.

She tried to go on with her letter, reminding herself that she was only an elderly woman who had got up too early in the morning and journeyed too far, that the despair creeping over her was merely her despair, her personal weakness, and that even if she got a sunstroke and went mad the rest of the world would go on. But suddenly, at the edge of her mind, Religion appeared, poor little talkative Christianity, and she knew that all its divine words from "Let there be Light" to "It is finished" only amounted to "boum." Then she was terrified over an area larger than usual; the universe, never comprehensible to her intellect, offered no repose to her soul, the mood of the last two months took definite form at last, and she realized that she didn't want to write to her children, didn't want to communicate with anyone, not even with God. She sat motionless with horror, and, when old Mohammed Latif came up to her, thought he would notice a difference. For a time she thought, "I am going to be ill," to comfort herself, then she surrendered to the vision. She lost all interest, even in Aziz, and the affectionate and sincere words that she had spoken to him seemed no longer hers but the air's.

CHAPTER 15

Miss Quested and Aziz and a guide continued the slightly tedious expedition. They did not talk much, for the sun was getting high. The air felt like a warm bath into which hotter water is trickling constantly, the temperature rose and rose, the boulders said, "I am alive," the small stones answered, "I am almost alive." Between the chinks lay the ashes of little plants. They meant to climb to the rocking-stone on the summit, but it was too far, and they contented themselves with the big group of caves. *En route* for these, they encountered several isolated caves, which the guide persuaded them to visit, but really there was nothing to see; they lit a match, admired its reflection in the polish, tested the echo and came out again. Aziz was "pretty sure they should come on some interesting old carvings soon," but only meant he wished there were some carvings. His deeper thoughts were about the breakfast. Symptoms of disorganization had appeared as he left the camp. He ran over the menu: an English breakfast, porridge and mutton chops, but some Indian dishes to cause conversation, and pan afterwards. He had never liked Miss Quested as much as Mrs. Moore, and had little to say to her, less than ever now that she would marry a British official.

Nor had Adela much to say to him. If his mind was with the breakfast, hers was mainly with her marriage. Simla next week, get rid of Antony, a view of Thibet, tiresome wedding bells, Agra in October, see Mrs. Moore comfortably off from Bombay—the procession passed before her again, blurred by the heat, and then she turned to the more serious business of her life at Chandrapore. There were real difficulties here—Ronny's limitations and her own—but she enjoyed facing difficulties, and decided that if she could control her peevishness (always her weak point), and neither rail against Anglo-India nor succumb to it, their married life ought to be happy and profitable. She mustn't be too theoretical; she would deal with each problem as it came up, and trust to Ronny's common sense and her own. Luckily, each had abundance of common sense and good will.

But as she toiled over a rock that resembled an inverted saucer, she thought, "What about love?" The rock was nicked by a double row of footholds, and somehow the question was suggested by them. Where had she seen footholds before? Oh yes, they were the pattern traced in the dust by the wheels of the Nawab Bahadur's car. She and Ronny—no, they did not love each other.

"Do I take you too fast?" enquired Aziz, for she had paused, a doubtful expression on her face. The discovery had come so suddenly that she felt like a mountaineer whose rope had broken. Not to love the man one's going to marry! Not to find it out till this moment! Not even to have asked oneself the question until now! Something else to think out. Vexed rather than appalled, she stood still, her eyes on the sparkling rock. There was esteem and animal contact at dusk, but the emotion that links them was absent. Ought she to break her engagement off? She was inclined to think not—it would cause so much trouble to others; besides, she wasn't convinced that love is necessary to a successful union. If love is everything, few marriages would survive the honeymoon. "No, I'm all right, thanks," she said, and, her emotions well under control, resumed the climb, though she felt a bit dashed. Aziz held her hand, the guide adhered to the surface like a lizard and scampered about as if governed by a personal centre of gravity.

"Are you married, Dr. Aziz?" she asked, stopping again, and frowning.

"Yes, indeed, do come and see my wife"—for he felt it more artistic to have his wife alive for a moment.

"Thank you," she said absently.

"She is not in Chandrapore just now."

"And have you children?"

"Yes, indeed, three," he replied in firmer tones.

"Are they a great pleasure to you?"

"Why, naturally, I adore them," he laughed.

"I suppose so." What a handsome little Oriental he was, and no doubt his wife and children were beautiful too, for people usually get what they already possess. She did not admire him with any personal warmth, for there was nothing of the vagrant in her blood, but she guessed he might attract women of his own race and rank, and she regretted that neither she nor Ronny had physical charm. It does make a difference in a relationship—beauty, thick hair, a fine skin. Probably this man had several wives—Mohammedans always insist on their full four, according to Mrs. Turton. And having no one else to speak to on that eternal rock, she gave rein to the subject of marriage and said in her honest, decent, inquisitive way: "Have you one wife or more than one?"

The question shocked the young man very much. It challenged a new conviction of his community, and new convictions are more sensitive than old. If she had said, "Do you worship one god or several?" he would not have objected. But to ask an educated Indian Moslem how many wives he has—appalling, hideous! He was in trouble how to conceal his confusion. "One, one in my own particular case," he sputtered, and let go of her hand. Quite a number of caves were at the top of the track, and thinking, "Damn the English even at their best," he plunged into one of them to recover his balance. She followed at her leisure, quite unconscious that she had said the wrong thing, and not seeing him, she also went into a cave, thinking with half her mind "sight-seeing bores me," and wondering with the other half about marriage.

CHAPTER 16

He waited in his cave a minute, and lit a cigarette, so that he could remark on rejoining her, "I bolted in to get out of the draught," or something of the sort. When he returned, he found the guide, alone, with his head on one side. He had heard a noise, he said, and then Aziz heard it too: the noise of a motor-car. They were now on the outer shoulder of the Kawa Dol, and by scrambling twenty yards they got a glimpse of the plain. A car was coming towards the hills down the Chandrapore road. But they could not get a good view of it, because the precipitous bastion curved at the top, so that the base was not easily seen and the car disappeared as it came nearer. No doubt it would stop almost exactly beneath them, at the place where the pukka road degenerated into a path, and the elephant had turned to sidle into the hills.

He ran back, to tell the strange news to his guest. The guide explained that she had gone into a cave. "Which cave?"

He indicated the group vaguely.

"You should have kept her in sight, it was your duty," said Aziz severely. "Here are twelve caves at least. How am I to know which contains my guest? Which is the cave I was in myself?"

The same vague gesture. And Aziz, looking again, could not even be sure he had returned to the same group. Caves appeared in every direction—it seemed their original spawning place—and the orifices were always the same size. He thought, "Merciful Heavens, Miss Quested is lost," then pulled himself together, and began to look for her calmly.

"Shout!" he commanded.

When they had done this for awhile, the guide explained that to shout is useless, because a Marabar cave can hear no sound but its own. Aziz wiped his head, and sweat began to stream inside his clothes. The place was so confusing; it was partly a terrace, partly a zigzag, and full of grooves that led this way and that like snake-tracks. He tried to go into every one, but he never knew where he had started. Caves got behind caves or confabulated in pairs, and some were at the entrance of a gully.

"Come here!" he called gently, and when the guide was in reach, he struck him in the face for a punishment. The man fled, and he was left alone. He thought, "This is the end of my career, my guest is lost." And then he discovered the simple and sufficient explanation of the mystery.

Miss Quested wasn't lost. She had joined the people in the car—friends of hers, no doubt, Mr. Heaslop perhaps. He had a sudden glimpse of her, far down the gully—only a glimpse, but there she was quite plain, framed between rocks, and speaking to another lady. He was so relieved that he did not think her conduct odd. Accustomed to sudden changes of plan, he supposed that she had run down the Kawa Dol impulsively, in the hope of a little drive. He started back alone towards his camp, and almost at once caught sight of something which would have disquieted him very much a moment before: Miss Quested's field-glasses. They were lying at the verge of a cave, half-way down an entrance tunnel. He tried to hang them over his shoulder, but the leather strap had broken, so he put them into his pocket instead. When he had gone a few steps, he thought she might have dropped something else, so he went back to look.

But the previous difficulty recurred: he couldn't identify the cave. Down in the plain he heard the car starting; however, he couldn't catch a second glimpse of that. So he scrambled down the valley-face of the hill towards Mrs. Moore, and here he was more successful: the colour and confusion of his little camp soon appeared, and in the midst of it he saw an Englishman's topi, and beneath it—oh joy!—smiled not Mr. Heaslop, but Fielding.

"Fielding! Oh, I have so wanted you!" he cried, dropping the "Mr." for the first time.

And his friend ran to meet him, all so pleasant and jolly, no dignity, shouting explanations and apologies about the train. Fielding had come in the newly arrived car—Miss Derek's car—that other lady was Miss Derek. Chatter, chatter, all the servants leaving their cooking to listen. Excellent Miss Derek! She had met Fielding by chance at the post office, said, "Why haven't you gone to the Marabar?" heard how he missed the train, offered to run him there and then. Another nice English lady. Where was she? Left with car and chauffeur while Fielding found camp. Car couldn't get up—no, of course not—hundreds of people must go down to escort Miss Derek and show her the way. The elephant in person...

"Aziz, can I have a drink?"

"Certainly not." He flew to get one.

"Mr. Fielding!" called Mrs. Moore, from her patch of shade; they had not spoken yet, because his arrival had coincided with the torrent from the hill.

"Good morning again!" he cried, relieved to find all well.

"Mr. Fielding, have you seen Miss Quested?"

"But I've only just arrived. Where is she?"

"I do not know."

"Aziz! Where have you put Miss Quested to?" Aziz, who was returning with a drink in his hand, had to think for a moment. His heart was full of new happiness. The picnic, after a nasty shock or two, had developed into something beyond his dreams, for Fielding had not only come, but brought an uninvited guest. "Oh, she's all right," he said; "she went down to see Miss Derek. Well, here's luck! Chin-chin!"

"Here's luck, but chin-chin I do refuse," laughed Fielding, who detested the phrase. "Here's to India!"

"Here's luck, and here's to England!"

Miss Derek's chauffeur stopped the cavalcade which was starting to escort his mistress up, and informed it that she had gone back with the other young lady to Chandrapore; she had sent him to say so. She was driving herself.

"Oh yes, that's quite likely," said Aziz. "I knew they'd gone for a spin."

"Chandrapore? The man's made a mistake," Fielding exclaimed.

"Oh no, why?" He was disappointed, but made light of it; no doubt the two young ladies were great friends. He would prefer to give breakfast to all four; still, guests must do as they wish, or they become prisoners. He went away cheerfully to inspect the porridge and the ice.

"What's happened?" asked Fielding, who felt at once that something had gone queer. All the way out Miss Derek had chattered about the picnic, called it an unexpected treat, and said that she preferred Indians who didn't invite her to their entertainments to those who did it. Mrs. Moore sat swinging her foot, and appeared sulky and stupid. She said: "Miss Derek is most unsatisfactory and restless, always in a hurry, always wanting something new; she will do anything in the world except go back to the Indian lady who pays her."

Fielding, who didn't dislike Miss Derek, replied: "She wasn't in a hurry when I left her. There was no question of returning to Chandrapore. It looks to me as if Miss Quested's in the hurry."

"Adela?—she's never been in a hurry in her life," said the old lady sharply.

"I say it'll prove to be Miss Quested's wish, in fact I know it is," persisted the schoolmaster. He was annoyed—chiefly with himself. He had begun by missing a train—a sin he was never guilty of—and now that he did arrive it was to upset Aziz' arrangements for the second time. He wanted someone to share the blame, and frowned at Mrs. Moore rather magisterially. "Aziz is a charming fellow," he announced.

"I know," she answered, with a yawn.

"He has taken endless trouble to make a success of our picnic."

They knew one another very little, and felt rather awkward at being drawn together by an Indian. The racial problem can take subtle forms. In their case it had induced a sort of jealousy, a mutual suspicion. He tried to goad her enthusiasm; she scarcely spoke. Aziz fetched them to breakfast.

"It is quite natural about Miss Quested," he remarked, for he had been working the incident a little in his mind, to get rid of its roughnesses. "We were having an interesting talk with our guide, then the car was seen, so she decided to go down to her friend." Incurably inaccurate, he already thought that this was what had occurred. He was inaccurate because he was sensitive. He did not like to remember Miss Quested's remark about polygamy, because it was unworthy of a guest, so he put it from his mind, and with it the knowledge that he had bolted into a cave to get away from her. He was inaccurate because he desired to honour her, and—facts being entangled—he had to arrange them in her vicinity, as one tidies the ground after extracting a weed. Before breakfast was over, he had told a good many lies. "She ran to her friend, I to mine," he went on, smiling. "And now I am with my friends and they are with me and each other, which is happiness."

Loving them both, he expected them to love each other. They didn't want to. Fielding thought with hostility, "I knew these women would make trouble," and Mrs. Moore thought, "This man, having missed the train, tries to blame us"; but her thoughts were feeble; since her faintness in the cave she was sunk in apathy and cynicism. The wonderful India of her opening weeks, with its cool nights and acceptable hints of infinity, had vanished.

Fielding ran up to see one cave. He wasn't impressed. Then they got on the elephant and the picnic began to unwind out of the corridor and escaped under the precipice towards the railway station, pursued by stabs of hot air. They came to the place where he had quitted the car. A disagreeable thought now struck him, and he said: "Aziz, exactly where and how did you leave Miss Quested?"

"Up there." He indicated the Kawa Dol cheerfully.

"But how——" A gully, or rather a crease, showed among the rocks at this place; it was scurfy with cactuses. "I suppose the guide helped her."

"Oh, rather, most helpful."

"Is there a path off the top?"

"Millions of paths, my dear fellow."

Fielding could see nothing but the crease. Everywhere else the glaring granite plunged into the earth.

"But you saw them get down safe?"

"Yes, yes, she and Miss Derek, and go off in the car."

"Then the guide came back to you?"

"Exactly. Got a cigarette?"

"I hope she wasn't ill," pursued the Englishman. The crease continued as a nullah across the plain, the water draining off this way towards the Ganges.

"She would have wanted me, if she was ill, to attend her."

"Yes, that sounds sense."

"I see you're worrying, let's talk of other things," he said kindly. "Miss Quested was always to do what she wished, it was our arrangement. I see you are worrying on my account, but really I don't mind, I never notice trifles."

"I do worry on your account. I consider they have been impolite!" said Fielding, lowering his voice. "She had no right to dash away from your party, and Miss Derek had no right to abet her."

So touchy as a rule, Aziz was unassailable. The wings that uplifted him did not falter, because he was a Mogul emperor who had done his duty. Perched on his elephant, he watched the Marabar Hills recede, and saw again, as provinces of his kingdom, the grim untidy plain, the frantic and feeble movements of the buckets, the white shrines, the shallow graves, the suave sky, the snake that looked like a tree. He had given his guests as good a time as he could, and if they came late or left early that was not his affair. Mrs. Moore slept, swaying against the rods of the howdah, Mohammed Latif embraced her with efficiency and respect, and by his own side sat Fielding, whom he began to think of as "Cyril."

"Aziz, have you figured out what this picnic will cost you?"

"Sh! my dear chap, don't mention that part. Hundreds and hundreds of rupees. The completed account will be too awful; my friends' servants have robbed me right and left, and as for an elephant, she apparently eats gold. I can trust you not to repeat this. And M.L.—please employ initials, he listens—is far the worst of all."

"I told you he's no good."

"He is plenty of good for himself; his dishonesty will ruin me."

"Aziz, how monstrous!"

"I am delighted with him really, he has made my guests comfortable; besides, it is my duty to employ him, he is my cousin. If money goes, money comes. If money stays, death comes. Did you ever hear that useful Urdu proverb? Probably not, for I have just invented it."

"My proverbs are: A penny saved is a penny earned; A stitch in time saves nine; Look before you leap; and the British Empire rests on them. You will never kick us out, you know, until you cease employing M.L.'s and such."

"Oh, kick you out? Why should I trouble over that dirty job? Leave it to the politicians... No, when I was a student I got excited over your damned countrymen, certainly; but if they'll let me get on with my profession and not be too rude to me officially, I really don't ask for more."

"But you do; you take them to a picnic."

"This picnic is nothing to do with English or Indian; it is an expedition of friends."

So the cavalcade ended, partly pleasant, partly not; the Brahman cook was picked up, the train arrived, pushing its burning throat over the plain, and the twentieth century took over from the sixteenth. Mrs. Moore entered her carriage, the three men went to theirs, adjusted the shutters, turned on the electric fan and tried to get some sleep. In the twilight, all resembled corpses, and the train itself seemed dead though it moved—a coffin from the scientific north which troubled the scenery four times a day. As it left the Marabars, their nasty little cosmos disappeared, and gave place to the Marabars seen from a distance, finite and rather romantic. The train halted once under a pump, to drench the stock of coal in its tender. Then it caught sight of the main line in the distance, took courage, and bumped forward, rounded the civil station, surmounted the level-crossing (the rails were scorching now), and clanked to a stand-still. Chandrapore, Chandrapore! The expedition was over.

And as it ended, as they sat up in the gloom and prepared to enter ordinary life, suddenly the long drawn strangeness of the morning snapped. Mr. Haq, the Inspector of Police, flung open the door of their carriage and said in shrill tones: "Dr. Aziz, it is my highly painful duty to arrest you."

"Hullo, some mistake," said Fielding, at once taking charge of the situation.

"Sir, they are my instructions. I know nothing."

"On what charge do you arrest him?"

"I am under instructions not to say."

"Don't answer me like that. Produce your warrant."

"Sir, excuse me, no warrant is required under these particular circumstances. Refer to Mr. McBryde."

"Very well, so we will. Come along, Aziz, old man; nothing to fuss about, some blunder."

"Dr. Aziz, will you kindly come?—a closed conveyance stands in readiness."

The young man sobbed—his first sound—and tried to escape out of the opposite door on to the line.

"That will compel me to use force," Mr. Haq wailed.

"Oh, for God's sake——" cried Fielding, his own nerves breaking under the contagion, and pulled him back before a scandal started, and shook him like a baby. A second later, and he would have been out, whistles blowing, a man-hunt... "Dear fellow, we're coming to McBryde together, and enquire what's gone wrong—he's a decent fellow, it's all unintentional... he'll apologize. Never, never act the criminal."

"My children and my name!" he gasped, his wings broken.

"Nothing of the sort. Put your hat straight and take my arm. I'll see you through."

"Ah, thank God, he comes," the Inspector exclaimed. They emerged into the midday heat, arm in arm. The station was seething. Passengers and porters rushed out of every recess, many Government servants, more police. Ronny escorted Mrs. Moore. Mohammed Latif began wailing. And before they could make their way through the chaos, Fielding was called off by the authoritative tones of Mr. Turton, and Aziz went on to prison alone.

CHAPTER 17

The Collector had watched the arrest from the interior of the waiting-room, and throwing open its perforated doors of zinc, he was now revealed like a god in a shrine. When Fielding entered the doors clapped to, and were guarded by a servant, while a punkah, to mark the importance of the moment, flapped dirty petticoats over their heads. The Collector could not speak at first. His face was white, fanatical, and rather beautiful—the expression that all English faces were to wear at Chandrapore for many days. Always brave and unselfish, he was now fused by some white and generous heat; he would have killed himself, obviously, if he had thought it right to do so. He spoke at last. "The worst thing in my whole career has happened," he said. "Miss Quested has been insulted in one of the Marabar caves."

"Oh no, oh no, no," gasped the other, feeling sickish.

"She escaped—by God's grace."

"Oh no, no, but not Aziz... not Aziz..."

He nodded.

"Absolutely impossible, grotesque."

"I called you to preserve you from the odium that would attach to you if you were seen accompanying him to the Police Station," said Turton, paying no attention to his protest, indeed scarcely hearing it.

He repeated "Oh no," like a fool. He couldn't frame other words. He felt that a mass of madness had arisen and tried to overwhelm them all; it had to be shoved back into its pit somehow, and he didn't know how to do it, because he did not understand madness: he had always gone about sensibly and quietly until a difficulty came right. "Who lodges this infamous charge?" he asked, pulling himself together.

"Miss Derek and—the victim herself..." He nearly broke down, unable to repeat the girl's name.

"Miss Quested herself definitely accuses him of——"

He nodded and turned his face away.

"Then she's mad."

"I cannot pass that last remark," said the Collector, waking up to the knowledge that they differed, and trembling with fury. "You will withdraw it instantly. It is the type of remark you have permitted yourself to make ever since you came to Chandrapore."

"I'm excessively sorry, sir; I certainly withdraw it unconditionally." For the man was half mad himself.

"Pray, Mr. Fielding, what induced you to speak to me in such a tone?"

"The news gave me a very great shock, so I must ask you to forgive me. I cannot believe that Dr. Aziz is guilty."

He slammed his hand on the table. "That—that is a repetition of your insult in an aggravated form."

"If I may venture to say so, no," said Fielding, also going white, but sticking to his point. "I make no reflection on the good faith of the two ladies, but the charge they are bringing against Aziz rests upon some mistake, and five minutes will clear it up. The man's manner is perfectly natural; besides, I know him to be incapable of infamy."

"It does indeed rest upon a mistake," came the thin, biting voice of the other. "It does indeed. I have had twenty-five years' experience of this country"—he paused, and "twenty-five years" seemed to fill the waiting-room with their staleness and ungenerosity—"and during those twenty-five years I have never known anything but disaster result when English people and Indians attempt to be intimate socially. Intercourse, yes. Courtesy, by all means. Intimacy—never, never. The whole weight of my authority is against it. I have been in charge at Chandrapore for six years, and if everything has gone smoothly, if there has been mutual respect and esteem, it is because both peoples kept to this simple rule. New-comers set our traditions aside, and in an instant what you see happens, the work of years is undone and the good name of my District ruined for a generation. I—I—can't see the end of this day's work, Mr. Fielding. You, who are imbued with modern ideas—no doubt you can. I wish I had never lived to see its beginning, I know that. It is the end of me. That a lady, that a young lady engaged to my most valued subordinate—that she—an English girl fresh from England—that I should have lived——"

Involved in his own emotions, he broke down. What he had said was both dignified and pathetic, but had it anything to do with Aziz? Nothing at all, if Fielding was right. It is impossible to regard a tragedy from two points of view, and whereas Turton had decided to avenge the girl, he hoped to save the man. He wanted to get away and talk to McBryde, who had always been friendly to him, was on the whole sensible, and could, anyhow, be trusted to keep cool.

"I came down particularly on your account—while poor Heaslop got his mother away. I regarded it as the most friendly thing I could do. I meant to tell you that there will be an informal meeting at the club this evening to discuss the situation, but I am doubtful whether you will care to come. Your visits there are always infrequent."

"I shall certainly come, sir, and I am most grateful to you for all the trouble you have taken over me. May I venture to ask—where Miss Quested is."

He replied with a gesture; she was ill.

"Worse and worse, appalling," he said feelingly.

But the Collector looked at him sternly, because he was keeping his head. He had not gone mad at the phrase "an English girl fresh from England," he had not rallied to the banner of race. He was still after facts, though the herd had decided on emotion. Nothing enrages Anglo-India more than the lantern of reason if it is exhibited for one moment after its extinction is decreed. All over Chandrapore that day the Europeans were putting aside their normal personalities and sinking themselves in their community. Pity, wrath, heroism, filled them, but the power of putting two and two together was annihilated.

Terminating the interview, the Collector walked on to the platform. The confusion there was revolting. A chuprassi of Ronny's had been told to bring up some trifles belonging to the ladies, and was appropriating for himself various articles to which he had no right; he was a camp follower of the angry English. Mohammed Latif made no attempt to resist him. Hassan flung off his turban, and wept. All the comforts that had been provided so liberally were rolled about and wasted in the sun. The Collector took in the situation at a glance, and his sense of justice functioned though he was insane with rage. He spoke the necessary word, and the looting stopped. Then he drove off to his bungalow and gave rein to his passions again. When he saw the coolies asleep in the ditches or the shopkeepers rising to salute him on their little platforms, he said to himself: "I know what you're like at last; you shall pay for this, you shall squeal."

CHAPTER 18

Mr. McBryde, the District Superintendent of Police, was the most reflective and best educated of the Chandrapore officials. He had read and thought a good deal, and, owing to a somewhat unhappy marriage, had evolved a complete philosophy of life. There was much of the cynic about him, but nothing of the bully; he never lost his temper or grew rough, and he received Aziz with courtesy, was almost reassuring. "I have to detain you until you get bail," he said, "but no doubt your friends will be applying for it, and of course they will be allowed to visit you, under regulations. I am given certain information, and have to act on it—I'm not your judge." Aziz was led off weeping. Mr. McBryde was shocked at his downfall, but no Indian ever surprised him, because he had a theory about climatic zones. The theory ran: "All unfortunate natives are criminals at heart, for the simple reason that they live south of latitude 30. They are not to blame, they have not a dog's chance—we should be like them if we settled here." Born at Karachi, he seemed to contradict his theory, and would sometimes admit as much with a sad, quiet smile.

"Another of them found out," he thought, as he set to work to draft his statement to the Magistrate.

He was interrupted by the arrival of Fielding.

He imparted all he knew without reservations. Miss Derek had herself driven in the Mudkul car about an hour ago, she and Miss Quested both in a terrible state. They had gone straight to his bungalow where he happened to be, and there and then he had taken down the charge and arranged for the arrest at the railway station.

"What is the charge, precisely?"

"That he followed her into the cave and made insulting advances. She hit at him with her field-glasses; he pulled at them and the strap broke, and that is how she got away. When we searched him just now, they were in his pocket."

"Oh no, oh no, no; it'll be cleared up in five minutes," he cried again.

"Have a look at them."

The strap had been newly broken, the eye-piece was jammed. The logic of evidence said "Guilty."

"Did she say any more?"

"There was an echo that appears to have frightened her. Did you go into those caves?"

"I saw one of them. There was an echo. Did it get on her nerves?"

"I couldn't worry her overmuch with questions. She'll have plenty to go through in the witness-box. They don't bear thinking about, these next weeks. I wish the Marabar Hills and all they contain were at the bottom of the sea. Evening after evening one saw them from the club, and they were just a harmless name... Yes, we start already." For a visiting card was brought; Vakil Mahmoud Ali, legal adviser to the prisoner, asked to be allowed to see him. McBryde sighed, gave permission, and continued: "I heard some more from Miss Derek—she is an old friend of us both and talks freely; well—her account is that you went off to locate the camp, and almost at once she heard stones falling on the Kawa Dol and saw Miss Quested running straight down the face of a precipice.

Well. She climbed up a sort of gully to her, and found her practically done for—her helmet off——"

"Was a guide not with her?" interrupted Fielding.

"No. She had got among some cactuses. Miss Derek saved her life coming just then—she was beginning to fling herself about. She helped her down to the car. Miss Quested couldn't stand the Indian driver, cried, 'Keep him away'—and it was that that put our friend on the track of what had happened. They made straight for our bungalow, and are there now. That's the story as far as I know it yet. She sent the driver to join you. I think she behaved with great sense."

"I suppose there's no possibility of my seeing Miss Quested?" he asked suddenly.

"I hardly think that would do. Surely."

"I was afraid you'ld say that. I should very much like to."

"She is in no state to see anyone. Besides, you don't know her well."

"Hardly at all... But you see I believe she's under some hideous delusion, and that that wretched boy is innocent."

The policeman started in surprise, and a shadow passed over his face, for he could not bear his dispositions to be upset. "I had no idea that was in your mind," he said, and looked for support at the signed deposition, which lay before him.

"Those field-glasses upset me for a minute, but I've thought since: it's impossible that, having attempted to assault her, he would put her glasses into his pocket."

"Quite possible, I'm afraid; when an Indian goes bad, he goes not only very bad, but very queer."

"I don't follow."

"How should you? When you think of crime you think of English crime. The psychology here is different. I dare say you'll tell me next that he was quite normal when he came down from the hill to greet you. No reason he should not be. Read any of the Mutiny records; which, rather than the Bhagavad Gita, should be your Bible in this country. Though I'm not sure that the one and the other are not closely connected. Am I not being beastly? But, you see, Fielding, as I've said to you once before, you're a schoolmaster, and consequently you come across these people at their best. That's what puts you wrong. They can be charming as boys. But I know them as they really are, after they have developed into men. Look at this, for instance." He held up Aziz' pocket-case. "I am going through the contents. They are not edifying. Here is a letter from a friend who apparently keeps a brothel."

"I don't want to hear his private letters."

"It'll have to be quoted in Court, as bearing on his morals. He was fixing up to see women at Calcutta."

"Oh, that'll do, that'll do."

McBryde stopped, naively puzzled. It was obvious to him that any two sahibs ought to pool all they knew about any Indian, and he could not think where the objection came in.

"I dare say you have the right to throw stones at a young man for doing that, but I haven't. I did the same at his age."

So had the Superintendent of Police, but he considered that the conversation had taken a turn that was undesirable. He did not like Fielding's next remark either.

"Miss Quested really cannot be seen? You do know that for a certainty?"

"You have never explained to me what's in your mind here. Why on earth do you want to see her?"

"On the off chance of her recanting before you send in that report and he's committed for trial, and the whole thing goes to blazes. Old man, don't argue about this, but do of your goodness just ring up your wife or Miss Derek and enquire. It'll cost you nothing."

"It's no use ringing up them," he replied, stretching out for the telephone. "Callendar settles a question like that, of course. You haven't grasped that she's seriously ill."

"He's sure to refuse, it's all he exists for," said the other desperately.

The expected answer came back: the Major would not hear of the patient being troubled.

"I only wanted to ask her whether she is certain, dead certain, that it was Aziz who followed her into the cave."

"Possibly my wife might ask her that much."

"But *I* wanted to ask her. I want someone who believes in him to ask her."

"What difference does that make?"

"She is among people who disbelieve in Indians."

"Well, she tells her own story, doesn't she?"

"I know, but she tells it to you."

McBryde raised his eyebrows, murmuring: "A bit too fine-spun. Anyhow, Callendar won't hear of you seeing her. I'm sorry to say he gave a bad account just now. He says that she is by no means out of danger."

They were silent. Another card was brought into the office—Hamidullah's. The opposite army was gathering.

"I must put this report through now, Fielding."

"I wish you wouldn't."

"How can I not?"

"I feel that things are rather unsatisfactory as well as most disastrous. We are heading for a most awful smash. I can see your prisoner, I suppose."

He hesitated. "His own people seem in touch with him all right."

"Well, when he's done with them."

"I wouldn't keep you waiting; good heavens, you take precedence of any Indian visitor, of course. I meant what's the good. Why mix yourself up with pitch?"

"I say he's innocent——"

"Innocence or guilt, why mix yourself up? What's the good?"

"Oh, good, good," he cried, feeling that every earth was being stopped. "One's got to breathe occasionally, at least I have. I mayn't see her, and now I mayn't see him. I promised him to come up here with him to you, but Turton called me off before I could get two steps."

"Sort of all-white thing the Burra Sahib would do," he muttered sentimentally. And trying not to sound patronizing, he stretched his hand over the table, and said: "We shall all have to hang together, old man, I'm afraid. I'm your junior in years, I know, but very much your senior in service; you don't happen to know this poisonous country as well as I do, and you must take it from me that the general situation is going to be nasty at Chandrapore during the next few weeks, very nasty indeed."

"So I have just told you."

"But at a time like this there's no room for—well—personal views. The man who doesn't toe the line is lost."

"I see what you mean."

"No, you don't see entirely. He not only loses himself, he weakens his friends. If you leave the line, you leave a gap in the line. These jackals"—he pointed at the lawyers' cards—"are looking with all their eyes for a gap."

"Can I visit Aziz?" was his answer.

"No." Now that he knew of Turton's attitude, the policeman had no doubts. "You may see him on a magistrate's order, but on my own responsibility I don't feel justified. It might lead to more complications."

He paused, reflecting that if he had been either ten years younger or ten years longer in India, he would have responded to McBryde's appeal. The bit between his teeth, he then said, "To whom do I apply for an order?"

"City Magistrate."

"That sounds comfortable!"

"Yes, one can't very well worry poor Heaslop."

More "evidence" appeared at this moment—the table-drawer from Aziz' bungalow, borne with triumph in a corporal's arms.

"Photographs of women. Ah!"

"That's his wife," said Fielding, wincing.

"How do you know that?"

"He told me."

McBryde gave a faint, incredulous smile, and started rummaging in the drawer. His face became inquisitive and slightly bestial. "Wife indeed, I know those wives!" he was thinking. Aloud he said: "Well, you must trot off now, old man, and the Lord help us, the Lord help us all..."

As if his prayer had been heard, there was a sudden rackety-dacket on a temple bell.

CHAPTER 19

Hamidullah was the next stage. He was waiting outside the Superintendent's office, and sprang up respectfully when he saw Fielding. To the Englishman's passionate "It's all a mistake," he answered, "Ah, ah, has some evidence come?"

"It will come," said Fielding, holding his hand.

"Ah, yes, Mr. Fielding; but when once an Indian has been arrested, we do not know where it will stop." His manner was deferential. "You are very good to greet me in this public fashion, I appreciate it; but, Mr. Fielding, nothing convinces a magistrate except evidence. Did Mr. McBryde make any remark when my card came in? Do you think my application annoyed him, will prejudice him against my friend at all? If so, I will gladly retire."

"He's not annoyed, and if he was, what does it matter?"

"Ah, it's all very well for you to speak like that, but we have to live in this country."

The leading barrister of Chandrapore, with the dignified manner and Cambridge degree, had been rattled. He too loved Aziz, and knew he was calumniated; but faith did not rule his heart, and he prated of "policy" and "evidence" in a way that saddened the Englishman. Fielding, too, had his anxieties—he didn't like the field-glasses or the discrepancy over the guide—but he relegated them to the edge of his mind, and forbade them to infect its core. Aziz *was* innocent, and all action must be based on that, and the people who said he was guilty were wrong, and it was hopeless to try to propitiate them. At the moment when he was throwing in his lot with Indians, he realized the profundity of the gulf that divided him from them. They always do something disappointing. Aziz had tried to run away from the police, Mohammed Latif had not checked the pilfering. And now Hamidullah!—instead of raging and denouncing, he temporized. Are Indians cowards? No, but they are bad starters and occasionally jib. Fear is everywhere; the British Raj rests on it; the respect and courtesy Fielding himself enjoyed were unconscious acts of propitiation. He told Hamidullah to cheer up, all would end well; and Hamidullah did cheer up, and became pugnacious and sensible. McBryde's remark, "If you leave the line, you leave a gap in the line," was being illustrated.

"First and foremost, the question of bail..."

Application must be made this afternoon. Fielding wanted to stand surety. Hamidullah thought the Nawab Bahadur should be approached.

"Why drag in him, though?"

To drag in everyone was precisely the barrister's aim. He then suggested that the lawyer in charge of the case would be a Hindu; the defence would then make a wider appeal. He mentioned one or two names—men from a distance who would not be intimidated by local conditions—and said he should prefer Amritrao, a Calcutta barrister, who had a high reputation professionally and personally, but who was notoriously anti-British.

Fielding demurred; this seemed to him going to the other extreme. Aziz must be cleared, but with a minimum of racial hatred. Amritrao was loathed at the club. His retention would be regarded as a political challenge.

"Oh no, we must hit with all our strength. When I saw my friend's private papers carried in just now in the arms of a dirty policeman, I said to myself, 'Amritrao is the man to clear up this.'"

There was a lugubrious pause. The temple bell continued to jangle harshly. The interminable and disastrous day had scarcely reached its afternoon. Continuing their work, the wheels of Dominion now propelled a messenger on a horse from the Superintendent to the Magistrate with an official report of arrest. "Don't complicate, let the cards play themselves," entreated Fielding, as he watched the man disappear into dust. "We're bound to win, there's nothing else we can do. She will never be able to substantiate the charge."

This comforted Hamidullah, who remarked with complete sincerity, "At a crisis, the English are really unequalled."

"Good-bye, then, my dear Hamidullah (we must drop the 'Mr.' now). Give Aziz my love when you see him, and tell him to keep calm, calm, calm. I shall go back to the College now. If you want me, ring me up; if you don't, don't, for I shall be very busy."

"Good-bye, my dear Fielding, and you actually are on our side against your own people?"

"Yes. Definitely."

He regretted taking sides. To slink through India unlabelled was his aim. Henceforward he would be called "anti-British," "seditious"—terms that bored him, and diminished his utility. He foresaw that besides being a tragedy, there would be a muddle; already he saw several tiresome little knots, and each time his eye returned to them, they were larger. Born in freedom, he was not afraid of muddle, but he recognized its existence.

This section of the day concluded in a queer vague talk with Professor Godbole. The interminable affair of the Russell's Viper was again in question. Some weeks before, one of the masters at the College, an unpopular Parsi, had found a Russell's Viper nosing round his class-room. Perhaps it had crawled in of itself, but perhaps it had not, and the staff still continued to interview their Principal about it, and to take up his time with their theories. The reptile is so poisonous that he did not like to cut them short, and this they knew. Thus when his mind was bursting with other troubles and he was debating whether he should compose a letter of appeal to Miss Quested, he was obliged to listen to a speech which lacked both basis and conclusion, and floated through air. At the end of it Godbole said, "May I now take my leave?"—always an indication that he had not come to his point yet. "Now I take my leave, I must tell you how glad I am to hear that after all you succeeded in reaching the Marabar. I feared my unpunctuality had prevented you, but you went (a far pleasanter method) in Miss Derek's car. I hope the expedition was a successful one."

"The news has not reached you yet, I can see."

"Oh yes."

"No; there has been a terrible catastrophe about Aziz."

"Oh yes. That is all round the College."

"Well, the expedition where that occurs can scarcely be called a successful one," said Fielding, with an amazed stare.

"I cannot say. I was not present."

He stared again—a most useless operation, for no eye could see what lay at the bottom of the Brahman's mind, and yet he had a mind and a heart too, and all his friends trusted him, without knowing why. "I am most frightfully cut up," he said.

"So I saw at once on entering your office. I must not detain you, but I have a small private difficulty on which I want your help; I am leaving your service shortly, as you know."

"Yes, alas!"

"And am returning to my birthplace in Central India to take charge of education there. I want to start a High School there on sound English lines, that shall be as like Government College as possible."

"Well?" he sighed, trying to take an interest.

"At present there is only vernacular education at Mau. I shall feel it my duty to change all that. I shall advise His Highness to sanction at least a High School in the Capital, and if possible another in each pargana."

Fielding sunk his head on his arms; really, Indians were sometimes unbearable.

"The point—the point on which I desire your help is this: what name should be given to the school?"

"A name? A name for a school?" he said, feeling sickish suddenly, as he had done in the waiting-room.

"Yes, a name, a suitable title, by which it can be called, by which it may be generally known."

"Really—I have no names for schools in my head. I can think of nothing but our poor Aziz. Have you grasped that at the present moment he is in prison?"

"Oh yes. Oh no, I do not expect an answer to my question now. I only meant that when you are at leisure, you might think the matter over, and suggest two or three alternative titles for schools. I had thought of the 'Mr. Fielding High School,' but failing that, the 'King-Emperor George the Fifth.'"

"Godbole!"

The old fellow put his hands together, and looked sly and charming.

"Is Aziz innocent or guilty?"

"That is for the Court to decide. The verdict will be in strict accordance with the evidence, I make no doubt."

"Yes, yes, but your personal opinion. Here's a man we both like, generally esteemed; he lives here quietly doing his work. Well, what's one to make of it? Would he or would he not do such a thing?"

"Ah, that is rather a different question from your previous one, and also more difficult: I mean difficult in our philosophy. Dr. Aziz is a most worthy young man, I have a great regard for him;

but I think you are asking me whether the individual can commit good actions or evil actions, and that is rather difficult for us." He spoke without emotion and in short tripping syllables.

"I ask you: did he do it or not? Is that plain? I know he didn't, and from that I start. I mean to get at the true explanation in a couple of days. My last notion is that it's the guide who went round with them. Malice on Miss Quested's part—it couldn't be that, though Hamidullah thinks so. She has certainly had some appalling experience. But you tell me, oh no—because good and evil are the same."

"No, not exactly, please, according to our philosophy. Because nothing can be performed in isolation. All perform a good action, when one is performed, and when an evil action is performed, all perform it. To illustrate my meaning, let me take the case in point as an example. I am informed that an evil action was performed in the Marabar Hills, and that a highly esteemed English lady is now seriously ill in consequence. My answer to that is this: that action was performed by Dr. Aziz." He stopped and sucked in his thin cheeks. "It was performed by the guide." He stopped again. "It was performed by you." Now he had an air of daring and of coyness. "It was performed by me." He looked shyly down the sleeve of his own coat. "And by my students. It was even performed by the lady herself. When evil occurs, it expresses the whole of the universe. Similarly when good occurs."

"And similarly when suffering occurs, and so on and so forth, and everything is anything and nothing something," he muttered in his irritation, for he needed the solid ground.

"Excuse me, you are now again changing the basis of our discussion. We were discussing good and evil. Suffering is merely a matter for the individual. If a young lady has sunstroke, that is a matter of no significance to the universe. Oh no, not at all. Oh no, not the least. It is an isolated matter, it only concerns herself. If she thought her head did not ache, she would not be ill, and that would end it. But it is far otherwise in the case of good and evil.

They are not what we think them, they are what they are, and each of us has contributed to both."

"You're preaching that evil and good are the same."

"Oh no, excuse me once again. Good and evil are different, as their names imply. But, in my own humble opinion, they are both of them aspects of my Lord. He is present in the one, absent in the other, and the difference between presence and absence is great, as great as my feeble mind can grasp. Yet absence implies presence, absence is not non-existence, and we are therefore entitled to repeat, 'Come, come, come, come.'" And in the same breath, as if to cancel any beauty his words might have contained, he added, "But did you have time to visit any of the interesting Marabar antiquities?"

Fielding was silent, trying to meditate and rest his brain.

"Did you not even see the tank by the usual camping ground?" he nagged.

"Yes, yes," he answered distractedly, wandering over half a dozen things at once.

"That is good, then you saw the Tank of the Dagger." And he related a legend which might have been acceptable if he had told it at the tea-party a fortnight ago. It concerned a Hindu Rajah who had slain his own sister's son, and the dagger with which he performed the deed remained clamped to his hand until in the course of years he came to the Marabar Hills, where he was thirsty and wanted to drink but saw a thirsty cow and ordered the water to be offered to her first, which, when done, "dagger fell from his hand, and to commemorate miracle he built Tank." Professor Godbole's conversations frequently culminated in a cow. Fielding received this one in gloomy silence.

In the afternoon he obtained a permit and saw Aziz, but found him unapproachable through misery. "You deserted me," was the only coherent remark. He went away to write his letter to Miss Quested. Even if it reached her, it would do no good, and probably the McBrydes would withhold it. Miss Quested did pull him up short. She was such a dry, sensible girl, and quite without malice: the last person in Chandrapore wrongfully to accuse an Indian.

CHAPTER 20

Although Miss Quested had not made herself popular with the English, she brought out all that was fine in their character. For a few hours an exalted emotion gushed forth, which the women felt even more keenly than the men, if not for so long. "What can we do for our sister?" was the only thought of Mesdames Callendar and Lesley, as they drove through the pelting heat to enquire. Mrs. Turton was the only visitor admitted to the sick-room. She came out ennobled by an unselfish sorrow. "She is my own darling girl," were the words she spoke, and then, remembering that she had called her "not pukka" and resented her engagement to young Heaslop, she began to cry. No one had ever seen the Collector's wife cry. Capable of tears—yes, but always reserving them for some adequate occasion, and now it had come. Ah, why had they not all been kinder to the stranger, more patient, given her not only hospitality but their hearts? The tender core of the heart that is so seldom used—they employed it for a little, under the stimulus of remorse. If all is over (as Major Callendar implied), well, all is over, and nothing can be done, but they retained some responsibility in her grievous wrong that they couldn't define. If she wasn't one of them, they ought to have made her one, and they could never do that now, she had passed beyond their invitation. "Why don't one think more of other people?" sighed pleasure-loving Miss Derek.

These regrets only lasted in their pure form for a few hours. Before sunset, other considerations adulterated them, and the sense of guilt (so strangely connected with our first sight of any suffering) had begun to wear away.

People drove into the club with studious calm—the jog-trot of country gentlefolk between green hedgerows, for the natives must not suspect that they were agitated. They exchanged the usual drinks, but everything tasted different, and then they looked out at the palisade of cactuses stabbing the purple throat of the sky; they realized that they were thousands of miles from any scenery that they understood. The club was fuller than usual, and several parents had brought their children into the rooms reserved for adults, which gave the air of the Residency at Lucknow. One young mother—a brainless but most beautiful girl—sat on a low ottoman in the smoking-room with her baby in her arms; her husband was away in the district, and she dared not return to her bungalow in case the "niggers attacked." The wife of a small railway official, she was generally snubbed; but this evening, with her abundant figure and masses of corn-gold hair, she symbolized all that is worth fighting and dying for; more permanent a symbol, perhaps, than poor Adela. "Don't worry, Mrs. Blakiston, those drums are only Mohurram," the men would tell her.

"Then they've started," she moaned, clasping the infant and rather wishing he would not blow bubbles down his chin at such a moment as this. "No, of course not, and anyhow, they're not coming to the club." "And they're not coming to the Burra Sahib's bungalow either, my dear, and that's where you and your baby'll sleep tonight," answered Mrs. Turton, towering by her side like Pallas Athene, and determining in the future not to be such a snob.

The Collector clapped his hands for silence. He was much calmer than when he had flown out at Fielding. He was indeed always calmer when he addressed several people than in a *tête-à-tête.* "I want to talk specially to the ladies," he said. "Not the least cause for alarm. Keep cool, keep cool. Don't go out more than you can help, don't go into the city, don't talk before your servants. That's all."

"Harry, is there any news from the city?" asked his wife, standing at some distance from him, and also assuming her public-safety voice. The rest were silent during the august colloquy.

"Everything absolutely normal."

"I had gathered as much. Those drums are merely Mohurram, of course."

"Merely the preparations for it—the Procession is not till next week."

"Quite so, not till Monday."

"Mr. McBryde's down there disguised as a Holy Man," said Mrs. Callendar.

"That's exactly the sort of thing that must not be said," he remarked, pointing at her. "Mrs. Callendar, be more careful than that, please, in these times."

"I... well, I..." She was not offended, his severity made her feel safe.

"Any more questions? Necessary questions."

"Is the—where is he——" Mrs. Lesley quavered.

"Jail. Bail has been refused."

Fielding spoke next. He wanted to know whether there was an official bulletin about Miss Quested's health, or whether the grave reports were due to gossip. His question produced a bad effect, partly because he had pronounced her name; she, like Aziz, was always referred to by a periphrasis.

"I hope Callendar may be able to let us know how things are going before long."

"I fail to see how that last question can be termed a necessary question," said Mrs. Turton.

"Will all ladies leave the smoking-room now, please?" he cried, clapping his hands again. "And remember what I have said.

We look to you to help us through a difficult time, and you can help us by behaving as if everything is normal. It is all I ask. Can I rely on you?"

"Yes, indeed, Burra Sahib," they chorused out of peaked, anxious faces. They moved out, subdued yet elated, Mrs. Blakiston in their midst like a sacred flame. His simple words had reminded them that they were an outpost of Empire. By the side of their compassionate love for Adela another sentiment sprang up which was to strangle it in the long run. Its first signs were prosaic and small. Mrs. Turton made her loud, hard jokes at bridge, Mrs. Lesley began to knit a comforter.

When the smoking-room was clear, the Collector sat on the edge of a table, so that he could dominate without formality. His mind whirled with contradictory impulses. He wanted to avenge Miss Quested and punish Fielding, while remaining scrupulously fair. He wanted to flog every native that he saw, but to do nothing that would lead to a riot or to the necessity for military intervention. The dread of having to call in the troops was vivid to him; soldiers put one thing straight, but leave a dozen others crooked, and they love to humiliate the civilian administration. One soldier was in the room this evening—a stray subaltern from a Gurkha regiment; he was a little drunk, and regarded his presence as providential. The Collector sighed. There seemed nothing for it but the old weary business of compromise and moderation. He longed for the good old days when an Englishman could satisfy his own honour and no questions asked afterwards. Poor young Heaslop had taken a step in this direction, by refusing bail, but the Collector couldn't feel this was wise of poor young Heaslop. Not only would the Nawab Bahadur and others be angry, but the Government of India itself also watches—and behind it is that caucus of cranks and cravens, the British Parliament. He had constantly to remind himself that, in the eyes of the law, Aziz was not yet guilty, and the effort fatigued him.

The others, less responsible, could behave naturally. They had started speaking of "women and children"—that phrase that exempts the male from sanity when it has been repeated a few times. Each felt that all he loved best in the world was at stake, demanded revenge, and was filled with a not unpleasing glow, in which the chilly and half-known features of Miss Quested vanished, and were replaced by all that is sweetest and warmest in the private life. "But it's the women and children," they repeated, and the Collector knew he ought to stop them intoxicating themselves, but he hadn't the heart. "They ought to be compelled to give hostages," etc. Many of the said women and children were leaving for the Hill Station in a few days, and the suggestion was made that they should be packed off at once in a special train.

"*And* a jolly suggestion," the subaltern cried. "The army's got to come in sooner or later. (A special train was in his mind inseparable from troops.) This would never have happened if Barabas Hill was under military control. Station a bunch of Gurkhas at the entrance of the cave was all that was wanted."

"Mrs. Blakiston was saying if only there were a few Tommies," remarked someone.

"English no good," he cried, getting his loyalties mixed. "Native troops for this country. Give me the sporting type of native, give me Gurkhas, give me Rajputs, give me Jats, give me the Punjabi, give me Sikhs, give me Marathas, Bhils, Afridis and Pathans, and really if it comes to that, I don't mind if you give me the scums of the bazaars. Properly led, mind. I'd lead them anywhere——"

The Collector nodded at him pleasantly, and said to his own people: "Don't start carrying arms about. I want everything to go on precisely as usual, until there's cause for the contrary. Get the womenfolk off to the hills, but do it quietly, and for Heaven's sake no more talk of special trains. Never mind what you think or feel. Possibly I have feelings too. One isolated Indian has attempted—is charged with an attempted crime." He flipped his forehead hard with his finger-nail, and they all realized that he felt as deeply as they did, and they loved him, and determined not to increase his difficulties. "Act upon that fact until there are more facts," he concluded. "Assume every Indian is an angel."

They murmured, "Right you are, Burra Sahib... Angels... Exactly..." From the subaltern: "Exactly what I said. The native's all right if you get him alone. Lesley! Lesley! You remember the one I had a knock with on your Maidan last month. Well, he was all right. Any native who plays polo is all right. What you've got to stamp on is these educated classes, and, mind, I do know what I'm talking about this time."

The smoking-room door opened, and let in a feminine buzz. Mrs. Turton called out, "She's better," and from both sections of the community a sigh of joy and relief rose. The Civil Surgeon, who had brought the good news, came in. His cumbrous, pasty face looked ill-tempered. He surveyed the company, saw Fielding crouched below him on an ottoman, and said, "H'm!"

Everyone began pressing him for details. "No one's out of danger in this country as long as they have a temperature," was his answer. He appeared to resent his patient's recovery, and no one who knew the old Major and his ways was surprised at this.

"Squat down, Callendar; tell us all about it."

"Take me some time to do that."

"How's the old lady?"

"Temperature."

"My wife heard she was sinking."

"So she may be. I guarantee nothing. I really can't be plagued with questions, Lesley."

"Sorry, old man."

"Heaslop's just behind me."

At the name of Heaslop a fine and beautiful expression was renewed on every face. Miss Quested was only a victim, but young Heaslop was a martyr; he was the recipient of all the evil intended against them by the country they had tried to serve; he was bearing the sahib's cross. And they fretted because they could do nothing for him in return; they felt so craven sitting on softness and attending the course of the law.

"I wish to God I hadn't given my jewel of an assistant leave. I'ld cut my tongue out first. To feel I'm responsible, that's what hits me. To refuse, and then give in under pressure. That is what I did, my sons, that is what I did."

Fielding took his pipe from his mouth and looked at it thoughtfully. Thinking him afraid, the other went on: "I understood an Englishman was to accompany the expedition. That is why I gave in."

"No one blames you, my dear Callendar," said the Collector, looking down. "We are all to blame in the sense that we ought to have seen the expedition was insufficiently guaranteed, and stopped it. I knew about it myself; we lent our car this morning to take the ladies to the station. We are all implicated in that sense, but not an atom of blame attaches to you personally."

"I don't feel that. I wish I could. Responsibility is a very awful thing, and I've no use for the man who shirks it." His eyes were directed on Fielding. Those who knew that Fielding had undertaken to accompany and missed the early train were sorry for him; it was what is to be expected when a man mixes himself up with natives; always ends in some indignity. The Collector, who knew more, kept silent, for the official in him still hoped that Fielding would toe the line. The conversation turned to women and children again, and under its cover Major Callendar got hold of the subaltern, and set him on to bait the schoolmaster. Pretending to be more drunk than he really was, he began to make semi-offensive remarks.

"Heard about Miss Quested's servant?" reinforced the Major.

"No, what about him?"

"Heaslop warned Miss Quested's servant last night never to lose sight of her. Prisoner got hold of this and managed to leave him behind. Bribed him. Heaslop has just found out the whole story, with names and sums—a well-known pimp to those people gave the money, Mohammed Latif by name. So much for the servant. What about the Englishman—our friend here? How did they get rid of him? Money again."

Fielding rose to his feet, supported by murmurs and exclamations, for no one yet suspected his integrity.

"Oh, I'm being misunderstood, apologies," said the Major offensively. "I didn't mean they bribed Mr. Fielding."

"Then what do you mean?"

"They paid the other Indian to make you late—Godbole. He was saying his prayers. I know those prayers!"

"That's ridiculous..." He sat down again, trembling with rage; person after person was being dragged into the mud.

Having shot this bolt, the Major prepared the next. "Heaslop also found out something from his mother. Aziz paid a herd of natives to suffocate her in a cave. That was the end of her, or would have been only she got out. Nicely planned, wasn't it? Neat. Then he could go on with the girl. He and she and a guide, provided by the same Mohammed Latif. Guide now can't be found. Pretty." His voice broke into a roar. "It's not the time for sitting down. It's the time for action. Call in the troops and clear the bazaars."

The Major's outbursts were always discounted, but he made everyone uneasy on this occasion. The crime was even worse than they had supposed—the unspeakable limit of cynicism, untouched since 1857. Fielding forgot his anger on poor old Godbole's behalf, and became thoughtful; the evil was propagating in every direction, it seemed to have an existence of its own, apart from anything that was done or said by individuals, and he understood better why both Aziz and Hamidullah had been inclined to lie down and die. His adversary saw that he was in trouble, and now ventured to say, "I suppose nothing that's said inside the club will go outside the club?" winking the while at Lesley.

"Why should it?" responded Lesley.

"Oh, nothing. I only heard a rumour that a certain member here present has been seeing the prisoner this afternoon. You can't run with the hare and hunt with the hounds, at least not in this country."

"Does anyone here present want to?"

Fielding was determined not to be drawn again. He had something to say, but it should be at his own moment. The attack failed to mature, because the Collector did not support it. Attention shifted from him for a time. Then the buzz of women broke out again. The door had been opened by Ronny.

The young man looked exhausted and tragic, also gentler than usual. He always showed deference to his superiors, but now it came straight from his heart. He seemed to appeal for their protection in the insult that had befallen him, and they, in instinctive homage, rose to their feet. But every human act in the East is tainted with officialism, and while honouring him they condemned Aziz and India. Fielding realized this, and he remained seated. It was an ungracious, a caddish thing to do, perhaps an unsound thing to do, but he felt he had been passive long enough, and that he might be drawn into the wrong current if he did not make a stand. Ronny, who had not seen him, said in husky tones, "Oh please—please all sit down, I only want to listen what has been decided."

"Heaslop, I'm telling them I'm against any show of force," said the Collector apologetically. "I don't know whether you will feel as I do, but that is how I am situated. When the verdict is obtained, it will be another matter."

"You are sure to know best; I have no experience, Burra Sahib."

"How is your mother, old boy?"

"Better, thank you. I wish everyone would sit down."

"Some have never got up," the young soldier said.

"And the Major brings us an excellent report of Miss Quested," Turton went on.

"I do, I do, I'm satisfied."

"You thought badly of her earlier, did you not, Major? That's why I refused bail."

Callendar laughed with friendly inwardness, and said, "Heaslop, Heaslop, next time bail's wanted, ring up the old doctor before giving it; his shoulders are broad, and, speaking in the strictest confidence, don't take the old doctor's opinion too seriously. He's a blithering idiot, we can always leave it at that, but he'll do the little he can towards keeping in quod the——" He broke off with affected politeness. "Oh, but he has one of his friends here."

The subaltern called, "Stand up, you swine."

"Mr. Fielding, what has prevented you from standing up?" said the Collector, entering the fray at last. It was the attack for which Fielding had waited, and to which he must reply.

"May I make a statement, sir?"

"Certainly."

Seasoned and self-contained, devoid of the fervours of nationality or youth, the schoolmaster did what was for him a comparatively easy thing. He stood up and said, "I believe Dr. Aziz to be innocent."

"You have a right to hold that opinion if you choose, but pray is that any reason why you should insult Mr. Heaslop?"

"May I conclude my statement?"

"Certainly."

"I am waiting for the verdict of the courts. If he is guilty I resign from my service, and leave India. I resign from the club now."

"Hear, hear!" said voices, not entirely hostile, for they liked the fellow for speaking out.

"You have not answered my question. Why did you not stand when Mr. Heaslop entered?"

"With all deference, sir, I am not here to answer questions, but to make a personal statement, and I have concluded it."

"May I ask whether you have taken over charge of this District?"

Fielding moved towards the door.

"One moment, Mr. Fielding. You are not to go yet, please. Before you leave the club, from which you do very well to resign, you will express some detestation of the crime, and you will apologize to Mr. Heaslop."

"Are you speaking to me officially, sir?"

The Collector, who never spoke otherwise, was so infuriated that he lost his head. He cried, "Leave this room at once, and I deeply regret that I demeaned myself to meet you at the station. You have sunk to the level of your associates; you are weak, weak, that is what is wrong with you——"

"I want to leave the room, but cannot while this gentleman prevents me," said Fielding lightly; the subaltern had got across his path.

"Let him go," said Ronny, almost in tears.

It was the only appeal that could have saved the situation. Whatever Heaslop wished must be done. There was a slight scuffle at the door, from which Fielding was propelled, a little more quickly than is natural, into the room where the ladies were playing cards. "Fancy if I'd fallen or got angry," he thought. Of course he was a little angry. His peers had never offered him violence or called him weak before, besides Heaslop had heaped coals of fire on his head. He wished he had not picked the quarrel over poor suffering Heaslop, when there were cleaner issues at hand.

However, there it was, done, muddled through, and to cool himself and regain mental balance he went on to the upper verandah for a moment, where the first object he saw was the Marabar Hills. At this distance and hour they leapt into beauty; they were Monsalvat, Walhalla, the towers of a cathedral, peopled with saints and heroes, and covered with flowers. What miscreant lurked in them, presently to be detected by the activities of the law? Who was the guide, and had he been found yet? What was the "echo" of which the girl complained? He did not know, but presently he would know. Great is information, and she shall prevail. It was the last moment of the light, and as he gazed at the Marabar Hills they seemed to move graciously towards him like a queen, and their charm became the sky's. At the moment they vanished they were everywhere, the cool benediction of the night descended, the stars sparkled, and the whole universe was a hill. Lovely, exquisite moment—but passing the Englishman with averted face and on swift wings. He experienced nothing himself; it was as if someone had told him there was such a moment, and he was obliged to believe. And he felt dubious and discontented suddenly, and wondered whether he was really and truly successful as a human being. After forty years' experience, he had learnt to manage his life and make the best of it on advanced European lines, had developed his personality, explored his limitations, controlled his passions—and he had done it all without becoming either pedantic or worldly. A creditable achievement, but as the moment passed, he felt he ought to have been working at something else the whole time,—he didn't know at what, never would know, never could know, and that was why he felt sad.

CHAPTER 21

Dismissing his regrets, as inappropriate to the matter in hand, he accomplished the last section of the day by riding off to his new allies. He was glad that he had broken with the club, for he would have picked up scraps of gossip there, and reported them down in the city, and he was glad to be denied this opportunity. He would miss his billiards, and occasional tennis, and cracks with McBryde, but really that was all, so light did he travel. At the entrance of the bazaars, a tiger made his horse shy—a youth dressed up as a tiger, the body striped brown and yellow, a mask over the face. Mohurram was working up. The city beat a good many drums, but seemed good-tempered. He was invited to inspect a small tazia—a flimsy and frivolous erection, more like a crinoline than the tomb of the grandson of the Prophet, done to death at Kerbela. Excited children were pasting coloured paper over its ribs. The rest of the evening he spent with the Nawab Bahadur, Hamidullah, Mahmoud Ali, and others of the confederacy. The campaign was also working up. A telegram had been sent to the famous Amritrao, and his acceptance received. Application for bail was to be renewed—it could not well be withheld now that Miss Quested was out of danger. The conference was serious and sensible, but marred by a group of itinerant musicians, who were allowed to play in the compound. Each held a large earthenware jar, containing pebbles, and jerked it up and down in time to a doleful chant. Distracted by the noise, he suggested their dismissal, but the Nawab Bahadur vetoed it; he said that musicians, who had walked many miles, might bring good luck.

Late at night, he had an inclination to tell Professor Godbole of the tactical and moral error he had made in being rude to Heaslop, and to hear what he would say. But the old fellow had gone to bed, and slipped off unmolested to his new job in a day or two: he always did possess the knack of slipping off.

CHAPTER 22

Adela lay for several days in the McBrydes' bungalow. She had been touched by the sun, also hundreds of cactus spines had to be picked out of her flesh. Hour after hour Miss Derek and Mrs. McBryde examined her through magnifying glasses, always coming on fresh colonies, tiny hairs that might snap off and be drawn into the blood if they were neglected. She lay passive beneath their fingers, which developed the shock that had begun in the cave. Hitherto she had not much minded whether she was touched or not: her senses were abnormally inert and the only contact she anticipated was that of mind. Everything now was transferred to the surface of her body, which began to avenge itself, and feed unhealthily. People seemed very much alike, except that some would come close while others kept away. "In space things touch, in time things part," she repeated to herself while the thorns were being extracted—her brain so weak that she could not decide whether the phrase was a philosophy or a pun.

They were kind to her, indeed over-kind, the men too respectful, the women too sympathetic; whereas Mrs. Moore, the only visitor she wanted, kept away. No one understood her trouble, or knew why she vibrated between hard commonsense and hysteria. She would begin a speech as if nothing particular had happened. "I went into this detestable cave," she would say dryly, "and I remember scratching the wall with my finger-nail, to start the usual echo, and then as I was saying there was this shadow, or sort of shadow, down the entrance tunnel, bottling me up. It seemed like an age, but I suppose the whole thing can't have lasted thirty seconds really. I hit at him with the glasses, he pulled me round the cave by the strap, it broke, I escaped, that's all. He never actually touched me once. It all seems such nonsense." Then her eyes would fill with tears. "Naturally I'm upset, but I shall get over it." And then she would break down entirely, and the women would feel she was one of themselves and cry too, and men in the next room murmur: "Good God, good God!" No one realized that she thought tears vile, a degradation more subtle than anything endured in the Marabar, a negation of her advanced outlook and the natural honesty of her mind. Adela was always trying to "think the incident out," always reminding herself that no harm had been done. There was "the shock," but what is that? For a time her own logic would convince her, then she would hear the echo again, weep, declare she was unworthy of Ronny, and hope her assailant would get the maximum penalty. After one of these bouts, she longed to go out into the bazaars and ask pardon from everyone she met, for she felt in some vague way that she was leaving the world worse than she found it. She felt that it was her crime, until the intellect, reawakening, pointed out to her that she was inaccurate here, and set her again upon her sterile round.

If only she could have seen Mrs. Moore! The old lady had not been well either, and was disinclined to come out, Ronny reported. And consequently the echo flourished, raging up and down like a nerve in the faculty of her hearing, and the noise in the cave, so unimportant intellectually, was prolonged over the surface of her life. She had struck the polished wall—for no reason—and before the comment had died away, he followed her, and the climax was the falling of her field-glasses. The sound had spouted after her when she escaped, and was going on still like a river that gradually floods the plain. Only Mrs. Moore could drive it back to its source and seal the broken reservoir. Evil was loose... she could even hear it entering the lives of others... And Adela spent days in this atmosphere of grief and depression. Her friends kept up their spirits by demanding holocausts of natives, but she was too worried and weak to do that.

When the cactus thorns had all been extracted, and her temperature fallen to normal, Ronny came to fetch her away. He was worn with indignation and suffering, and she wished she could comfort him; but intimacy seemed to caricature itself, and the more they spoke the more wretched and self-conscious they became. Practical talk was the least painful, and he and McBryde now told her one or two things which they had concealed from her during the crisis, by the doctor's orders. She learnt for the first time of the Mohurram troubles. There had nearly been a riot. The last day of the festival, the great procession left its official route, and tried to enter the civil station, and a telephone had been cut because it interrupted the advance of one of the larger paper towers. McBryde and his police had pulled the thing straight—a fine piece of work. They passed on to another and very painful subject: the trial. She would have to appear in court, identify the prisoner, and submit to cross-examination by an Indian lawyer.

"Can Mrs. Moore be with me?" was all she said.

"Certainly, and I shall be there myself," Ronny replied. "The case won't come before me; they've objected to me on personal grounds. It will be at Chandrapore—we thought at one time it would be transferred elsewhere."

"Miss Quested realizes what all that means, though," said McBryde sadly. "The case will come before Das."

Das was Ronny's assistant—own brother to the Mrs. Bhattacharya whose carriage had played them false last month. He was courteous and intelligent, and with the evidence before him could only come to one conclusion; but that he should be judge over an English girl had convulsed the station with wrath, and some of the women had sent a telegram about it to Lady Mellanby, the wife of the Lieutenant-Governor.

"I must come before someone."

"That's—that's the way to face it. You have the pluck, Miss Quested." He grew very bitter over the arrangements, and called them "the fruits of democracy." In the old days an Englishwoman would not have had to appear, nor would any Indian have dared to discuss her private affairs. She would have made her deposition, and judgment would have followed. He apologized to her for the condition of the country, with the result that she gave one of her sudden little shoots of tears. Ronny wandered miserably about the room while she cried, treading upon the flowers of the Kashmir carpet that so inevitably covered it or drumming on the brass Benares bowls. "I do this less every day, I shall soon be quite well," she said, blowing her nose and feeling hideous.

"What I need is something to do. That is why I keep on with this ridiculous crying."

"It's not ridiculous, we think you wonderful," said the policeman very sincerely. "It only bothers us that we can't help you more. Your stopping here—at such a time—is the greatest honour this house——" He too was overcome with emotion. "By the way, a letter came here for you while you were ill," he continued. "I opened it, which is a strange confession to make. Will you forgive me? The circumstances are peculiar. It is from Fielding."

"Why should he write to me?"

"A most lamentable thing has happened. The defence got hold of him."

"He's a crank, a crank," said Ronny lightly.

"That's your way of putting it, but a man can be a crank without being a cad. Miss Quested had better know how he behaved to you. If you don't tell her, somebody else will." He told her. "He is now the mainstay of the defence, I needn't add. He is the one righteous Englishman in a horde of tyrants. He receives deputations from the bazaar, and they all chew betel nut and smear one another's hands with scent. It is not easy to enter into the mind of such a man. His students are on strike—out of enthusiasm for him they won't learn their lessons. If it weren't for Fielding one would never have had the Mohurram trouble. He has done a very grave disservice to the whole community. The letter lay here a day or two, waiting till you were well enough, then the situation got so grave that I decided to open it in case it was useful to us."

"Is it?" she said feebly.

"Not at all. He only has the impertinence to suggest you have made a mistake."

"Would that I had!" She glanced through the letter, which was careful and formal in its wording. "Dr. Aziz is innocent," she read. Then her voice began to tremble again. "But think of his behaviour to you, Ronny. When you had already to bear so much for my sake! It was shocking of him. My dear, how can I repay you? How can one repay when one has nothing to give? What is the use of personal relationships when everyone brings less and less to them? I feel we ought all to go back into the desert for centuries and try and get good. I want to begin at the beginning. All the things I thought I'd learnt are just a hindrance, they're not knowledge at all. I'm not fit for personal relationships. Well, let's go, let's go. Of course Mr. Fielding's letter doesn't count; he can think and write what he likes, only he shouldn't have been rude to you when you had so much to bear. That's what matters... I don't want your arm, I'm a magnificent walker, so don't touch me, please."

Mrs. McBryde wished her an affectionate good-bye—a woman with whom she had nothing in common and whose intimacy oppressed her. They would have to meet now, year after year, until one of their husbands was superannuated. Truly Anglo-India had caught her with a vengeance, and perhaps it served her right for having tried to take up a line of her own. Humbled yet repelled, she gave thanks. "Oh, we must help one another, we must take the rough with the smooth," said Mrs. McBryde. Miss Derek was there too, still making jokes about her comic Maharajah and Rani. Required as a witness at the trial, she had refused to send back the Mudkul car; they would be frightfully sick. Both Mrs. McBryde and Miss Derek kissed her, and called her by her Christian name. Then Ronny drove her back. It was early in the morning, for the day, as the hot weather advanced, swelled like a monster at both ends, and left less and less room for the movements of mortals.

As they neared his bungalow, he said: "Mother's looking forward to seeing you, but of course she's old, one mustn't forget that. Old people never take things as one expects, in my opinion." He seemed warning her against approaching disappointment, but she took no notice. Her friendship with Mrs. Moore was so deep and real that she felt sure it would last, whatever else happened. "What can I do to make things easier for you? it's you who matter," she sighed.

"Dear old girl to say so."

"Dear old boy." Then she cried: "Ronny, she isn't ill too?"

He reassured her; Major Callendar was not dissatisfied.

"But you'll find her—irritable. We are an irritable family. Well, you'll see for yourself. No doubt my own nerves are out of order, and I expected more from mother when I came in from the office than she felt able to give. She is sure to make a special effort for you; still, I don't want your home-coming to be a disappointing one. Don't expect too much."

The house came in sight. It was a replica of the bungalow she had left. Puffy, red, and curiously severe, Mrs. Moore was revealed upon a sofa. She didn't get up when they entered, and the surprise of this roused Adela from her own troubles.

"Here you are both back," was the only greeting.

Adela sat down and took her hand. It withdrew, and she felt that just as others repelled her, so did she repel Mrs. Moore.

"Are you all right? You appeared all right when I left," said Ronny, trying not to speak crossly, but he had instructed her to give the girl a pleasant welcome, and he could not but feel annoyed.

"I am all right," she said heavily. "As a matter of fact I have been looking at my return ticket. It is interchangeable, so I have a much larger choice of boats home than I thought."

"We can go into that later, can't we?"

"Ralph and Stella may be wanting to know when I arrive."

"There is plenty of time for all such plans. How do you think our Adela looks?"

"I am counting on you to help me through; it is such a blessing to be with you again, everyone else is a stranger," said the girl rapidly.

But Mrs. Moore showed no inclination to be helpful. A sort of resentment emanated from her. She seemed to say: "Am I to be bothered forever?" Her Christian tenderness had gone, or had developed into a hardness, a just irritation against the human race; she had taken no interest at the arrest, asked scarcely any questions, and had refused to leave her bed on the awful last night of Mohurram, when an attack was expected on the bungalow.

"I know it's all nothing; I must be sensible, I do try——" Adela continued, working again towards tears.

"I shouldn't mind if it had happened anywhere else; at least I really don't know where it did happen."

Ronny supposed that he understood what she meant: she could not identify or describe the particular cave, indeed almost refused to have her mind cleared up about it, and it was recognized that the defence would try to make capital out of this during the trial. He reassured her: the Marabar caves were notoriously like one another; indeed, in the future they were to be numbered in sequence with white paint.

"Yes, I mean that, at least not exactly; but there is this echo that I keep on hearing."

"Oh, what of the echo?" asked Mrs. Moore, paying attention to her for the first time.

"I can't get rid of it."

"I don't suppose you ever will."

Ronny had emphasized to his mother that Adela would arrive in a morbid state, yet she was being positively malicious.

"Mrs. Moore, what is this echo?"

"Don't you know?"

"No—what is it? oh, do say! I felt you would be able to explain it... this will comfort me so..."

"If you don't know, you don't know; I can't tell you."

"I think you're rather unkind not to say."

"Say, say, say," said the old lady bitterly. "As if anything can be said! I have spent my life in saying or in listening to sayings; I have listened too much. It is time I was left in peace. Not to die," she added sourly. "No doubt you expect me to die, but when I have seen you and Ronny married, and seen the other two and whether they want to be married—I'll retire then into a cave of my own." She smiled, to bring down her remark into ordinary life and thus add to its bitterness. "Somewhere where no young people will come asking questions and expecting answers. Some shelf."

"Quite so, but meantime a trial is coming on," said her son hotly, "and the notion of most of us is that we'd better pull together and help one another through, instead of being disagreeable. Are you going to talk like that in the witness-box?"

"Why should I be in the witness-box?"

"To confirm certain points in our evidence."

"I have nothing to do with your ludicrous law courts," she said, angry. "I will not be dragged in at all."

"I won't have her dragged in, either; I won't have any more trouble on my account," cried Adela, and again took the hand, which was again withdrawn. "Her evidence is not the least essential."

"I thought she would want to give it. No one blames you, mother, but the fact remains that you dropped off at the first cave, and encouraged Adela to go on with him alone, whereas if you'd been well enough to keep on too nothing would have happened. He planned it, I know. Still, you fell into his trap just like Fielding and Antony before you... Forgive me for speaking so plainly, but you've no right to take up this high and mighty attitude about law courts. If you're ill, that's different; but you say you're all right and you seem so, in which case I thought you'ld want to take your part, I did really."

"I'll not have you worry her whether she's well or ill," said Adela, leaving the sofa and taking his arm; then dropped it with a sigh and sat down again. But he was pleased she had rallied to him and surveyed his mother patronizingly. He had never felt easy with her. She was by no means the dear old lady outsiders supposed, and India had brought her into the open.

"I shall attend your marriage, but not your trial," she informed them, tapping her knee; she had become very restless, and rather ungraceful. "Then I shall go to England."

"You can't go to England in May, as you agreed."

"I have changed my mind."

"Well, we'd better end this unexpected wrangle," said the young man, striding about. "You appear to want to be left out of everything, and that's enough."

"My body, my miserable body," she sighed. "Why isn't it strong? Oh, why can't I walk away and be gone? Why can't I finish my duties and be gone? Why do I get headaches and puff when I walk? And all the time this to do and that to do and this to do in your way and that to do in her way, and everything sympathy and confusion and bearing one another's burdens. Why can't this be done and that be done in my way and they be done and I at peace? Why has anything to be done, I cannot see. Why all this marriage, marriage?... The human race would have become a single person centuries ago if marriage was any use. And all this rubbish about love, love in a church, love in a cave, as if there is the least difference, and I held up from my business over such trifles!"

"What do you want?" he said, exasperated. "Can you state it in simple language? If so, do."

"I want my pack of patience cards."

"Very well, get them."

He found, as he expected, that the poor girl was crying. And, as always, an Indian close outside the window, a mali in this case, picking up sounds. Much upset, he sat silent for a moment, thinking over his mother and her senile intrusions. He wished he had never asked her to visit India, or become under any obligation to her.

"Well, my dear girl, this isn't much of a home-coming," he said at last. "I had no idea she had this up her sleeve."

Adela had stopped crying. An extraordinary expression was on her face, half relief, half horror. She repeated, "Aziz, Aziz."

They all avoided mentioning that name. It had become synonymous with the power of evil. He was "the prisoner," "the person in question," "the defence," and the sound of it now rang out like the first note of new symphony.

"Aziz... have I made a mistake?"

"You're over-tired," he cried, not much surprised.

"Ronny, he's innocent; I made an awful mistake."

"Well, sit down anyhow." He looked round the room, but only two sparrows were chasing one another. She obeyed and took hold of his hand. He stroked it and she smiled, and gasped as if she had risen to the surface of the water, then touched her ear.

"My echo's better."

"That's good. You'll be perfectly well in a few days, but you must save yourself up for the trial. Das is a very good fellow, we shall all be with you."

"But Ronny, dear Ronny, perhaps there oughtn't to be any trial."

"I don't quite know what you're saying, and I don't think you do."

"If Dr. Aziz never did it he ought to be let out."

A shiver like impending death passed over Ronny. He said hurriedly, "He was let out—until the Mohurram riot, when he had to be put in again." To divert her, he told her the story, which was held to be amusing. Nureddin had stolen the Nawab Bahadur's car and driven Aziz into a ditch in the dark. Both of them had fallen out, and Nureddin had cut his face open. Their wailing had been drowned by the cries of the faithful, and it was quite a time before they were rescued by the police. Nureddin was taken to the Minto Hospital, Aziz restored to prison, with an additional charge against him of disturbing the public peace. "Half a minute," he remarked when the anecdote was over, and went to the telephone to ask Callendar to look in as soon as he found it convenient, because she hadn't borne the journey well.

When he returned, she was in a nervous crisis, but it took a different form—she clung to him, and sobbed, "Help me to do what I ought. Aziz is good. You heard your mother say so."

"Heard what?"

"He's good; I've been so wrong to accuse him."

"Mother never said so."

"Didn't she?" she asked, quite reasonable, open to every suggestion anyway.

"She never mentioned that name once."

"But, Ronny, I heard her."

"Pure illusion. You can't be quite well, can you, to make up a thing like that."

"I suppose I can't. How amazing of me!"

"I was listening to all she said, as far as it could be listened to; she gets very incoherent."

"When her voice dropped she said it—towards the end, when she talked about love—love—I couldn't follow, but just then she said: 'Doctor Aziz never did it.'"

"Those words?"

"The idea more than the words."

"Never, never, my dear girl. Complete illusion. His name was not mentioned by anyone. Look here—you are confusing this with Fielding's letter."

"That's it, that's it," she cried, greatly relieved. "I knew I'd heard his name somewhere. I am so grateful to you for clearing this up—it's the sort of mistake that worries me, and proves I'm neurotic."

"So you won't go saying he's innocent again, will you? for every servant I've got is a spy." He went to the window. The mali had gone, or rather had turned into two small children—impossible they should know English, but he sent them packing. "They all hate us," he explained. "It'll be all right after the verdict, for I will say this for them, they do accept the accomplished fact; but at present they're pouring out money like water to catch us tripping, and a remark like yours is the very thing they look out for. It would enable them to say it was a put-up job on the part of us officials. You see what I mean."

Mrs. Moore came back, with the same air of ill-temper, and sat down with a flump by the card-table. To clear the confusion up, Ronny asked her point-blank whether she had mentioned the prisoner. She could not understand the question and the reason of it had to be explained. She replied: "I never said his name," and began to play patience.

"I thought you said, 'Aziz is an innocent man,' but it was in Mr. Fielding's letter."

"Of course he is innocent," she answered indifferently: it was the first time she had expressed an opinion on the point.

"You see, Ronny, I was right," said the girl.

"You were not right, she never said it."

"But she thinks it."

"Who cares what she thinks?"

"Red nine on black ten——" from the card-table.

"She can think, and Fielding too, but there's such a thing as evidence, I suppose."

"I know, but——"

"Is it again my duty to talk?" asked Mrs. Moore, looking up. "Apparently, as you keep interrupting me."

"Only if you have anything sensible to say."

"Oh, how tedious... trivial..." and as when she had scoffed at love, love, love, her mind seemed to move towards them from a great distance and out of darkness. "Oh, why is everything still my duty? when shall I be free from your fuss? Was he in the cave and were you in the cave and on and on... and Unto us a Son is born, unto us a Child is given... and am I good and is he bad and are we saved?... and ending everything the echo."

"I don't hear it so much," said Adela, moving towards her. "You send it away, you do nothing but good, you are so good."

"I am not good, no, bad." She spoke more calmly and resumed her cards, saying as she turned them up, "A bad old woman, bad, bad, detestable. I used to be good with the children growing up, also I meet this young man in his mosque, I wanted him to be happy. Good, happy, small people. They do not exist, they were a dream... But I will not help you to torture him for what he never did. There are different ways of evil and I prefer mine to yours."

"Have you any evidence in the prisoner's favour?" said Ronny in the tones of the just official. "If so, it is your bounden duty to go into the witness-box for him instead of for us. No one will stop you."

"One knows people's characters, as you call them," she retorted disdainfully, as if she really knew more than character but could not impart it. "I have heard both English and Indians speak well of him, and I felt it isn't the sort of thing he would do."

"Feeble, mother, feeble."

"Most feeble."

"And most inconsiderate to Adela."

Adela said: "It would be so appalling if I was wrong. I should take my own life."

He turned on her with: "What was I warning you just now? You know you're right, and the whole station knows it."

"Yes, he... This is very, very awful. I'm as certain as ever he followed me... only, wouldn't it be possible to withdraw the case? I dread the idea of giving evidence more and more, and you are all so good to women here and you have so much more power than in England—look at Miss Derek's motor-car. Oh, of course it's out of the question, I'm ashamed to have mentioned it; please forgive me."

"That's all right," he said inadequately. "Of course I forgive you, as you call it. But the case has to come before a magistrate now; it really must, the machinery has started."

"She has started the machinery; it will work to its end."

Adela inclined towards tears in consequence of this unkind remark, and Ronny picked up the list of steamship sailings with an excellent notion in his head. His mother ought to leave India at once: she was doing no good to herself or to anyone else there.

CHAPTER 23

Lady Mellanby, wife to the Lieutenant-Governor of the Province, had been gratified by the appeal addressed to her by the ladies of Chandrapore. She could not do anything—besides, she was sailing for England; but she desired to be informed if she could show sympathy in any other way. Mrs. Turton replied that Mr. Heaslop's mother was trying to get a passage, but had delayed too long, and all the boats were full; could Lady Mellanby use her influence? Not even Lady Mellanby could expand the dimensions of a P. and O., but she was a very, very nice woman, and she actually wired offering the unknown and obscure old lady accommodation in her own reserved cabin. It was like a gift from heaven; humble and grateful, Ronny could not but reflect that there are compensations for every woe. His name was familiar at Government House owing to poor Adela, and now Mrs. Moore would stamp it on Lady Mellanby's imagination, as they journeyed across the Indian Ocean and up the Red Sea. He had a return of tenderness for his mother—as we do for our relatives when they receive conspicuous and unexpected honour. She was not negligible, she could still arrest the attention of a high official's wife.

So Mrs. Moore had all she wished; she escaped the trial, the marriage, and the hot weather; she would return to England in comfort and distinction, and see her other children. At her son's suggestion, and by her own desire, she departed. But she accepted her good luck without enthusiasm. She had come to that state where the horror of the universe and its smallness are both visible at the same time—the twilight of the double vision in which so many elderly people are involved. If this world is not to our taste, well, at all events there is Heaven, Hell, Annihilation—one or other of those large things, that huge scenic background of stars, fires, blue or black air. All heroic endeavour, and all that is known as art, assumes that there is such a background, just as all practical endeavour, when the world is to our taste, assumes that the world is all. But in the twilight of the double vision, a spiritual muddledom is set up for which no high-sounding words can be found; we can neither act nor refrain from action, we can neither ignore nor respect Infinity. Mrs. Moore had always inclined to resignation. As soon as she landed in India it seemed to her good, and when she saw the water flowing through the mosque-tank, or the Ganges, or the moon, caught in the shawl of night with all the other stars, it seemed a beautiful goal and an easy one. To be one with the universe! So dignified and simple. But there was always some little duty to be performed first, some new card to be turned up from the diminishing pack and placed, and while she was pottering about, the Marabar struck its gong.

What had spoken to her in that scoured-out cavity of the granite? What dwelt in the first of the caves? Something very old and very small. Before time, it was before space also. Something snub-nosed, incapable of generosity—the undying worm itself. Since hearing its voice, she had not entertained one large thought, she was actually envious of Adela. All this fuss over a frightened girl! Nothing had happened, "and if it had," she found herself thinking with the cynicism of a withered priestess, "if it had, there are worse evils than love." The unspeakable attempt presented itself to her as love: in a cave, in a church—Boum, it amounts to the same. Visions are supposed to entail profundity, but—— Wait till you get one, dear reader! The abyss also may be petty, the serpent of eternity made of maggots; her constant thought was: "Less attention should be paid to my future daughter-in-law and more to me, there is no sorrow like my sorrow," although when the attention was paid she rejected it irritably.

Her son couldn't escort her to Bombay, for the local situation continued acute, and all officials had to remain at their posts. Antony couldn't come either, in case he never returned to give his evidence. So she travelled with no one who could remind her of the past. This was a relief. The heat had drawn back a little before its next advance, and the journey was not unpleasant. As she left Chandrapore the moon, full again, shone over the Ganges and touched the shrinking channels into threads of silver, then veered and looked into her window. The swift and comfortable mail-train slid with her through the night, and all the next day she was rushing through Central India, through landscapes that were baked and bleached but had not the hopeless melancholy of the plain. She watched the indestructible life of man and his changing faces, and the houses he has built for himself and God, and they appeared to her not in terms of her own trouble but as things to see. There was, for instance, a place called Asirgarh which she passed at sunset and identified on a map—an enormous fortress among wooded hills. No one had ever mentioned Asirgarh to her, but it had huge and noble bastions and to the right of them was a mosque. She forgot it. Ten minutes later, Asirgarh reappeared. The mosque was to the left of the bastions now. The train in its descent through the Vindyas had described a semicircle round Asirgarh. What could she connect it with except its own name? Nothing; she knew no one who lived there. But it had looked at her twice and seemed to say: "I do not vanish." She woke in the middle of the night with a start, for the train was falling over the western cliff. Moonlit pinnacles rushed up at her like the fringes of a sea; then a brief episode of plain, the real sea, and the soupy dawn of Bombay. "I have not seen the right places," she thought, as she saw embayed in the platforms of the Victoria Terminus the end of the rails that had carried her over a continent and could never carry her back. She would never visit Asirgarh or the other untouched places; neither Delhi nor Agra nor the Rajputana cities nor Kashmir, nor the obscurer marvels that had sometimes shone through men's speech: the bilingual rock of Girnar, the statue of Shri Belgola, the ruins of Mandu and Hampi, temples of Khajraha, gardens of Shalimar. As she drove through the huge city which the West has built and abandoned with a gesture of despair, she longed to stop, though it was only Bombay, and disentangle the hundred Indias that passed each other in its streets. The feet of the horses moved her on, and presently the boat sailed and thousands of coco-nut palms appeared all round the anchorage and climbed the hills to wave her farewell. "So you thought an echo was India; you took the Marabar caves as final?" they laughed. "What have we in common with them, or they with Asirgarh? Good-bye!" Then the steamer rounded Colaba, the continent swung about, the cliff of the Ghats melted into the haze of a tropic sea. Lady Mellanby turned up and advised her not to stand in the heat: "We are safely out of the frying-pan," said Lady Mellanby, "it will never do to fall into the fire."

CHAPTER 24

Making sudden changes of gear, the heat accelerated its advance after Mrs. Moore's departure until existence had to be endured and crime punished with the thermometer at a hundred and twelve. Electric fans hummed and spat, water splashed on to screens, ice clinked, and outside these defences, between a greyish sky and a yellowish earth, clouds of dust moved hesitatingly. In Europe life retreats out of the cold, and exquisite fireside myths have resulted—Balder, Persephone—but here the retreat is from the source of life, the treacherous sun, and no poetry adorns it because disillusionment cannot be beautiful. Men yearn for poetry though they may not confess it; they desire that joy shall be graceful and sorrow august and infinity have a form, and India fails to accommodate them. The annual helter-skelter of April, when irritability and lust spread like a canker, is one of her comments on the orderly hopes of humanity. Fish manage better; fish, as the tanks dry, wriggle into the mud and wait for the rains to uncake them. But men try to be harmonious all the year round, and the results are occasionally disastrous. The triumphant machine of civilization may suddenly hitch and be immobilized into a car of stone, and at such moments the destiny of the English seems to resemble their predecessors', who also entered the country with intent to refashion it, but were in the end worked into its pattern and covered with its dust.

Adela, after years of intellectualism, had resumed her morning kneel to Christianity. There seemed no harm in it, it was the shortest and easiest cut to the unseen, and she could tack her troubles on to it. Just as the Hindu clerks asked Lakshmi for an increase in pay, so did she implore Jehovah for a favourable verdict. God who saves the King will surely support the police. Her deity returned a consoling reply, but the touch of her hands on her face started prickly heat, and she seemed to swallow and expectorate the same insipid clot of air that had weighed on her lungs all the night. Also the voice of Mrs. Turton disturbed her. "Are you ready, young lady?" it pealed from the next room.

"Half a minute," she murmured. The Turtons had received her after Mrs. Moore left. Their kindness was incredible, but it was her position not her character that moved them; she was the English girl who had had the terrible experience, and for whom too much could not be done. No one, except Ronny, had any idea of what passed in her mind, and he only dimly, for where there is officialism every human relationship suffers. In her sadness she said to him, "I bring you nothing but trouble; I was right on the Maidan, we had better just be friends," but he protested, for the more she suffered the more highly he valued her. Did she love him? This question was somehow draggled up with the Marabar, it had been in her mind as she entered the fatal cave. Was she capable of loving anyone?

"Miss Quested, Adela, what d'ye call yourself, it's half-past seven; we ought to think of starting for that Court when you feel inclined."

"She's saying her prayers," came the Collector's voice.

"Sorry, my dear; take your time... Was your chhota hazri all right?"

"I can't eat; might I have a little brandy?" she asked, deserting Jehovah.

When it was brought, she shuddered, and said she was ready to go.

"Drink it up; not a bad notion, a peg."

"I don't think it'll really help me, Burra Sahib."

"You sent brandy down to the Court, didn't you, Mary?"

"I should think I did, champagne too."

"I'll thank you this evening, I'm all to pieces now," said the girl, forming each syllable carefully as if her trouble would diminish if it were accurately defined. She was afraid of reticence, in case something that she herself did not perceive took shape beneath it, and she had rehearsed with Mr. McBryde in an odd, mincing way her terrible adventure in the cave, how the man had never actually touched her but dragged her about, and so on. Her aim this morning was to announce, meticulously, that the strain was appalling, and she would probably break down under Mr. Amritrao's cross-examination and disgrace her friends. "My echo has come back again badly," she told them.

"How about aspirin?"

"It is not a headache, it is an echo."

Unable to dispel the buzzing in her ears, Major Callendar had diagnosed it as a fancy, which must not be encouraged. So the Turtons changed the subject. The cool little lick of the breeze was passing over the earth, dividing night from day; it would fail in ten minutes, but they might profit by it for their drive down into the city.

"I am sure to break down," she repeated.

"You won't," said the Collector, his voice full of tenderness.

"Of course she won't, she's a real sport."

"But Mrs. Turton..."

"Yes, my dear child?"

"If I do break down, it is of no consequence. It would matter in some trials, not in this. I put it to myself in the following way: I can really behave as I like, cry, be absurd, I am sure to get my verdict, unless Mr. Das is most frightfully unjust."

"You're bound to win," he said calmly, and did not remind her that there was bound to be an appeal. The Nawab Bahadur had financed the defence, and would ruin himself sooner than let an "innocent Moslem perish," and other interests, less reputable, were in the background too. The case might go up from court to court, with consequences that no official could foresee. Under his very eyes, the temper of Chandrapore was altering. As his car turned out of the compound, there was a tap of silly anger on its paint—a pebble thrown by a child. Some larger stones were dropped near the mosque. In the Maidan, a squad of native police on motor cycles waited to escort them through the bazaars. The Collector was irritated and muttered, "McBryde's an old woman"; but Mrs. Turton said, "Really, after Mohurram a show of force will do no harm; it's ridiculous to pretend they don't hate us, do give up that farce." He replied in an odd, sad voice, "I don't hate them, I don't know why," and he didn't hate them; for if he did, he would have had to condemn his own career as a bad investment. He retained a contemptuous affection for the pawns he had moved about for so many years, they must be worth his pains. "After all, it's our women who make everything more difficult out here," was his inmost thought, as he caught sight of some obscenities upon a long blank wall, and beneath his chivalry to Miss Quested resentment lurked, waiting its day—perhaps there is a grain of resentment in all chivalry. Some students had gathered in front of the City Magistrate's Court—hysterical boys whom he would have faced if alone, but he told the driver to work round to the rear of the building. The students jeered, and Rafi (hiding behind a comrade that he might not be identified) called out the English were cowards.

They gained Ronny's private room, where a group of their own sort had collected. None were cowardly, all nervy, for queer reports kept coming in. The Sweepers had just struck, and half the commodes of Chandrapore remained desolate in consequence—only half, and Sweepers from the District, who felt less strongly about the innocence of Dr. Aziz, would arrive in the afternoon, and break the strike, but why should the grotesque incident occur? And a number of Mohammedan ladies had sworn to take no food until the prisoner was acquitted; their death would make little difference, indeed, being invisible, they seemed dead already, nevertheless it was disquieting. A new spirit seemed abroad, a rearrangement, which no one in the stern little band of whites could explain. There was a tendency to see Fielding at the back of it: the idea that he was weak and cranky had been dropped. They abused Fielding vigorously: he had been seen driving up with the two counsels, Amritrao and Mahmoud Ali; he encouraged the Boy Scout movement for seditious reasons; he received letters with foreign stamps on them, and was probably a Japanese spy. This morning's verdict would break the renegade, but he had done his country and the Empire incalculable disservice. While they denounced him, Miss Quested lay back with her hands on the arms of her chair and her eyes closed, reserving her strength. They noticed her after a time, and felt ashamed of making so much noise.

"Can we do nothing for you?" Miss Derek said.

"I don't think so, Nancy, and I seem able to do nothing for myself."

"But you're strictly forbidden to talk like that; you're wonderful."

"Yes indeed," came the reverent chorus.

"My old Das is all right," said Ronny, starting a new subject in low tones.

"Not one of them's all right," contradicted Major Callendar.

"Das is, really."

"You mean he's more frightened of acquitting than convicting, because if he acquits he'll lose his job," said Lesley with a clever little laugh.

Ronny did mean that, but he cherished "illusions" about his own subordinates (following the finer traditions of his service here), and he liked to maintain that his old Das really did possess moral courage of the Public School brand. He pointed out that—from one point of view—it was good that an Indian was taking the case. Conviction was inevitable; so better let an Indian pronounce it, there would be less fuss in the long run. Interested in the argument, he let Adela become dim in his mind.

"In fact, you disapprove of the appeal I forwarded to Lady Mellanby," said Mrs. Turton with considerable heat. "Pray don't apologize, Mr. Heaslop; I am accustomed to being in the wrong."

"I didn't mean that..."

"All right. I said don't apologize."

"Those swine are always on the look-out for a grievance," said Lesley, to propitiate her.

"Swine, I should think so," the Major echoed. "And what's more, I'll tell you what. What's happened is a damn good thing really, barring of course its application to present company. It'll make them squeal and it's time they did squeal. I've put the fear of God into them at the hospital anyhow. You should see the grandson of our so-called leading loyalist." He tittered brutally as he described poor Nureddin's present appearance.

"His beauty's gone, five upper teeth, two lower and a nostril... Old Panna Lal brought him the looking-glass yesterday and he blubbered... I laughed; I laughed, I tell you, and so would you; that used to be one of these buck niggers, I thought, now he's all septic; damn him, blast his soul—er—I believe he was unspeakably immoral—er——" He subsided, nudged in the ribs, but added,

"I wish I'd had the cutting up of my late assistant too; nothing's too bad for these people."

"At last some sense is being talked," Mrs. Turton cried, much to her husband's discomfort.

"That's what I say; I say there's not such a thing as cruelty after a thing like this."

"Exactly, and remember it afterwards, you men. You're weak, weak, weak. Why, they ought to crawl from here to the caves on their hands and knees whenever an Englishwoman's in sight, they oughtn't to be spoken to, they ought to be spat at, they ought to be ground into the dust, we've been far too kind with our Bridge Parties and the rest."

She paused. Profiting by her wrath, the heat had invaded her. She subsided into a lemon squash, and continued between the sips to murmur, "Weak, weak." And the process was repeated. The issues Miss Quested had raised were so much more important than she was herself that people inevitably forgot her.

Presently the case was called.

Their chairs preceded them into the Court, for it was important that they should look dignified. And when the chuprassies had made all ready, they filed into the ramshackly room with a condescending air, as if it was a booth at a fair. The Collector made a small official joke as he sat down, at which his entourage smiled, and the Indians, who could not hear what he said, felt that some new cruelty was afoot, otherwise the sahibs would not chuckle.

The Court was crowded and of course very hot, and the first person Adela noticed in it was the humblest of all who were present, a person who had no bearing officially upon the trial: the man who pulled the punkah. Almost naked, and splendidly formed, he sat on a raised platform near the back, in the middle of the central gangway, and he caught her attention as she came in, and he seemed to control the proceedings. He had the strength and beauty that sometimes come to flower in Indians of low birth. When that strange race nears the dust and is condemned as untouchable, then nature remembers the physical perfection that she accomplished elsewhere, and throws out a god—not many, but one here and there, to prove to society how little its categories impress her. This man would have been notable anywhere: among the thin-hammed, flat-chested mediocrities of Chandrapore he stood out as divine, yet he was of the city, its garbage had nourished him, he would end on its rubbish heaps. Pulling the rope towards him, relaxing it rhythmically, sending swirls of air over others, receiving none himself, he seemed apart from human destinies, a male fate, a winnower of souls. Opposite him, also on a platform, sat the little assistant magistrate, cultivated, self-conscious, and conscientious. The punkah wallah was none of these things: he scarcely knew that he existed and did not understand why the Court was fuller than usual, indeed he did not know that it was fuller than usual, didn't even know he worked a fan, though he thought he pulled a rope. Something in his aloofness impressed the girl from middle-class England, and rebuked the narrowness of her sufferings. In virtue of what had she collected this roomful of people together? Her particular brand of opinions, and the suburban Jehovah who sanctified them—by what right did they claim so much importance in the world, and assume the title of civilization? Mrs. Moore—she looked round, but Mrs. Moore was far away on the sea; it was the kind of question they might have discussed on the voyage out before the old lady had turned disagreeable and queer.

While thinking of Mrs. Moore she heard sounds, which gradually grew more distinct. The epoch-making trial had started, and the Superintendent of Police was opening the case for the prosecution.

Mr. McBryde was not at pains to be an interesting speaker; he left eloquence to the defence, who would require it. His attitude was, "Everyone knows the man's guilty, and I am obliged to say so in public before he goes to the Andamans." He made no moral or emotional appeal, and it was only by degrees that the studied negligence of his manner made itself felt, and lashed part of the audience to fury. Laboriously did he describe the genesis of the picnic. The prisoner had met Miss Quested at an entertainment given by the Principal of Government College, and had there conceived his intentions concerning her: prisoner was a man of loose life, as documents found upon him at his arrest would testify, also his fellow-assistant, Dr. Panna Lal, was in a position to throw light on his character, and Major Callendar himself would speak. Here Mr. McBryde paused. He wanted to keep the proceedings as clean as possible, but Oriental Pathology, his favourite theme, lay around him, and he could not resist it. Taking off his spectacles, as was his habit before enunciating a general truth, he looked into them sadly, and remarked that the darker races are physically attracted by the fairer, but not *vice versa*—not a matter for bitterness this, not a matter for abuse, but just a fact which any scientific observer will confirm.

"Even when the lady is so uglier than the gentleman?" The comment fell from nowhere, from the ceiling perhaps. It was the first interruption, and the Magistrate felt bound to censure it. "Turn that man out," he said. One of the native policemen took hold of a man who had said nothing, and turned him out roughly.

Mr. McBryde resumed his spectacles and proceeded. But the comment had upset Miss Quested. Her body resented being called ugly, and trembled.

"Do you feel faint, Adela?" asked Miss Derek, who tended her with loving indignation.

"I never feel anything else, Nancy. I shall get through, but it's awful, awful."

This led to the first of a series of scenes. Her friends began to fuss around her, and the Major called out, "I must have better arrangements than this made for my patient; why isn't she given a seat on the platform? She gets no air."

Mr. Das looked annoyed and said: "I shall be happy to accommodate Miss Quested with a chair up here in view of the particular circumstances of her health." The chuprassies passed up not one chair but several, and the entire party followed Adela on to the platform, Mr. Fielding being the only European who remained in the body of the hall.

"That's better," remarked Mrs. Turton, as she settled herself.

"Thoroughly desirable change for several reasons," replied the Major.

The Magistrate knew that he ought to censure this remark, but did not dare to. Callendar saw that he was afraid, and called out authoritatively, "Right, McBryde, go ahead now; sorry to have interrupted you."

"Are you all right yourselves?" asked the Superintendent.

"We shall do, we shall do."

"Go on, Mr. Das, we are not here to disturb you," said the Collector patronizingly. Indeed, they had not so much disturbed the trial as taken charge of it.

While the prosecution continued, Miss Quested examined the hall—timidly at first, as though it would scorch her eyes. She observed to left and right of the punkah man many a half-known face. Beneath her were gathered all the wreckage of her silly attempt to see India—the people she had met at the Bridge Party, the man and his wife who hadn't sent their carriage, the old man who would lend his car, various servants, villagers, officials, and the prisoner himself. There he sat—strong, neat little Indian with very black hair, and pliant hands. She viewed him without special emotion. Since they last met, she had elevated him into a principle of evil, but now he seemed to be what he had always been—a slight acquaintance. He was negligible, devoid of significance, dry like a bone, and though he was "guilty" no atmosphere of sin surrounded him. "I suppose he *is* guilty. Can I possibly have made a mistake?" she thought. For this question still occurred to her intellect, though since Mrs. Moore's departure it had ceased to trouble her conscience.

Pleader Mahmoud Ali now arose, and asked with ponderous and ill-judged irony whether his client could be accommodated on the platform too: even Indians felt unwell sometimes, though naturally Major Callendar did not think so, being in charge of a Government Hospital. "Another example of their exquisite sense of humour," sang Miss Derek. Ronny looked at Mr. Das to see how he would handle the difficulty, and Mr. Das became agitated, and snubbed Pleader Mahmoud Ali severely.

"Excuse me——" It was the turn of the eminent barrister from Calcutta. He was a fine-looking man, large and bony, with grey closely cropped hair. "We object to the presence of so many European ladies and gentlemen upon the platform," he said in an Oxford voice. "They will have the effect of intimidating our witnesses. Their place is with the rest of the public in the body of the hall. We have no objection to Miss Quested remaining on the platform, since she has been unwell; we shall extend every courtesy to her throughout, despite the scientific truths revealed to us by the District Superintendent of Police; but we do object to the others."

"Oh, cut the cackle and let's have the verdict," the Major growled.

The distinguished visitor gazed at the Magistrate respectfully.

"I agree to that," said Mr. Das, hiding his face desperately in some papers. "It was only to Miss Quested that I gave permission to sit up here. Her friends should be so excessively kind as to climb down."

"Well done, Das, quite sound," said Ronny with devastating honesty.

"Climb down, indeed, what incredible impertinence!" Mrs. Turton cried.

"Do come quietly, Mary," murmured her husband.

"Hi! my patient can't be left unattended."

"Do you object to the Civil Surgeon remaining, Mr. Amritrao?"

"I should object. A platform confers authority."

"Even when it's one foot high; so come along all," said the Collector, trying to laugh.

"Thank you very much, sir," said Mr. Das, greatly relieved. "Thank you, Mr. Heaslop; thank you ladies all."

And the party, including Miss Quested, descended from its rash eminence. The news of their humiliation spread quickly, and people jeered outside. Their special chairs followed them. Mahmoud Ali (who was quite silly and useless with hatred) objected even to these; by whose authority had special chairs been introduced, why had the Nawab Bahadur not been given one? etc. People began to talk all over the room, about chairs ordinary and special, strips of carpet, platforms one foot high.

But the little excursion had a good effect on Miss Quested's nerves. She felt easier now that she had seen all the people who were in the room. It was like knowing the worst. She was sure now that she should come through "all right"—that is to say, without spiritual disgrace, and she passed the good news on to Ronny and Mrs. Turton. They were too much agitated with the defeat to British prestige to be interested. From where she sat, she could see the renegade Mr. Fielding. She had had a better view of him from the platform, and knew that an Indian child perched on his knee. He was watching the proceedings, watching her. When their eyes met, he turned his away, as if direct intercourse was of no interest to him.

The Magistrate was also happier. He had won the battle of the platform, and gained confidence. Intelligent and impartial, he continued to listen to the evidence, and tried to forget that later on he should have to pronounce a verdict in accordance with it. The Superintendent trundled steadily forward: he had expected these outbursts of insolence—they are the natural gestures of an inferior race, and he betrayed no hatred of Aziz, merely an abysmal contempt.

The speech dealt at length with the "prisoner's dupes," as they were called—Fielding, the servant Antony, the Nawab Bahadur. This aspect of the case had always seemed dubious to Miss Quested, and she had asked the police not to develop it. But they were playing for a heavy sentence, and wanted to prove that the assault was premeditated. And in order to illustrate the strategy, they produced a plan of the Marabar Hills, showing the route that the party had taken, and the "Tank of the Dagger" where they had camped.

The Magistrate displayed interest in archæology.

An elevation of a specimen cave was produced; it was lettered "Buddhist Cave."

"Not Buddhist, I think, Jain..."

"In which cave is the offence alleged, the Buddhist or the Jain?" asked Mahmoud Ali, with the air of unmasking a conspiracy.

"All the Marabar caves are Jain."

"Yes, sir; then in which Jain cave?"

"You will have an opportunity of putting such questions later."

Mr. McBryde smiled faintly at their fatuity. Indians invariably collapse over some such point as this. He knew that the defence had some wild hope of establishing an alibi, that they had tried (unsuccessfully) to identify the guide, and that Fielding and Hamidullah had gone out to the Kawa Dol and paced and measured all one moonlit night. "Mr. Lesley says they're Buddhist, and he ought to know if anyone does. But may I call attention to the shape?" And he described what had occurred there. Then he spoke of Miss Derek's arrival, of the scramble down the gully, of the return of the two ladies to Chandrapore, and of the document Miss Quested signed on her arrival, in which mention was made of the field-glasses. And then came the culminating evidence:

the discovery of the field-glasses on the prisoner. "I have nothing to add at present," he concluded, removing his spectacles. "I will now call my witnesses. The facts will speak for themselves. The prisoner is one of those individuals who have led a double life. I dare say his degeneracy gained upon him gradually. He has been very cunning at concealing, as is usual with the type, and pretending to be a respectable member of society, getting a Government position even. He is now entirely vicious and beyond redemption, I am afraid. He behaved most cruelly, most brutally, to another of his guests, another English lady. In order to get rid of her, and leave him free for his crime, he crushed her into a cave among his servants. However, that is by the way."

But his last words brought on another storm, and suddenly a new name, Mrs. Moore, burst on the court like a whirlwind. Mahmoud Ali had been enraged, his nerves snapped; he shrieked like a maniac, and asked whether his client was charged with murder as well as rape, and who was this second English lady.

"I don't propose to call her."

"You don't because you can't, you have smuggled her out of the country; she is Mrs. Moore, she would have proved his innocence, she was on our side, she was poor Indians' friend."

"You could have called her yourself," cried the Magistrate. "Neither side called her, neither must quote her as evidence."

"She was kept from us until too late—I learn too late—this is English justice, here is your British Raj. Give us back Mrs. Moore for five minutes only, and she will save my friend, she will save the name of his sons; don't rule her out, Mr. Das; take back those words as you yourself are a father; tell me where they have put her, oh, Mrs. Moore..."

"If the point is of any interest, my mother should have reached Aden," said Ronny dryly; he ought not to have intervened, but the onslaught had startled him.

"Imprisoned by you there because she knew the truth." He was almost out of his mind, and could be heard saying above the tumult: "I ruin my career, no matter; we are all to be ruined one by one."

"This is no way to defend your case," counselled the Magistrate.

"I am not defending a case, nor are you trying one. We are both of us slaves."

"Mr. Mahmoud Ali, I have already warned you, and unless you sit down I shall exercise my authority."

"Do so; this trial is a farce, I am going." And he handed his papers to Amritrao and left, calling from the door histrionically yet with intense passion, "Aziz, Aziz—farewell forever." The tumult increased, the invocation of Mrs. Moore continued, and people who did not know what the syllables meant repeated them like a charm. They became Indianized into Esmiss Esmoor, they were taken up in the street outside. In vain the Magistrate threatened and expelled. Until the magic exhausted itself, he was powerless.

"Unexpected," remarked Mr. Turton.

Ronny furnished the explanation. Before she sailed, his mother had taken to talk about the Marabar in her sleep, especially in the afternoon when servants were on the verandah, and her disjointed remarks on Aziz had doubtless been sold to Mahmoud Ali for a few annas: that kind of thing never ceases in the East.

"I thought they'd try something of the sort. Ingenious." He looked into their wide-open mouths. "They get just like over their religion," he added calmly. "Start and can't stop. I'm sorry for your old Das, he's not getting much of a show."

"Mr. Heaslop, how disgraceful dragging in your dear mother," said Miss Derek, bending forward.

"It's just a trick, and they happened to pull it off. Now one sees why they had Mahmoud Ali—just to make a scene on the chance. It is his speciality." But he disliked it more than he showed.

It was revolting to hear his mother travestied into Esmiss Esmoor, a Hindu goddess.

"Esmiss Esmoor
Esmiss Esmoor
Esmiss Esmoor
Esmiss Esmoor..."

"Ronny——"

"Yes, old girl?"

"Isn't it all queer."

"I'm afraid it's very upsetting for you."

"Not the least. I don't mind it."

"Well, that's good."

She had spoken more naturally and healthily than usual. Bending into the middle of her friends, she said: "Don't worry about me, I'm much better than I was; I don't feel the least faint; I shall be all right, and thank you all, thank you, thank you for your kindness." She had to shout her gratitude, for the chant, Esmiss Esmoor, went on.

Suddenly it stopped. It was as if the prayer had been heard, and the relics exhibited. "I apologize for my colleague," said Mr. Amritrao, rather to everyone's surprise. "He is an intimate friend of our client, and his feelings have carried him away."

"Mr. Mahmoud Ali will have to apologize in person," the Magistrate said.

"Exactly, sir, he must. But we had just learnt that Mrs. Moore had important evidence which she desired to give. She was hurried out of the country by her son before she could give it; and this unhinged Mr. Mahmoud Ali—coming as it does upon an attempt to intimidate our only other European witness, Mr. Fielding. Mr. Mahmoud Ali would have said nothing had not Mrs. Moore been claimed as a witness by the police." He sat down.

"An extraneous element is being introduced into the case," said the Magistrate. "I must repeat that as a witness Mrs. Moore does not exist. Neither you, Mr. Amritrao, nor, Mr. McBryde, you, have any right to surmise what that lady would have said. She is not here, and consequently she can say nothing."

"Well, I withdraw my reference," said the Superintendent wearily. "I would have done so fifteen minutes ago if I had been given the chance. She is not of the least importance to me."

"I have already withdrawn it for the defence." He added with forensic humour: "Perhaps you can persuade the gentlemen outside to withdraw it too," for the refrain in the street continued.

"I am afraid my powers do not extend so far," said Das, smiling.

So peace was restored, and when Adela came to give her evidence the atmosphere was quieter than it had been since the beginning of the trial. Experts were not surprised. There is no stay in your native. He blazes up over a minor point, and has nothing left for the crisis. What he seeks is a grievance, and this he had found in the supposed abduction of an old lady. He would now be less aggrieved when Aziz was deported.

But the crisis was still to come.

Adela had always meant to tell the truth and nothing but the truth, and she had rehearsed this as a difficult task—difficult, because her disaster in the cave was connected, though by a thread, with another part of her life, her engagement to Ronny. She had thought of love just before she went in, and had innocently asked Aziz what marriage was like, and she supposed that her question had roused evil in him. To recount this would have been incredibly painful, it was the one point she wanted to keep obscure; she was willing to give details that would have distressed other girls, but this story of her private failure she dared not allude to, and she dreaded being examined in public in case something came out. But as soon as she rose to reply, and heard the sound of her own voice, she feared not even that. A new and unknown sensation protected her, like magnificent armour. She didn't think what had happened, or even remember in the ordinary way of memory, but she returned to the Marabar Hills, and spoke from them across a sort of darkness to Mr. McBryde. The fatal day recurred, in every detail, but now she was of it and not of it at the same time, and this double relation gave it indescribable splendour. Why had she thought the expedition "dull"? Now the sun rose again, the elephant waited, the pale masses of the rock flowed round her and presented the first cave; she entered, and a match was reflected in the polished walls—all beautiful and significant, though she had been blind to it at the time. Questions were asked, and to each she found the exact reply; yes, she had noticed the "Tank of the Dagger," but not known its name; yes, Mrs. Moore had been tired after the first cave and sat in the shadow of a great rock, near the dried-up mud. Smoothly the voice in the distance proceeded, leading along the paths of truth, and the airs from the punkah behind her wafted her on...

"...the prisoner and the guide took you on to the Kawa Dol, no one else being present?"

"The most wonderfully shaped of those hills. Yes." As she spoke, she created the Kawa Dol, saw the niches up the curve of the stone, and felt the heat strike her face. And something caused her to add: "No one else was present to my knowledge. We appeared to be alone."

"Very well, there is a ledge half-way up the hill, or broken ground rather, with caves scattered near the beginning of a nullah."

"I know where you mean."

"You went alone into one of those caves?"

"That is quite correct."

"And the prisoner followed you."

"Now we've got 'im," from the Major.

She was silent. The court, the place of question, awaited her reply. But she could not give it until Aziz entered the place of answer.

"The prisoner followed you, didn't he?" he repeated in the monotonous tones that they both used; they were employing agreed words throughout, so that this part of the proceedings held no surprises.

"May I have half a minute before I reply to that, Mr. McBryde?"

"Certainly."

Her vision was of several caves. She saw herself in one, and she was also outside it, watching its entrance, for Aziz to pass in. She failed to locate him. It was the doubt that had often visited her, but solid and attractive, like the hills, "I am not——" Speech was more difficult than vision. "I am not quite sure."

"I beg your pardon?" said the Superintendent of Police.

"I cannot be sure..."

"I didn't catch that answer." He looked scared, his mouth shut with a snap. "You are on that landing, or whatever we term it, and you have entered a cave. I suggest to you that the prisoner followed you."

She shook her head.

"What do you mean, please?"

"No," she said in a flat, unattractive voice. Slight noises began in various parts of the room, but no one yet understood what was occurring except Fielding. He saw that she was going to have a nervous breakdown and that his friend was saved.

"What is that, what are you saying? Speak up, please." The Magistrate bent forward.

"I'm afraid I have made a mistake."

"What nature of mistake?"

"Dr. Aziz never followed me into the cave."

The Superintendent slammed down his papers, then picked them up and said calmly: “Now, Miss Quested, let us go on. I will read you the words of the deposition which you signed two hours later in my bungalow.”

“Excuse me, Mr. McBryde, you cannot go on. I am speaking to the witness myself. And the public will be silent. If it continues to talk, I have the court cleared. Miss Quested, address your remarks to me, who am the Magistrate in charge of the case, and realize their extreme gravity. Remember you speak on oath, Miss Quested.”

“Dr. Aziz never——”

“I stop these proceedings on medical grounds,” cried the Major on a word from Turton, and all the English rose from their chairs at once, large white figures behind which the little magistrate was hidden. The Indians rose too, hundreds of things went on at once, so that afterwards each person gave a different account of the catastrophe.

“You withdraw the charge? Answer me,” shrieked the representative of Justice.

Something that she did not understand took hold of the girl and pulled her through. Though the vision was over, and she had returned to the insipidity of the world, she remembered what she had learnt. Atonement and confession—they could wait. It was in hard prosaic tones that she said, “I withdraw everything.”

“Enough—sit down. Mr. McBryde, do you wish to continue in the face of this?”

The Superintendent gazed at his witness as if she was a broken machine, and said, “Are you mad?”

“Don’t question her, sir; you have no longer the right.”

“Give me time to consider——”

“Sahib, you will have to withdraw; this becomes a scandal,” boomed the Nawab Bahadur suddenly from the back of the court.

"He shall not," shouted Mrs. Turton against the gathering tumult. "Call the other witnesses; we're none of us safe——" Ronny tried to check her, and she gave him an irritable blow, then screamed insults at Adela.

The Superintendent moved to the support of his friends, saying nonchalantly to the Magistrate as he did so, "Right, I withdraw."

Mr. Das rose, nearly dead with the strain. He had controlled the case, just controlled it. He had shown that an Indian can preside. To those who could hear him he said, "The prisoner is released without one stain on his character; the question of costs will be decided elsewhere."

And then the flimsy framework of the court broke up, the shouts of derision and rage culminated, people screamed and cursed, kissed one another, wept passionately. Here were the English, whom their servants protected, there Aziz fainted in Hamidullah's arms. Victory on this side, defeat on that—complete for one moment was the antithesis. Then life returned to its complexities, person after person struggled out of the room to their various purposes, and before long no one remained on the scene of the fantasy but the beautiful naked god. Unaware that anything unusual had occurred, he continued to pull the cord of his punkah, to gaze at the empty dais and the overturned special chairs, and rhythmically to agitate the clouds of descending dust.

CHAPTER 25

Miss Quested had renounced her own people. Turning from them, she was drawn into a mass of Indians of the shopkeeping class, and carried by them towards the public exit of the court. The faint, indescribable smell of the bazaars invaded her, sweeter than a London slum, yet more disquieting: a tuft of scented cotton wool, wedged in an old man's ear, fragments of pan between his black teeth, odorous powders, oils—the Scented East of tradition, but blended with human sweat as if a great king had been entangled in ignominy and could not free himself, or as if the heat of the sun had boiled and fried all the glories of the earth into a single mess. They paid no attention to her. They shook hands over her shoulder, shouted through her body—for when the Indian does ignore his rulers, he becomes genuinely unaware of their existence. Without part in the universe she had created, she was flung against Mr. Fielding.

"What do you want here?"

Knowing him for her enemy, she passed on into the sunlight without speaking.

He called after her, "Where are you going, Miss Quested?"

"I don't know."

"You can't wander about like that. Where's the car you came in?"

"I shall walk."

"What madness... there's supposed to be a riot on... the police have struck, no one knows what'll happen next. Why don't you keep to your own people?"

"Ought I to join them?" she said, without emotion. She felt emptied, valueless; there was no more virtue in her.

"You can't, it's too late. How are you to get round to the private entrance now? Come this way with me—quick—I'll put you into my carriage."

"Cyril, Cyril, don't leave me," called the shattered voice of Aziz.

"I'm coming back... This way, and don't argue." He gripped her arm. "Excuse manners, but I don't know anyone's position. Send my carriage back any time to-morrow, if you please."

"But where am I to go in it?"

"Where you like. How should I know your arrangements?"

The victoria was safe in a quiet side lane, but there were no horses, for the sais, not expecting the trial would end so abruptly, had led them away to visit a friend. She got into it obediently. The man could not leave her, for the confusion increased, and spots of it sounded fanatical. The main road through the bazaars was blocked, and the English were gaining the civil station by by-ways; they were caught like caterpillars, and could have been killed off easily.

"What—what have you been doing?" he cried suddenly. "Playing a game, studying life, or what?"

"Sir, I intend these for you, sir," interrupted a student, running down the lane with a garland of jasmine on his arm.

"I don't want the rubbish; get out."

"Sir, I am a horse, we shall be your horses," another cried as he lifted the shafts of the victoria into the air.

"Fetch my sais, Rafi; there's a good chap."

"No, sir, this is an honour for us."

Fielding wearied of his students. The more they honoured him the less they obeyed. They lassoed him with jasmine and roses, scratched the splash-board against a wall, and recited a poem, the noise of which filled the lane with a crowd.

"Hurry up, sir; we pull you in a procession." And, half affectionate, half impudent, they bundled him in.

"I don't know whether this suits you, but anyhow you're safe," he remarked. The carriage jerked into the main bazaar, where it created some sensation. Miss Quested was so loathed in Chandrapore that her recantation was discredited, and the rumour ran that she had been stricken by the Deity in the middle of her lies. But they cheered when they saw her sitting by the heroic Principal (some addressed her as Mrs. Moore!), and they garlanded her to match him. Half gods, half guys, with sausages of flowers round their necks, the pair were dragged in the wake of Aziz' victorious landau. In the applause that greeted them some derision mingled. The English always stick together! That was the criticism. Nor was it unjust. Fielding shared it himself, and knew that if some misunderstanding occurred, and an attack was made on the girl by his allies, he would be obliged to die in her defence. He didn't want to die for her, he wanted to be rejoicing with Aziz.

Where was the procession going? To friends, to enemies, to Aziz' bungalow, to the Collector's bungalow, to the Minto Hospital where the Civil Surgeon would eat dust and the patients (confused with prisoners) be released, to Delhi, Simla. The students thought it was going to Government College. When they reached a turning, they twisted the victoria to the right, ran it by side lanes down a hill and through a garden gate into the mango plantation, and, as far as Fielding and Miss Quested were concerned, all was peace and quiet. The trees were full of glossy foliage and slim green fruit, the tank slumbered; and beyond it rose the exquisite blue arches of the garden-house. "Sir, we fetch the others; sir, it is a somewhat heavy load for our arms," were heard. Fielding took the refugee to his office, and tried to telephone to McBryde. But this he could not do; the wires had been cut. All his servants had decamped. Once more he was unable to desert her. He assigned her a couple of rooms, provided her with ice and drinks and biscuits, advised her to lie down, and lay down himself—there was nothing else to do. He felt restless and thwarted as he listened to the retreating sounds of the procession, and his joy was rather spoilt by bewilderment. It was a victory, but such a queer one.

At that moment Aziz was crying, "Cyril, Cyril..." Crammed into a carriage with the Nawab Bahadur, Hamidullah, Mahmoud Ali, his own little boys, and a heap of flowers, he was not content; he wanted to be surrounded by all who loved him. Victory gave no pleasure, he had suffered too much. From the moment of his arrest he was done for, he had dropped like a wounded animal; he had despaired, not through cowardice, but because he knew that an Englishwoman's word would always outweigh his own. "It is fate," he said; and, "It is fate," when he was imprisoned anew after Mohurram. All that existed, in that terrible time, was affection, and affection was all that he felt in the first painful moments of his freedom. "Why isn't Cyril following? Let us turn back." But the procession could not turn back. Like a snake in a drain, it advanced down the narrow bazaar towards the basin of the Maidan, where it would turn about itself, and decide on its prey.

"Forward, forward," shrieked Mahmoud Ali, whose every utterance had become a yell. "Down with the Collector, down with the Superintendent of Police."

"Mr. Mahmoud Ali, this is not wise," implored the Nawab Bahadur: he knew that nothing was gained by attacking the English, who had fallen into their own pit and had better be left there; moreover, he had great possessions and deprecated anarchy.

"Cyril, again you desert," cried Aziz.

"Yet some orderly demonstration is necessary," said Hamidullah, "otherwise they will still think we are afraid."

"Down with the Civil Surgeon... rescue Nureddin."

"Nureddin?"

"They are torturing him."

"Oh, my God..."—for this, too, was a friend.

"They are not. I will not have my grandson made an excuse for an attack on the hospital," the old man protested.

"They are Callendar boasted so before the trial. I heard through the tatties; he said, 'I have tortured that nigger.'"

"Oh, my God, my God... He called him a nigger, did he?"

"They put pepper instead of antiseptic on the wounds."

"Mr. Mahmoud Ali, impossible; a little roughness will not hurt the boy, he needs discipline."

"Pepper. Civil Surgeon said so. They hope to destroy us one by one; they shall fail."

The new injury lashed the crowd to fury. It had been aimless hitherto, and had lacked a grievance. When they reached the Maidan and saw the sallow arcades of the Minto they shambled towards it howling. It was near midday. The earth and sky were insanely ugly, the spirit of evil again strode abroad. The Nawab Bahadur alone struggled against it, and told himself that the rumour must be untrue. He had seen his grandson in the ward only last week. But he too was carried forward over the new precipice. To rescue, to maltreat Major Callendar in revenge, and then was to come the turn of the civil station generally.

But disaster was averted, and averted by Dr. Panna Lal.

Dr. Panna Lal had offered to give evidence for the prosecution in the hope of pleasing the English, also because he hated Aziz. When the case broke down, he was in a very painful position. He saw the crash coming sooner than most people, slipped from the court before Mr. Das had finished, and drove Dapple off through the bazaars, in flight from the wrath to come. In the hospital he should be safe, for Major Callendar would protect him. But the Major had not come, and now things were worse than ever, for here was a mob, entirely desirous of his blood, and the orderlies were mutinous and would not help him over the back wall, or rather hoisted him and let him drop back, to the satisfaction of the patients. In agony he cried, "Man can but die the once," and waddled across the compound to meet the invasion, salaaming with one hand and holding up a pale yellow umbrella in the other. "Oh, forgive me," he whined as he approached the victorious landau. "Oh, Dr. Aziz, forgive the wicked lies I told." Aziz was silent, the others thickened their throats and threw up their chins in token of scorn. "I was afraid, I was mislaid," the suppliant continued. "I was mislaid here, there, and everywhere as regards your character. Oh, forgive the poor old hakim who gave you milk when ill! Oh, Nawab Bahadur, whoever merciful, is it my poor little dispensary you require? Take every cursed bottle." Agitated, but alert, he saw them smile at his indifferent English, and suddenly he started playing the buffoon, flung down his umbrella, trod through it, and struck himself upon the nose. He knew what he was doing, and so did they. There was nothing pathetic or eternal in the degradation of such a man. Of ignoble origin, Dr. Panna Lal possessed nothing that could be disgraced, and he wisely decided to make the other Indians feel like kings, because it would put them into better tempers. When he found they wanted Nureddin, he skipped like a goat, he scuttled like a hen to do their bidding, the hospital was saved, and to the end of his life he could not understand why he had not obtained promotion on the morning's work. "Promptness, sir, promptness similar to you," was the argument he employed to Major Callendar when claiming it.

When Nureddin emerged, his face all bandaged, there was a roar of relief as though the Bastille had fallen. It was the crisis of the march, and the Nawab Bahadur managed to get the situation into hand. Embracing the young man publicly, he began a speech about Justice, Courage, Liberty, and Prudence, ranged under heads, which cooled the passion of the crowd. He further announced that he should give up his British-conferred title, and live as a private gentleman, plain Mr. Zulfiqar, for which reason he was instantly proceeding to his country seat. The landau turned, the crowd accompanied it, the crisis was over. The Marabar caves had been a terrible strain on the local administration; they altered a good many lives and wrecked several careers, but they did not break up a continent or even dislocate a district.

"We will have rejoicings to-night," the old man said. "Mr. Hamidullah, I depute you to bring out our friends Fielding and Amritrao, and to discover whether the latter will require special food. The others will keep with me. We shall not go out to Dilkusha until the cool of the evening, of course. I do not know the feelings of other gentlemen; for my own part, I have a slight headache, and I wish I had thought to ask our good Panna Lal for aspirin."

For the heat was claiming its own. Unable to madden, it stupefied, and before long most of the Chandrapore combatants were asleep. Those in the civil station kept watch a little, fearing an attack, but presently they too entered the world of dreams—that world in which a third of each man's life is spent, and which is thought by some pessimists to be a premonition of eternity.

CHAPTER 26

Evening approached by the time Fielding and Miss Quested met and had the first of their numerous curious conversations. He had hoped, when he woke up, to find someone had fetched her away, but the College remained isolated from the rest of the universe. She asked whether she could have "a sort of interview," and, when he made no reply, said, "Have you any explanation of my extraordinary behaviour?"

"None," he said curtly. "Why make such a charge if you were going to withdraw it?"

"Why, indeed."

"I ought to feel grateful to you, I suppose, but——"

"I don't expect gratitude. I only thought you might care to hear what I have to say."

"Oh, well," he grumbled, feeling rather school boyish. "I don't think a discussion between us is desirable. To put it frankly, I belong to the other side in this ghastly affair."

"Would it not interest you to hear my side?"

"Not much."

"I shouldn't tell you in confidence, of course. So you can hand on all my remarks to your side, for there is one great mercy that has come out of all to-day's misery: I have no longer any secrets.

My echo has gone—I call the buzzing sound in my ears an echo. You see, I have been unwell ever since that expedition to the caves, and possibly before it."

The remark interested him rather; it was what he had sometimes suspected himself. "What kind of illness?" he enquired.

She touched her head at the side, then shook it.

"That was my first thought, the day of the arrest: hallucination."

"Do you think that would be so?" she asked with great humility. "What should have given me an hallucination?"

"One of three things certainly happened in the Marabar," he said, getting drawn into a discussion against his will. "One of four things. Either Aziz is guilty, which is what your friends think; or you invented the charge out of malice, which is what my friends think; or you have had an hallucination. I'm very much inclined"—getting up and striding about—"now that you tell me that you felt unwell before the expedition—it's an important piece of evidence—I believe that you yourself broke the strap of the field-glasses; you were alone in that cave the whole time."

"Perhaps..."

"Can you remember when you first felt out of sorts?"

"When I came to tea with you there, in that garden-house."

"A somewhat unlucky party. Aziz and old Godbole were both ill after it too."

"I was not ill—it is far too vague to mention: it is all mixed up with my private affairs. I enjoyed the singing... but just about then a sort of sadness began that I couldn't detect at the time... no, nothing as solid as sadness: living at half pressure expresses it best. Half pressure. I remember going on to polo with Mr. Heaslop at the Maidan. Various other things happened—it doesn't matter what, but I was under par for all of them. I was certainly in that state when I saw the caves, and you suggest (nothing shocks or hurts me)—you suggest that I had an hallucination there, the sort of thing—though in an awful form—that makes some women think they've had an offer of marriage when none was made."

"You put it honestly, anyhow."

"I was brought up to be honest; the trouble is it gets me nowhere."

Liking her better, he smiled and said, "It'll get us to heaven."

"Will it?"

"If heaven existed."

"Do you not believe in heaven, Mr. Fielding, may I ask?" she said, looking at him shyly.

"I do not. Yet I believe that honesty gets us there."

"How can that be?"

"Let us go back to hallucinations. I was watching you carefully through your evidence this morning, and if I'm right, the hallucination (what you call half pressure—quite as good a word) disappeared suddenly."

She tried to remember what she had felt in court, but could not; the vision disappeared whenever she wished to interpret it. "Events presented themselves to me in their logical sequence," was what she said, but it hadn't been that at all.

"My belief—and of course I was listening carefully, in hope you would make some slip—my belief is that poor McBryde exorcised you. As soon as he asked you a straightforward question, you gave a straightforward answer, and broke down."

"Exorcise in that sense. I thought you meant I'd seen a ghost."

"I don't go to that length!"

"People whom I respect very much believe in ghosts," she said rather sharply. "My friend Mrs. Moore does."

"She's an old lady."

"I think you need not be impolite to her, as well as to her son."

"I did not intend to be rude. I only meant it is difficult, as we get on in life, to resist the supernatural. I've felt it coming on me myself. I still jog on without it, but what a temptation, at forty-five, to pretend that the dead live again; one's own dead; no one else's matter."

"Because the dead don't live again."

"I fear not."

"So do I."

There was a moment's silence, such as often follows the triumph of rationalism. Then he apologized handsomely enough for his behaviour to Heaslop at the club.

"What does Dr. Aziz say of me?" she asked, after another pause.

"He—he has not been capable of thought in his misery, naturally he's very bitter," said Fielding, a little awkward, because such remarks as Aziz had made were not merely bitter, they were foul. The underlying notion was, "It disgraces me to have been mentioned in connection with such a hag." It enraged him that he had been accused by a woman who had no personal beauty; sexually, he was a snob. This had puzzled and worried Fielding. Sensuality, as long as it is straight-forward, did not repel him, but this derived sensuality—the sort that classes a mistress among motor-cars if she is beautiful, and among eye-flies if she isn't—was alien to his own emotions, and he felt a barrier between himself and Aziz whenever it arose. It was, in a new form, the old, old trouble that eats the heart out of every civilization: snobbery, the desire for possessions, creditable appendages; and it is to escape this rather than the lusts of the flesh that saints retreat into the Himalayas. To change the subject, he said, "But let me conclude my analysis. We are agreed that he is not a villain and that you are not one, and we aren't really sure that it was an hallucination. There's a fourth possibility which we must touch on: was it somebody else?"

"The guide."

"Exactly, the guide. I often think so. Unluckily Aziz hit him on the face, and he got a fright and disappeared. It is most unsatisfactory, and we hadn't the police to help us, the guide was of no interest to them."

"Perhaps it was the guide," she said quietly; the question had lost interest for her suddenly.

"Or could it have been one of that gang of Pathans who have been drifting through the district?"

"Someone who was in another cave, and followed me when the guide was looking away? Possibly."

At that moment Hamidullah joined them, and seemed not too pleased to find them closeted together. Like everyone else in Chandrapore, he could make nothing of Miss Quested's conduct. He had overheard their last remark. "Hullo, my dear Fielding," he said. "So I run you down at last. Can you come out at once to Dilkusha?"

"At once?"

"I hope to leave in a moment, don't let me interrupt," said Adela.

"The telephone has been broken; Miss Quested can't ring up her friends," he explained.

"A great deal has been broken, more than will ever be mended," said the other. "Still, there should be some way of transporting this lady back to the civil lines. The resources of civilization are numerous." He spoke without looking at Miss Quested, and he ignored the slight movement she made towards him with her hand.

Fielding, who thought the meeting might as well be friendly, said, "Miss Quested has been explaining a little about her conduct of this morning."

"Perhaps the age of miracles has returned. One must be prepared for everything, our philosophers say."

"It must have seemed a miracle to the onlookers," said Adela, addressing him nervously. "The fact is that I realized before it was too late that I had made a mistake, and had just enough presence of mind to say so. That is all my extraordinary conduct amounts to."

"All it amounts to, indeed," he retorted, quivering with rage but keeping himself in hand, for he felt she might be setting another trap. "Speaking as a private individual, in a purely informal conversation, I admired your conduct, and I was delighted when our warm-hearted students garlanded you. But, like Mr. Fielding, I am surprised; indeed, surprise is too weak a word. I see you drag my best friend into the dirt, damage his health and ruin his prospects in a way you cannot conceive owing to your ignorance of our society and religion, and then suddenly you get up in the witness-box: 'Oh no, Mr. McBryde, after all I am not quite sure, you may as well let him go.' Am I mad? I keep asking myself. Is it a dream, and if so, when did it start? And without doubt it is a dream that has not yet finished. For I gather you have not done with us yet, and it is now the turn of the poor old guide who conducted you round the caves."

"Not at all, we were only discussing possibilities," interposed Fielding.

"An interesting pastime, but a lengthy one. There are one hundred and seventy million Indians in this notable peninsula, and of course one or other of them entered the cave. Of course some Indian is the culprit, we must never doubt that. And since, my dear Fielding, these possibilities will take you some time"—here he put his arm over the Englishman's shoulder and swayed him to and fro gently—"don't you think you had better come out to the Nawab Bahadur's—or I should say to Mr. Zulfiqar's, for that is the name he now requires us to call him by."

"Gladly, in a minute..."

"I have just settled my movements," said Miss Quested. "I shall go to the Dak Bungalow."

"Not the Turtons'?" said Hamidullah, goggle-eyed. "I thought you were their guest."

The Dak Bungalow of Chandrapore was below the average, and certainly servant less. Fielding, though he continued to sway with Hamidullah, was thinking on independent lines, and said in a moment: "I have a better idea than that, Miss Quested. You must stop here at the College. I shall be away at least two days, and you can have the place entirely to yourself, and make your plans at your convenience."

"I don't agree at all," said Hamidullah, with every symptom of dismay. "The idea is a thoroughly bad one. There may quite well be another demonstration to-night, and suppose an attack is made on the College. You would be held responsible for this lady's safety, my dear fellow."

"They might equally attack the Dak Bungalow."

"Exactly, but the responsibility there ceases to be yours."

"Quite so. I have given trouble enough."

"Do you hear? The lady admits it herself. It's not an attack from our people I fear—you should see their orderly conduct at the hospital; what we must guard against is an attack secretly arranged by the police for the purpose of discrediting you. McBryde keeps plenty of roughs for this purpose, and this would be the very opportunity for him."

"Never mind. She is not going to the Dak Bungalow," said Fielding. He had a natural sympathy for the down-trodden—that was partly why he rallied from Aziz—and had become determined not to leave the poor girl in the lurch. Also, he had a new-born respect for her, consequent on their talk. Although her hard schoolmistressy manner remained, she was no longer examining life, but being examined by it; she had become a real person.

"Then where is she to go? We shall never have done with her!" For Miss Quested had not appealed to Hamidullah. If she had shown emotion in court, broke down, beat her breast, and invoked the name of God, she would have summoned forth his imagination and generosity—he had plenty of both. But while relieving the Oriental mind, she had chilled it, with the result that he could scarcely believe she was sincere, and indeed from his standpoint she was not. For her behaviour rested on cold justice and honesty; she had felt, while she recanted, no passion of love for those whom she had wronged. Truth is not truth in that exacting land unless there go with it kindness and more kindness and kindness again, unless the Word that was with God also is God. And the girl's sacrifice—so creditable according to Western notions—was rightly rejected, because, though it came from her heart, it did not include her heart. A few garlands from students was all that India ever gave her in return.

"But where is she to have her dinner, where is she to sleep? I say here, here, and if she is hit on the head by roughs, she is hit on the head. That is my contribution. Well, Miss Quested?"

"You are very kind. I should have said yes, I think, but I agree with Mr. Hamidullah. I must give no more trouble to you. I believe my best plan is to return to the Turtons, and see if they will allow me to sleep, and if they turn me away I must go to the Dak. The Collector would take me in, I know, but Mrs. Turton said this morning that she would never see me again." She spoke without bitterness, or, as Hamidullah thought, without proper pride. Her aim was to cause the minimum of annoyance.

"Far better stop here than expose yourself to insults from that preposterous woman."

"Do you find her preposterous? I used to. I don't now."

"Well, here's our solution," said the barrister, who had terminated his slightly minatory caress and strolled to the window. "Here comes the City Magistrate. He comes in a third-class band-ghari for purposes of disguise, he comes unattended, but here comes the City Magistrate."

"At last," said Adela sharply, which caused Fielding to glance at her.

"He comes, he comes, he comes. I cringe. I tremble."

"Will you ask him what he wants, Mr. Fielding?"

"He wants you, of course."

"He may not even know I'm here."

"I'll see him first, if you prefer."

When he had gone, Hamidullah said to her bitingly: "Really, really. Need you have exposed Mr. Fielding to this further discomfort? He is far too considerate." She made no reply, and there was complete silence between them until their host returned.

"He has some news for you," he said. "You'll find him on the verandah. He prefers not to come in."

"Does he tell me to come out to him?"

"Whether he tells you or not, you will go, I think," said Hamidullah.

She paused, then said, "Perfectly right," and then said a few words of thanks to the Principal for his kindness to her during the day.

"Thank goodness, that's over," he remarked, not escorting her to the verandah, for he held it unnecessary to see Ronny again.

"It was insulting of him not to come in."

"He couldn't very well after my behaviour to him at the Club. Heaslop doesn't come out badly. Besides, Fate has treated him pretty roughly to-day. He has had a cable to the effect that his mother's dead, poor old soul."

"Oh, really. Mrs. Moore. I'm sorry," said Hamidullah rather indifferently.

"She died at sea."

"The heat, I suppose."

"Presumably."

"May is no month to allow an old lady to travel in."

"Quite so. Heaslop ought never to have let her go, and he knows it. Shall we be off?"

"Let us wait until the happy couple leave the compound clear... they really are intolerable dawdling there. Ah well, Fielding, you don't believe in Providence, I remember. I do. This is Heaslop's punishment for abducting our witness in order to stop us establishing our alibi."

"You go rather too far there. The poor old lady's evidence could have had no value, shout and shriek Mahmoud Ali as he will. She couldn't see through the Kawa Dol even if she had wanted to. Only Miss Quested could have saved him."

"She loved Aziz, he says, also India, and he loved her."

"Love is of no value in a witness, as a barrister ought to know. But I see there is about to be an Esmiss Esmoor legend at Chandrapore, my dear Hamidullah, and I will not impede its growth."

The other smiled, and looked at his watch. They both regretted the death, but they were middle-aged men, who had invested their emotions elsewhere, and outbursts of grief could not be expected from them over a slight acquaintance. It's only one's own dead who matter. If for a moment the sense of communion in sorrow came to them, it passed. How indeed is it possible for one human being to be sorry for all the sadness that meets him on the face of the earth, for the pain that is endured not only by men, but by animals and plants, and perhaps by the stones? The soul is tired in a moment, and in fear of losing the little she does understand, she retreats to the permanent lines which habit or chance have dictated, and suffers there. Fielding had met the dead woman only two or three times, Hamidullah had seen her in the distance once, and they were far more occupied with the coming gathering at Dilkusha, the "victory" dinner, for which they would be most victoriously late.

They agreed not to tell Aziz about Mrs. Moore till the morrow, because he was fond of her, and the bad news might spoil his fun.

"Oh, this is unbearable!" muttered Hamidullah. For Miss Quested was back again.

"Mr. Fielding, has Ronny told you of this new misfortune?"

He bowed.

"Ah me!" She sat down, and seemed to stiffen into a monument.

"Heaslop is waiting for you, I think."

"I do so long to be alone. She was my best friend, far more to me than to him. I can't bear to be with Ronny... I can't explain... Could you do me the very great kindness of letting me stop after all?"

Hamidullah swore violently in the vernacular.

"I should be pleased, but does Mr. Heaslop wish it?"

"I didn't ask him, we are too much upset—it's so complex, not like what unhappiness is supposed to be. Each of us ought to be alone, and think. Do come and see Ronny again."

"I think he should come in this time," said Fielding, feeling that this much was due to his own dignity. "Do ask him to come."

She returned with him. He was half miserable, half arrogant—indeed, a strange mix-up—and broke at once into uneven speech. "I came to bring Miss Quested away, but her visit to the Turtons has ended, and there is no other arrangement so far, mine are bachelor quarters now——"

Fielding stopped him courteously. "Say no more, Miss Quested stops here. I only wanted to be assured of your approval. Miss Quested, you had better send for your own servant if he can be found, but I will leave orders with mine to do all they can for you, also I'll let the Scouts know. They have guarded the College ever since it was closed, and may as well go on. I really think you'll be as safe here as anywhere. I shall be back Thursday."

Meanwhile Hamidullah, determined to spare the enemy no incidental pain, had said to Ronny: "We hear, sir, that your mother has died. May we ask where the cable came from?"

"Aden."

"Ah, you were boasting she had reached Aden, in court."

"But she died on leaving Bombay," broke in Adela. "She was dead when they called her name this morning. She must have been buried at sea."

Somehow this stopped Hamidullah, and he desisted from his brutality, which had shocked Fielding more than anyone else. He remained silent while the details of Miss Quested's occupation of the College were arranged, merely remarking to Ronny, "It is clearly to be understood, sir, that neither Mr. Fielding nor any of us are responsible for this lady's safety at Government College," to which Ronny agreed. After that, he watched the semi-chivalrous behavings of the three English with quiet amusement; he thought Fielding had been incredibly silly and weak, and he was amazed by the younger people's want of proper pride. When they were driving out to Dilkusha, hours late, he said to Amritrao, who accompanied them: "Mr. Amritrao, have you considered what sum Miss Quested ought to pay as compensation?"

"Twenty thousand rupees."

No more was then said, but the remark horrified Fielding. He couldn't bear to think of the queer honest girl losing her money and possibly her young man too. She advanced into his consciousness suddenly. And, fatigued by the merciless and enormous day, he lost his usual sane view of human intercourse, and felt that we exist not in ourselves, but in terms of each others' minds—a notion for which logic offers no support and which had attacked him only once before, the evening after the catastrophe, when from the verandah of the club he saw the fists and fingers of the Marabar swell until they included the whole night sky.

CHAPTER 27

"Aziz, are you awake?"

"No, so let us have a talk; let us dream plans for the future."

"I am useless at dreaming."

"Good night then, dear fellow."

The Victory Banquet was over, and the revellers lay on the roof of plain Mr. Zulfiqar's mansion, asleep, or gazing through mosquito nets at the stars. Exactly above their heads hung the constellation of the Lion, the disc of Regulus so large and bright that it resembled a tunnel, and when this fancy was accepted all the other stars seemed tunnels too.

"Are you content with our day's work, Cyril?" the voice on his left continued.

"Are you?"

"Except that I ate too much. 'How is stomach, how head?'—I say, Panna Lal and Callendar 'll get the sack."

"There'll be a general move at Chandrapore."

"And you'll get promotion."

"They can't well move me down, whatever their feelings."

"In any case we spend our holidays together, and visit Kashmir, possibly Persia, for I shall have plenty of money. Paid to me on account of the injury sustained by my character," he explained with cynical calm. "While with me you shall never spend a single pie. This is what I have always wished, and as the result of my misfortunes it has come."

"You have won a great victory..." began Fielding.

"I know, my dear chap, I know; your voice need not become so solemn and anxious. I know what you are going to say next: Let, oh let Miss Quested off paying, so that the English may say, 'Here is a native who has actually behaved like a gentleman; if it was not for his black face we would almost allow him to join our club.' The approval of your compatriots no longer interests me, I have become anti-British, and ought to have done so sooner, it would have saved me numerous misfortunes."

"Including knowing me."

"I say, shall we go and pour water on to Mohammed Latif's face? He is so funny when this is done to him asleep."

The remark was not a question but a full-stop. Fielding accepted it as such and there was a pause, pleasantly filled by a little wind which managed to brush the top of the house. The banquet, though riotous, had been agreeable, and now the blessings of leisure—unknown to the West, which either works or idles—descended on the motley company. Civilization strays about like a ghost here, revisiting the ruins of empire, and is to be found not in great works of art or mighty deeds, but in the gestures well-bred Indians make when they sit or lie down. Fielding, who had dressed up in native costume, learnt from his excessive awkwardness in it that all his motions were makeshifts, whereas when the Nawab Bahadur stretched out his hand for food or Nureddin applauded a song, something beautiful had been accomplished which needed no development. This restfulness of gesture—it is the Peace that passeth Understanding, after all, it is the social equivalent of Yoga. When the whirring of action ceases, it becomes visible, and reveals a civilization which the West can disturb but will never acquire. The hand stretches out for ever, the lifted knee has the eternity though not the sadness of the grave. Aziz was full of civilization this evening, complete, dignified, rather hard, and it was with diffidence that the other said: "Yes, certainly you must let off Miss Quested easily. She must pay all your costs, that is only fair, but do not treat her like a conquered enemy."

"Is she wealthy? I depute you to find out."

"The sums mentioned at dinner when you all got so excited—they would ruin her, they are perfectly preposterous. Look here..."

"I am looking, though it gets a bit dark. I see Cyril Fielding to be a very nice chap indeed and my best friend, but in some ways a fool. You think that by letting Miss Quested off easily I shall make a better reputation for myself and Indians generally. No, no. It will be put down to weakness and the attempt to gain promotion officially. I have decided to have nothing more to do with British India, as a matter of fact. I shall seek service in some Moslem State, such as Hyderabad, Bhopal, where Englishmen cannot insult me anymore. Don't counsel me otherwise."

"In the course of a long talk with Miss Quested..."

"I don't want to hear your long talks."

"Be quiet. In the course of a long talk with Miss Quested I have begun to understand her character. It's not an easy one, she being a prig. But she is perfectly genuine and very brave. When she saw she was wrong, she pulled herself up with a jerk and said so. I want you to realize what that means. All her friends around her, the entire British Raj pushing her forward. She stops, sends the whole thing to smithereens. In her place I should have funked it. But she stopped, and almost did she become a national heroine, but my students ran us down a side street before the crowd caught flame. Do treat her considerately. She really mustn't get the worst of both worlds. I know what all these"—he indicated the shrouded forms on the roof—"will want, but you mustn't listen to them. Be merciful. Act like one of your six Mogul Emperors, or all the six rolled into one."

"Not even Mogul Emperors showed mercy until they received an apology."

"She'll apologize if that's the trouble," he cried, sitting up. "Look, I'll make you an offer. Dictate to me whatever form of words you like, and this time to-morrow I'll bring it back signed. This is not instead of any public apology she may make you in law. It's an addition."

"'Dear Dr. Aziz, I wish you had come into the cave; I am an awful old hag, and it is my last chance.' Will she sign that?"

"Well good night, good night, it's time to go to sleep, after that."

"Good night, I suppose it is."

"Oh, I wish you wouldn't make that kind of remark," he continued after a pause. "It is the one thing in you I can't put up with."

"I put up with all things in you, so what is to be done?"

"Well, you hurt me by saying it; good night."

There was silence, then dreamily but with deep feeling the voice said: "Cyril, I have had an idea which will satisfy your tender mind: I shall consult Mrs. Moore." Opening his eyes, and beholding thousands of stars, he could not reply, they silenced him.

"Her opinion will solve everything; I can trust her so absolutely. If she advises me to pardon this girl, I shall do so. She will counsel me nothing against my real and true honour, as you might."

"Let us discuss that to-morrow morning."

"Is it not strange? I keep on forgetting she has left India. During the shouting of her name in court I fancied she was present. I had shut my eyes, I confused myself on purpose to deaden the pain. Now this very instant I forgot again. I shall be obliged to write. She is now far away, well on her way towards Ralph and Stella."

"To whom?"

"To those other children."

"I have not heard of other children."

"Just as I have two boys and a girl, so has Mrs. Moore. She told me in the mosque."

"I knew her so slightly."

"I have seen her but three times, but I know she is an Oriental."

"You are so fantastic... Miss Quested, you won't treat her generously; while over Mrs. Moore there is this elaborate chivalry. Miss Quested anyhow behaved decently this morning, whereas the old lady never did anything for you at all, and it's pure conjecture that she would have come forward in your favour, it only rests on servants' gossip. Your emotions never seem in proportion to their objects, Aziz."

"Is emotion a sack of potatoes, so much the pound, to be measured out? Am I a machine? I shall be told I can use up my emotions by using them, next."

"I should have thought you could. It sounds common sense. You can't eat your cake and have it, even in the world of the spirit."

"If you are right, there is no point in any friendship; it all comes down to give and take, or give and return, which is disgusting, and we had better all leap over this parapet and kill ourselves. Is anything wrong with you this evening that you grow so materialistic?"

"Your unfairness is worse than my materialism."

"I see. Anything further to complain of?" He was good-tempered and affectionate but a little formidable. Imprisonment had made channels for his character, which would never fluctuate as widely now as in the past. "Because it is far better you put all your difficulties before me, if we are to be friends for ever. You do not like Mrs. Moore, and are annoyed because I do; however, you will like her in time."

When a person, really dead, is supposed to be alive, an unhealthiness infects the conversation. Fielding could not stand the tension any longer and blurted out: "I'm sorry to say Mrs. Moore's dead."

But Hamidullah, who had been listening to all their talk, and did not want the festive evening spoilt, cried from the adjoining bed: "Aziz, he is trying to pull your leg; don't believe him, the villain."

"I do not believe him," said Aziz; he was inured to practical jokes, even of this type.

Fielding said no more. Facts are facts, and everyone would learn of Mrs. Moore's death in the morning. But it struck him that people are not really dead until they are felt to be dead. As long as there is some misunderstanding about them, they possess a sort of immortality. An experience of his own confirmed this. Many years ago he had lost a great friend, a woman, who believed in the Christian heaven, and assured him that after the changes and chances of this mortal life they would meet in it again. Fielding was a blank, frank atheist, but he respected every opinion his friend held: to do this is essential in friendship. And it seemed to him for a time that the dead awaited him, and when the illusion faded it left behind it an emptiness that was almost guilt: "This really is the end," he thought, "and I gave her the final blow." He had tried to kill Mrs. Moore this evening, on the roof of the Nawab Bahadur's house; but she still eluded him, and the atmosphere remained tranquil. Presently the moon rose—the exhausted crescent that precedes the sun—and shortly after men and oxen began their interminable labour, and the gracious interlude, which he had tried to curtail, came to its natural conclusion.

CHAPTER 28

Dead she was—committed to the deep while still on the southward track, for the boats from Bombay cannot point towards Europe until Arabia has been rounded; she was further in the tropics than ever achieved while on shore, when the sun touched her for the last time and her body was lowered into yet another India—the Indian Ocean. She left behind her sore discomfort, for a death gives a ship a bad name. Who was this Mrs. Moore? When Aden was reached, Lady Mellanby cabled, wrote, did all that was kind, but the wife of a Lieutenant-Governor does not bargain for such an experience; and she repeated: "I had only seen the poor creature for a few hours when she was taken ill; really this has been needlessly distressing, it spoils one's home-coming." A ghost followed the ship up the Red Sea, but failed to enter the Mediterranean. Somewhere about Suez there is always a social change: the arrangements of Asia weaken and those of Europe begin to be felt, and during the transition Mrs. Moore was shaken off. At Port Said the grey blustery north began. The weather was so cold and bracing that the passengers felt it must have broken in the land they had left, but it became hotter steadily there in accordance with its usual law.

The death took subtler and more lasting shapes in Chandrapore. A legend sprang up that an Englishman had killed his mother for trying to save an Indian's life—and there was just enough truth in this to cause annoyance to the authorities. Sometimes it was a cow that had been killed—or a crocodile with the tusks of a boar had crawled out of the Ganges. Nonsense of this type is more difficult to combat than a solid lie. It hides in rubbish heaps and moves when no one is looking. At one period two distinct tombs containing Esmiss Esmoor's remains were reported: one by the tannery, the other up near the goods station. Mr. McBryde visited them both and saw signs of the beginning of a cult—earthenware saucers and so on. Being an experienced official, he did nothing to irritate it, and after a week or so, the rash died down. "There's propaganda behind all this," he said, forgetting that a hundred years ago, when Europeans still made their home in the country-side and appealed to its imagination, they occasionally became local demons after death—not a whole god, perhaps, but part of one, adding an epithet or gesture to what already existed, just as the gods contribute to the great gods, and they to the philosophic Brahm.

Ronny reminded himself that his mother had left India at her own wish, but his conscience was not clear. He had behaved badly to her, and he had either to repent (which involved a mental overturn), or to persist in unkindness towards her. He chose the latter course. How tiresome she had been with her patronage of Aziz! What a bad influence upon Adela! And now she still gave trouble with ridiculous "tombs," mixing herself up with natives. She could not help it, of course, but she had attempted similar exasperating expeditions in her lifetime, and he reckoned it against her. The young man had much to worry him—the heat, the local tension, the approaching visit of the Lieutenant-Governor, the problems of Adela—and threading them all together into a grotesque garland were these Indianizations of Mrs. Moore. What does happen to one's mother when she dies? Presumably she goes to heaven, anyhow she clears out. Ronny's religion was of the sterilized Public School brand, which never goes bad, even in the tropics. Wherever he entered, mosque, cave, or temple, he retained the spiritual outlook of the Fifth Form, and condemned as "weakening" any attempt to understand them. Pulling himself together, he dismissed the mater from his mind. In due time he and his half-brother and -sister would put up a tablet to her in the Northamptonshire church where she had worshipped, recording the dates of her birth and death and the fact that she had been buried at sea. This would be sufficient.

And Adela—she would have to depart too; he hoped she would have made the suggestion herself ere now. He really could not marry her—it would mean the end of his career. Poor lamentable Adela... She remained at Government College, by Fielding's courtesy—unsuitable and humiliating, but no one would receive her at the civil station. He postponed all private talk until the award against her was decided. Aziz was suing her for damages in the sub-judge's court. Then he would ask her to release him. She had killed his love, and it had never been very robust; they would never have achieved betrothal but for the accident to the Nawab Bahadur's car. She belonged to the callow academic period of his life which he had outgrown—Grasmere, serious talks and walks, that sort of thing.

CHAPTER 29

The visit of the Lieutenant-Governor of the Province formed the next stage in the decomposition of the Marabar. Sir Gilbert, though not an enlightened man, held enlightened opinions. Exempted by a long career in the Secretariate from personal contact with the peoples of India, he was able to speak of them urbanely, and to deplore racial prejudice. He applauded the outcome of the trial, and congratulated Fielding on having taken "the broad, the sensible, the only possible charitable view from the first. Speaking confidentially..." he proceeded. Fielding deprecated confidences, but Sir Gilbert insisted on imparting them; the affair had been "mishandled by certain of our friends up the hill" who did not realize that "the hands of the clock move forward, not back," etc., etc. One thing he could guarantee: the Principal would receive a most cordial invitation to rejoin the club, and he begged, nay commanded him, to accept. He returned to his Himalayan altitudes well satisfied; the amount of money Miss Quested would have to pay, the precise nature of what had happened in the caves—these were local details, and did not concern him.

Fielding found himself drawn more and more into Miss Quested's affairs. The College remained closed and he ate and slept at Hamidullah's, so there was no reason she should not stop on if she wished. In her place he would have cleared out, sooner than submit to Ronny's half-hearted and distracted civilities, but she was waiting for the hour-glass of her sojourn to run through. A house to live in, a garden to walk in during the brief moment of the cool—that was all she asked, and he was able to provide them. Disaster had shown her her limitations, and he realized now what a fine loyal character she was. Her humility was touching. She never repined at getting the worst of both worlds; she regarded it as the due punishment of her stupidity. When he hinted to her that a personal apology to Aziz might be seemly, she said sadly: "Of course. I ought to have thought of it myself, my instincts never help me. Why didn't I rush up to him after the trial? Yes, of course I will write him an apology, but please will you dictate it?" Between them they concocted a letter, sincere, and full of moving phrases, but it was not moving as a letter. "Shall I write another?" she enquired. "Nothing matters if I can undo the harm I have caused. I can do this right, and that right; but when the two are put together they come wrong. That's the defect of my character. I have never realized it until now. I thought that if I was just and asked questions I would come through every difficulty." He replied: "Our letter is a failure for a simple reason which we had better face: you have no real affection for Aziz, or Indians generally." She assented. "The first time I saw you, you were wanting to see India, not Indians, and it occurred to me: Ah, that won't take us far. Indians know whether they are liked or not—they cannot be fooled here. Justice never satisfies them, and that is why the British Empire rests on sand." Then she said: "Do I like anyone, though?" Presumably she liked Heaslop, and he changed the subject, for this side of her life did not concern him.

His Indian friends were, on the other hand, a bit above themselves. Victory, which would have made the English sanctimonious, made them aggressive. They wanted to develop an offensive, and tried to do so by discovering new grievances and wrongs, many of which had no existence. They suffered from the usual disillusion that attends warfare. The aims of battle and the fruits of conquest are never the same; the latter have their value and only the saint rejects them, but their hint of immortality vanishes as soon as they are held in the hand. Although Sir Gilbert had been courteous, almost obsequious, the fabric he represented had in no wise bowed its head. British officialism remained, as all-pervading and as unpleasant as the sun; and what was next to be done against it was not very obvious, even to Mahmoud Ali. Loud talk and trivial lawlessness were attempted, and behind them continued a genuine but vague desire for education. "Mr. Fielding, we must all be educated promptly."

Aziz was friendly and domineering. He wanted Fielding to "give in to the East," as he called it, and live in a condition of affectionate dependence upon it. "You can trust me, Cyril." No question of that, and Fielding had no roots among his own people. Yet he really couldn't become a sort of Mohammed Latif. When they argued about it something racial intruded—not bitterly, but inevitably, like the colour of their skins: coffee-colour versus pinko-grey. And Aziz would conclude: "Can't you see that I'm grateful to you for your help and want to reward you?" And the other would retort: "If you want to reward me, let Miss Quested off paying."

The insensitiveness about Adela displeased him. It would, from every point of view, be right to treat her generously, and one day he had the notion of appealing to the memory of Mrs. Moore. Aziz had this high and fantastic estimate of Mrs. Moore. Her death had been a real grief to his warm heart; he wept like a child and ordered his three children to weep also. There was no doubt that he respected and loved her. Fielding's first attempt was a failure. The reply was: "I see your trick. I want revenge on them. Why should I be insulted and suffer and the contents of my pockets read and my wife's photograph taken to the police station? Also I want the money – to educate my little boys, as I explained to her." But he began to weaken, and Fielding was not ashamed to practise a little necromancy. Whenever the question of compensation came up, he introduced the dead woman's name.

Just as other propagandists invented her a tomb, so did he raise a questionable image of her in the heart of Aziz, saying nothing that he believed to be untrue, but producing something that was probably far from the truth. Aziz yielded suddenly. He felt it was Mrs. Moore's wish that he should spare the woman who was about to marry her son, that it was the only honour he could pay her, and he renounced with a passionate and beautiful outburst the whole of the compensation money, claiming only costs. It was fine of him, and, as he foresaw, it won him no credit with the English. They still believed he was guilty, they believed it to the end of their careers, and retired Anglo-Indians in Tunbridge Wells or Cheltenham still murmur to each other: "That Marabar case which broke down because the poor girl couldn't face giving her evidence—that was another bad case."

When the affair was thus officially ended, Ronny, who was about to be transferred to another part of the Province, approached Fielding with his usual constraint and said: "I wish to thank you for the help you have given Miss Quested. She will not of course trespass on your hospitality further; she has as a matter of fact decided to return to England. I have just arranged about her passage for her. I understand she would like to see you."

"I shall go round at once."

On reaching the College, he found her in some upset. He learnt that the engagement had been broken by Ronny. "Far wiser of him," she said pathetically. "I ought to have spoken myself, but I drifted on wondering what would happen. I would willingly have gone on spoiling his life through inertia—one has nothing to do, one belongs nowhere and becomes a public nuisance without realizing it." In order to reassure him, she added: "I speak only of India. I am not astray in England. I fit in there—no, don't think I shall do harm in England. When I am forced back there, I shall settle down to some career. I have sufficient money left to start myself, and heaps of friends of my own type. I shall be quite all right." Then sighing: "But oh, the trouble I've brought on everyone here... I can never get over it. My carefulness as to whether we should marry or not... and in the end Ronny and I part and aren't even sorry. We ought never to have thought of marriage. Weren't you amazed when our engagement was originally announced?"

"Not much. At my age one's seldom amazed," he said, smiling. "Marriage is too absurd in any case. It begins and continues for such very slight reasons. The social business props it up on one side, and the theological business on the other, but neither of them are marriage, are they? I've friends who can't remember why they married, no more can their wives. I suspect that it mostly happens haphazard, though afterwards various noble reasons are invented. About marriage I am cynical."

"I am not. This false start has been all my own fault. I was bringing to Ronny nothing that ought to be brought, that was why he rejected me really. I entered that cave thinking: Am I fond of him? I have not yet told you that, Mr. Fielding. I didn't feel justified. Tenderness, respect, personal intercourse—I tried to make them take the place—of——"

"I no longer want love," he said, supplying the word.

"No more do I. My experiences here have cured me. But I want others to want it."

"But to go back to our first talk (for I suppose this is our last one)—when you entered that cave, who did follow you, or did no one follow you? Can you now say? I don't like it left in air."

"Let us call it the guide," she said indifferently. "It will never be known. It's as if I ran my finger along that polished wall in the dark, and cannot get further. I am up against something, and so are you. Mrs. Moore—she did know."

"How could she have known what we don't?"

"Telepathy, possibly."

The pert, meagre word fell to the ground. Telepathy? What an explanation! Better withdraw it, and Adela did so. She was at the end of her spiritual tether, and so was he. Were there worlds beyond which they could never touch, or did all that is possible enter their consciousness? They could not tell. They only realized that their outlook was more or less similar, and found in this a satisfaction. Perhaps life is a mystery, not a muddle; they could not tell. Perhaps the hundred Indias which fuss and squabble so tiresomely are one, and the universe they mirror is one. They had not the apparatus for judging.

"Write to me when you get to England."

"I shall, often. You have been excessively kind. Now that I'm going, I realize it. I wish I could do something for you in return, but I see you've all you want."

"I think so," he replied after a pause. "I have never felt more happy and secure out here. I really do get on with Indians, and they do trust me. It's pleasant that I haven't had to resign my job. It's pleasant to be praised by an L.-G. Until the next earthquake I remain as I am."

"Of course this death has been troubling me."

"Aziz was so fond of her too."

"But it has made me remember that we must all die: all these personal relations we try to live by are temporary. I used to feel death selected people, it is a notion one gets from novels, because some of the characters are usually left talking at the end. Now 'death spares no one' begins to be real."

"Don't let it become too real, or you'll die yourself. That is the objection to meditating upon death. We are subdued to what we work in. I have felt the same temptation, and had to sheer off. I want to go on living a bit."

"So do I."

A friendliness, as of dwarfs shaking hands, was in the air. Both man and woman were at the height of their powers—sensible, honest, even subtle. They spoke the same language, and held the same opinions, and the variety of age and sex did not divide them. Yet they were dissatisfied. When they agreed, "I want to go on living a bit," or, "I don't believe in God," the words were followed by a curious backwash as though the universe had displaced itself to fill up a tiny void, or as though they had seen their own gestures from an immense height—dwarfs talking, shaking hands and assuring each other that they stood on the same footing of insight. They did not think they were wrong, because as soon as honest people think they are wrong instability sets up. Not for them was an infinite goal behind the stars, and they never sought it. But wistfulness descended on them now, as on other occasions; the shadow of the shadow of a dream fell over their clear-cut interests, and objects never seen again seemed messages from another world.

"And I do like you so very much, if I may say so," he affirmed.

"I'm glad, for I like you. Let's meet again."

"We will, in England, if I ever take home leave."

"But I suppose you're not likely to do that yet."

"Quite a chance. I have a scheme on now as a matter of fact."

"Oh, that would be very nice."

So it petered out. Ten days later Adela went off, by the same route as her dead friend. The final beat up before the monsoon had come. The country was stricken and blurred. Its houses, trees and fields were all modelled out of the same brown paste, and the sea at Bombay slid about like broth against the quays. Her last Indian adventure was with Antony, who followed her on to the boat and tried to blackmail her. She had been Mr. Fielding's mistress, Antony said. Perhaps Antony was discontented with his tip. She rang the cabin bell and had him turned out, but his statement created rather a scandal, and people did not speak to her much during the first part of the voyage. Through the Indian Ocean and the Red Sea she was left to herself, and to the dregs of Chandrapore.

With Egypt the atmosphere altered. The clean sands, heaped on each side of the canal, seemed to wipe off everything that was difficult and equivocal, and even Port Said looked pure and charming in the light of a rose-grey morning. She went on shore there with an American missionary, they walked out to the Lesseps statue, they drank the tonic air of the Levant. "To what duties, Miss Quested, are you returning in your own country after your taste of the tropics?" the missionary asked.

"Observe, I don't say to what do you turn, but to what do you *re*-turn. Every life ought to contain both a turn and a *re*-turn. This celebrated pioneer (he pointed to the statue) will make my question clear. He turns to the East, he *re*-turns to the West. You can see it from the cute position of his hands, one of which holds a string of sausages." The missionary looked at her humorously, in order to cover the emptiness of his mind. He had no idea what he meant by "turn" and "return," but he often used words in pairs, for the sake of moral brightness. "I see," she replied. Suddenly, in the Mediterranean clarity, she had seen. Her first duty on returning to England was to look up those other children of Mrs. Moore's, Ralph and Stella, then she would turn to her profession. Mrs. Moore had tended to keep the products of her two marriages apart, and Adela had not come across the younger branch so far.

CHAPTER 30

Another local consequence of the trial was a Hindu-Moslem entente. Loud protestations of amity were exchanged by prominent citizens, and there went with them a genuine desire for a good understanding. Aziz, when he was at the hospital one day, received a visit from rather a sympathetic figure: Mr. Das. The magistrate sought two favours from him: a remedy for shingles and a poem for his brother-in-law's new monthly magazine. He accorded both.

"My dear Das, why, when you tried to send me to prison, should I try to send Mr. Bhattacharya a poem? Eh? That is naturally entirely a joke. I will write him the best I can, but I thought your magazine was for Hindus."

"It is not for Hindus, but Indians generally," he said timidly.

"There is no such person in existence as the general Indian."

"There was not, but there may be when you have written a poem. You are our hero; the whole city is behind you, irrespective of creed."

"I know, but will it last?"

"I fear not," said Das, who had much mental clearness. "And for that reason, if I may say so, do not introduce too many Persian expressions into the poem, and not too much about the bulbul."

"Half a sec," said Aziz, biting his pencil. He was writing out a prescription. "Here you are... Is not this better than a poem?"

"Happy the man who can compose both."

"You are full of compliments to-day."

"I know you bear me a grudge for trying that case," said the other, stretching out his hand impulsively. "You are so kind and friendly, but always I detect irony beneath your manner."

"No, no, what nonsense!" protested Aziz. They shook hands, in a half-embrace that typified the entente. Between people of distant climes there is always the possibility of romance, but the various branches of Indians know too much about each other to surmount the unknowable easily. The approach is prosaic. "Excellent," said Aziz, patting a stout shoulder and thinking, "I wish they did not remind me of cow-dung"; Das thought, "Some Moslems are very violent." They smiled wistfully, each spying the thought in the other's heart, and Das, the more articulate, said: "Excuse my mistakes, realize my limitations. Life is not easy as we know it on the earth."

"Oh, well, about this poem—how did you hear I sometimes scribbled?" he asked, much pleased, and a good deal moved—for literature had always been a solace to him, something that the ugliness of facts could not spoil.

"Professor Godbole often mentioned it, before his departure for Mau."

"How did he hear?"

"He too was a poet; do you not divine each other?"

Flattered by the invitation, he got to work that evening. The feel of the pen between his fingers generated bulbuls at once. His poem was again about the decay of Islam and the brevity of love; as sad and sweet as he could contrive, but not nourished by personal experience, and of no interest to these excellent Hindus. Feeling dissatisfied, he rushed to the other extreme, and wrote a satire, which was too libellous to print. He could only express pathos or venom, though most of his life had no concern with either. He loved poetry—science was merely an acquisition, which he laid aside when unobserved like his European dress—and this evening he longed to compose a new song which should be acclaimed by multitudes and even sung in the fields. In what language shall it be written? And what shall it announce? He vowed to see more of Indians who were not Mohammedans, and never to look backward. It is the only healthy course. Of what help, in this latitude and hour, are the glories of Cordova and Samarcand? They have gone, and while we lament them the English occupy Delhi and exclude us from East Africa. Islam itself, though true, throws cross-lights over the path to freedom. The song of the future must transcend creed.

The poem for Mr. Bhattacharya never got written, but it had an effect. It led him towards the vague and bulky figure of a mother-land. He was without natural affection for the land of his birth, but the Marabar Hills drove him to it. Half closing his eyes, he attempted to love India. She must imitate Japan. Not until she is a nation will her sons be treated with respect. He grew harder and less approachable. The English, whom he had laughed at or ignored, persecuted him everywhere; they had even thrown nets over his dreams. "My great mistake has been taking our rulers as a joke," he said to Hamidullah next day; who replied with a sigh: "It is far the wisest way to take them, but not possible in the long run. Sooner or later a disaster such as yours occurs, and reveals their secret thoughts about our character. If God himself descended from heaven into their club and said you were innocent, they would disbelieve him. Now you see why Mahmoud Ali and self waste so much time over intrigues and associate with creatures like Ram Chand."

"I cannot endure committees. I shall go right away."

"Where to? Turtons and Burtons, all are the same."

"But not in an Indian state."

"I believe the Politicals are obliged to have better manners. It amounts to no more."

"I do want to get away from British India, even to a poor job. I think I could write poetry there. I wish I had lived in Babur's time and fought and written for him. Gone, gone, and not even any use to say 'Gone, gone,' for it weakens us while we say it. We need a king, Hamidullah; it would make our lives easier. As it is, we must try to appreciate these quaint Hindus. My notion now is to try for some post as doctor in one of their states."

"Oh, that is going much too far."

"It is not going as far as Mr. Ram Chand."

"But the money, the money—they will never pay an adequate salary, those savage Rajahs."

"I shall never be rich anywhere, it is outside my character."

"If you had been sensible and made Miss Quested pay——"

"I chose not to. Discussion of the past is useless," he said, with sudden sharpness of tone. "I have allowed her to keep her fortune and buy herself a husband in England, for which it will be very necessary. Don't mention the matter again."

"Very well, but your life must continue a poor man's; no holidays in Kashmir for you yet, you must stick to your profession and rise to a highly paid post, not retire to a jungle-state and write poems. Educate your children, read the latest scientific periodicals, compel European doctors to respect you. Accept the consequences of your own actions like a man."

Aziz winked at him slowly and said: "We are not in the law courts. There are many ways of being a man; mine is to express what is deepest in my heart."

"To such a remark there is certainly no reply," said Hamidullah, moved. Recovering himself and smiling, he said: "Have you heard this naughty rumour that Mohammed Latif has got hold of?"

"Which?"

"When Miss Quested stopped in the College, Fielding used to visit her... rather too late in the evening, the servants say."

"A pleasant change for her if he did," said Aziz, making a curious face.

"But you understand my meaning?"

The young man winked again and said: "Just! Still, your meaning doesn't help me out of my difficulties. I am determined to leave Chandrapore. The problem is, for where? I am determined to write poetry. The problem is, about what? You give me no assistance." Then, surprising both Hamidullah and himself, he had an explosion of nerves. "But who does give me assistance? No one is my friend. All are traitors, even my own children. I have had enough of friends."

"I was going to suggest we go behind the purdah, but your three treacherous children are there, so you will not want to."

"I am sorry, it is ever since I was in prison my temper is strange; take me, forgive me."

"Nureddin's mother is visiting my wife now. That is all right, I think."

"They come before me separately, but not so far together. You had better prepare them for the united shock of my face."

"No, let us surprise them without warning, far too much nonsense still goes on among our ladies. They pretended at the time of your trial they would give up purdah; indeed, those of them who can write composed a document to that effect, and now it ends in humbug. You know how deeply they all respect Fielding, but not one of them has seen him. My wife says she will, but always when he calls there is some excuse—she is not feeling well, she is ashamed of the room, she has no nice sweets to offer him, only Elephants' Ears, and if I say Elephants' Ears are Mr. Fielding's favourite sweet, she replies that he will know how badly hers are made, so she cannot see him on their account. For fifteen years, my dear boy, have I argued with my begum, for fifteen years, and never gained a point, yet the missionaries inform us our women are down-trodden. If you want a subject for a poem, take this: The Indian lady as she is and not as she is supposed to be."

CHAPTER 31

Aziz had no sense of evidence. The sequence of his emotions decided his beliefs, and led to the tragic coolness between himself and his English friend. They had conquered but were not to be crowned. Fielding was away at a conference, and after the rumour about Miss Quested had been with him undisturbed for a few days, he assumed it was true. He had no objection on moral grounds to his friends amusing themselves, and Cyril, being middle-aged, could no longer expect the pick of the female market, and must take his amusement where he could find it. But he resented him making up to this particular woman, whom he still regarded as his enemy; also, why had he not been told? What is friendship without confidences? He himself had told things sometimes regarded as shocking, and the Englishman had listened, tolerant, but surrendering nothing in return.

He met Fielding at the railway station on his return, agreed to dine with him, and then started taxing him by the oblique method, outwardly merry. An avowed European scandal there was—Mr. McBryde and Miss Derek. Miss Derek's faithful attachment to Chandrapore was now explained: Mr. McBryde had been caught in her room, and his wife was divorcing him. "That pure-minded fellow. However, he will blame the Indian climate. Everything is our fault really. Now, have I not discovered an important piece of news for you, Cyril?"

"Not very," said Fielding, who took little interest in distant sins. "Listen to mine." Aziz' face lit up. "At the conference, it was settled..."

"This evening will do for schoolmastery. I should go straight to the Minto now, the cholera looks bad. We begin to have local cases as well as imported. In fact, the whole of life is somewhat sad. The new Civil Surgeon is the same as the last, but does not yet dare to be. That is all any administrative change amounts to. All my suffering has won nothing for us. But look here, Cyril, while I remember it. There's gossip about you as well as McBryde. They say that you and Miss Quested became also rather too intimate friends. To speak perfectly frankly, they say you and she have been guilty of impropriety."

"They would say that."

"It's all over the town, and may injure your reputation. You know, everyone is by no means your supporter. I have tried all I could to silence such a story."

"Don't bother. Miss Quested has cleared out at last."

"It is those who stop in the country, not those who leave it, whom such a story injures. Imagine my dismay and anxiety. I could scarcely get a wink of sleep. First my name was coupled with her and now it is yours."

"Don't use such exaggerated phrases."

"As what?"

"As dismay and anxiety."

"Have I not lived all my life in India? Do I not know what produces a bad impression here?" His voice shot up rather crossly.

"Yes, but the scale, the scale. You always get the scale wrong, my dear fellow. A pity there is this rumour, but such a very small pity—so small that we may as well talk of something else."

"You mind for Miss Quested's sake, though. I can see from your face."

"As far as I do mind. I travel light."

"Cyril, that boastfulness about travelling light will be your ruin. It is raising up enemies against you on all sides, and makes me feel excessively uneasy."

"What enemies?"

Since Aziz had only himself in mind, he could not reply. Feeling a fool, he became angrier. "I have given you list after list of the people who cannot be trusted in this city. In your position I should have the sense to know I was surrounded by enemies. You observe I speak in a low voice. It is because I see your sais is new. How do I know he isn't a spy?" He lowered his voice: "Every third servant is a spy."

"Now, what is the matter?" he asked, smiling.

"Do you contradict my last remark?"

"It simply doesn't affect me. Spies are as thick as mosquitoes, but it's years before I shall meet the one that kills me. You've something else in your mind."

"I've not; don't be ridiculous."

"You have. You're cross with me about something or other."

Any direct attack threw him out of action. Presently he said: "So you and Madamsell Adela used to amuse one another in the evening, naughty boy."

Those drab and high-minded talks had scarcely made for dalliance. Fielding was so startled at the story being taken seriously, and so disliked being called a naughty boy, that he lost his head and cried: "You little rotter! Well, I'm damned. Amusement indeed. Is it likely at such a time?"

"Oh, I beg your pardon, I'm sure. The licentious Oriental imagination was at work," he replied, speaking gaily, but cut to the heart; for hours after his mistake he bled inwardly.

"You see, Aziz, the circumstances... also the girl was still engaged to Heaslop, also I never felt..."

"Yes, yes; but you didn't contradict what I said, so I thought it was true. Oh dear, East and West. Most misleading. Will you please put your little rotter down at his hospital?"

"You're not offended?"

"Most certainly I am not."

"If you are, this must be cleared up later on."

"It has been," he answered, dignified. "I believe absolutely what you say, and of that there need be no further question."

"But the way I said it must be cleared up. I was unintentionally rude. Unreserved regrets."

"The fault is entirely mine."

Tangles like this still interrupted their intercourse. A pause in the wrong place, an intonation misunderstood, and a whole conversation went awry. Fielding had been startled, not shocked, but how convey the difference? There is always trouble when two people do not think of sex at the same moment, always mutual resentment and surprise, even when the two people are of the same race. He began to recapitulate his feelings about Miss Quested. Aziz cut him short with: "But I believe you, I believe. Mohammed Latif shall be severely punished for inventing this."

"Oh, leave it alone, like all gossip—it's merely one of those half-alive things that try to crowd out real life. Take no notice, it'll vanish, like poor old Mrs. Moore's tombs."

"Mohammed Latif has taken to intriguing. We are already much displeased with him. Will it satisfy you if we send him back to his family without a present?"

"We'll discuss M.L. at dinner."

His eyes went clotted and hard. "Dinner. This is most unlucky—— I forgot. I have promised to dine with Das."

"Bring Das to me."

"He will have invited other friends."

"You are coming to dinner with me as arranged," said Fielding, looking away. "I don't stand this. You are coming to dinner with me. You come."

They had reached the hospital now. Fielding continued round the Maidan alone. He was annoyed with himself, but counted on dinner to pull things straight. At the post office he saw the Collector. Their vehicles were parked side by side while their servants competed in the interior of the building. "Good morning; so you are back," said Turton icily. "I should be glad if you will put in your appearance at the club this evening."

"I have accepted re-election, sir. Do you regard it as necessary I should come? I should be glad to be excused; indeed, I have a dinner engagement this evening."

"It is not a question of your feelings, but of the wish of the Lieutenant-Governor. Perhaps you will ask me whether I speak officially. I do. I shall expect you this evening at six. We shall not interfere with your subsequent plans."

He attended the grim little function in due course. The skeletons of hospitality rattled—"Have a peg, have a drink." He talked for five minutes to Mrs. Blakiston, who was the only surviving female. He talked to McBryde, who was defiant about his divorce, conscious that he had sinned as a sahib. He talked to Major Roberts, the new Civil Surgeon; and to young Milner, the new City Magistrate; but the more the club changed, the more it promised to be the same thing. "It is no good," he thought, as he returned past the mosque, "we all build upon sand; and the more modern the country gets, the worse'll be the crash. In the old eighteenth century, when cruelty and injustice raged, an invisible power repaired their ravages. Everything echoes now; there's no stopping the echo. The original sound may be harmless, but the echo is always evil." This reflection about an echo lay at the verge of Fielding's mind. He could never develop it. It belonged to the universe that he had missed or rejected. And the mosque missed it too. Like himself, those shallow arcades provided but a limited asylum. "There is no God but God" doesn't carry us far through the complexities of matter and spirit; it is only a game with words, really, a religious pun, not a religious truth.

He found Aziz overtired and dispirited, and he determined not to allude to their misunderstanding until the end of the evening; it would be more acceptable then. He made a clean breast about the club—said he had only gone under compulsion, and should never attend again unless the order was renewed. "In other words, probably never; for I am going quite soon to England."

"I thought you might end in England," he said very quietly, then changed the conversation. Rather awkwardly they ate their dinner, then went out to sit in the Mogul garden-house.

"I am only going for a little time. On official business. My service is anxious to get me away from Chandrapore for a bit. It is obliged to value me highly, but does not care for me. The situation is somewhat humorous."

"What is the nature of the business? Will it leave you much spare time?"

"Enough to see my friends."

"I expected you to make such a reply. You are a faithful friend. Shall we now talk about something else?"

"Willingly. What subject?"

"Poetry," he said, with tears in his eyes. "Let us discuss why poetry has lost the power of making men brave. My mother's father was also a poet, and fought against you in the Mutiny. I might equal him if there was another mutiny. As it is, I am a doctor, who has won a case and has three children to support, and whose chief subject of conversation is official plans."

"Let us talk about poetry." He turned his mind to the innocuous subject. "You people are sadly circumstanced. Whatever are you to write about? You cannot say, 'The rose is faded,' for evermore. We know it's faded. Yet you can't have patriotic poetry of the 'India, my India' type, when it's nobody's India."

"I like this conversation. It may lead to something interesting."

"You are quite right in thinking that poetry must touch life. When I knew you first, you used it as an incantation."

"I was a child when you knew me first. Everyone was my friend then. The Friend: a Persian expression for God. But I do not want to be a religious poet either."

"I hoped you would be."

"Why, when you yourself are an atheist?"

"There is something in religion that may not be true, but has not yet been sung."

"Explain in detail."

"Something that the Hindus have perhaps found."

"Let them sing it."

"Hindus are unable to sing."

"Cyril, you sometimes make a sensible remark. That will do for poetry for the present. Let us now return to your English visit."

"We haven't discussed poetry for two seconds," said the other, smiling.

But Aziz was addicted to cameos. He held the tiny conversation in his hand, and felt it epitomized his problem. For an instant he recalled his wife, and, as happens when a memory is intense, the past became the future, and he saw her with him in a quiet Hindu jungle native state, far away from foreigners. He said: "I suppose you will visit Miss Quested."

"If I have time. It will be strange seeing her in Hampstead."

"What is Hampstead?"

"An artistic and thoughtful little suburb of London——"

"And there she lives in comfort: you will enjoy seeing her... Dear me, I've got a headache this evening. Perhaps I am going to have cholera. With your permission, I'll leave early."

"When would you like the carriage?"

"Don't trouble—I'll bike."

"But you haven't got your bicycle. My carriage fetched you—let it take you away."

"Sound reasoning," he said, trying to be gay. "I have not got my bicycle. But I am seen too often in your carriage. I am thought to take advantage of your generosity by Mr. Ram Chand." He was out of sorts and uneasy. The conversation jumped from topic to topic in a broken-backed fashion. They were affectionate and intimate, but nothing clicked tight.

"Aziz, you have forgiven me the stupid remark I made this morning?"

"When you called me a little rotter?"

"Yes, to my eternal confusion. You know how fond I am of you."

"That is nothing, of course, we all of us make mistakes. In a friendship such as ours a few slips are of no consequence."

But as he drove off, something depressed him—a dull pain of body or mind, waiting to rise to the surface. When he reached the bungalow he wanted to return and say something very affectionate; instead, he gave the sais a heavy tip, and sat down gloomily on the bed, and Hassan massaged him incompetently. The eye-flies had colonized the top of an almeira; the red stains on the durry were thicker, for Mohammed Latif had slept here during his imprisonment and spat a good deal; the table drawer was scarred where the police had forced it open; everything in Chandrapore was used up, including the air. The trouble rose to the surface now: he was suspicious; he suspected his friend of intending to marry Miss Quested for the sake of her money, and of going to England for that purpose.

"Huzoor?"—for he had muttered.

"Look at those flies on the ceiling. Why have you not drowned them?"

"Huzoor, they return."

"Like all evil things."

To divert the conversation, Hassan related how the kitchen-boy had killed a snake, good, but killed it by cutting it in two, bad, because it becomes two snakes.

"When he breaks a plate, does it become two plates?"

"Glasses and a new teapot will similarly be required, also for myself a coat."

Aziz sighed. Each for himself. One man needs a coat, another a rich wife; each approaches his goal by a clever detour. Fielding had saved the girl a fine of twenty thousand rupees, and now followed her to England. If he desired to marry her, all was explained; she would bring him a larger dowry. Aziz did not believe his own suspicions—better if he had, for then he would have denounced and cleared the situation up. Suspicion and belief could in his mind exist side by side. They sprang from different sources, and need never intermingle. Suspicion in the Oriental is a sort of malignant tumour, a mental malady, that makes him self-conscious and unfriendly suddenly; he trusts and mistrusts at the same time in a way the Westerner cannot comprehend. It is his demon, as the Westerner's is hypocrisy. Aziz was seized by it, and his fancy built a satanic castle, of which the foundation had been laid when he talked at Dilkusha under the stars. The girl had surely been Cyril's mistress when she stopped in the College—Mohammed Latif was right. But was that all? Perhaps it was Cyril who followed her into the cave... No; impossible. Cyril hadn't been on the Kawa Dol at all. Impossible. Ridiculous. Yet the fancy left him trembling with misery. Such treachery—if true—would have been the worst in Indian history; nothing so vile, not even the murder of Afzul Khan by Sivaji. He was shaken, as though by a truth, and told Hassan to leave him.

Next day he decided to take his children back to Mussoorie. They had come down for the trial, that he might bid them farewell, and had stayed on at Hamidullah's for the rejoicings. Major Roberts would give him leave, and during his absence Fielding would go off to England. The idea suited both his beliefs and his suspicions. Events would prove which was right, and preserve, in either case, his dignity.

Fielding was conscious of something hostile, and because he was really fond of Aziz his optimism failed him. Travelling light is less easy as soon as affection is involved. Unable to jog forward in the serene hope that all would come right, he wrote an elaborate letter in the rather modern style: "It is on my mind that you think me a prude about women. I had rather you thought anything else of me. If I live impeccably now, it is only because I am well on the forties—a period of revision. In the eighties I shall revise again. And before the nineties come—I shall be revised! But, alive or dead, I am absolutely devoid of morals. Do kindly grasp this about me." Aziz did not care for the letter at all. It hurt his delicacy. He liked confidences, however gross, but generalizations and comparisons always repelled him. Life is not a scientific manual. He replied coldly, regretting his inability to return from Mussoorie before his friend sailed: "But I must take my poor little holiday while I can. All must be economy henceforward, all hopes of Kashmir have vanished forever and ever. When you return I shall be slaving far away in some new post."

And Fielding went, and in the last gutterings of Chandrapore—heaven and earth both looking like toffee—the Indian's bad fancies were confirmed. His friends encouraged them, for though they had liked the Principal, they felt uneasy at his getting to know so much about their private affairs. Mahmoud Ali soon declared that treachery was afoot. Hamidullah murmured, "Certainly of late he no longer addressed us with his former frankness," and warned Aziz "not to expect too much—he and she are, after all, both members of another race." "Where are my twenty thousand rupees?" he thought. He was absolutely indifferent to money—not merely generous with it, but promptly paying his debts when he could remember to do so—yet these rupees haunted his mind, because he had been tricked about them, and allowed them to escape overseas, like so much of the wealth of India. Cyril would marry Miss Quested—he grew certain of it, all the unexplained residue of the Marabar contributing. It was the natural conclusion of the horrible senseless picnic, and before long he persuaded himself that the wedding had actually taken place.

CHAPTER 32

Egypt was charming—a green strip of carpet and walking up and down it four sorts of animals and one sort of man. Fielding's business took him there for a few days. He re-embarked at Alexandria—bright blue sky, constant wind, clean low coast-line, as against the intricacies of Bombay. Crete welcomed him next with the long snowy ridge of its mountains, and then came Venice. As he landed on the piazzetta a cup of beauty was lifted to his lips, and he drank with a sense of disloyalty. The buildings of Venice, like the mountains of Crete and the fields of Egypt, stood in the right place, whereas in poor India everything was placed wrong. He had forgotten the beauty of form among idol temples and lumpy hills; indeed, without form, how can there be beauty? Form stammered here and there in a mosque, became rigid through nervousness even, but oh these Italian churches! San Giorgio standing on the island which could scarcely have risen from the waves without it, the Salute holding the entrance of a canal which, but for it, would not be the Grand Canal! In the old undergraduate days he had wrapped himself up in the many-coloured blanket of St. Mark's, but something more precious than mosaics and marbles was offered to him now: the harmony between the works of man and the earth that upholds them, the civilization that has escaped muddle, the spirit in a reasonable form, with flesh and blood subsisting. Writing picture post-cards to his Indian friends, he felt that all of them would miss the joys he experienced now, the joys of form, and that this constituted a serious barrier. They would see the sumptuousness of Venice, not its shape, and though Venice was not Europe, it was part of the Mediterranean harmony. The Mediterranean is the human norm. When men leave that exquisite lake, whether through the Bosphorus or the Pillars of Hercules, they approach the monstrous and extraordinary; and the southern exit leads to the strangest experience of all. Turning his back on it yet again, he took the train northward, and tender romantic fancies that he thought were dead for ever, flowered when he saw the buttercups and daisies of June.

Part 3

Temple

CHAPTER 33

Some hundreds of miles westward of the Marabar Hills, and two years later in time, Professor Narayan Godbole stands in the presence of God. God is not born yet—that will occur at midnight—but He has also been born centuries ago, nor can He ever be born, because He is the Lord of the Universe, who transcends human processes. He is, was not, is not, was. He and Professor Godbole stood at opposite ends of the same strip of carpet.

> *"Tukaram, Tukaram,*
> *Thou art my father and mother and everybody.*
> *Tukaram, Tukaram,*
> *Thou art my father and mother and everybody.*
> *Tukaram, Tukaram,*
> *Thou art my father and mother and everybody.*
> *Tukaram, Tukaram,*
> *Thou art my father and mother and everybody.*
> *Tukaram..."*

This corridor in the palace at Mau opened through other corridors into a courtyard. It was of beautiful hard white stucco, but its pillars and vaulting could scarcely be seen behind coloured rags, iridescent balls, chandeliers of opaque pink glass, and murky photographs framed crookedly. At the end was the small but famous shrine of the dynastic cult, and the God to be born was largely a silver image the size of a teaspoon. Hindus sat on either side of the carpet where they could find room, or overflowed into the adjoining corridors and the courtyard—Hindus, Hindus only, mild-featured men, mostly villagers, for whom anything outside their villages passed in a dream. They were the toiling ryot, whom some call the real India. Mixed with them sat a few tradesmen out of the little town, officials, courtiers, scions of the ruling house. Schoolboys kept inefficient order. The assembly was in a tender, happy state unknown to an English crowd, it seethed like a beneficent potion. When the villagers broke cordon for a glimpse of the silver image, a most beautiful and radiant expression came into their faces, a beauty in which there was nothing personal, for it caused them all to resemble one another during the moment of its indwelling, and only when it was withdrawn did they revert to individual clods. And so with the music. Music there was, but from so many sources that the sum-total was untrammelled. The braying banging crooning melted into a single mass which trailed round the palace before joining the thunder. Rain fell at intervals throughout the night.

It was the turn of Professor Godbole's choir. As Minister of Education, he gained this special honour. When the previous group of singers dispersed into the crowd, he pressed forward from the back, already in full voice, that the chain of sacred sounds might be uninterrupted. He was barefoot and in white, he wore a pale blue turban; his gold pince-nez had caught in a jasmine garland, and lay sideways down his nose. He and the six colleagues who supported him clashed their cymbals, hit small drums, droned upon a portable harmonium, and sang:

"Tukaram, Tukaram,
Thou art my father and mother and everybody.
Tukaram, Tukaram,

Thou art my father and mother and everybody.
Tukaram, Tukaram..."

They sang not even to the God who confronted them, but to a saint; they did not one thing which the non-Hindu would feel dramatically correct; this approaching triumph of India was a muddle (as we call it), a frustration of reason and form. Where was the God Himself, in whose honour the congregation had gathered? Indistinguishable in the jumble of His own altar, huddled out of sight amid images of inferior descent, smothered under rose-leaves, overhung by oleographs, outblazed by golden tablets representing the Rajah's ancestors, and entirely obscured, when the wind blew, by the tattered foliage of a banana. Hundreds of electric lights had been lit in His honour (worked by an engine whose thumps destroyed the rhythm of the hymn). Yet His face could not be seen. Hundreds of His silver dishes were piled around Him with the minimum of effect. The inscriptions which the poets of the State had composed were hung where they could not be read, or had twitched their drawing-pins out of the stucco, and one of them (composed in English to indicate His universality) consisted, by an unfortunate slip of the draughtsman, of the words, "God si Love."

God si Love. Is this the first message of India?

"*Tukaram, Tukaram...,*"

continued the choir, reinforced by a squabble behind the purdah curtain, where two mothers tried to push their children at the same moment to the front. A little girl's leg shot out like an eel. In the courtyard, drenched by the rain, the small Europeanized band stumbled off into a waltz. "Nights of Gladness" they were playing. The singers were not perturbed by this rival, they lived beyond competition. It was long before the tiny fragment of Professor Godbole that attended to outside things decided that his pince-nez was in trouble, and that until it was adjusted he could not choose a new hymn. He laid down one cymbal, with the other he clashed the air, with his free hand he fumbled at the flowers round his neck. A colleague assisted him. Singing into one another's grey moustaches, they disentangled the chain from the tinsel into which it had sunk. Godbole consulted the music-book, said a word to the drummer, who broke rhythm, made a thick little blur of sound, and produced a new rhythm. This was more exciting, the inner images it evoked more definite, and the singers' expressions became fatuous and languid. They loved all men, the whole universe, and scraps of their past, tiny splinters of detail, emerged for a moment to melt into the universal warmth. Thus Godbole, though she was not important to him, remembered an old woman he had met in Chandrapore days. Chance brought her into his mind while it was in this heated state, he did not select her, she happened to occur among the throng of soliciting images, a tiny splinter, and he impelled her by his spiritual force to that place where completeness can be found. Completeness, not reconstruction. His senses grew thinner, he remembered a wasp seen he forgot where, perhaps on a stone. He loved the wasp equally, he impelled it likewise, he was imitating God. And the stone where the wasp clung—could he... no, he could not, he had been wrong to attempt the stone, logic and conscious effort had seduced, he came back to the strip of red carpet and discovered that he was dancing upon it. Up and down, a third of the way to the altar and back again, clashing his cymbals, his little legs twinkling, his companions dancing with him and each other. Noise, noise, the Europeanized band louder, incense on the altar, sweat, the blaze of lights, wind in the bananas, noise, thunder, eleven-fifty by his wrist-watch, seen as he threw up his hands and detached the tiny reverberation that was his soul. Louder shouts in the crowd. He danced on. The boys and men who were squatting in the aisles were lifted forcibly and dropped without changing their shapes into the laps of their neighbours. Down the path thus cleared advanced a litter. It was the aged ruler of the state, brought against the advice of his physicians to witness the Birth ceremony.

No one greeted the Rajah, nor did he wish it; this was no moment for human glory. Nor could the litter be set down, lest it defiled the temple by becoming a throne. He was lifted out of it while its feet remained in air, and deposited on the carpet close to the altar, his immense beard was straightened, his legs tucked under him, a paper containing red powder was placed in his hand. There he sat, leaning against a pillar, exhausted with illness, his eyes magnified by many unshed tears.

He had not to wait long. In a land where all else was unpunctual, the hour of the Birth was chronometrically observed. Three minutes before it was due, a Brahman brought forth a model of the village of Gokul (the Bethlehem in that nebulous story) and placed it in front of the altar. The model was on a wooden tray about a yard square; it was of clay, and was gaily blue and white with streamers and paint. Here, upon a chair too small for him and with a head too large, sat King Kansa, who is Herod, directing the murder of some Innocents, and in a corner, similarly proportioned, stood the father and mother of the Lord, warned to depart in a dream. The model was not holy, but more than a decoration, for it diverted men from the actual image of the God, and increased their sacred bewilderment. Some of the villagers thought the Birth had occurred, saying with truth that the Lord must have been born, or they could not see Him. But the clock struck midnight, and simultaneously the rending note of the conch broke forth, followed by the trumpeting of elephants; all who had packets of powder threw them at the altar, and in the rosy dust and incense, and clanging and shouts, Infinite Love took upon itself the form of *Shri Krishna*, and saved the world. All sorrow was annihilated, not only for Indians, but for foreigners, birds, caves, railways, and the stars; all became joy, all laughter; there had never been disease nor doubt, misunderstanding, cruelty, fear. Some jumped in the air, others flung themselves prone and embraced the bare feet of the universal lover; the women behind the purdah slapped and shrieked; the little girl slipped out and danced by herself, her black pigtails flying. Not an orgy of the body; the tradition of that shrine forbade it. But the human spirit had tried by a desperate contortion to ravish the unknown, flinging down science and history in the struggle, yes, beauty herself. Did it succeed? Books written afterwards say "Yes." But how, if there is such an event, can it be remembered afterwards? How can it be expressed in anything but itself? Not only from the unbeliever are mysteries hid, but the adept himself cannot retain them. He may think, if he chooses, that he has been with God, but as soon as he thinks it, it becomes history, and falls under the rules of time.

A cobra of papier-mâché now appeared on the carpet, also a wooden cradle swinging from a frame. Professor Godbole approached the latter with a red silk napkin in his arms. The napkin was God, not that it was, and the image remained in the blur of the altar. It was just a napkin, folded into a shape which indicated a baby's. The Professor dandled it and gave it to the Rajah, who, making a great effort, said, "I name this child Shri Krishna," and tumbled it into the cradle. Tears poured from his eyes, because he had seen the Lord's salvation. He was too weak to exhibit the silk baby to his people, his privilege in former years. His attendants lifted him up, a new path was cleared through the crowd, and he was carried away to a less sacred part of the palace. There, in a room accessible to Western science by an outer staircase, his physician, Dr. Aziz, awaited him. His Hindu physician, who had accompanied him to the shrine, briefly reported his symptoms. As the ecstasy receded, the invalid grew fretful. The bumping of the steam engine that worked the dynamo disturbed him, and he asked for what reason it had been introduced into his home. They replied that they would enquire, and administered a sedative.

Down in the sacred corridors, joy had seethed to jollity. It was their duty to play various games to amuse the newly born God, and to simulate his sports with the wanton dairymaids of Brindaban.

Butter played a prominent part in these. When the cradle had been removed, the principal nobles of the state gathered together for an innocent frolic. They removed their turbans, and one put a lump of butter on his forehead, and waited for it to slide down his nose into his mouth. Before it could arrive, another stole up behind him, snatched the melting morsel, and swallowed it himself. All laughed exultantly at discovering that the divine sense of humour coincided with their own. "God si love!" There is fun in heaven. God can play practical jokes upon Himself, draw chairs away from beneath His own posteriors, set His own turbans on fire, and steal His own petticoats when He bathes. By sacrificing good taste, this worship achieved what Christianity has shirked: the inclusion of merriment. All spirit as well as all matter must participate in salvation, and if practical jokes are banned, the circle is incomplete. Having swallowed the butter, they played another game which chanced to be graceful: the fondling of Shri Krishna under the similitude of a child. A pretty red and gold ball is thrown, and he who catches it chooses a child from the crowd, raises it in his arms, and carries it round to be caressed. All stroke the darling creature for the Creator's sake, and murmur happy words. The child is restored to his parents, the ball thrown on, and another child becomes for a moment the World's Desire. And the Lord bounds hither and thither through the aisles, chance, and the sport of chance, irradiating little mortals with His immortality... When they had played this long enough—and being exempt from boredom, they played it again and again, they played it again and again—they took many sticks and hit them together, whack smack, as though they fought the Pandava wars, and threshed and churned with them, and later on they hung from the roof of the temple, in a net, a great black earthenware jar, which was painted here and there with red, and wreathed with dried figs. Now came a rousing sport. Springing up, they struck at the jar with their sticks. It cracked, broke, and a mass of greasy rice and milk poured on to their faces. They ate and smeared one another's mouths, and dived between each other's legs for what had been pashed upon the carpet. This way and that spread the divine mess, until the line of schoolboys, who had somewhat fended off the crowd, broke for their share. The corridors, the courtyard, were filled with benign confusion. Also the flies awoke and claimed their share of God's bounty. There was no quarrelling, owing to the nature of the gift, for blessed is the man who confers it on another, he imitates God. And those "imitations," those "substitutions," continued to flicker through the assembly for many hours, awaking in each man, according to his capacity, an emotion that he would not have had otherwise. No definite image survived; at the Birth it was questionable whether a silver doll or a mud village, or a silk napkin, or an intangible spirit, or a pious resolution, had been born. Perhaps all these things! Perhaps none! Perhaps all birth is an allegory! Still, it was the main event of the religious year. It caused strange thoughts. Covered with grease and dust, Professor Godbole had once more developed the life of his spirit. He had, with increasing vividness, again seen Mrs. Moore, and round her faintly clinging forms of trouble. He was a Brahman, she Christian, but it made no difference, it made no difference whether she was a trick of his memory or a telepathic appeal. It was his duty, as it was his desire, to place himself in the position of the God and to love her, and to place himself in her position and to say to the God, "Come, come, come, come." This was all he could do. How inadequate! But each according to his own capacities, and he knew that his own were small. "One old Englishwoman and one little, little wasp," he thought, as he stepped out of the temple into the grey of a pouring wet morning. "It does not seem much, still it is more than I am myself."

CHAPTER 34

Dr. Aziz left the palace at the same time. As he returned to his house—which stood in a pleasant garden further up the main street of the town—he could see his old patron paddling and capering in the slush ahead. "Hullo!" he called, and it was the wrong remark, for the devotee indicated by circular gestures of his arms that he did not desire to be disturbed. He added, "Sorry," which was right, for Godbole twisted his head till it didn't belong to his body, and said in a strained voice that had no connection with his mind: "He arrived at the European Guest House perhaps—at least possibly."

"Did he? Since when?"

But time was too definite. He waved his arm more dimly and disappeared. Aziz knew who "he" was—Fielding—but he refused to think about him, because it disturbed his life, and he still trusted the floods to prevent him from arriving. A fine little river issued from his garden gate and gave him much hope. It was impossible that anyone could get across from Deora in such weather as this. Fielding's visit was official. He had been transferred from Chandrapore, and sent on a tour through Central India to see what the remoter states were doing with regard to English education. He had married, he had done the expected with Miss Quested, and Aziz had no wish to see him again.

"Dear old Godbole," he thought, and smiled. He had no religious curiosity, and had never discovered the meaning of this annual antic, but he was well assured that Godbole was a dear old man. He had come to Mau through him and remained on his account. Without him he could never have grasped problems so totally different from those of Chandrapore. For here the cleavage was between Brahman and non-Brahman; Moslems and English were quite out of the running, and sometimes not mentioned for days. Since Godbole was a Brahman, Aziz was one also for purposes of intrigue: they would often joke about it together. The fissures in the Indian soil are infinite: Hinduism, so solid from a distance, is riven into sects and clans, which radiate and join, and change their names according to the aspect from which they are approached. Study it for years with the best teachers, and when you raise your head, nothing they have told you quite fits. Aziz, the day of his inauguration, had remarked: "I study nothing, I respect"—making an excellent impression. There was now a minimum of prejudice against him. Nominally under a Hindu doctor, he was really chief medicine man to the court. He had to drop inoculation and such Western whims, but even at Chandrapore his profession had been a game, centring round the operating table, and here in the backwoods he let his instruments rust, ran his little hospital at half steam, and caused no undue alarm.

His impulse to escape from the English was sound. They had frightened him permanently, and there are only two reactions against fright: to kick and scream on committees, or to retreat to a remote jungle, where the sahib seldom comes. His old lawyer friends wanted him to stop in British India and help agitate, and might have prevailed, but for the treachery of Fielding. The news had not surprised him in the least. A rift had opened between them after the trial when Cyril had not joined in his procession; those advocacies of the girl had increased it; then came the post-cards from Venice, so cold, so unfriendly that all agreed that something was wrong; and finally, after a silence, the expected letter from Hampstead. Mahmoud Ali was with him at the time. "Some news that will surprise you. I am to marry someone whom you know..." He did not read further. "Here it comes, answer for me——" and he threw it to Mahmoud Ali. Subsequent letters he destroyed unopened. It was the end of a foolish experiment. And though sometimes at the back of his mind he felt that Fielding had made sacrifices for him, it was now all confused with his genuine hatred of the English. "I am an Indian at last," he thought, standing motionless in the rain.

Life passed pleasantly, the climate was healthy so that the children could be with him all the year round, and he had married again—not exactly a marriage, but he liked to regard it as one—and he read his Persian, wrote his poetry, had his horse, and sometimes got some shikar while the good Hindus looked the other way. His poems were all on one topic—Oriental womanhood. "The purdah must go," was their burden, "otherwise we shall never be free." And he declared (fantastically) that India would not have been conquered if women as well as men had fought at Plassy. "But we do not show our women to the foreigner"—not explaining how this was to be managed, for he was writing a poem.. Bulbuls and roses would still persist, the pathos of defeated Islam remained in his blood and could not be expelled by modernities. Illogical poems—like their writer. Yet they struck a true note: there cannot be a mother-land without new homes. In one poem—the only one funny old Godbole liked—he had skipped over the mother-land (whom he did not truly love) and gone straight to internationality. "Ah, that is bhakti; ah, my young friend, that is different and very good. Ah, India, who seems not to move, will go straight there while the other nations waste their time. May I translate this particular one into Hindi? In fact, it might be rendered into Sanskrit almost, it is so enlightened. Yes, of course, all your other poems are very good too. His Highness was saying to Colonel Maggs last time he came that we are proud of you"—simpering slightly.

Colonel Maggs was the Political Agent for the neighbourhood and Aziz' dejected opponent. The Criminal Investigation Department kept an eye on Aziz ever since the trial—they had nothing actionable against him, but Indians who have been unfortunate must be watched, and to the end of his life he remained under observation, thanks to Miss Quested's mistake. Colonel Maggs learnt with concern that a suspect was coming to Mau, and, adopting a playful manner, rallied the old Rajah for permitting a Moslem doctor to approach his sacred person. A few years ago, the Rajah would have taken the hint, for the Political Agent then had been a formidable figure, descending with all the thunders of Empire when it was most inconvenient, turning the polity inside out, requiring motor-cars and tiger-hunts, trees cut down that impeded the view from the Guest House, cows milked in his presence, and generally arrogating the control of internal affairs. But there had been a change of policy in high quarters. Local thunders were no longer endorsed, and the group of little states that composed the agency discovered this and began comparing notes with fruitful result. To see how much, or how little, Colonel Maggs would stand, became an agreeable game at Mau, which was played by all the departments of State. He had to stand the appointment of Dr. Aziz. The Rajah did not take the hint, but replied that Hindus were less exclusive than formerly, thanks to the enlightened commands of the Viceroy, and he felt it his duty to move with the times.

Yes, all had gone well hitherto, but now, when the rest of the state was plunged in its festival, he had a crisis of a very different sort. A note awaited him at his house. There was no doubt that Fielding had arrived overnight, nor much doubt that Godbole knew of his arrival, for the note was addressed to him, and he had read it before sending it on to Aziz, and had written in the margin, "Is not this delightful news, but unfortunately my religious duties prevent me from taking any action." Fielding announced that he had inspected Mudkul (Miss Derek's former preserve), that he had nearly been drowned at Deora, that he had reached Mau according to time-table, and hoped to remain there two days, studying the various educational innovations of his old friend. Nor had he come alone. His wife and her brother accompanied him. And then the note turned into the sort of note that always did arrive from the State Guest House. Wanting something. No eggs. Mosquito nets torn. When would they pay their respects to His Highness? Was it correct that a torchlight procession would take place? If so, might they view it? They didn't want to give trouble, but if they might stand in a balcony, or if they might go out in a boat... Aziz tore the note up. He had had enough of showing Miss Quested native life. Treacherous hideous harridan! Bad people altogether. He hoped to avoid them, though this might be difficult, for they would certainly be held up for several days at Mau. Down country, the floods were even worse, and the pale grey faces of lakes had appeared in the direction of the Asirgarh railway station.

CHAPTER 35

Long before he discovered Mau, another young Mohammedan had retired there—a saint. His mother said to him, "Free prisoners." So he took a sword and went up to the fort. He unlocked a door, and the prisoners streamed out and resumed their previous occupations, but the police were too much annoyed and cut off the young man's head. Ignoring its absence, he made his way over the rocks that separate the fort and the town, killing policemen as he went, and he fell outside his mother's house, having accomplished her orders. Consequently there are two shrines to him to-day—that of the Head above, and that of the Body below—and they are worshipped by the few Mohammedans who live near, and by Hindus also. "There is no God but God"; that symmetrical injunction melts in the mild airs of Mau; it belongs to pilgrimages and universities, not to feudalism and agriculture. When Aziz arrived, and found that even Islam was idolatrous, he grew scornful, and longed to purify the place, like Alamgir. But soon he didn't mind, like Akbar. After all, this saint had freed prisoners, and he himself had lain in prison. The Shrine of the Body lay in his own garden and produced a weekly crop of lamps and flowers, and when he saw them he recalled his sufferings. The Shrine of the Head made a nice short walk for the children. He was off duty the morning after the great pujah, and he told them to come.

Jemila held his hand. Ahmed and Karim ran in front, arguing what the body looked like as it came staggering down, and whether they would have been frightened if they met it. He didn't want them to grow up superstitious, so he rebuked them, and they answered yes father, for they were well brought up, but, like himself, they were impervious to argument, and after a polite pause they continued saying what their natures compelled them to say.

A slim, tall eight-sided building stood at the top of the slope, among some bushes. This was the Shrine of the Head. It had not been roofed, and was indeed merely a screen. Inside it crouched a humble dome, and inside that, visible through a grille, was a truncated gravestone, swathed in calico. The inner angles of the screen were cumbered with bees' nests, and a gentle shower of broken wings and other aerial oddments kept falling, and had strewn the damp pavement with their flue. Ahmed, apprized by Mohammed Latif of the character of the bee, said, "They will not hurt us, whose lives are chaste," and pushed boldly in; his sister was more cautious. From the shrine they went to a mosque, which, in size and design, resembled a fire-screen; the arcades of Chandrapore had shrunk to a flat piece of ornamental stucco, with protuberances at either end to suggest minarets. The funny little thing didn't even stand straight, for the rock on which it had been put was slipping down the hill. It, and the shrine, were a strange outcome of the protests of Arabia.

They wandered over the old fort, now deserted, and admired the various views. The scenery, according to their standards, was delightful—the sky grey and black, bellyfuls of rain all over it, the earth pocked with pools of water and slimy with mud. A magnificent monsoon—the best for three years, the tanks already full, bumper crops possible. Out towards the river (the route by which the Fieldings had escaped from Deora) the downpour had been enormous, the mails had to be pulled across by ropes. They could just see the break in the forest trees where the gorge came through, and the rocks above that marked the site of the diamond mine, glistening with wet. Close beneath was the suburban residence of the Junior Rani, isolated by floods, and Her Highness, lax about purdah, to be seen paddling with her handmaidens in the garden and waving her sari at the monkeys on the roof. But better not look close beneath, perhaps—nor towards the European Guest House either. Beyond the Guest House rose another grey-green gloom of hills, covered with temples like little white flames. There were over two hundred gods in that direction alone, who visited each other constantly, and owned numerous cows, and all the betel-leaf industry, besides having shares in the Asirgarh motor omnibus. Many of them were in the palace at this moment, having the time of their lives; others, too large or proud to travel, had sent symbols to represent them. The air was thick with religion and rain.

Their white shirts fluttering, Ahmed and Karim ran about over the fort, shrieking with joy. Presently they intersected a line of prisoners, who were looking aimlessly at an old bronze gun. "Which of you is to be pardoned?" they asked. For to-night was the procession of the Chief God, when He would leave the palace, escorted by the whole power of the State, and pass by the Jail, which stood down in the town now. As He did so, troubling the waters of our civilization, one prisoner would be released, and then He would proceed to the great Mau tank that stretched as far as the Guest House garden, where something else would happen, some final or subsidiary apotheosis, after which He would submit to the experience of sleep. The Aziz family did not grasp as much as this, being Moslem, but the visit to the Jail was common knowledge. Smiling, with downcast eyes, the prisoners discussed with the gentry their chances of salvation. Except for the irons on their legs, they resembled other men, nor did they feel different. Five of them, who had not yet been brought to trial, could expect no pardon, but all who had been convicted were full of hope. They did not distinguish between the God and the Rajah in their minds, both were too far above them; but the guard was better educated, and ventured to enquire after His Highness's health.

"It always improves," replied the medicine man. As a matter of fact, the Rajah was dead, the ceremony overnight had overtaxed his strength. His death was being concealed lest the glory of the festival were dimmed. The Hindu physician, the Private Secretary, and a confidential servant remained with the corpse, while Aziz had assumed the duty of being seen in public, and misleading people. He had liked the ruler very much, and might not prosper under his successor, yet he could not worry over such problems yet, for he was involved in the illusion he helped to create. The children continued to run about, hunting for a frog to put in Mohammed Latif's bed, the little fools. Hundreds of frogs lived in their own garden, but they must needs catch one up on the fort. They reported two topis below. Fielding and his brother-in-law, instead of resting after their journey, were climbing the slope to the saint's tomb!

"Throw stones?" asked Karim.

"Put powdered glass in their pan?"

"Ahmed, come here for such wickedness." He raised his hand to smite his firstborn, but allowed it to be kissed instead. It was sweet to have his sons with him at this moment, and to know they were affectionate and brave. He pointed out that the Englishmen were State guests, so must not be poisoned, and received, as always, gentle yet enthusiastic assent to his words.

The two visitors entered the octagon, but rushed out at once pursued by some bees. Hither and thither they ran, beating their heads; the children shrieked with derision, and out of heaven, as if a plug had been pulled, fell a jolly dollop of rain. Aziz had not meant to greet his former friend, but the incident put him into an excellent temper. He felt compact and strong. He shouted out, "Hullo, gentlemen, are you in trouble?"

The brother-in-law exclaimed; a bee had got him.

"Lie down in a pool of water, my dear sir—here are plenty. Don't come near me... I cannot control them, they are State bees;

complain to His Highness of their behaviour." There was no real danger, for the rain was increasing. The swarm retired to the shrine. He went up to the stranger and pulled a couple of stings out of his wrist, remarking, "Come, pull yourself together and be a man."

"How do you do, Aziz, after all this time? I heard you were settled in here," Fielding called to him, but not in friendly tones. "I suppose a couple of stings don't signify."

"Not the least. I'll send an embrocation over to the Guest House. I heard you were settled in there."

"Why have you not answered my letters?" he asked, going straight for the point, but not reaching it, owing to buckets of rain. His companion, new to the country, cried, as the drops drummed on his topi, that the bees were renewing their attack. Fielding checked his antics rather sharply, then said: "Is there a short cut down to our carriage? We must give up our walk. The weather's pestilential."

"Yes. That way."

"Are you not coming down yourself?"

Aziz sketched a comic salaam; like all Indians, he was skilful in the slighter impertinences. "I tremble, I obey," the gesture said, and it was not lost upon Fielding. They walked down a rough path to the road—the two men first; the brother-in-law (boy rather than man) next, in a state over his arm, which hurt; the three Indian children last, noisy and impudent—all six wet through.

"How goes it, Aziz?"

"In my usual health."

"Are you making anything out of your life here?"

"How much do you make out of yours?"

"Who is in charge of the Guest House?" he asked, giving up his slight effort to recapture their intimacy, and growing more official; he was older and sterner.

"His Highness's Private Secretary, probably."

"Where is he, then?"

"I don't know."

"Because not a soul's been near us since we arrived."

"Really."

"I wrote beforehand to the Durbar, and asked if a visit was convenient. I was told it was, and arranged my tour accordingly; but the Guest House servants appear to have no definite instructions, we can't get any eggs, also my wife wants to go out in the boat."

"There are two boats."

"Exactly, and no oars."

"Colonel Maggs broke the oars when here last."

"All four?"

"He is a most powerful man."

"If the weather lifts, we want to see your torchlight procession from the water this evening," he pursued. "I wrote to Godbole about it, but he has taken no notice; it's a place of the dead."

"Perhaps your letter never reached the Minister in question."

"Will there be any objection to English people watching the procession?"

"I know nothing at all about the religion here. I should never think of watching it myself."

"We had a very different reception both at Mudkul and Deora, they were kindness itself at Deora, the Maharajah and Maharani wanted us to see everything."

"You should never have left them."

"Jump in, Ralph"—they had reached the carriage.

"Jump in, Mr. Quested, and Mr. Fielding."

"Who on earth is Mr. Quested?"

"Do I mispronounce that well known name? Is he not your wife's brother?"

"Who on earth do you suppose I've married?"

"I'm only Ralph Moore," said the boy, blushing, and at that moment there fell another pailful of the rain, and made a mist round their feet. Aziz tried to withdraw, but it was too late.

"Quested? Quested? Don't you know that my wife was Mrs. Moore's daughter?"

He trembled, and went purplish grey; he hated the news, hated hearing the name Moore.

"Perhaps this explains your odd attitude?"

"And pray what is wrong with my attitude?"

"The preposterous letter you allowed Mahmoud Ali to write for you."

"This is a very useless conversation, I consider."

"However did you make such a mistake?" said Fielding, more friendly than before, but scathing and scornful. "It's almost unbelievable. I should think I wrote you half a dozen times, mentioning my wife by name. Miss Quested! What an extraordinary notion!" From his smile, Aziz guessed that Stella was beautiful. "Miss Quested is our best friend, she introduced us, but... what an amazing notion. Aziz, we must thrash this misunderstanding out later on. It is clearly some devilry of Mahmoud Ali's. He knows perfectly well I married Miss Moore. He called her 'Heaslop's sister' in his insolent letter to me."

The name woke furies in him. "So she is, and here is Heaslop's brother, and you his brother-in-law, and good-bye." Shame turned into a rage that brought back his self-respect. "What does it matter to me who you marry? Don't trouble me here at Mau is all I ask. I do not want you, I do not want one of you in my private life, with my dying breath I say it. Yes, yes, I made a foolish blunder; despise me and feel cold. I thought you married my enemy. I never read your letter. Mahmoud Ali deceived me. I thought you'd stolen my money, but"—he clapped his hands together, and his children gathered round him—"it's as if you stole it. I forgive Mahmoud Ali all things, because he loved me." Then pausing, while the rain exploded like pistols, he said, "My heart is for my own people henceforward," and turned away. Cyril followed him through the mud, apologizing, laughing a little, wanting to argue and reconstruct, pointing out with irrefragable logic that he had married, not Heaslop's betrothed, but Heaslop's sister. What difference did it make at this hour of the day? He had built his life on a mistake, but he had built it. Speaking in Urdu, that the children might understand, he said: "Please do not follow us, whomever you marry. I wish no Englishman or Englishwoman to be my friend."

He returned to the house excited and happy. It had been an uneasy, uncanny moment when Mrs. Moore's name was mentioned, stirring memories. "Esmiss Esmoor..."—as though she was coming to help him. She had always been so good, and that youth whom he had scarcely looked at was her son, Ralph Moore, Stella and Ralph, whom he had promised to be kind to, and Stella had married Cyril.

CHAPTER 36

All the time the palace ceased not to thrum and tum-tum. The revelation was over, but its effect lasted, and its effect was to make men feel that the revelation had not yet come. Hope existed despite fulfilment, as it will be in heaven. Although the God had been born, His procession—loosely supposed by many to be the birth—had not taken place. In normal years, the middle hours of this day were signalized by performances of great beauty in the private apartments of the Rajah. He owned a consecrated troupe of men and boys, whose duty it was to dance various actions and meditations of his faith before him. Seated at his ease, he could witness the Three Steps by which the Saviour ascended the universe to the discomfiture of Indra, also the death of the dragon, the mountain that turned into an umbrella, and the saddhu who (with comic results) invoked the God before dining. All culminated in the dance of the milk maidens before Krishna, and in the still greater dance of Krishna before the milk maidens, when the music and the musicians swirled through the dark blue robes of the actors into their tinsel crowns, and all became one. The Rajah and his guests would then forget that this was a dramatic performance, and would worship the actors. Nothing of the sort could occur to-day, because death interrupts. It interrupted less here than in Europe, its pathos was less poignant, its irony less cruel.

There were two claimants to the throne, unfortunately, who were in the palace now and suspected what had happened, yet they made no trouble, because religion is a living force to the Hindus, and can at certain moments fling down everything that is petty and temporary in their natures. The festival flowed on, wild and sincere, and all men loved each other, and avoided by instinct whatever could cause inconvenience or pain.

Aziz could not understand this, any more than an average Christian could. He was puzzled that Mau should suddenly be purged from suspicion and self-seeking. Although he was an outsider, and excluded from their rites, they were always particularly charming to him at this time; he and his household received small courtesies and presents, just because he was outside. He had nothing to do all day, except to send the embrocation over to the Guest House, and towards sunset he remembered it, and looked round his house for a local palliative, for the dispensary was shut. He found a tin of ointment belonging to Mohammed Latif, who was unwilling it should be removed, for magic words had been spoken over it while it was being boiled down, but Aziz promised that he would bring it back after application to the stings: he wanted an excuse for a ride.

The procession was beginning to form as he passed the palace. A large crowd watched the loading of the State palanquin, the prow of which protruded in the form of a silver dragon's head through the lofty half-opened door. Gods, big and little, were getting aboard. He averted his eyes, for he never knew how much he was supposed to see, and nearly collided with the Minister of Education. "Ah, you might make me late"—meaning that the touch of a non-Hindu would necessitate another bath; the words were spoken without moral heat. "Sorry," said Aziz. The other smiled, and again mentioned the Guest House party, and when he heard that Fielding's wife was not Miss Quested after all, remarked "Ah, no, he married the sister of Mr. Heaslop. Ah, exactly, I have known that for over a year"—also without heat. "Why did you not tell me? Your silence plunged me into a pretty pickle." Godbole, who had never been known to tell anyone anything, smiled again, and said in deprecating tones: "Never be angry with me. I am, as far as my limitations permit, your true friend; besides, it is my holy festival." Aziz always felt like a baby in that strange presence, a baby who unexpectedly receives a toy. He smiled also, and turned his horse into a lane, for the crush increased. The Sweepers' Band was arriving. Playing on sieves and other emblems of their profession, they marched straight at the gate of the palace with the air of a victorious army. All other music was silent, for this was ritually the moment of the Despised and Rejected; the God could not issue from his temple until the unclean Sweepers played their tune, they were the spot of filth without which the spirit cannot cohere. For an instant the scene was magnificent. The doors were thrown open, and the whole court was seen inside, barefoot and dressed in white robes; in the fairway stood the Ark of the Lord, covered with cloth of gold and flanked by peacock fans and by stiff circular banners of crimson. It was full to the brim with statuettes and flowers. As it rose from the earth on the shoulders of its bearers, the friendly sun of the monsoons shone forth and flooded the world with colour, so that the yellow tigers painted on the palace walls seemed to spring, and pink and green skeins of cloud to link up the upper sky. The palanquin moved... The lane was full of State elephants, who would follow it, their howdahs empty out of humility. Aziz did not pay attention to these sanctities, for they had no connection with his own; he felt bored, slightly cynical, like his own dear Emperor Babur, who came down from the north and found in Hindustan no good fruit, no fresh water or witty conversation, not even a friend.

The lane led quickly out of the town on to high rocks and jungle. Here he drew reign and examined the great Mau tank, which lay exposed beneath him to its remotest curve. Reflecting the evening clouds, it filled the nether-world with an equal splendour, so that earth and sky leant toward one another, about to clash in ecstasy. He spat, cynical again, more cynical than before. For in the centre of the burnished circle a small black blot was advancing—the Guest House boat. Those English had improvised something to take the place of oars, and were proceeding in their work of patrolling India. The sight endeared the Hindus by comparison, and looking back at the milk-white hump of the palace, he hoped that they would enjoy carrying their idol about, for at all events it did not pry into other people's lives. This pose of "seeing India" which had seduced him to Miss Quested at Chandrapore was only a form of ruling India; no sympathy lay behind it; he knew exactly what was going on in the boat as the party gazed at the steps down which the image would presently descend, and debated how near they might row without getting into trouble officially.

He did not give up his ride, for there would be servants at the Guest House whom he could question; a little information never comes amiss. He took the path by the sombre promontory that contained the royal tombs. Like the palace, they were of snowy stucco, and gleamed by their internal light, but their radiance grew ghostly under approaching night. The promontory was covered with lofty trees, and the fruit-bats were unhooking from the boughs and making kissing sounds as they grazed the surface of the tank; hanging upside down all the day, they had grown thirsty. The signs of the contented Indian evening multiplied; frogs on all sides, cow-dung burning eternally; a flock of belated hornbills overhead, looking like winged skeletons as they flapped across the gloaming. There was death in the air, but not sadness; a compromise had been made between destiny and desire, and even the heart of man acquiesced.

The European Guest House stood two hundred feet above the water, on the crest of a rocky and wooded spur that jutted from the jungle. By the time Aziz arrived, the water had paled to a film of mauve-grey, and the boat vanished entirely. A sentry slept in the Guest House porch, lamps burned in the cruciform of the deserted rooms. He went from one room to another, inquisitive, and malicious. Two letters lying on the piano rewarded him, and he pounced and read them promptly. He was not ashamed to do this. The sanctity of private correspondence has never been ratified by the East. Moreover, Mr. McBryde had read all his letters in the past, and spread their contents. One letter—the more interesting of the two—was from Heaslop to Fielding. It threw light on the mentality of his former friend, and it hardened him further against him. Much of it was about Ralph Moore, who appeared to be almost an imbecile. "Hand on my brother whenever suits you. I write to you because he is sure to make a bad bunderbust." Then: "I quite agree—life is too short to cherish grievances, also I'm relieved you feel able to come into line with the Oppressors of India to some extent. We need all the support we can get. I hope that next time Stella comes my way she will bring you with her, when I will make you as comfortable as a bachelor can—it's certainly time we met. My sister's marriage to you coming after my mother's death and my own difficulties did upset me, and I was unreasonable. It is about time we made it up properly, as you say—let us leave it at faults on both sides. Glad about your son and heir. When next any of you write to Adela, do give her some sort of message from me, for I should like to make my peace with her too. You are lucky to be out of British India at the present moment. Incident after incident, all due to propaganda, but we can't lay our hands on the connecting thread. The longer one lives here, the more certain one gets that everything hangs together. My personal opinion is, it's the Jews."

Thus far the red-nosed boy. Aziz was distracted for a moment by blurred sounds coming from over the water; the procession was under way. The second letter was from Miss Quested to Mrs. Fielding. It contained one or two interesting touches. The writer hoped that "Ralph will enjoy his India more than I did mine," and appeared to have given him money for this purpose—"my debt which I shall never repay in person." What debt did Miss Quested imagine she owed the country? He did not relish the phrase.

Talk of Ralph's health. It was all "Stella and Ralph," even "Cyril" and "Ronny"—all so friendly and sensible, and written in a spirit he could not command. He envied the easy intercourse that is only possible in a nation whose women are free. These five people were making up their little difficulties, and closing their broken ranks against the alien. Even Heaslop was coming in. Hence the strength of England, and in a spurt of temper he hit the piano, and since the notes had swollen and stuck together in groups of threes, he produced a remarkable noise.

"Oh, oh, who is that?" said a nervous and respectful voice; he could not remember where he had heard its tones before. Something moved in the twilight of an adjoining room. He replied, "State doctor, ridden over to enquire, very little English," slipped the letters into his pocket, and to show that he had free entry to the Guest House, struck the piano again.

Ralph Moore came into the light.

What a strange-looking youth, tall, prematurely aged, the big blue eyes faded with anxiety, the hair impoverished and tousled! Not a type that is often exported imperially. The doctor in Aziz thought, "Born of too old a mother," the poet found him rather beautiful.

"I was unable to call earlier owing to pressure of work. How are the celebrated bee-stings?" he asked patronizingly.

"I—I was resting, they thought I had better; they throb rather."

His timidity and evident "newness" had complicated effects on the malcontent. Speaking threateningly, he said, "Come here, please, allow me to look." They were practically alone, and he could treat the patient as Callendar had treated Nureddin.

"You said this morning——"

"The best of doctors make mistakes. Come here, please, for the diagnosis under the lamp. I am pressed for time."

"Aough——"

"What is the matter, pray?"

"Your hands are unkind."

He started and glanced down at them. The extraordinary youth was right, and he put them behind his back before replying with outward anger: "What the devil have my hands to do with you? This is a most strange remark. I am a qualified doctor, who will not hurt you."

"I don't mind pain, there is no pain."

"No pain?"

"Not really."

"Excellent news," sneered Aziz.

"But there is cruelty."

"I have brought you some salve, but how to put it on in your present nervous state becomes a problem," he continued, after a pause.

"Please leave it with me."

"Certainly not. It returns to my dispensary at once." He stretched forward, and the other retreated to the farther side of a table. "Now, do you want me to treat your stings, or do you prefer an English doctor? There is one at Asirgarh. Asirgarh is forty miles away, and the Ringnod dam broken. Now you see how you are placed. I think I had better see Mr. Fielding about you; this is really great nonsense, your present behaviour."

"They are out in a boat," he replied, glancing about him for support.

Aziz feigned intense surprise. "They have not gone in the direction of Mau, I hope. On a night like this the people become most fanatical." And, as if to confirm him, there was a sob, as though the lips of a giant had parted; the procession was approaching the Jail.

"You should not treat us like this," he challenged, and this time Aziz was checked, for the voice, though frightened, was not weak.

"Like what?"

"Dr. Aziz, we have done you no harm."

"Aha, you know my name, I see. Yes, I am Aziz. No, of course your great friend Miss Quested did me no harm at the Marabar."

Drowning his last words, all the guns of the State went off. A rocket from the Jail garden gave the signal. The prisoner had been released, and was kissing the feet of the singers. Rose-leaves fall from the houses, sacred spices and coco-nut are brought forth... It was the half-way moment; the God had extended His temple, and paused exultantly. Mixed and confused in their passage, the rumours of salvation entered the Guest House. They were startled and moved on to the porch, drawn by the sudden illumination. The bronze gun up on the fort kept flashing, the town was a blur of light, in which the houses seemed dancing, and the palace waving little wings. The water below, the hills and sky above, were not involved as yet; there was still only a little light and song struggling among the shapeless lumps of the universe. The song became audible through much repetition; the choir was repeating and inverting the names of deities.

"Radhakrishna Radhakrishna,
Radhakrishna Radhakrishna,
Krishnaradha Radhakrishna,
Radhakrishna Radhakrishna,"

they sang, and woke the sleeping sentry in the Guest House; he leant upon his iron-tipped spear.

"I must go back now, good night," said Aziz, and held out his hand, completely forgetting that they were not friends, and focusing his heart on something more distant than the caves, something beautiful. His hand was taken, and then he remembered how detestable he had been, and said gently, "Don't you think me unkind anymore?"

"No."

"How can you tell, you strange fellow?"

"Not difficult, the one thing I always know."

"Can you always tell whether a stranger is your friend?"

"Yes."

"Then you are an Oriental." He unclasped as he spoke, with a little shudder. Those words—he had said them to Mrs. Moore in the mosque in the beginning of the cycle, from which, after so much suffering, he had got free. Never be friends with the English! Mosque, caves, mosque, caves. And here he was starting again. He handed the magic ointment to him. "Take this, think of me when you use it. I shall never want it back. I must give you one little present, and it is all I have got; you are Mrs. Moore's son."

"I am that," he murmured to himself; and a part of Aziz' mind that had been hidden seemed to move and force its way to the top.

"But you are Heaslop's brother also, and alas, the two nations cannot be friends."

"I know. Not yet."

"Did your mother speak to you about me?"

"Yes." And with a swerve of voice and body that Aziz did not follow he added, "In her letters, in her letters. She loved you."

"Yes, your mother was my best friend in all the world." He was silent, puzzled by his own great gratitude. What did this eternal goodness of Mrs. Moore amount to? To nothing, if brought to the test of thought. She had not borne witness in his favour, nor visited him in the prison, yet she had stolen to the depths of his heart, and he always adored her. "This is our monsoon, the best weather," he said, while the lights of the procession waved as though embroidered on an agitated curtain. "How I wish she could have seen them, our rains. Now is the time when all things are happy, young and old. They are happy out there with their savage noise, though we cannot follow them; the tanks are all full so they dance, and this is India. I wish you were not with officials, then I would show you my country, but I cannot. Perhaps I will just take you out on the water now, for one short half-hour."

Was the cycle beginning again? His heart was too full to draw back. He must slip out in the darkness, and do this one act of homage to Mrs. Moore's son. He knew where the oars were—hidden to deter the visitors from going out—and he brought the second pair, in case they met the other boat; the Fieldings had pushed themselves out with long poles, and might get into difficulties, for the wind was rising.

Once on the water, he became easy. One kind action was with him always a channel for another, and soon the torrent of his hospitality gushed forth and he began doing the honours of Mau and persuading himself that he understood the wild procession, which increased in lights and sounds as the complications of its ritual developed. There was little need to row, for the freshening gale blew them in the direction they desired. Thorns scratched the keel, they ran into an islet and startled some cranes. The strange temporary life of the August flood-water bore them up and seemed as though it would last forever.

The boat was a rudderless dinghy. Huddled up in the stern, with the spare pair of oars in his arms, the guest asked no questions about details. There was presently a flash of lightning, followed by a second flash—little red scratches on the ponderous sky. "Was that the Rajah?" he asked.

"What—what do you mean?"

"Row back."

"But there's no Rajah—nothing——"

"Row back, you will see what I mean."

Aziz found it hard work against the advancing wind. But he fixed his eyes on the pin of light that marked the Guest House and backed a few strokes.

"There..."

Floating in the darkness was a king, who sat under a canopy, in shining royal robes...

"I can't tell you what that is, I'm sure," he whispered. "His Highness is dead. I think we should go back at once."

They were close to the promontory of the tombs, and had looked straight into the chhatri of the Rajah's father through an opening in the trees. That was the explanation. He had heard of the image—made to imitate life at enormous expense—but he had never chanced to see it before, though he frequently rowed on the lake. There was only one spot from which it could be seen, and Ralph had directed him to it. Hastily he pulled away, feeling that his companion was not so much a visitor as a guide. He remarked, "Shall we go back now?"

"There is still the procession."

"I'd rather not go nearer—they have such strange customs, and might hurt you."

"A little nearer."

Aziz obeyed. He knew with his heart that this was Mrs. Moore's son, and indeed until his heart was involved he knew nothing. "Radhakrishna Radhakrishna Radhakrishna Radhakrishna Krishnaradha," went the chant, then suddenly changed, and in the interstice he heard, almost certainly, the syllables of salvation that had sounded during his trial at Chandrapore.

"Mr. Moore, don't tell anyone that the Rajah is dead. It is a secret still, I am supposed not to say. We pretend he is alive until after the festival, to prevent unhappiness. Do you want to go still nearer?"

"Yes."

He tried to keep the boat out of the glare of the torches that began to star the other shore. Rockets kept going off, also the guns. Suddenly, closer than he had calculated, the palanquin of Krishna appeared from behind a ruined wall, and descended the carven glistening water-steps. On either side of it the singers tumbled, a woman prominent, a wild and beautiful young saint with flowers in her hair. She was praising God without attributes—thus did she apprehend Him. Others praised Him without attributes, seeing Him in this or that organ of the body or manifestation of the sky. Down they rushed to the foreshore and stood in the small waves, and a sacred meal was prepared, of which those who felt worthy partook. Old Godbole detected the boat, which was drifting in on the gale, and he waved his arms—whether in wrath or joy Aziz never discovered. Above stood the secular power of Mau—elephants, artillery, crowds—and high above them a wild tempest started, confined at first to the upper regions of the air. Gusts of wind mixed darkness and light, sheets of rain cut from the north, stopped, cut from the south, began rising from below, and across them struggled the singers, sounding every note but terror, and preparing to throw God away, God Himself, (not that God can be thrown) into the storm. Thus was He thrown year after year, and were others thrown—little images of Ganpati, baskets of ten-day corn, tiny tazias after Mohurram—scapegoats, husks, emblems of passage; a passage not easy, not now, not here, not to be apprehended except when it is unattainable; the God to be thrown was an emblem of that.

The village of Gokul reappeared upon its tray. It was the substitute for the silver image, which never left its haze of flowers; on behalf of another symbol, it was to perish. A servitor took it in his hands, and tore off the blue and white streamers. He was naked, broad-shouldered, thin-waisted—the Indian body again triumphant—and it was his hereditary office to close the gates of salvation. He entered the dark waters, pushing the village before him, until the clay dolls slipped off their chairs and began to gutter in the rain, and King Kansa was confounded with the father and mother of the Lord. Dark and solid, the little waves sipped, then a great wave washed and then English voices cried "Take care!"

The boats had collided with each other.

The four outsiders flung out their arms and grappled, and, with oars and poles sticking out, revolved like a mythical monster in the whirlwind. The worshippers howled with wrath or joy, as they drifted forward helplessly against the servitor. Who awaited them, his beautiful dark face expressionless, and as the last morsels melted on his tray, it struck them.

The shock was minute, but Stella, nearest to it, shrank into her husband's arms, then reached forward, then flung herself against Aziz, and her motions capsized them. They plunged into the warm, shallow water, and rose struggling into a tornado of noise. The oars, the sacred tray, the letters of Ronny and Adela, broke loose and floated confusedly. Artillery was fired, drums beaten, the elephants trumpeted, and drowning all an immense peal of thunder, unaccompanied by lightning, cracked like a mallet on the dome.

That was the climax, as far as India admits of one. The rain settled in steadily to its job of wetting everybody and everything through, and soon spoiled the cloth of gold on the palanquin and the costly disc-shaped banners. Some of the torches went out, fireworks didn't catch, there began to be less singing, and the tray returned to Professor Godbole, who picked up a fragment of the mud adhering and smeared it on his forehead without much ceremony. Whatever had happened had happened, and while the intruders picked themselves up, the crowds of Hindus began a desultory move back into the town. The image went back too, and on the following day underwent a private death of its own, when some curtains of magenta and green were lowered in front of the dynastic shrine. The singing went on even longer... ragged edges of religion... unsatisfactory and undramatic tangles... "God is love." Looking back at the great blur of the last twenty-four hours, no man could say where was the emotional centre of it, any more than he could locate the heart of a cloud.

CHAPTER 37

Friends again, yet aware that they could meet no more, Aziz and Fielding went for their last ride in the Mau jungles. The floods had abated and the Rajah was officially dead, so the Guest House party were departing next morning, as decorum required. What with the mourning and the festival, the visit was a failure.

Fielding had scarcely seen Godbole, who promised every day to show him over the King-Emperor George Fifth High School, his main objective, but always made some excuse. This afternoon Aziz let out what had happened: the King-Emperor had been converted into a granary, and the Minister of Education did not like to admit this to his former Principal. The school had been opened only last year by the Agent to the Governor-General, and it still flourished on paper; he hoped to start it again before its absence was remarked and to collect its scholars before they produced children of their own. Fielding laughed at the tangle and waste of energy, but he did not travel as lightly as in the past; education was a continuous concern to him, because his income and the comfort of his family depended on it. He knew that few Indians think education good in itself, and he deplored this now on the widest grounds. He began to say something heavy on the subject of Native States, but the friendliness of Aziz distracted him. This reconciliation was a success, anyhow. After the funny shipwreck there had been no more nonsense or bitterness, and they went back laughingly to their old relationship as if nothing had happened. Now they rode between jolly bushes and rocks. Presently the ground opened into full sunlight and they saw a grassy slope bright with butterflies, also a cobra, which crawled across doing nothing in particular, and disappeared among some custard apple trees. There were round white clouds in the sky, and white pools on the earth; the hills in the distance were purple. The scene was as park-like as England, but did not cease being queer. They drew rein, to give the cobra elbow-room, and Aziz produced a letter that he wanted to send to Miss Quested. A charming letter. He wanted to thank his old enemy for her fine behaviour two years back: perfectly plain was it now that she had behaved well. "As I fell into our largest Mau tank under circumstances our other friends will relate, I thought how brave Miss Quested was, and decided to tell her so, despite my imperfect English. Through you I am happy here with my children instead of in a prison, of that I make no doubt. My children shall be taught to speak of you with the greatest affection and respect."

"Miss Quested will be greatly pleased. I am glad you have seen her courage at last."

"I want to do kind actions all round and wipe out the wretched business of the Marabar forever. I have been so disgracefully hasty, thinking you meant to get hold of my money: as bad a mistake as the cave itself."

"Aziz, I wish you would talk to my wife. She too believes that the Marabar is wiped out."

"How so?"

"I don't know, perhaps she might tell you, she won't tell me. She has ideas I don't share—indeed, when I'm away from her I think them ridiculous. When I'm with her, I suppose because I'm fond of her, I feel different, I feel half dead and half blind. My wife's after something. You and I and Miss Quested are, roughly speaking, not after anything. We jog on as decently as we can, you a little in front—a laudable little party. But my wife is not with us."

"What are you meaning? Is Stella not faithful to you, Cyril? This fills me with great concern."

Fielding hesitated. He was not quite happy about his marriage. He was passionate physically again—the final flare-up before the clinkers of middle age—and he knew that his wife did not love him as much as he loved her, and he was ashamed of pestering her. But during the visit to Mau the situation had improved. There seemed a link between them at last—that link outside either participant that is necessary to every relationship. In the language of theology, their union had been blessed. He could assure Aziz that Stella was not only faithful to him, but likely to become more so; and trying to express what was not clear to himself, he added dully that different people had different points of view. "If you won't talk about the Marabar to Stella, why won't you talk to Ralph? He is a wise boy really. And (same metaphor) he rides a little behind her, though with her."

"Tell him also, I have nothing to say to him, but he is indeed a wise boy and has always one Indian friend. I partly love him because he brought me back to you to say good-bye. For this is good-bye, Cyril, though to think about it will spoil our ride and make us sad."

"No, we won't think about it." He too felt that this was their last free intercourse. All the stupid misunderstandings had been cleared up, but socially they had no meeting-place. He had thrown in his lot with Anglo-India by marrying a countrywoman, and he was acquiring some of its limitations, and already felt surprise at his own past heroism. Would he to-day defy all his own people for the sake of a stray Indian? Aziz was a memento, a trophy, they were proud of each other, yet they must inevitably part. And, anxious to make what he could of this last afternoon, he forced himself to speak intimately about his wife, the person most dear to him.

He said: "From her point of view, Mau has been a success. It calmed her—both of them suffer from restlessness. She found something soothing, some solution of her queer troubles here." After a silence—myriads of kisses around them as the earth drew the water in—he continued: "Do you know anything about this Krishna business?"

"My dear chap, officially they call it Gokul Ashtami. All the State offices are closed, but how else should it concern you and me?"

"Gokul is the village where Krishna was born—well, more or less born, for there's the same hovering between it and another village as between Bethlehem and Nazareth. What I want to discover is its spiritual side, if it has one."

"It is useless discussing Hindus with me. Living with them teaches me no more. When I think I annoy them, I do not. When I think I don't annoy them, I do. Perhaps they will sack me for tumbling on to their dolls'-house; on the other hand, perhaps they will double my salary. Time will prove. Why so curious about them?"

"It's difficult to explain. I never really understood or liked them, except an occasional scrap of Godbole. Does the old fellow still say 'Come, come?'"

"Oh, presumably."

Fielding sighed, opened his lips, shut them, then said with a little laugh, "I can't explain, because it isn't in words at all, but why do my wife and her brother like Hinduism, though they take no interest in its forms? They won't talk to me about this. They know I think a certain side of their lives is a mistake, and are shy. That's why I wish you would talk to them, for at all events you're Oriental."

Aziz refused to reply. He didn't want to meet Stella and Ralph again, knew they didn't want to meet him, was incurious about their secrets, and felt good old Cyril to be a bit clumsy.

Something—not a sight, but a sound—flitted past him, and caused him to re-read his letter to Miss Quested. Hadn't he wanted to say something else to her? Taking out his pen, he added: "For my own part, I shall henceforth connect you with the name that is very sacred in my mind, namely, Mrs. Moore." When he had finished, the mirror of the scenery was shattered, the meadow disintegrated into butterflies. A poem about Mecca—the Caaba of Union—the thorn-bushes where pilgrims die before they have seen the Friend—they flitted next; he thought of his wife; and then the whole semi-mystic, semi-sensuous overturn, so characteristic of his spiritual life, came to end like a landslip and rested in its due place, and he found himself riding in the jungle with his dear Cyril.

"Oh, shut up," he said. "Don't spoil our last hour with foolish questions. Leave Krishna alone, and talk about something sensible."

They did. All the way back to Mau they wrangled about politics. Each had hardened since Chandrapore, and a good knock about proved enjoyable. They trusted each other, although they were going to part, perhaps because they were going to part. Fielding had "no further use for politeness," he said, meaning that the British Empire really can't be abolished because it's rude. Aziz retorted, "Very well, and we have no use for you," and glared at him with abstract hate. Fielding said: "Away from us, Indians go to seed at once. Look at the King-Emperor High School! Look at you, forgetting your medicine and going back to charms. Look at your poems."—"Jolly good poems, I'm getting published Bombay side."—"Yes, and what do they say? Free our women and India will be free. Try it, my lad. Free your own lady in the first place, and see who'll wash Ahmed Karim and Jamila's faces. A nice situation!"

Aziz grew more excited. He rose in his stirrups and pulled at his horse's head in the hope it would rear. Then he should feel in a battle. He cried: "Clear out, all you Turtons and Burtons.

We wanted to know you ten years back—now it's too late. If we see you and sit on your committees, it's for political reasons, don't you make any mistake." His horse did rear. "Clear out, clear out, I say. Why are we put to so much suffering? We used to blame you, now we blame ourselves, we grow wiser. Until England is in difficulties we keep silent, but in the next European war—aha, aha! Then is our time." He paused, and the scenery, though it smiled, fell like a gravestone on any human hope. They cantered past a temple to Hanuman—God so loved the world that he took monkey's flesh upon him—and past a Saivite temple, which invited to lust, but under the semblance of eternity, its obscenities bearing no relation to those of our flesh and blood. They splashed through butterflies and frogs; great trees with leaves like plates rose among the brushwood. The divisions of daily life were returning, the shrine had almost shut.

"Who do you want instead of the English? The Japanese?" jeered Fielding, drawing rein.

"No, the Afghans. My own ancestors."

"Oh, your Hindu friends will like that, won't they?"

"It will be arranged—a conference of Oriental statesmen."

"It will indeed be arranged."

"Old story of 'We will rob every man and rape every woman from Peshawar to Calcutta,' I suppose, which you get some nobody to repeat and then quote every week in the *Pioneer* in order to frighten us into retaining you! We know!" Still he couldn't quite fit in Afghans at Mau, and, finding he was in a corner, made his horse rear again until he remembered that he had, or ought to have, a mother-land. Then he shouted: "India shall be a nation! No foreigners of any sort! Hindu and Moslem and Sikh and all shall be one! Hurrah! Hurrah for India! Hurrah! Hurrah!"

India a nation! What an apotheosis! Last comer to the drab nineteenth-century sisterhood! Waddling in at this hour of the world to take her seat! She, whose only peer was the Holy Roman Empire, she shall rank with Guatemala and Belgium perhaps! Fielding mocked again. And Aziz in an awful rage danced this way and that, not knowing what to do, and cried: "Down with the English anyhow. That's certain. Clear out, you fellows, double quick, I say. We may hate one another, but we hate you most. If I don't make you go, Ahmed will, Karim will, if it's fifty five-hundred years we shall get rid of you, yes, we shall drive every blasted Englishman into the sea, and then"—he rode against him furiously—"and then," he concluded, half kissing him, "you and I shall be friends."

"Why can't we be friends now?" said the other, holding him affectionately. "It's what I want. It's what you want."

But the horses didn't want it—they swerved apart; the earth didn't want it, sending up rocks through which riders must pass single file; the temples, the tank, the jail, the palace, the birds, the carrion, the Guest House, that came into view as they issued from the gap and saw Mau beneath: they didn't want it, they said in their hundred voices, "No, not yet," and the sky said, "No, not there."

Weybridge, 1924

OTHER BOOKS YOU MAY LIKE

- The Imitation of Christ by Thomas À Kempis, ISBN: 9789388118057
- The Knowledge of the Holy by AW Tozer, ISBN: 9789389157130
- The Law by Neville Goddard, ISBN: 9789390492886
- The Law of Success by Napoleon Hill, ISBN: 9788180320927
- The Light of Asia by Sir Edwin Arnold, ISBN: 9789380914923
- The Magic of Believing by Claudie Bristol, ISBN: 9789388118149
- The Magic of Faith by Joseph Murphy, ISBN: 9789388118743
- The Miracles of Your Mind by Joseph Murphy, ISBN: 9788180320743
- The Origin of Species by Charles Darwin, ISBN: 9788180320453
- The Power of Awareness by Neville Goddard, ISBN: 9789387669406
- The Power of Positive Thinking by Norman Vincent Peale, ISBN: 9789388118569
- The Power of Your Subconscious Mind by Joseph Murphy, ISBN: 9788180320958
- The Problem of Increasing Human Energy by Nikola Tesla, ISBN: 9789354990953
- The Psychopathology of Everyday Life by Sigmund Freud, ISBN: 9789388118071
- The Pursuit of God by AW Tozer, ISBN: 9789389157147
- The Red Badge of Courage by Stephen Crane, ISBN: 9789354990977
- The Richest Man in Babylon by George S. Clason, ISBN: 9789387669369
- The Science of Getting Rich by Wallace D. Wattles, ISBN: 9788180320972
- The World as I See It by Albert Einstein, ISBN: 9789388118125
- The Yoga Sutras of Patanjali by Patanjali, ISBN: 9789389716351
- Think and Grow Rich by Napoleon Hill, ISBN: 9788180320255
- Thought Vibration by William Walker Atkinson, ISBN: 9789389157154
- Who were the Shudras by Dr B.R. Ambedkar, ISBN: 9789354991028
- Wuthering Heights by Emily Brontë, ISBN: 9788193545898
- Your Faith is Your Fortune by Neville Goddard, ISBN: 9789389157161
- Zen in the Art of Archery by Eugen Herrigel, ISBN: 9789354991059

Develop your reading habit | Gift books to your friends